The Hunters and the Hunted

The scout led the Emeri horsemen into the gorge and pointed out where the fleeing slaves and the raiders who had rescued them had rested. "We will catch up with them today."

The Emeri officer had little liking for his task—to hunt down a bunch of pitiable scarecrows led by wild Shumai—unworthy targets for Emeri arrows, good for nothing but easy slaughter.

As the gorge narrowed, a long, quavering shout came from ahead. The scout stopped, holding up his hand. Then there was a strange, distant rushing sound, growing into a rumble.

"Weapons ready!" the officer called—then turned and saw a tower of rushing water rounding the turn of the gorge ahead.

A man screamed and ran for the steep bank. He did not reach it.

The Breaking of Northwall

Paul O. Williams

A Del Rey Book

BALLANTINE BOOKS • NEW YORK

A Del Rey Book
Published by Ballantine Books

Copyright © 1980 by Paul O. Williams

All rights reserved under International and Pan-American
Copyright Conventions. Published in the United States by
Ballantine Books, a division of Random House, Inc., New
York, and simultaneously in Canada by Random House of
Canada, Limited, Toronto, Canada.

Library of Congress Catalog Card Number: 80-68217

ISBN 0-345-29259-6

Manufactured in the United States of America

First Edition: February 1981
Second Printing: October 1981

Cover art by: Darrell K. Sweet

Map by: Chris Barbieri

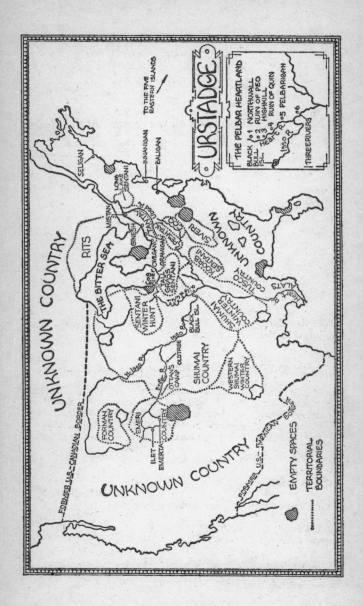

To Nancy, who also knows all the seasons of the Heart

1

ONCE more toward evening Adai the Jestan toiled slowly up the wide, curving stone steps to the highest tower. The cupped wear in the limestone made her hug the right wall, her ringed hand clicking on the stone.

The two guards flashed knowing glances at one another as she arrived at the station. "No sign yet, Jestana," said the taller. "Nothing but clear river. But before the week is out, the Sentani will come."

"The Sentani," she murmured, leaning over the north wall. The trees, save the oaks, were largely bare already, and their brown, clinging leaves were soon to go. The wind was chill, and the sunset glowed brick red from under the edges of a thick layer of cloud. The dry grasses on the high tops of the river bluffs lay down before the wind. Far to the west, across the river and beyond the swamps, a prairie fire near the horizon sent up a long trail of smoke.

"The Shumai are driving the wild ones," she said.

"It is late for them. Perhaps it is a natural fire," said the tall guard.

"You needn't reassure me, Tanbar," she replied. "It is the Shumai."

"Perhaps he will stay the winter at Northwall, Jestana."

"His exile is over. Who would spend another winter at Northwall when he could be here? There is little metal for working. There are few comforts, few rolls to read. No. Something has happened."

"But Jestak is not just anyone. He might want to stay. Or perhaps he will send word with the Sentani."

"How is it possible? They would surely harm him. I don't understand. Since he went to the eastern cities, I don't understand at all. What trouble. I am sure he did nothing so bad he had to take reticence to protect himself." And she turned to go.

"We will have you called if we see," Tanbar called. "Don't worry. Remember, he has the tattoo."

"The tattoo. The tattoo. I don't understand. Where did he get that? We send him east to be educated, a great opportunity, and he returns rangy and wild, and late, and tattooed with the snake sign of savages. From Northwall all we get is silence, enigma, messages from Sentani, hints of fraternization with Shumai, the murderers." The Jestana muttered this as she toiled downward around the curve of stairs.

"What tattoo?" asked the shorter guard. "You mean that Jestak has the mark of the Sentani? How is that possible?"

"I don't know, Din. I only saw it once, when the family sent him to Northwall as punishment for his waste of the years in the east. It is all very strange. He has not been any credit to his family, surely. He has become different, independent. But he is not a nobody. He took reticence even though they put him to scrubbing for it. He keeps his own counsel. He has been through a great deal, that is clear. He is like no Pelbar I have ever known—though I remember when he was as much a Pelbar as any of us. That day he left on the eastern track, what he had been vanished with him. When he finally returned—two years late—he was another man."

"He was gone, then, six years?"

"Yes, almost. He would not give any details about what happened. All the family knew was that he did not learn the law he was sent, at great expense, to learn. He knew some, surely. But not what was needed to open any trade with Innanigan or Stanigan. So we remain in this waste, trading with savages only—when we can do that—and shut off from the ancient learning."

"We have our own. I always have felt your family was wrong in this desire."

"Yes. Everyone has been through that."

"Isn't it time we all knew what went on with Jestak? The Jestan have been too close-mouthed about it. Northwall has been incredibly silent. It is not good to divide us, especially now, Tanbar."

"I am not at liberty to tell all the Pelbar the business of the Jestan, Din. However, I will tell you what I can, with the understanding that it be kept in confidence."

"Agreed," and they touched palms in the simple but absolute Pelbar ceremony of swearing.

"All I know was what I saw at the family council at which Jestak was exiled. They tried to break his right of reticence, when they saw that the menial work would not do it. They charged him with secrecy and waste of resources, failure to carry out the design with which he was assigned and to which he swore.

"Jestak himself said little. He said he was guilty as charged, but would give no details, and even seemed a little eager for exile. True, we tend to be rigid. A thing sworn to must be done in spite of unforeseen difficulties. He had little life here under the conditions he had to undergo. Jestak simply sat under the lockstone while the accusations were read. No amount of questioning would draw from him what had happened. He did say that a fight in Innanigan had caused his failure to enter the conclave of learning. A fight. A Pelbar in a fight. All his training in diplomacy seems to have failed him. One would think him a tribesman. His only defense was that he had to fight and that he had won. 'You would never accept any of my statements anyway,' he said.

"Whatever happened must have been serious, we think, because some of the extra time could be on account of some punishment. All else I can tell you is that he came home with a variety of skills that were wholly unexpected. They are not such things as the Pelbar develop. Things like the endless running of the outside tribesmen, various ways of swimming, the handling of boats, the mastery of the body, though not by our disciplines. He still is a good metalworker, in fact has taught us some new casting techniques, and some automatic work. His literary and artistic skills have fallen sadly backward—except for song. And even there it seems impossible for him to stay with Pelbar harmonies. He continually ruins his songs by introducing wild improvisation.

"The surprise, of course, came with his sentence, a serious one."

"What was that?"

"He was condemned at the spring equinox to go to Northwall alone and to remain until the sun again rose the next year through the split in the spring rocks. He smiled. Then he asked permission to go right away.

"The family was so angry with him that they agreed instantly, and even pushed through the vote. It was almost like a death sentence to one regarded as incorrigible. Adai

and even Odosi cried aloud and had to be subdued. Then
came the shock."

"Was not all that shocking enough? We thought you had
sent him in the autumn."

"No. He sent himself. It was then that he unlaced his left
sleeve, and bared his arm as he had never done since he
returned. Holding up his forearm, he showed the snake tattoo of the Sentani. He smiled and said, 'They will not hurt
me, you know. I will go with them to Northwall, in response to your commands.' "

"Aiii."

"Yes. I saw it, and being close, I also saw the scars on
his arm that no one else appeared to see. At least no one
has mentioned it, and I now, to you, have mentioned it for
the first time—except to my wife."

"Something has befallen him on his eastern journey."

"Yes, but what it all comes to, nobody now knows."

"At least," said Dindani, "he will be safe from the Sentani, since they have honored his tattoo, as Northwall has
told us. Perhaps he will come south with them at the Rain-
month truce."

"Perhaps. That is my view. He is staying through to the
spring equinox, though his year of exile is over. He is
showing them that he cares nothing for their punishments."

"That will not go well with him."

"No. But the family is becoming more aware of the fact
that all the strangeness may bring about some change in
our relations with the Sentani, and this has even been
brought up in the council, though the Protector has denied
it. But that business of the marriage last spring, and the
one they call Winnt. Somehow Jestak apparently had a
hand in that."

"Ah."

"But I have little hope for much."

"Well, hope cannot hurt us. It would be nice to go
freely."

The gentle clashing of arms, growing louder, announced
the arrival of replacements, and the two friends prepared
their gear for descent into the growing gloom of the city
below.

II

As the wind made dry sounds in the oak leaves, Jestak had gone north from Pelbarigan at an easy run, his pack slapping lightly at his back. He saw, here and there, the marks of the northing Sentani hunters. He would have to walk in on them, arm up, or else be attacked as a stray Pelbar before he could reveal his earned brotherhood. But he had little fear. Despite his stay since spring in Pelbarigan, his instincts were awake. This track had a beetle trail in it. That one had dried since the hunter passed, and its edges had crumbled down into the pressed sole. He was quite sure they were well ahead.

In spite of all the apparent shame, he was glad to be gone. He had not remembered, in his childhood, the great shut stone walls of Pelbarigan as he now saw them, barring out the cold but also the light—the enemy but also the light wind and bird song. Northwall, only half as large, containing only about a thousand people, would at least compromise more between Pelbar security and the wide-ranging freedom of the Sentani. And perhaps there he could see some way to put into use some of the ideas he had learned from the ancient men of the East Islands. His head was dizzy with them. They seemed to make sense, and yet they did not apply to any situation he had known, except perhaps his own life. Men seemed inexorably divided. No one really reached across the tribal boundaries, and even within Pelbarigan there were parties with strongly divergent ideas.

The Saltstream prophets had spoken to him because he was a Pelbar, from so far west that he was to them only a whisper in a dream, and yet he had the sign of the Sentani. That had been a matter of chance. But they saw in it the workings of a prophecy. Their sense of prophecy was different from that of Pel, the one who had organized Pelbar society in the old time. They saw it as inevitable tendencies, given the forces of unity and conjunction in the world. He was not sure how the evidence of the time of fire fit in this at all.

He was nearly at the River of the Cattails, passing the ruin called Quin, when the first warning came. It was not a matter of hearing. It was knowing. And when he first took that knowledge, he stopped in two steps, and was still beneath the alders in another, rolling up his sleeve.

"Out, Pelbar, and meet the arrow," called a sharp voice.

"I claim immunity," Jestak returned, in clear Sentani dialect, immediately standing, arm up, tattoo forward. He was met with a laugh of a dozen voices together.

"Did you paint that on, toolman? Here, Dar, spit on it and wipe it away. You will learn not to imitate the sacred signs of the Sentani."

Jestak did not reply. The one called Dar had sauntered up to him, put his bow beneath his chin, and looked at the tattoo.

"Aiii," he called. "It is a tattoo, Mokil. It bears the sign of the eastern band of the long lakes and the star of Nok-ush for the right eye."

Mokil, a short, wide-shouldered man, strode forward for a look. He paused, looking then at the position of the sun. Without a word, he held out his two palms, against which Jestak put his own, and then the two men touched foreheads.

"You will explain to us, no doubt," he muttered. "But not now. We are late. Run with us to the foot of Highkill, where the main band stays. Then we will learn of you. There will be time enough to redress the wrong then if you have usurped these marks."

"Redress? But you have just sworn to me."

"I swore to the tattoo and the bonds of all bands. To you, too, if they are true. Come."

Without a word, the men began their long trot north toward Highkill, Jestak in their midst, matching their easy strides with his own, feeling at home as he had in the eastern lake country, with Igon in front of him.

Highkill was a small branch valley to the great river, with a stream in it, called Antler, and a wide-mouthed park between the limestone bluffs and the river. Like two stone towers, they overlooked everything else in the countryside, and so, with sentinels on each high knob, the Sentani bands habitually rested at the site on their northward run. At the base of the south knob was a small ruin, fused and crumbled blocks of artificial stone from the former time, but blasted and puddled by the heat of death of the time of fire.

The Sentani were arranged in seven bands, each at the star point of their governmental symbol, each with its band name. They were, despite their free habits, a strict and ordered people, and so, when Mokil's party loped through the southern apex into the star, though a Pelbar was running with the rest—so strange an occurrence that most of the 343 men in the winter hunt had never seen its like—there was no general rush to the northpoint. Instead, two men from each point followed for news of the strange Pelbar.

Not only did they follow, but then ate in silence the fish soup and ankle root prepared for the northpoint men. Finally, Mokil motioned the men to sit down and Jestak to stand before him.

"Now, Pelbar, you will tell us of the tattoo? Where did you get it and by what right do you wear it?"

"I was given it at the long lake in the east named Tcham, by the people of Nokush, of the lake Sentani, because of my friendship with Igon of that band. Igon and I are brothers, and, to save my life, and thus take back his own, which I had saved, Igon asked the Nokush to mark me as their own."

One old man shook his head. "What of the ordeal?" he said. "Did you undergo the preparatory ordeal? Or is Nokush now giving out our saving sign to any riffraff that comes along. Atou."

Jestak slipped off his tunic, showing the marks of the ordeal plainly enough, as well as many other scars. A general murmur went through the men. Here was one who had suffered sufficiently, and beyond sufficiently, and thus was safe, sure, and adopted according to rite.

"What are you called?"

"Jestak of the Jestan, the Pelbarigan metalworkers, eldest of the sons of Adai, and her husband, Steltan. I was born and grew in Pelbarigan, but now I have traveled east and north to the Bitter Sea, through the eastern Sentani lands, and to the eastern cities. I have lived in Innanigan and have sailed east to the East Islands, living for a time at Saltstream."

"Ah, Pelbar. How can all of this be true for one so young?" Mokil asked. "You name places that are only distant dreams or never heard of. You must tell us of this, if only for our entertainment in this far place. But first tell us why you are here, when every Pelbar has shut himself away from our arrows and the first snow is almost come."

"I am exiled from Pelbarigan to Northwall for a year. It was to start at spring equinox, which is safer, but I left soon after the sentence, hoping to go north with you."

"Exiled. What have you done? Are you a criminal, then?"

"Only by Pelbar custom. I did not fulfill commands I had accepted, and I have never told the Pelbar even so much of what has happened to me as I have just told you. We are a shut people. In Pelbarigan there are strong factions. We theorize endlessly. They would never have understood, believed, or accepted what I now see. It would have put my family in a bad position if I were to have told them everything. It was simpler this way, and has saved endless wrangling. Besides, a winter shut into Pelbarigan is not a thing I can relish anymore. I need some time to think and room to move, and Northwall will give me both."

"Pah. They are as shut up as any Pelbar, with their endless smoky fires and stone piled high on stone. You have made no bargain, Jestak."

"We shall see. Perhaps, with your permission, I may visit you on the deep snows. I have learned the methods of the Rits northwest of the Bitter Sea for cold travel."

"Hah, then. You have lived with them, too. How you have kept from being killed is a miracle. Just today it was by a flea's whisker. But we have kept you standing, and now you must sit and tell us, and the men from the starpoints, about all these wild lies. Unless you are more of a man than any, these things could hardly be so. Come. Sit. We will see who will be the first to catch you up."

Jestak bowed and went to the bearskin to Mokil's left. "I thank you all for your hospitality and your company," he began.

All bowed and murmured, and lifted the left hand with the last two fingers together.

"This is a long story, and I am telling it to you frankly and openly because the Sentani I have found are people of great honesty of mind and are able to entertain wide-ranging stories. They are, I have come to feel, only held back by a rigidity of custom and nomadic habit from being the great power of the northeast lands. Please do not be offended. I learned frank speech from Igon, but I have not mastered the degree of openness beyond which offense is given. My Sentani instincts are imperfect."

"No offense, Pelbar. Go on."

"Over seven years ago I was sent east by my family to learn law of the councils of Innanigan. Their hope was somehow to open trade from these central lands, since now the Pelbar work is traded only to you, to the Shumai, and occasionally, from Threerivers, to a north group of the Tusco, and these only by truce and with difficulty, as you know."

"Anyone who would deal with the Shumai would have difficulty," said Juk, a graying hunter. "But how did your family hope to accomplish such a fantastic thing?"

"They did not know. The Pelbar are a shut-up people. I was supposed to find out, with help. They had no idea of the difficult journey they sent me on, or how wild and impossible is the eastern track once one has passed the tall grass and groves. We had trained in running, and in secrecy, in order to make the trek, but it was of no use.

"We were no more than into the foothills of the high eastern rises than we were set on by a small band of Peshtak. In the fight, which was short, because we were only five, three of us were immediately killed. My companion, Brus, had managed to spear one of the Peshtak, and consequently they flayed him alive and tied him in a field of anthills. He died slowly and horribly. They seemed to enjoy it. Of all the peoples I have met, they alone hurt for pleasure.

"I was taken northward well over two hundred ayas, apparently in preparation for a central meeting of bands at which I was to suffer some sort of torture. The capture was bad enough, and I bear its scars, but the Peshtak made a fatal error. They passed too close to the high lands near the Ubed, which flows north into the Bitter Sea. They were surprised and taken by the Tantal, and I with them.

"So my former captors were enslaved with me, not that that made them more agreeable, but they had little chance to carry out their cruelties, because the Tantal saw me as of some value, as I have a strong frame. We were put in a large timber barge and made to pole it, then row it, north, downriver to the edge of the Bitter Sea to their central city."

"Gramigan."

"No. Gramigan lies west and is smaller. We went to Ginesh, which stands on the high ground above the marsh that lies at the emptying of the Ubed into the Bitter Sea. The Bitter Sea is fresh water, and I do not know why it has that name except for its cold, or perhaps the blasted areas near the ruins there, left from the time of fire, in which nothing grows.

"It was there I met Igon. He had been taken some six months earlier, and was one of only four Sentani who had been enslaved. Since our dialects are fairly close, and since he was ill and I helped him get well, we became friends.

"We were all in a large log slave house by the river's edge, a mixture of the Sentani, Peshtak, four Shumai all the way from the east arm of the plains, a large number of Rits from the northwest, because they are so docile that—"

"More docile than the Pelbar?"

"I took care not to be docile, lest they mount a force even so far as these western lands in order to enslave us. They are many. The peoples near them are very wary of them. We here could, I am sure, withstand them, but it would be much trouble. It would be costly in any case, even if they got so far through the eastern Shumai bands near the river's edge to the north. The Stone Creek Shumai, for example."

"The Shumai? Surely those rabble could not stop men of discipline and resource. They have never beaten us."

"Well, we can let that go. But have you ever known Shumai? I knew the four captives of Ginesh, and found them to be intelligent people of a curious blend of gentleness and steel hardness. They have very agile minds. They kept to themselves, of course, and tended to despise the rest, but they were honest and fair, and not cruel for the sake of cruelty.

"I think you may not realize how much even you depend on the Shumai. Even though we are all hostile, still the Shumai coppers are in your buckles and knife handles, even though Pelbar made them. In the same way, the Shumai wear guard tunics made by us from Sentani trade fibers. They also buy your wild rice, through us, and our beaver felts, from your hunting, are often bought by the

Shumai. We need each other, or there would be no truce weeks, and our hostilities would be more bitter."

"They are bitter enough. Go on with your story."

"When I met Igon, he was ill, as were many of the others. The Shumai alone seemed to keep up strength, but I saw it might be because they would eat rodents they caught in the loghouse, and no other peoples would. Igon needed meat. All the Tantal fed us was grain mush, and that was not plentiful. They were used to working and mal-feeding their slaves to death, then simply dumping them in the river and supplying the gap with more captives. They had become habituated to using slave labor, but they feared a healthy person—or even anyone who had been around very long. None of us, except the Rits, proved easy to handle.

"Though you may not know it, the Pelbar do fish. And we are the only people who do it with a line, rather than a spear or net. I was able to catch enough fish, and to teach the others, to get back Igon's strength. We had to do it secretly, at night, under a corner of the loghouse that protruded over a caving bank. The rate of our dying began to slow, and the Tantal began to grow upset and suspicious. They accused us of stealing, and beat some of us as examples, but they only succeeded in building our solidarity.

"Perhaps it was for this reason that they apparently determined to eliminate us all in the late fall and get along without slaves for the winter. You see, one of our duties was in bringing in the wood and trade ships from the Bitter Sea mouth of the river. It was shallow, so the slavemasters would swim us out to the ships, which bore sail, and then we would tow and row them up into the Ubed to the wharf areas."

"Bore sail?"

"They are propelled by the wind, by means of large pieces of cloth held up on poles. We were forced out into the water as the season grew later and later, and a few began to die of the water cold. Igon was a fine swimmer. He had taught me the stroke of the lakes, which conserved energy, and that perhaps saved my life.

"We determined, though there was a slight chance of it, to meet the next ship far enough out, by fast swimming, to try to take it, and start off down the shore of the Bitter Sea eastward enough ahead of pursuit to escape. There were only eight of us in on this plan. The three Shumai (one having died), Igon and his friends, and I. There was little chance of success. We did not dare bring in the Peshtak, who are treacherous until their last breath, or the Rits, who are so remote in their normal life, which demands great cooperation against the hard winter, that they had developed little sense of defense, never needing it."

"Jestak, I am dizzy with all these strange tribes."

"As was I, Mokil, living through it. You have no idea how it would be to a Pelbar. Our solution to life has been to shut away its harsh side, and as a result, we are far more inexperienced than the Sentani, who wander across vast stretches of land every year."

"There is plenty of empty land, Pelbar, if you wanted to use it."

"Yes, but it is not the Pelbar way."

"I could never understand how the Pelbar started their peculiar manner of life," said Dar.

"Nor I. It happened centuries ago, and our history and religion explains it to some degree. But we——"

"Your story, Pelbar."

"Yes. As it happened, by chance, we had made the right plan, because soon after a hard west wind came up and blew for several days. The Tantal were anxious to get in the last of their ships before winter, and one, coming from the west, fast, looked to their sentinels to be in trouble if we used our usual methods of docking it. So we were swum far out, to catch the ship well before it would go to leeward and beach on the east shore.

"We knew it was our chance, so the eight of us swam slightly ahead, even outdistancing the following boats with our overseers. There were twelve Tantal on board, but they were busy and worried, and we acted exhausted, so they gave us less heed than was usual. There was a sharp fight. All three Shumai were killed. They led, with great fury, because of the death of their comrade. And before they died, they killed the swordsmen, the two bowmen, and the man with the lash, and we began to let the ship drive downwind, with the overseers' boats trying to follow into bow range.

"But the Rits stopped them, swarmed on the boats, and came after. We took on twenty-two of them before we had to let drive downwind ahead of the swarm of Tantal that put out after us."

"You left some?"

"Yes. They called to us to go. Those on board insisted that all had agreed. They had had their plan too, so as it was, seven were lost to the Tantal. It has always troubled me, but Zepherre, their leader, said they had all agreed ahead of time that all would support the escape of some. As they saw it, they needed to return and alert their whole people to organize and provide a defense against the growing threat of the Tantal and their slavery culture.

"When the wind died finally, we had to work back north and west to the archipelago called Cwebb, to drop off the Rits. By that time it was really winter, and we came west again across the Bitter Sea with snow at our backs and some furious winds. Finally we grounded and burned the boat over a hundred ayas north of the valley of the Nokushi, and had a hard time of it getting there. The Rits had instructed us carefully in winter travel, though. They are used to it, and do it with long slats of wood, a device they claim came down from the ancients.

"Anyhow, we made the journey, and Igon was reunited with his family, as were Tishtak and Moggon. The other Sentani, whose name is Pokinnikani, was of the central band of the tall grass, but—"

"Aiii, Pelbar," said Yall, a southpoint man, "Pokinnikani is alive then. I have met his family at the summergathering as they mourned his loss, some years ago now. They knew nothing of what had happened to him."

"He was alive when I left the valley of the Nokushi," returned Jestak. "But that was some time ago. He had not planned to return to his band until a good opportunity afforded, since he would have to cross Peshtak country alone unless he went well to the north. But if all is well, he is home again."

"And you, Jestak," said Mokil. "You became a Sentani then?"

"No. It was not that easy. It was agreeable to me, but of course it was up to them. I felt then the first inklings of my understanding that all the tribes are alike men. We western peoples all speak dialects of the same tongue, and I have come to be convinced that before the time of fire, we were all one people somehow."

"Ahhh. Pah," said Mokil, and there was a general murmur of disapproval from around the circle.

Jestak merely laughed and shrugged. "I have seen much of the world, although I am young. I am now both a Sentani and a Pelbar, the only one since anyone knows. I have eaten with the Shumai in prison and later in Innanigan, and I have slept curled up between Rits so we wouldn't freeze. I have fed fish soup to a dying Peshtak because his fellows would not come near him because he stank, and I pitied him. I have even seen softness among the Tantal toward their prisoners. They are not monsters, though they have embraced a culture that includes much cruelty. I have been in the eastern cities—three of them—and then to the East Islands, and found such astonishing likenesses among us all that I see no need for us to be so hostile to one another. It is fear. It comes from the fact that men are so few, and so are swallowed up by the greatness of the land."

The Sentani plainly disagreed, and some got up to drift back to their own pointbands.

Jestak also arose. "Please wait," he said. "Only one more moment. I have found, among the scattered ruins from here to the eastern coast, printed in the stone, or the artificial stone, some of the same symbols. And the same sequences. The ancients were a people of one language, I think. They in Innanigan say it was so, but they fear the knowledge and so only the learned will talk much of it. I do not know what it all means, but it must mean something."

"It means, Pelbar, that it is time to sleep. You will take your hour on the sentinel circle, with the brown squad, at moonrise," said Mokil. Jestak was relieved. Clearly the Sentani thought he was odd, but with their usual solidarity and politeness to strangers who were officially Sentani, of whatever band, they did not press the point. Mokil had both ended the conversation and accepted Jestak into his starpoint.

Jestak saluted him, hands out, palms up, and said, "Yes, point leader."

Mokil gestured, and, as the circle broke up, pointed to a young man with a long gash down his leg, and said, "Sleep all night, Winnt. Jestak watches for you." Then he stumped off, slightly bowlegged, to his roll of furs on the leaf mat.

III

Morning rose gray and raw, and the Sentani, rolling stiffly out of their fur sacks, prepared for the day's run northward, drinking only a tea of sumac berries and eating cold banton cakes.

Kicking ashes from the fire, one of the younger men of the north starpoint squinted at Jestak and remarked, "Tell me, Pelbar, if we ever fight against your people, on which side will you be?"

Jestak was glad he had a mouthful of the hard cake, and he chewed as slowly as he could. But a dozen men were waiting. "I don't know," he finally said. "I have wondered. I hope it never comes to that. I could not fight either."

"But it has come and will come," said Rede, the same man.

"Maybe. Maybe I can stop it," said Jestak.

"That," said another, "is smoke in the wind. You are in a position to betray somebody no matter what you do."

"I have thought of all of this, of course. If the time comes, I am willing to pay what must be paid. All I have decided is that I can be a victim if the need arises, but not a betrayer."

"I don't envy you, Jestak," said Juk. "In my grandfather's time, so he said, we seldom met the Shumai, and the Pelbar were only great blocks of stone we passed, except for truceweeks. But clashes are growing more frequent—though not much with the Pelbar." But then the horn sounded, and the first point began its northward run for the day.

By then it was clear that the night's sleep had not cured Winnt. For all his gameness and refusal to murmur, he was not running well. By high sun his squad of the northpoint men were three ayas behind the last of the others. By nightfall they were nearly walking, and could see the winking fires of the main body far ahead. Winnt refused to give in, and no one else mentioned it. When they finally reached the camp, Winnt could do nothing but lie down. He had ripped his calf on a snag in the river while netting fish, and the whole lower leg was angry and swollen. Mokil was clearly worried. No one was allowed to stop the northward movement of the Sentani winter hunt through the river area of the three Pelbar cities because of the possibility of attack from a body of the Shumai from the west. Although the Sentani are willing enough to fight, they preferred to go about their own business, and the numbers would be bound to be against them anyway, if the Shumai migration caught them. At Koorb they were counting on the dried meat and furs that the hunt would produce, as well as the trade goods it would bring from the Pelbar.

"We will see how it is in the morning, Winnt, boy," said Mokil. The young hunter did not answer, but stared, hard-faced, at the darkening river.

"Did you see any of the woolly deer on your way north, Mokil?" Jestak asked.

"A few."

"No herds, or even groups of ten to twenty?"

"No. Three or four was the most. Why do you ask?"

"The Shumai tend to follow the woolly deer in the fall, as a kind of guide to the movement of the wild cattle. On the years when the deer move south late, so do the Shumai. We have seen one or two at once at Pelbarigan. This means that larger numbers will come soon, and with them the Shumai. If the deer haven't herded, but are drifting south in scattered groups, as they sometimes do, then the Shumai bands will tend to be small, too. But otherwise we can expect a large number."

"What is it you are getting at?"

"We are only a day and a half from Northwall. I will stay behind, with Winnt, if you agree, and get him there as quickly as I can. He will be safe there."

"They will kill him."

"No. I am your guarantee. They would never kill him in any case, though they might refuse to help. With me there they would restrict him, to be sure, to only a small part of the city, lest the Sentani learn its defenses. But they would care for his leg. Later he could rejoin you, or he could stay all winter, if need be."

"Jestak," murmured Winnt. "I am Sentani. This is a mere scratch. How can I stay in a stinking city all winter?"

"If those red lines creep up to your thigh and beyond," said Jestak, "that scratch may kill you. As it is, you may lose the leg if it progresses."

"Lose the leg?" said Mokil.

"We would have to cut if off to save him if it putrefies," said Jestak.

The revulsion of the Sentani hunters at this idea was universal. All conveyed the idea, without saying anything, that they would rather die.

"Winnt would have to agree, of course, and I see he would not, but lives have been saved by such a process," said Jestak.

"What for?" Dar snorted.

"For the love of the sun and air, for worship of Aven, for useful work, for the love of family. Surely you have cripples sometimes. At Nokush I saw a few. Of course they did not depend so on running as you, being lake men, and having more year-round village living. But at any rate, my offer is to help Winnt to Northwall and keep him safe, if his infection allows it, until he can rejoin you."

"We will see in the morning," said Mokil.

In the morning, a few snowflakes drifted by on a harsh wind. All the starpoints were ready to run early except the north. Mokil was restless. The other men sat, silent, waiting his decision, ready to go, but clustered around Winnt, whose leg was larger than it had been, and more immobile.

"Dar," Mokil said. "You and Jestak take Winnt to Northwall. Then you can come on when it is safe, or you can stay, as you see fit. Jestak, you give me a message to leave at the message stone to tell them of your coming. Might they send a party to help you?"

"No. They would think that a trick to lure some men to their deaths."

"Do you think, Pelbar," said a tall, thin man, Bron, "that those walls could keep us out if we really wanted to get in?"

"Yes," said Jestak, quietly. "Or if by some chance you got in, you would never get out again."

"No matter," said Mokil hastily. "We are hunting giant beaver and flat-horned deer. We are not invading. Dar is in charge, Jestak, but he will listen to your counsel before making decisions. Now what, Jestak, would you do right away? We must hurry. The starpoints are beginning to leave already."

"I would have Dar and me carry Winnt on a litter about nine ayas upriver to a place I know of, and hide there until nightfall. Then I would move north again until dawn. That should put us just south of the Ruin of Peo, and just over a day from Northwall.

"That will be the most dangerous place, as the Shumai sometimes camp there, but again, I know a place we can hide for the day. Then on the next night we can move to within sight of Northwall if Winnt is able to go that fast."

"I will go," said Winnt.

"How does that seem to you, Dar?"

"I am agreeable, although I do not like all this hiding. But we have little choice."

"I am sure," remarked Bron, "that the Pelbar has plenty of places to hide."

Jestak looked at him a little hard, but said nothing. He did turn and spit into the fire.

"Peace," said Mokil. "We cannot stay longer. Good-bye to the three of you. May Atou be with you all." And he placed his hands against all three in turn, kneeling to salute Winnt, whose hard young face tightened to avoid a flash of tears. Without another word, the north starpoint began its northward run, and Dar and Jestak commenced work on a litter.

It was ready before the sun cleared the bare trees on the west side of the river. Gently, they lifted Winnt onto it, he grimacing so as not to cry out. As they smoothed the furs around him, Dar stopped. "I thought I heard a dog," he whispered.

"You did. A Shumai dog. I heard one before we rolled out this morning."

"Aiii. Atou," said Dar.

"Let us try this, then, Dar. Surely if they come across the river, having been drawn by the campsmoke, they will turn and follow the main body up the trail. There is another trail back from here almost an ayas east. They should be coming from the west. This trail is very small and much rougher. You must promise never to tell of it or use this knowledge against the Pelbar. But I have used it when the area was alive with Sentani. I even sat, once, on that pinnacle and watched a small band of Shumai skinning deer where we are now."

"Let us not wait," said Dar. "I agree."

The two men tried to trot slowly with Winnt, but it

proved too painful for him. The trail led upward toward high ground, through brush and forest. Unlike the main trail, it had many climbs and dips. Twice in the first hour they went waist deep in streams, holding Winnt high. They never crossed the streams, but went first down, then up, to pick up the trail again.

Three times before high sun, they rested, but never for long. At such times they were very still, as if listening for the distant bay of the Shumai dog. Past noon they heard it again, one dog, far to the west.

"Good," Jestak whispered. "There is only one dog. That means a small band. If they follow the starband, it will do them no good, and now that the Sentani are free to run, they will be gone before any more can gather."

"Maybe," said Dar. "The Shumai never go beyond Northwall very much anyhow."

"Never," said Jestak. "Even to follow the black short-horns, in fall. It leaves them too far from the long grass before winter comes."

"Where did you learn so much of them?" Winnt asked.

"It is Pelbar business to know as much as we can about where all the peoples are and go—if we can. And now you and I will have to go if we are to reach the shelter. This way it is taking us longer," said Jestak, rising and standing by the lead end of the litter. Dar grunted and stood, dusting himself. The snow began to fall a little more heavily, and they began to worry about tracks.

Toward evening the trail dipped toward the river through scrub oak and briars. The men took no more breaks now and moved at a swinging pace that was nearly a trot. Dar was beginning to pant heavily, but he dared not ask a rest from a mere Pelbar.

"Winnt, boy, what have you been eating," he panted at one point.

The wetting in the cold streams and the long struggle to keep up the pace in spite of the terrain told on both men, and Winnt was beginning to groan in his pain, fighting to keep still.

Finally, they stopped in a small, cup-shaped depression, having skirted a prairie-crowned crest in the woods. "Look north, Dar," said Jestak. "What do you see?"

"Nothing to remark," said Dar.

"Look by the base of that bark oak. Anything?"

"Still no."

"Good. That is as far as we have to go." And Jestak signaled to take up the litter again, and they moved slowly across the grassy cup to the oak, which stood near a tumbled rock outcrop. Here Jestak signaled that they should put the litter down. Walking to the outcrop, he lifted down a rock, then put his shoulder against a large boulder. It swung on a pivot, leaving an opening into which the men could easily slide the litter. Once they were inside, Dar and Jestak crawled back to the opening and studied the growing darkness.

"No dogs, Jestak."

"No. And no tracks, with this snow."

"Not until tomorrow, anyhow. Then we can see. We can never go on tonight."

"True."

After Jestak had swung down the gatestone and fastened it, the inside was completely dark. He moved, though, with sureness, along the south wall until he reached the shelf of the lamp, and there, with flint and steel, he started some tinder and ignited the small oil flame.

"Ahhh," said Winnt. Though neither Sentani said anything, they both suddenly saw further into the mystery of how the Pelbar cities communicated with one another. The interior was not large, but it was still more than the Sentani were used to outside of Koorb. Four bows waited in racks by the gatestone, and bundles of arrows by them. Two long swords hung overhead on the wall. Bunks lay along the north wall, and supplies and kitchen goods along the south. In the rear of the waycave was a well that drilled down through solid rock into a seepage stratum in the limestone, guiding some of the water off into a small pool. The walls were plastered smooth and covered with paintings of a fineness that even in the dim light the two Sentani recognized as something they had never seen before. Behind the bunks on the north wall was a passage leading to a side room that followed two bends to a small fissure drilled out through the rock and shaped to look natural. A similar small room and vent system led out the south wall near the basin. A hole in the floor by the basin served as a drain, and in the south vent room was a latrine cut deep in the rock and washed by the overflow conducted from the well pool.

As the two Sentani rested, Jestak busied himself with housekeeping. "We may take no lights into the vent rooms at night," he said. "But a lamp in this room cannot be seen." He emptied the permanent rodent traps into the latrine, washed them out, and reset them. Lighting a larger lamp, he placed it under a ring and tripod, and began heating water in a copper bowl. From a raised stone chest he brought down filled pads and spread them on three of the ten bunks. Another stone box produced some biscuit, hard as iron, called "traveler's rock" by the Pelbar, who eat it only dipped in tea to soften it. Dried apples hung in loops of cord in one vent room, and Jestak took one down for them.

Without much talk the two men heated tea and mixed dried meat with apples, a few herbs from a pottery cannister, and the traveler's rock. Over the small flame this took some time, but they were too tired to be in much of a hurry, and Winnt was dazed with his pain and fatigue. After they ate, and fed Winnt slowly and carefully, they washed his leg with warm water and Pelbar soap from the small supply in the waycave. Winnt put his belt in his mouth and bit down hard on it to keep from crying out, but even so his muffled gasps and cries grew almost unbearable to the other two.

"I think it will break soon. See there," said Dar, gesturing. "We can't go on until it does, Jestak. We must wait here until tomorrow night anyhow."

"I can go. Do not stay on my account," said Winnt, faintly. "I will be running again before long." The other two exchanged glances.

"To be sure," Jestak returned. "But as Dar says, let us stay here awhile. As it is, I think I am ready for sleep."

But Jestak did not sleep right away. Near the lamp he prayed in the Pelbar manner, which is to put the heels of the hands to the eyes and curl the fingers against the forehead. Once in their fursacks, the two well men spent a restless night, too fatigued to sleep deeply, and too distracted by the moans of Winnt, who rolled and pitched, dozed and woke. Toward morning, he let out a long wail and fell unconscious. The other two were at his side immediately, and the light of the lamp showed his wound was draining. The tanned leg, now puffed and misshapen, with lines of purple, lay like an old fire, with a gray cast in the dim flame. Pelbar textiles, woven from Shumai trade fibers, absorbed the matter and washed the wound. After Dar could see sunlight from the fissure in the vent room,

Jestak said gently to the reawakened Winnt, "Good. You will not lose the leg now. You are winning against the infection. Rest and we will be able to travel tonight."

It was not that easy. Winnt was still in much pain, but he and Dar, neither of whom had ever been in so confined a place before, were restless before the sun had set. The dust of snow of the day before was gone with the cold light of the Buckmonth sun, though, so they had no tracks to worry about for the present. A quarter moon would light the path somewhat, and as Jestak eased back the gatestone, and replaced the key rock, all were eager to be gone. They listened in the dark for a few minutes. No dogs. Nothing but wind in dry weeds, dry leaves.

That night was a nightmare for Winnt, as the two carriers moved rapidly on a path so faint, by the design of the Pelbar, that it was hard to see in daylight. The first pale showing of dawn found the men still several ayas south of the Ruin of Peo and Jestak's other shelter. Soon they would be out of the hills, and the flat land toward Peo would give them little cover. It is movement that catches the eye of the hunter, and Shumai in the area might easily see them.

"Jestak," said Dar. "How near are we to the river?"

"Not two ayas."

"Let us go there and spend the day in the willow thickets. Tonight we can move on, and bypass your shelter."

"We will have to cross the main trail. Shumai dogs can pick us up as a fresher scent."

"We will have to risk it."

As light grew, the two men moved into a slow jog, and Winnt put his broad sleeve in his mouth and bit hard against the painful jarring. It was nearly full light when they crossed the main trail. Dar and Jestak put the litter down a short distance beyond, and Dar returned to check the trail. He came back frowning.

"A large party of Shumai are behind the starband," he said. "But I think they are far behind. They cannot have passed until sometime last night. I don't think they will catch up."

"No one outruns the Shumai," said Jestak. "Or so they say. The question is, will they go beyond Northwall? Surely the starband has passed there before now."

"And," said Winnt from the litter, "will they then turn back and lie between Northwall and us?"

"Come," returned Dar. "Let us get on to the willows."

By full day they were in a thick willow tangle by the edge of the water at the lower end of a bend, where they could see both upriver and down. Dar had carefully put several mansnares on their path. When he returned, he found Jestak bending over a strange piece of equipment he had never seen before. Winnt was watching, as Jestak fixed a large, convex piece of glass over the tiny kettle he carried, focusing the slanting sun rays on the water inside.

"We can have no fire," he said, "but this will help warm some water." He nested the kettle in his fur mittens. Dar and Winnt looked puzzled. "Winnt," continued Jestak, "since you are here, move this as the sun moves, so the rays always fall within the water through the glass top. I will lash those driftwood logs into a narrow raft. If we get trapped by the water, we will need it."

Jestak had a small knife in his pack, and a linksaw, and with them, and much caution and patience, he spent much of the day fashioning a raft, lashed and pegged. It was ungainly, but solid, and its narrowness, he hoped, would let them pole it rapidly.

In midafternoon, he took his turn at sleeping, and Dar watched. The wind began to rise, and the waves from the river made it impossible to hear very much. Dar washed Winnt's leg with the sun-warmed water and repacked Jestak's gear while he slept.

"Dar," said Winnt. "I don't like it. I can almost taste the Shumai. Let's move near the raft."

"Yes, I, too—" began Dar, but was interrupted by a snap and a wild yell as the furthest of the mansnares was sprung. Jestak was up instantly. The two men rushed Winnt to the raft, threw their gear on, and pushed off as they heard the next snare sprung. Poling out, as Winnt strung the two bows, Jestak and Dar strained to get out of spear range before the Shumai should reach shore.

The dog was first in sight, a long-haired, gray animal, almost waist high, forcing the willows and running down the water's edge to make the long leap onto the raft. Dar's pole caught him in midair in the ribs and parried the jump. The dog fell into the water, rose, and continued his pursuit, snarling and snapping. Winnt, grunting in pain, rolled sideways and put an arrow through his neck, and at that moment, four Shumai came in sight, three with spears, one with an axe. All yelled with a peculiar, quavering falsetto as they saw the men on the raft. The man in the lead raised his weapon and ran onto the water's edge to throw it, only to trip the mansnare Dar had hidden and fall headlong, with three wooden stakes protruding through his back.

The man behind him stooped instantly, picked up the spear, and threw it with great force at Dar, but Jestak's pole reached over and struck it down in front of the raft into the water.

"Atou," said Dar. Winnt's next arrow passed by the dodging man in the lead, and the second man's spear stuck into the raft across his body, its shaft slapping him sharply as it swayed downward from the fastened tip.

Two more Shumai appeared on the shore, but Dar had taken up a bow and nocked an arrow, as Jestak continued poling outward into the main channel. There were now three spearmen, though none dared throw, knowing that Dar could shoot any man who, in the act of launching his spear, was too off-balance to dodge.

"Ready, Winnt," Jestak muttered. "If they all throw at once, you shoot just before they release. Take the center man."

That was the Shumai plan, but Winnt's arrow disrupted their aim, hitting the left man in the arm as Dar's thudded into the center one in the midsection. Two spears fell wide, but one aimed true at Winnt, and Jestak, in lunging for it, was raked across the palm. Winnt twisted, but was pinned to the logs by it, as it passed through his coat at the waist and sliced through skin and flesh at waist level. Another arrow from Dar was casually dodged by the axeman, as if in contempt. That ended the exchange of weapons. In the gathering dusk, the enemies looked at each other across the stretch of rippling water in a momentary silence. The man with the arrow in his arm was removing it impassively, while the others showed their rage, lifting their remaining spears in a final loonlike call of defiance.

The long raft began to spin in the current. Dar took up one of Jestak's crude paddles, while Jestak worked the spear out of the log, and Winnt's coat, with his good hand, holding the other against his leg.

"So much for that," said Dar. "Now what?"

"Now we paddle upriver on the west shore," said Jestak. "They will have no boats here. They may run north and build rafts to intercept us, but we will have to risk that. We aren't that far from Northwall."

With much effort, they made for an island about an ayas upriver, passing over to the west side out of sight. There Winnt bound up Jestak's hand, while Jestak, in turn, sewed up Winnt's side, which was cut through, but not deeply. Both men grimaced in pain but did not cry out. Dar was in mid-island, watching. When Jestak whistled softly, he returned.

"Well," he said, "we have killed four men and a dog and wounded one other. Not bad. But they will not take that lightly."

"No, but it is only a small band. The question is, will they be able to link up with any others? I have some other ideas, anyway. I have spent time at Northwall and know the area well."

"We never see Pelbar outside the walls except at truce-weeks."

"Nevertheless we go often enough."

The two men poled up the west side of the wooded island and then paddled out into the open stream. As they appeared, they heard the faint cry of the Shumai, who saw them in spite of the dark.

"Good," said Jestak.

"I see no good in it," returned Winnt. His leg was improving, in spite of all the misuse of the last days, and with it his spirits had begun to return.

"If we work hard all night, we will be at Northwall before daybreak," Jestak explained. "They will follow on the shore, naturally, but they cannot both keep us in sight and cross Arkan Creek, which runs into the main Heart River just south of Northwall. They will get across, of course, but we should gain on them there and then pass behind Rabbit-brush Island. If they then put out from shore, to catch us at the head of the island, as we turn to cross to the city, then we break the raft, by severing these withes here, and allow part of the raft to drift back downriver, with some refuse or other to make them think we are there and have a stratagem. They will then turn in pursuit, and we can make for the city around the head of the island. Winnt, you may have to sit up and paddle. Can you do that?"

"Yes."

"Does that sound all right to you, Dar?"

The dark Sentani laughed. "What am I comparing it to?" he asked. "It is not like eating deer tongue in summer along the banks of the Sentan, with a woman playing the pellute by my side, and singing of love. But I am willing to try it. I have one question. What if there are Shumai on Rabbitbrush?"

"Ah, yes. That would not be good. I had thought of that, but think that they will not be of the same group and will know nothing of us. Perhaps that will make the difference." And the two men bent to their paddles in silence as the night deepened and grew chill, and the stars wheeled toward dawn.

Dar could see that the Pelbar knew the shape of the river by instinct, where each channel crossing lay, where to find the easiest water to pole or paddle in, and how to avoid snags. He surmised that the Pelbar traveled the river by night undetected.

Before the sky began to lighten, Rabbitbrush Island loomed ahead, and to the east, the black, looming cube of Northwall, high over the bluffs. They could see small fires on Rabbitbrush. Counting them, Dar saw eighteen.

"That will mean," he said, out of the silence of their straining paddling, "there are at least fifty Shumai on Rabbitbrush. What do we do, Jestak?"

"We come in close under the willows and put holes in their boats. Then we carry on as before. They will have little watch tonight, except perhaps a couple of men on the Northwall side. These boats will be temporary makeshifts put together for immediate use. If we are out in the main river before they are aware of us, then we will be safely to Northwall before they can stop us."

Coming slowly up to the foot of the island, the men found rough skin-covered boats and quietly put cross-shaped slits in the hides with their short swords. Working their way upriver, they accounted for twenty-five boats without being seen when Jestak touched Dar's shoulder. "This one is larger," he whispered. "Let us put Winnt in it, and let the raft go."

As they were doing this, they could hear, faintly, from the east bank, the yells of the Shumai following. The camp was being aroused. There was no time to waste. The raft was pushed free, with a Shumai hide bundle on it taken from the shore stuff, and the two worked the boat toward the swampy willow head of the island. Fires began to blaze up behind them. They could hear men calling, then a general call for silence. The Shumai who had followed them were coming out from shore now, probably on a raft. The two groups began hailing each other, as the boat of fugitives waited at the tip of the island. A distant yell told them that the raft had been discovered drifting downstream. The eastern sky was just beginning to show signs of pink. Calls from the island told Jestak that the Shumai there understood, and were making for the boats. "Now," he said, and they pushed free from the north end of the island and strained for the eastern bank, slightly upstream, above the mouth of Arkan Creek.

They had not gone fifty arms before a call behind them told them they had been discovered. In spite of the strain, Dar laughed at the thought of swarms of men launching boats that promptly sank. The Shumai on the river saw them now, too, but the current was dead against them, and their raft could not hope to catch the fugitive boat. They turned and headed for the east bank. Plainly they hoped to beach there and run north to intercept the three. Winnt, leaning up, said quietly, "They have picked up some others. I count fifteen."

"Winnt," grunted Jestak, between strokes, "get into my pack and find a long copper whistle on the right. Put it in my right pocket."

Winnt obeyed without question, growing used to the Pelbar's strange equipment and strange requests. The Shumai were now on shore below, and beginning their run, with high, quavering cries.

As the boat grounded, Jestak stooped and threw his pack far out into the river, and the two men picked up the litter and began to run toward Northwall. It was dawn. Watch fires along the wall showed that the city was alerted to something. Jestak in the lead, they headed straight for the blank wall, which showed no gate anywhere, but only a plain face of stone. Dar panted, "Jestak, how . . . will we . . . get in?"

"They will open."

From the south, they could see several Shumai coming out of the brush by the creek and running across the forefield in an attempt to head them off. A long horn blast sounded from the wall. Without stopping, Jestak took the crosspiece of the litter in his left hand, swept the whistle to his mouth, and returned a long, piercing shrill, then dropped the whistle from his mouth and ran on. The Shumai were gaining. More could be seen behind, running fast. Halfway down the face of the wall, toward the north, a small light showed, and Jestak immediately ran for it. It would be close. The Shumai were almost within spear range, coming from the south, when, with a spray of coals, a long cloud of smoke shot out from the wall, separating the two parties. The Shumai ran through it, yelling and coughing. As Jestak neared the wall, a portion of it tipped and rose, and the three ran through into a dark, walled corridor. "Keep running," gasped Jestak.

Before the stone closed, three Shumai were inside, and one launched a spear as the floor trap tipped from under them and they disappeared, screaming. Soon, a door at the end of the corridor opened, and a short man strode toward the group on the floor.

"Well, Jestak . . ." he began, then stopped, as he saw his nephew holding the head of Dar, panting and weeping, as the Shumai spear that had pierced the Sentani drained his blood from both front and back.

"We . . . it was . . . we have . . . it is all right. It is all right. Oh, Atou, Atou," said Dar, softly. And then he died.

 IV

SIMA PALL, the Northwall Protector, sat in the judgment hall on a low dais, robed in the dark-red mantle of her office. She bent over the low table in front of her, writing slowly, not seeming to notice the other four of the council as they entered. Her dark hair was piled in a stack of three buns, that of the others in two. Occasionally she dipped her pen, touched it to a small pad of fiber, and continued to write.

Last, Jestak entered, accompanied by his uncle, Manti the Jestan, chief of defenses of Northwall. Manti bowed low, turned to his left, and sat against the wall on a small curved bench. Jestak also bowed, somewhat stiffly, and remained standing.

Finally Sima Pall looked up. "We are assembled and in

order," she began, in a dry near-falsetto. She did not smile. "We have several matters to attend to, chiefly the ones involving you, Jestak the Jestan, and those involving the problems of defense which you have caused and which have come about in part by the concentration of Shumai outside our walls.

"First, I have a list of matters concerning you, Jestak, which of course we must have answers for.

"Primarily, you are sent to us as an exile from Pelbarigan, which is perhaps a suitable shame for you, but hardly a compliment to us. The document of your exile, you tell us, is in your pack in the river opposite the city. Is that correct?"

"Yes, Protector, but I know where it is and can recover it when the Shumai depart."

"Yes is sufficient. Second, you have not only sent advance message of your exile by hostile Sentani, but arrived with two more Sentani, not to mention your own wild man's tattoo. One of these Sentani is even now inside our walls, learning of our defenses while receiving medical care. Is that correct?"

"Yes."

"Yes, Protector, if you please. Third, not only did you come north in company of these Sentani, but you have aroused the hostility of the Shumai in protecting one of them. And furthermore, you have done what no Pelbar has ever before done. You have admitted two of the enemy to a waycave, thus revealing to them that such a system of communication exists and jeopardizing our entire communications and transportation system. Is that correct?"

"Yes, Protector. It was necessary to save—"

"Jestak!" hissed Manti.

"Fourth, you not only returned from the eastern cities without your mission completed, but two years late. And you have never revealed the particulars of your absence to anyone. Nor have you told those of Northwall, to whom you have the duty, of the fate of the others, and especially of Brus, whose mother is on the council." She waved her hand to the thin and anxious face on the far left.

Jestak shifted his glance to her and found her eyes boring into him. He dropped his look. "Brus and the others are dead," he said.

A wail went up from Brin Brunag, and at the same instant, Manti strode to Jestak, and said, "Have a care. We cannot indulge you. We have order here. You were not asked to speak."

"Peace, Manti," continued the Protector. "He would not have been exiled if he were a simple and easy case. I am sure we can reinstill Pelbar courtesy in him in a year's time. I expect also the particulars of this misfortune, as well as the explanation of how you failed your friends. You seem to have prospered yourself and made other friends."

A small man entered the chamber by a side door and whispered to Manti. The Protector arched her brows at this interruption. "I beg your indulgence, Protector and council," Manti blushed. "It seems the Shumai are at the message stone and demand the return of their three fellows who entered the pivot gate yesterday."

"They were dispatched, were they not?" chanted the Protector.

"Yes, in the floortrap."

"Then how can we return them? Surely that will stir their animosity even further, will it not?"

"As you say, Protector," said Manti.

"What a lot of river water!" Jestak burst in. "How can you say this? Here you trade with these people twice a year and know nothing of them. If you really want them angry, just do not return the bodies. They may bluster, but they well know a fight is a fight, and that they were the aggressors. You can't refuse the bodies. They will stay well into winter. They will refuse truceweeks. The Shumai custom is to honor their dead."

Silence followed Jestak's outburst. None of the council had ever confronted any such defiance of the Protector's clear decision before. Sima Pall controlled her rising anger, as became a Pelbar politician. She was in a quandary. Clearly Jestak spoke from knowledge, and if he were right, her decision might jeopardize the winter activity of Northwall, which was usually deserted by the outside tribes. Yet if she were to acknowledge that there might be something correct in what he said, her authority would have been successfully breached by the exile. Yet he was Manti's nephew. Manti sensed her dilemma, appalled as he was by his nephew's behavior.

"Your punishment, Jestak," she finally said, "is to deliver the bodies yourself to this Shumai. If they honor you and your opinion, then you will return to us and to this council. If not, as I fully anticipate, then the severest punishment in the Pelbar code, rejection from the cities, to fend as you best can, will have been in a sense administered."

Manti started. It seemed a death sentence, and it was hard to see his nephew receive it. He did not understand the slight smile on the thin face of the young man. Manti had seen a casting out once before, and had seen Omant the Oken cut down soon after he reached the river by Shumai hunters camped on the north field after fall truceweek.

"You, Manti, shall go with him, wearing, of course, the trucecape, which, under the circumstances, they will have to honor."

"A request, Protector," said Jestak.

"Are you in a position to make requests?"

"Only one to the political advantage of the Pelbar. Since we are two, send to them that only two of them be at the message stone and unarmed, as we will be."

"Granted," said the Protector. Then she rose and left the room by a small rear door. Jestak had the feeling that she was hastening to an upper window to witness his death with some self-satisfaction. But then she turned and gave him one glance from inside the door. And he was no longer sure.

All bowed and left. "Jestak, of all the moose-headed foolishness. You have thrown away your life. How can I stand there and see them cut you down? Surely they will conceal weapons. You know these Shumai. They are the wildest of all the tribes. How—"

"I do know them, Uncle. I do not think they will violate their truce. However, I shall conceal a weapon as well."

"No Pelbar ever violates a confidence. I forbid it."

"Nevertheless, Uncle, I will take a weapon. No confidence will be violated because they will never know I am armed unless they draw weapons first."

Manti was speechless with the enormity of what Jestak had just said. The young man took his shoulders and looked him in the face. "I'm sorry, Uncle. But you must trust me. Remember, though I am young, I have traveled farther, seen much more, interacted with more peoples, and survived more crises, than anyone in either Pelbarigan or Northwall. When you sent us to the east, you sent us like butterflies to the forge. You had no idea what you did.

I survived, but not by observing Pelbar niceties. Trust me, I beg of you."

The older man was completely nonplussed. He held his palms to his chest, in a gesture of exhausted compliance. "Good," said Jestak. "Now let us ready the bodies."

In accordance with Jestak's instructions, the three bodies, of which no care had been taken, were washed. Their clothing was also washed and arranged on them as well as could be. Much to the puzzlement and distaste of the Pelbar, Jestak placed herbs on wrists and ankles and around the waist, and a simple iron necklace was put around each of their necks. As the arrangement specified, with the third quadrant of the sun, the pivot stone raised, and the two men started across the forefield toward the message stone where the two Shumai waited. The bodies were on a drag, which Jestak carried across his shoulders, his hurt hand, bandaged, hanging over the crosspole. One of the two Shumai was the axeman from the camp by the river. He looked grim. The other man, young and light-haired, acted more casual. He, thought Jestak, is the one to watch.

As the agreement had it, Manti was to do the speaking, and Jestak, who knew the Shumai dialect, would translate if need be.

"Pelbar swine," said the axeman, "I see you have come from your pens to return our men as you said. That is good for you."

"Honored Shumai," returned Manti, when Jestak had made clear the western dialect, "we regret that circumstances were as they were, but we felt that we could do no other than defend ourselves and our kinsman."

It was clear that the axeman understood much of what was said. Nonetheless, Jestak translated, "Here, you fat fish belly. Take your men, and expect the same for any others you may send near Pelbar walls."

The Shumai's hand went to his side, but his axe was not there. Then he glanced at the three bodies. There was a silence. "You have honored them in the manner of the northeast bands," he said. "You are the one of the beach. The one who runs with the Sentani dogs. Your offal will rot on dishonored ground soon enough. Nonetheless, I thank you for your kindness to my men."

Jestak translated, and Manti was as much relieved as puzzled. "I am glad you are pleased with what we have done, and I hope the necessity never arises again to break the peace."

The Shumai shifted his eyes to Jestak, wanting to see how this courtesy would come out. "We did not wish to kill your men," he began, "but you forced it on us, the way a snake will rush beneath the hooves of the bulls. You have also served us another interesting turn. The first Sentani ever to be in Pelbar walls lies there now recovering from his wounds."

The axeman understood that Jestak was bestowing a further honor by informing him that one of his own allies had been killed. Here was a man he understood as little as did the Pelbar their own.

"Kaim," he said, turning to the younger man. "Take our companions to the shore, where our friends await them. And you, Pelbar," he continued, addressing Manti, "in order to maintain the odds, though they would still, after all, be in my favor, kindly return to your walls. I would have some extraneous words with this wild young one, who runs with the Sentani dogs."

Both companions were puzzled. Kaim, it was quite clear, had hoped for a fight, and some revenge. But the order was clear. Jestak translated it faithfully, and with some hesitancy, Manti bowed and retired.

"Now," said the axeman. "Do not think that you will kill me with the short sword under your coat. I am more than a match for you."

"I do not doubt it, Shumai, even perhaps without the knife in your inner belt. What do you wish with me?"

"You speak perfectly in the manner of my northern cousins, west of the Bitter Sea. And you have dressed the dead in their manner. That was a good thing, and has saved us the necessity of much starvation and hardship in avenging them. And yet you run with the Sentani weasels."

"They were dogs last time."

"No matter, Pelbar. You are disrupting the pattern of things, on which all order depends. Nonetheless, I thank you and would like to know how you survived acquaintance with Shumai."

Jestak briefly told him of his captivity with the Tantal, and his hard-won acquaintanceship with the northeast Shumai. "What," said the axeman, "were their names?"

"The eldest was Drok. Wan died before we escaped. The

other two were brothers, Ould and Nev. Do you know them?"

"No. But we will send word of their fate to their band. How were they buried?"

"Wan was thrown into the river by the Tantal. We could do nothing about it. The others were buried on a high hill on the south shore of the Bitter Sea, in lake Sentani country, by Igon and me. Their heads faced the sunrise. They were buried upright, and their hands held a broken spear."

"So again we owe you. Perhaps I will pay the debt by not killing you now. So the Pelbar thought to steal a gain on us by linking up with the eastern cities? But you were not able to do that, I see."

"Axeman, we western peoples have an entirely false picture of the eastern cities, their power, and where they are. Between here and the east most of the land is empty, with an occasional ruin. The eastern cities do not control much. Only as far west as the east slopes of the mountains. Between them and the eastern Sentani are the Peshtak and a tribe I never met, the Coo. Both are fierce and incredibly cruel—I think because they are crushed between two forces and are making themselves so dangerous that they will be left untouched. I am Pelbar enough to wish that we out here were all at peace with one another. When one is in the east, one thinks of us all as one group, and surely the easterners do. We are, to them, the barbarians of the west. I even lived with a Shumai in Innanigan."

The axeman laughed. "We get along well enough without peace, Pelbar. Would you have us all women, or ruled by women as you are? Where is the glory of peace?"

Jestak placed his palms on his chest. "I am, I suppose, a man without a tribe. The Pelbar are close-minded, the Shumai are too anxious to kill without a reason, and the Sentani, who lie somewhere between, are so anxious to avoid the Shumai and follow their old pattern of life that they never change. I do not understand."

"There is nothing to understand. It is the way of things. Do not question them. I noticed, by the way, that you killed no one. Therefore I do not owe you anyone. But do not think that I will not kill you if we again meet. Good luck until then. And good-bye. My name is Waldura."

"Good-bye. Mine is Jestak." The two men held their right hands out with palms flat, and placed them together three times in the Shumai sign of parting. Then both turned their backs on one another and walked back to their peoples.

The Protector was amazed. She had, as Jestak surmised, watched the whole episode from her upper window, and had witnessed with puzzlement the short conversation between Jestak and the axeman at the message stone, standing at their ease, gesturing, and finishing with the Shumai parting. She sat in the growing dusk, not even noticing when Comm brought her steaming bush tea and silently put it on the small table by her side. Finally, long after he had withdrawn, she smelled it and took a sip. It was nearly cold. She was a shrewd woman who had maintained her position for many years by decisions wise in the Pelbar manner, and by holding the tight organization of the city to its duties without slackening. But here was something new. It had, perhaps, been introduced by the Pelbarigan idea of communication with the eastern peoples, to set up trade. The fear had been that the tribesmen seemed to grow in numbers—not rapidly, though surely—but the Pelbar, with their strict ways and controls on birth, remained more or less the same. Plainly change of some sort was necessary, but the cautious Pelbar, after endless discussions, had been undecided as to what to do. Free birth would disrupt the social system, overinvolve the women who were needed for administration, and necessitate some enormous project, such as the building of a new city. The only sites were far from Threerivers, Pelbarigan, or Northwall. The builders, working deliberately and in Pelbar perfection, would be unprotected. It was an unacceptable solution. Nor could the existing cities easily be added to, without enormous labor for little gain, and without jeopardizing the food supplies of their fragile economy, for they did almost no unprotected farming, and their enemies did not trade foods very freely, but largely raw materials gathered from the wilderness.

Yet now she had witnessed this anomaly. Jestak. Plainly the project of the eastern cities was to bring change. But the changes that would come had been planned, and they had not occurred as planned. Although it was against Pelbar custom, the council would have to get from Jestak information about what happened. He had been largely silent on the matter. His reasons were not clear. Perhaps he had done some dishonorable thing, to which he would not confess. Perhaps some situation had arisen that had brought the deaths of his companions and he was unwilling to bring shame and blame to the planners and anguish to the families—here to the Brunag—and so took his right of reticence. But to bring a Sentani into Northwall as a friend and companion, as had never been done, and then to talk with a Shumai enemy on apparently equal terms—neither of these things had ever been heard of to her knowledge. She picked up a small baton and rapped on a hollow wood pipe hung by her chair. Comm soon appeared from behind the draped doorway to the outer room.

"Comm, this tea it cold."

"Yes, Protector." He removed the cup, not telling her that it had stood now a half quadrant. "Would you like some fresh?" he asked.

"No. Bring Manti." Comm bowed and left.

It was not long before the chief of defenses was ushered into the Protector's room. He bowed low. "Sit, Manti," she said, "and tell me what transpired at the message stone."

After this had been done, as far as Manti was able, she remarked, "Then he did not translate faithfully what you said?"

"No, Protector. But if I may be permitted to make an observation . . ."

"Yes, Manti. Do not stand on our ceremonies. There is more here that I must understand. Speak freely and I will not hold you to it."

"Yes, Protector. After Jestak called him a 'fish belly,' he seemed to respect him more. Especially, of course, when he saw how the bodies were arranged."

"A fish belly?"

"Yes, Protector. I had called him 'Honored Shumai,' and this Jestak rendered as 'fish belly.' I must say, as much as I understood it, although shocking, it was a good return to the typical Shumai insults."

The Protector came as near to a smile as she had since Jestak arrived. "But the Pelbar do not indulge themselves. It is unwise and undiplomatic."

"Yes, Protector. I think in this case, however, if I may be permitted to say so, Jestak was not indulging himself but rather using a diplomatic method common among the outside tribes, with which he is familiar. He says they are men of honor in their own way, even the wild Shumai."

"You say, Manti, that Jestak knew how the northeast Shumai bury their dead? Where do they range?"

"Jestak says west of the Bitter Sea, but I do not know where that is."

"The Bitter Sea. I have heard of it, but only once, as a rumor from the reports of a truceweek. The Bitter Sea. So there is one, and Jestak has been there. Manti, I think we will have to break a precedent. We must demand from Jestak a full report of all that transpired in the years in which he was away. We must insist that he break the right of reticence and protect him from any insults or prosecution that must befall his speaking."

"But, Protector, do you think . . ." But she had raised her hand for silence.

"Manti, you are acting like an old man, fidgeting and bowing. I remember when you called me Sima, and with some gentleness. Now please think of the frankness of those times, and talk to me as you would, without respect to courtesy or position. I would say this to no one else, nor would I like it to go beyond this room. Tell me, old Manti of the spicebushes, exactly what you think."

The man blushed, and finally the Protector stood and walked to him. "Embrace me, Manti, and tell me then. Once we committed that impropriety without much thought to Pelbar rules. I not only permit it. I demand it. Tell me, old man, exactly what your mind, and not your courtesies, thinks."

And against her shoulder, Manti murmured, "I think, Sima, that Jestak is a man of great ability. I know he has been through much, for I have seen some of his scars. He has a quick mind and a sense of command I have never seen in a Pelbar man, though it is common enough in the outside tribesmen. I think we must listen to him. Perhaps he is the first breath of a change of climate for the west. Perhaps it will be a bad change. But he drops information in conversation that no one else knows of. Perhaps we have been limited too long by our exclusive occupancy of these cities."

"Would you have preferred the death of the outside tribes?"

"No. Surely, no. But in a way, is not this a kind of death as well, never to paddle the rivers freely, as we see the Sentani do several times yearly?"

"Let us not take this any further, Manti, for these are

extraneous questions. Tell Comm, as you go out, to summon a council meeting, a private one, immediately in the council chamber, in spite of the hour."

"Yes, Protector." But she had not yet let go of him. "Old Manti." And she touched her lips to each of his sunnarrowed eyes. Then she let him go.

Winnt was mending. He was not accustomed to giving women so much authority, but here all was strange, and he, still weak, simply accepted everything with some of the helplessness of a child. Jestak looked in on him frequently. But his embarrassment chiefly came from the woman called Viret the Mejan, who attended to the sick and hurt, and who treated his body like her private possession, making free with it as if he were a baby and she the mother. She had even questioned him quite frankly on his circumcision, examining it like a strange flower, explaining, without much delicacy, that it was the first she had seen in all her medical practice. He thought he would die of embarrassment, but she would not permit his silence, and insisted he take his face from the bolster with which he had covered it. The buffeting of the journey, and especially the race for the wall, had left him weakened and passive, and he was in no condition to assert his dignity.

The young Pelbar man who accompanied the Mejana worked largely in silence and performed the bidding of the physician, washing and binding him with a gentleness unknown among the Sentani men—though common enough, Winnt reflected, among the women. His outcry when a company of curious women, several of them young, came during the time when two of the Pelbar nurses were bathing him, caused much merriment among them. He was determined to leave Northwall as soon as he was well. It was clear to him that he was indeed mending. Only his weakness prevented him from flinging them all from the room.

He was even more emotionally drained when, after a time, one of them returned, a small, dark-haired woman of no more than his own age, and said to him, in the millifluous Pelbar tones, "Jestak has told us in a manner in which no man should ever speak to a woman that we were wrong to come here as we did. The others were outraged at him, and put it down as one more of his wild and unacceptable traits. No woman will ever allow him to serve her. Several even told him so, but he was not ashamed. He said he thought he would like to marry a Shumai woman. A Shumai. He really said that. What is more, I think he half meant it. Do you understand me? Yes? Anyway, please forgive me, and us. We are not accustomed to strangers, and it may well be that we did offend you, though I don't understand how that could be. We do see the Sentani men, though, and the Shumai, from the walls at truceweeks, and they appear to be unfortunately lacking in the wisdom of women. Perhaps that is why they are so barbaric. Ah, I may have offended you again. At any rate, even though you are so thin and tattooed on the arm, I would accept your service if you were discerning enough to render it. What? I have offended you again? You are unaccountable."

She frowned. But then she put an apple on his stomach, quite abruptly, and left. Winnt lay in bewildered exasperation. Then, having nothing to do, he slowly ate the apple, core and seeds as well, leaving only the stem, which he tossed expertly into the box in the corner, wincing as his leg pulled from the motion.

As a result of the council meeting of the previous night, a general meeting of the Northwall leaders, including council, discipline chiefs, and defense segments, was called in the judgment hall. Jestak, of course, was commanded to be present as the focus of the meeting.

"Today," began the Protector, "we are going to talk freely. It will be necessary if we are to find out from Jestak the Jestan the results of his eastern trip, on which so much effort was placed, and which has failed so signally, and about which he has taken the right of reticence. Today, however, Jestak, we—the council, that is—must command you to break your reticence and relate to us the account of your journey and the reasons for its failure. In return, we release you from the penalties for any insults or improprieties that your speech will bring. This does not mean, of course, that you are to insult us gratuitously, as you have already, but rather that you are to give us the facts. Please, if you will, refrain from calling us 'fish belly.' "

Jestak smiled at that, and a murmur went around the room.

"The story would keep you here for days, Protector," said Jestak. "What would you like to hear in particular?"

"Start with your departure from Pelbarigan. We will question you as you go."

"As you know, we left Pelbarigan as soon as the tribes left the area after spring truceweeks. The training for running we had been given was the soundest training we had had. We ran eastward across the high grass and groves, all Sentani country, as the council had determined. We were able to avoid them successfully. However, the extent of the land was not about a hundred and fifty ayas, as had been surmised, but closer to three hundred, and beyond it lay a forest that was also Sentani country and stretched for another two hundred. At the rate of our running, in keeping with your commands, we were exhausted, and supplies were low, and we had not reached what was described to us as 'the safety and justice of the eastern cities.' The truth of the matter, as I later learned, is that a wide range of mountains lies between the forest Sentani country and the eastern cities, and this is occupied by two tribes more fierce than the Shumai, because more implacable, and without honor. These are called the Peshtak and the Coo."

"And just how did you learn these, ah, amazing, shall we call them, facts?"

"By being attacked, Protector. We were entering the western foothills of these mountains, having rested and restored our stocks as well as we could in hostile country. We were suddenly attacked, and all but I were killed."

"And why were you not killed?"

"I was not at the camp. Three were sleeping. Brus was watching, and I was at the river's edge, fishing from under willows. I ran to the camp when I heard the shouts, but I was taken as I entered. I never had a chance to defend anyone."

"Never had the chance?"

"No. I was in a net snare, held by four men, who hung me from a tree while they finished with the others, then brought me down still entangled."

"Jestak," interrupted the Brunaga. "You have not told how Brus was killed. I will have to hear that, even though I fear it."

"No, I have not. I would that you would release me from it, Eastcouncil, for it is something I would prefer not to relate."

"Tell it, Jestak," commanded the Protector.

"Although they kill, even the Shumai are not cruel for pleasure, Protector, as are the Peshtak. Brus killed an attacker with his sword, and so was tortured to death. He was strong, though, just like an outside tribesman, and joked as long as he could, and never cried out although the Peshtak tried a number of elaborations on their torture to make him."

Brin the Brunag was sobbing. "This," she said, "is the result of leaving the walls, but Brus would go. Who would listen to the counsel of a man?"

"We must hear all," said the Protector. "We must operate from knowledge. What did they do, Jestak? Did they whip him?"

"Yes, they whipped him."

"To death? You are holding back."

"Very well. They flayed him alive and put him in a place where the ants could eat him."

A general shriek went around the room. None had heard of anything of the sort, and the horror and dismay were universal. The Protector herself had not been prepared for this, and it took her some moments to recover.

Finally, she said, "Have you told it all?"

Jestak said nothing.

"Very well, then, where were you at the time?"

"I was tied to a tree to watch."

"They did not abuse you, then?"

"Only to beat me at this time. They meant to torture me in the future."

"To beat you only, but not severely, I take it."

Jestak did not answer, but merely took off his tunic and undercoat and turned his back to her. Another murmur went around the room, for his back was a mass of interlaced scars.

"All of that did not come from the Peshtak, of course," said Jestak, resuming his clothes. "About a third, I would say. Most came from the Tantal, and a little in Innanigan."

"Aiii," said the Protector. "It would seem you wandered around the east being beaten, even in the cities. Who are the Tantal? Go on, Jestak."

Jestak briefly recounted the story of his trip eastward, and his attempts to work in Innanigan in order to recover the lost funds and enroll for his law studies. The high-sun bells began to ring in harmony, and the Protector closed the meeting, saying, "You have told us enough wonders for today, Jestak. Even if half of them are true, we have some further material for thought. We will resume this meeting tomorrow and learn further of the difficulties of going beyond our walls." Jestak opened his mouth to answer, but thought better of it and merely bowed and retired with the rest.

Winnt was an expert on the pellute, the traditional stringed instrument manufactured only in the Pelbar cities, but played generally by all the western tribes. Mokil had taken his pellute and hung it without explanation at the message stone with his communication to Northwall from Jestak. That, of course, caused some puzzlement and consternation. The instrument, although old, needed no repair. It was of Pelbarigan manufacture. The artisans of Northwall examined it and merely laid it on a shelf until they learned what to do with it.

On the third day of his stay in Northwall, Winnt asked for it again. It was soon produced, and he spent some of his convalescence strumming and singing Sentani songs. He was so engaged when an elderly woman entered the room, as usual without asking leave. "Sentani," she opened abruptly, "where did you get that instrument?"

Irritated, Winnt did not respond immediately, but went on playing. She did not understand such insolence, in Pelbar terms, but simply waited, listening. Finally, Winnt said, "It has been my family's for many years."

"My grandfather made it," she said flatly. He stopped. "Your grandfather?"

"Yes. May I see it? Look here, on the base of the bowl. Here are the artisan's marks with the date, the 978th year of Pelbarigan, and the maker's name, Cilt the Ovel. He was my grandfather, and a famous maker of the pellute. I am astonished that it has lasted this long in all your wanderings."

Winnt studied the marks. "It has not been wandering long," he returned. "Most of the time it has been in the Fastness of Koorb, far to the south, our permanent home, in the loghouse of my family."

"It is well worn."

"Yes. It has been used continually."

"And skillfully repaired."

"My great uncle, who is beyond the days of running, spends his time in such repairs. He is slow and careful, and all say that he does it well."

"Indeed he does. May I play it?" And when Winnt handed it back to her, she sat on the side bench and, after expertly tuning it, struck up a sort of song that Winnt had never heard. After a time, she began to sing, in an old, quavering voice:

> Aven the Mother
> of everything living,
> bring us the wet winds, oh
> live in our stone.
>
> Bless us with showers,
> food to all giving,
> temper our metals,
> raise our seed sown.
>
> Save us from tribesmen,
> love, be forgiving,
> our prayers to you ever,
> we will intone.

This she played over, singing almost to herself, then played a sad and minor song, only humming gently. "It is a fine, sound instrument," she finally said, handing it back. "How do you play it?"

"I do not play very well lying down, but I will try." And Winnt strummed several songs, then launched into a complex and rapid hounka dance. By that time he had an audience of three women in the doorway, though he could not see them from where his bed lay. One was Cise, the giver of the apple. Finally Winnt launched into a simple song of his own, and since Sentani dialect is quite close to Pelbar, all could understand:

> Rains of summer, winds of fall,
> lashing our hall. I do not come.
> Snows of winter, breeze of spring,
> Never do bring greeting to kin.
>
> Under the highstone where I lie
> seasonless I, ages go by.
> Never the running, never love,
> Nor from above shines the sun.

Each line was distinct and surrounded with strummed melody, and the song as a whole, rendered in a gentle tenor chant, was something strange and new to the Pelbar. The old one, Sendi, asked him to play it again, watching his fingering carefully, as he went through the song as before, though some of the improvisations were quite different.

"That is not like the last time," she said.

"Well, no. We always vary the songs as we play them. Do you not do that?"

"No. They are always the same."

"Ah. The varying is much of the enjoyment for us."

"What is that song about?"

"It was written by Oman, a central leader, almost two hundred years ago. He was wounded in a fight and knew he would die, so he wrote his own lament."

"He had not a sense, then, of living forever?"

"Living forever? No. He was dying and knew that he was. He lies high on a rock ridge overlooking the Great Sentan River, near where it flows into the Heart. I have seen the place many times. It is sad and has the quality of his song."

"Does not your religion take into account life after death?"

"Life after death? No. What is that? There are the spirits of places and some are associated with men and women. Do you mean spirits?"

"No. I mean Armon, the place of peace and joy after death, where all go and there is no fighting and no hiding."

"I have never heard of it."

Sendi rose. "It is time for me to return to my weavers. We are working on shingle square capes, and they need much supervision. Good day, Sentani. My name is Sendi the Ieon. You are Winnt?"

"Yes. I am Winnt of the north starband of Koorb."

The old woman smoothed his cover slightly and departed through the now empty door.

That evening, as she arranged the reports of the month's work in ceramics, Cise was humming slightly to herself, repetitiously, as her mother and supervisor, Calen, called out each category of ware. The older woman was concentrating as well as she could, with all the untoward and strange events on her mind, and this extra interference began to grate. "Under the highstone," Cise sang audibly.

"Under what? What is that you are singing?" said Calen.

"Oh, it is a song," said Cise. "I am sorry, I didn't mean to disturb you."

"What is a highstone?"

"I don't know."

"Then how can you sing about it?"

"Oh. It is only something the Sentani was singing down in the infirmary this afternoon. I was going by with Savia and heard him singing to Sendi and so I listened. It seems his pellute was made many years ago by her grandfather."

"He was from Pelbarigan."

"Yes."

"It is a dreadful song. But what could one expect from a savage. Well, let us finish this general report. If this business of Jestak will not disrupt things too much, the Protector will want to view all reports tomorrow. What are you smiling about?"

"Nothing, my mother. Here. Here are the production marks for all coverless bowls."

"Jestak," Winnt was saying. "If I do not get out of here soon I will go mad. There is no window, even, from which I can see the river and the trees. Only this small yard. And everybody is coming in to see your pet barbarian. Especially the women. I have never seen so many women with so much to say."

Jestak smiled. "Another will be by soon."

"No. That mustn't be. I forbid it."

"Men do not forbid much here. You are mending. Perhaps tomorrow you could try standing, though we will have to ask the Mejana."

"Another woman. The worst of all. She treats me like a dog or a piece of meat, with all her poking and prodding. She has no decency or delicacy."

"She is as good a physician as there is in the west."

"And the one with the apple."

"Somebody gave you an apple?" And Jestak laughed outright. "Be careful or you will never get out."

"Aiii. What? Have I done something to commit myself?"

"Had it a bite out of it?"

"No. It was a good, sound apple."

"Beware of it if it has a bite out of it already. You might say that Sentani never eat food that has a bite out of it. Its spirit has already entered the first biter, or something. It would be best if you didn't, I think."

"Its spirit? What are you talking about?"

"They don't know anything about you, though if you

keep singing to them, they will begin to think you are really not a hairy barbarian after all."

"To them? I only sang for the old one, Sendi."

"I guess you did not see the crowd in the door."

"Aiii. A crowd in the door. Leg, get well so I may run."

"You will be the first Sentani ever to run from the Pelbar."

"Indeed I will. I will run so fast that I will melt snow. Is the snow deep?"

"No, but soon it will be, I think. When you are walking, I will take you to our woodshop. I would like to teach you how to make the snow gliders of the Rits so your trip will be easier."

"We have our own snowpads, which I can make."

"These are superior. I have used both. You can double your speed. I would simply give you the pair I have been working on, but if you can make them, then the whole starband will be able to have them. Here," he continued, "is the other person I mentioned to you. Ursa," he said, gesturing to the woman in the doorway, "is a naturalist, a student of wild things. Being Pelbar, she is unable to travel far and would like some information from you about things seen in your travels. Is that all right?"

"Can I refuse?" he murmured.

"Not really, I fear," whispered Jestak.

"Men do not whisper before women in Northwall," said Ursa decidedly. She was quite young, and somewhat wispy. Her hair was lighter than most of the Pelbar, who tended toward dark hair. She had a bit of the blondness of the Shumai, with an abundance of freckles on her thin, studious face. Her eyes were a rich blue that startled Winnt with their depth.

"Young man," she began without preamble. "I would like to ask you some questions." She rummaged among her papers. "I understand that you are a hunter. Perhaps you can give me some information about some of the flora and fauna . . ."

"The what?"

"The plants and animals of your acquaintance. I am particularly concerned with their ranges, which I have no opportunity to observe, and other information about their habits."

"Their habits?"

"Yes, their habits. Now, I understand that you were going north to hunt the caracajawat."

"The what?"

"These," she said, waving an illustration.

"Oh. The flat-horned deer."

"Well, they are not deer, really, but we can call them that if you would like. Now, if you please, tell me what you know about them."

Winnt sighed. "To start with, your picture is not right. Here, give it to me. See, here, where you have the legs so short? They come down like this. Here, can you give me a quill and a piece of paper?"

"Excuse me," said Jestak. "I see you are in good hands. I must report to Manti now." He raised his hand in the doorway.

"Oh. Yes," said Winnt. "You must report." He rolled his eyes. "Yes, all right, good-bye. Now, madam . . ."

"Madam?"

"Well, now. The legs, you see, must be long to manage the deep snow. They really go like this." And he began to sketch them in with an expertness that surprised the naturalist, who had expected, apparently, a series of grunts.

The judgment hall was crowded the next morning as Jestak went on. "The eastern cities are not as you suppose them to be. They are no solution to anyone's problem, though perhaps we might trade with them. There are eight of them, stretched out along the east coast of the continent. I rather suspect that they were not quite so severely damaged in the time of fire, and so retain a few devices from before that time. This is their defense, for surely they themselves are not especially inventive."

"I do not understand, Jestak. What time of fire? Do you mean the time that made the Ruin of Peo and that at Highkill, and the other three?"

"Protector, wherever I went, I encountered ruins. Not many, for they are very old, but it seems clear that people once occupied the whole land. There are pieces of roadway of artificial stone, not yet swallowed by the land, and even pieces of gigantic metal bridges. And all of them use the same alphabet in their words, what few there are. It is essentially like ours."

"Wait, Jestak. This is another concept altogether. Yet I

see I must indulge you a bit further so we may get back to the main story."

"The Sentani know of many ruins. So do the Shumai. I think that all the tribes must have once been one people before some terrible thing destroyed all, and only a very few remained, and they in isolation. And that they made the tribes, only eventually coming in contact with one another, and at that time becoming hostile."

All sat in silence for some time. Finally the Protector remarked. "It would seem, if what you say is true, that there must have once been a very fierce hostility."

"Perhaps," returned Jestak, "it involved a people from beyond the sea, for they in Innanigan mentioned that they believed there was such a place, and I did go to the islands over a thousand ayas out in the sea.

"But this is not the only thing. Except for the Rits, who speak another tongue, all the tribes speak dialects of one language. The farther I went from home, the stranger the dialects became, but with practice, I could understand them all. Except for the Rits. And some of their words were curiously like ours."

"Jestak, we must leave your speculations now and return to the record. What happened when you were at Innanigan? You have told us that you tried to work in order to recoup the lost funds and so follow your orders. Go on."

"I found it very difficult to get any but the simplest and most menial sort of work, and at that rate I would never get the money ahead for study. I tried to do the metalwork for which I was trained, but they would not allow it, saying that only certain people, belonging to a certain guild, were permitted to do it. Yet they let me do menial work in the metal shops, and I learned many skills that will do us good. But it was difficult, even living as cheaply as I could, to save money. It soon became clear to me that the Innanigani did not like strangers, and strangers tended to band together.

"There were almost no westerners, but I fell in with a Shumai, whose adventures were even more strange than mine."

"We are not concerned with the adventures of this Shumai, Jestak."

"Yes, and yet I became so. His name was Stantu. We lived together in one room in order to save money. He was trying to get together the resources to get home.

"The Innanigani are somewhat honest with each other only because their elaborate system of laws prevents them from being otherwise. They are always going to the judgment, and a whole class of people makes much money by specializing in legal matters. I became conscious of this as I spent much of my spare time trying to acquaint myself with their legal system in order to see what would have to be done for the Pelbar to treat with them, even though by that time I was convinced that actual trade would be much more difficult than anyone here had imagined. They are not just to foreigners and work to their own advantage always. While we would never cheat the Sentani or Shumai in truceweek trading, it is a matter of course for them to shortweight, to substitute, to miscalculate, always in their favor, and because of their superior weaponry, no one can seriously challenge them. Even the Peshtak, fierce as they are, defer in trading, though they know they are being wronged.

"Stantu discovered that the Innanigani money system allowed people to deposit their funds for use by others in a central money pool. They would then receive not only their own funds, after a time, but an additional percentage paid by those who wanted to make use of these funds.

"This is part of the secret of eastern strength, because this money pool is large and allows for money trading among the eight cities. Thus a group wanting to start a manufactury may get much funding soon and pay it back as they work. This way too, they may pay many workers to work for them. There is no central council, as here, because the system is too big. No central body makes the decisions for the group. Strangely enough, this sort of anarchy quaintly resembles that of the Shumai, for even the Sentani are highly organized. I began to see that in this way many minds are at work in the solving of economic problems, not a few, who cannot possibly be wise in all things."

"Are you purposely insulting us, Jestak? Are you not going beyond what you were asked?"

"I regret any insult, Protector, but I was only trying to give what information I could because no one else has been there."

"Stay closer to your story and leave matters of judgment to us."

"Stantu put his savings into a depository. Some time later, when he returned for them, for he felt he had enough for supplies and superior weapons, and a passage on a trading vessel far to the south and west, to the mouth of the Heart, he went—"

"Wait, Jestak. Are you saying then that you can go from the eastern cities to the mouth of our river by a boat?" The geographer, Hildre, was talking. Her world had recently been so revised by Jestak that her concepts were wholly jumbled in her mind. She had kept her draftsman busy now until very late at night to allow for Jestak's information. It was not working out, although she was very skillful at local matters.

"Well," said Jestak, "naturally. The river must flow downhill, and hence must eventually arrive at the sea. I saw a number of rivers doing that. If it is the same sea, that is, without land intervening, one must be able to travel there by water. The Innanigani have begun trading with the Alats who live at the mouth of the Heart. Much rice is grown there in the lowlands bordering the sea."

"Rice?"

"Not like the rice of the northern lakes that the Sentani trade. A different but closely related grain," said Jestak, patiently.

"Let us continue the main thread," the Protector repeated.

"One thing more, if you please, Protector," said Umer of the council. "Jestak, I do not understand your concept of long travel by boats. That on the Bitter Sea seemed so very far. I have even seen our river too rough for boats. But now you are speaking of infinite journeys by the great eastern sea."

"Ah, Umer, I wish you could see these boats. They are several times as large as this room, all of heavy wood, with sails to push them. Large ones, and many of them, and it takes much skill to move them. We will have to learn these concepts because the world is beginning to reawaken, and we are still in burrows. With such boats we could go to Pelbarigan anytime we chose, and nothing could stop us but low water."

"Jestak, if you please. We will form the judgments. May we go on?"

"Yes, Protector. Stantu was unable to get his money. He was informed that his claim was invalid because he was not a member of the eastern league. Of course they knew this when he put the money there in the first place, but they simply saw a way by their laws to cheat him."

"I imagine he began slaughtering in the Shumai manner."

"He came to get my short sword, and it was only with much difficulty that I stopped him. He nearly killed me, but I reasoned with him that we would first try to beat them at their own practice, and if that did not work, I would help him to kill them, and then we would escape."

"Ahhh. What you have forgotten. A Pelbar proposing such an action, such purposeful aggression. Clearly we had sent the wrong man." It was Brin speaking, but this time even the Protector shook her head slightly, and seeing this shift in the wind, Brin fell silent.

"I went to work at the writings of the law, and finally found a case in which it was established that if one entered into a contract knowing that its conditions were not to be met, then that contract was invalid. It did not mention that the contract was meant only for Innanigani.

"We took them to the judgment, and after much wrangling, we won. There was one party, even of the Innanigani, who saw the justice of our case. Stantu got his money back. But he got back only what he had put in, not the gain, because they decided that that contract had not been valid. So in a way the money people got something too, except it cost them much to go to judgment. And it cost me as well, nearly all I had saved. But that made little difference, because Innanigan was no longer safe for us. We were harassed from all sides. Stantu was imprisoned on a false charge, but we hid his money, and it must have been waiting for him when he got out."

"And you . . ."

"And I was set upon by a mob and once beaten, and then the second time I defended myself and cut down several of the swine and had to flee by the first means. That happened to be a trading vessel headed for the eastern islands. I worked on the ship and was sick much of the time because of its rocking on the waves. But finally I got used to it and loved the freedom of the open water. We used to see birds hundreds of ayas out, riding on the water much as our river gulls. But they must have lived out there much of their lives."

"What horror, Jestak, did you find on these eastern islands?"

"None, Protector. They were a haven of peace. They were like Pelbarigan or Northwall, though outdoors. If I had my way, I would never have left there, but of course I had my duty to you and so returned."

"Perhaps," mused the Protector, "we could all go there. But that being impossible, we must deal with things as they are."

"I wish, Protector, that you could indeed go there. It would be a revelation to you. There are five islands, only two very large at all. The one I stayed on for several months, Saltstream, was the largest, and the other, Midridge, was the highest. Even though small, it contained a mountain, and that with fire at the top coming from the earth itself."

The Protector struck her wooden gong. "That must suffice for now. These wonders, it would seem, continue to grow. Jestak, you must go with Hildre to sketch out some of these matters. Later, I would see you by myself."

The moon was already well risen when Jestak was bowed into the presence of the Protector, in the same small high room in which she had received Manti.

"Sit down," she said. Then she took out a polished wooden box, inlaid with bone and mica, and set it on the table between them. Slowly she raised the cover. Inside, crisp and brown, were several pages of printed material, with numbers on the corners.

"Do not touch these, Jestak. Just look at them. Try not to breathe on them because they are very fragile. Is this the writing that you saw on the ruins in the east?"

Jestak looked. "Yes, Protector. This I can read a little, for I saw several such in Innanigan. It is an old form of what we now write. See, here is our word for 'desk.' It is not greatly different. This is from a book."

"A book?"

"Yes. They have them in Innanigan. Instead of separate sheets of paper for writing, or a roll, they stack the sheets and fasten one side together, like this. Then each sheet has a number on each side. That confirms, I think, my idea that the destruction was less complete in the east."

"What?"

"At the time of fire, Protector."

"Ah, yes, so you have said. Then why, Jestak, have the eastern cities not prospered and spread this far west?"

"The destruction, even so, must have been great. They are really very few, and the land is so large that it is hard for a Pelbar to imagine it. Here in Northwall we number only a thousand. Innanigan is perhaps twenty times that many, but that too is so few. I imagine that the Pelbar might have begun with perhaps one couple or several people and that it has taken all this time to build what we have out of nothing. Surely we look much alike, and our variations can be accounted for by the taking in of stray tribesmen through the centuries."

"Jestak, you love to speculate."

"Where, Protector, did these pages come from?"

"I do not know, Jestak. It is a great secret, and so much so that it has been handed down through too many generations by word of mouth, from Protector to Protector. But I will tell you the rumors if you promise to hold strict confidence."

"I do so promise, Protector."

"It is said that these remained from the Ruin of Peo, from which the Pelbar first came, and that they remain from before what you call the time of fire."

The two looked at each other for a long time. "Jestak, this has now gone much beyond a matter of political advantage, of my dignity, or of your self-assertion. You are striking at the very roots of Pelbar society. We must move slowly, or all will be disrupted. But we must have the strength to move. You are so reckless. Remember that you must have Pelbar interest at all times. I beg this of you. And I have never said that to a man—but one and that was long ago. Perhaps you are right and that the world is reawakening. We have looked so long to the eastern cities as our one rumor of hope, and for so long the outside tribes have gained and gained in strength, in spite of their warring and their wild life. I fear I do not have the strength for so great changes as I seem to see coming."

"I will be faithful, Protector."

"Can you be faithful to all those to whom you have pledged faith? You are a tattooed Sentani. You have lived and spoken with the Shumai, and they seem to have some respect for you if they know you. Yet you are Pelbar and all these groups are hostile. Can you manage all that?"

"I don't know. As I told Mokil's band, I will be, if necessary, a victim, though not a betrayer."

"I hope that you can manage it, Jestak. One other thing. Why did you not tell in Pelbarigan what you have told us?"

"You, Protector, are far more reasonable than Excur, Protector of Pelbarigan. You will at least modify the strict courtesies of the Pelbar when you see a reason for it. In Pelbarigan, it would have all been 'Yes, Protector,' 'No, Protector,' 'I was wrong, Protector.' I would have been consigned to lifelong latrine duty as an outcast and a useless person. All I would have done, of course, is to have fled to the Sentani, in order to live like a human being. We are sometimes our worst enemies, Protector."

"And yet I fear I have let this go too far already."

"We must now ride with it, Protector. Things will change whether we will it or not, and we must adjust. That is one reason why I practically begged my exile here. In a city nearly twice this size, all hope of personal acquaintance is lost, and all becomes politics. In Pelbarigan I think they would not even have accepted the concept that there is a Bitter Sea."

"Now, Jestak, I am going to ask a favor of you."

"You have it, Protector."

"Let us declare a silence of one month before we go on with your story. We must absorb it slowly."

"As you wish, Protector."

"And one more thing."

"Yes, Protector?"

"You did make up that about the mountain with fire on top, did you not?"

"No, Protector. It was there. They call it a volcano."

"I see. Indulge me one final thing, Jestak. I have had to learn and change so much, to forgive you and see that I must not wish to see you die as I once thought possible. Now, since you are, in a roundabout way, almost a part of my family—no, do not ask of it—I must be sure of your loyalty, your personal loyalty in an embrace." She moved toward him and took him into her old arms, and he slowly put his around her. "You needn't be so tentative with your old aunt, Jestak." He smiled in the dark room and embraced her fully. "I knew a man who was this young and hard once," she said, "though not so tall." And with that she dismissed him, then stopped him and said, "I need not remind you that this does not change our official relationship, and I shall scold and chide you as always."

"Of course, Protector," said Jestak, himself now somewhat abashed by the newness of all this.

 V

IT was deep winter when Winnt, learning the snow sliders, went through the west pivot of Northwall, accompanied by Ursa on a similar pair. She had on a small pack with study materials. This was to be a combination excursion. Winnt was regaining his former strength and needed exercise and practice before beginning his trek northward. Ursa was to gain from his knowledge of the wilderness of the region. The area was free of the herds that the Shumai followed, and so safe. Pelbar were cutting ice on the river for storage in the deep caves under the city. The two stopped to watch for a time, then set off upriver, an unusual sight to the ice cutters, who seldom saw a Pelbar woman outside the walls, and surely never in the company of a Sentani.

"Look at that, Orge," said Aten. "She who is so deep in her birds and flowers that she has never looked at a man is going off with Jestak's pet barbarian." He rested on a block and gestured.

"That is just why. No need to be jealous. She sees only a source of information. He is a walking mouth to her. Don't worry. I didn't know you wished to serve her."

"Pffaf. Quit that. That may be her idea, of course, but what of him?"

"He is not strong enough to vanish. He has to return. Besides, he seemed to be a man of honor. I have played a game of tati with him, though it was hard, because every woman in Northwall seemed to be wandering in and out of his room. It was quite funny, really, especially in its effect on him. He is appalled at our women. Sentani women, he told me, are only equal to their men and do not administer

any more often than a man. They ask to enter. I guess with
hunters the men rule themselves, because the women can't
keep up. He said a few young ones go on the hunts, though
not the winter hunt."

"I have seen them going by on the river," said Aten,
"paddling with the men. They must be all bone and gris-
tle."

"Apparently so. Winnt keeps remarking on the softness
and weight of our women."

"An eye for them, eh."

"I am not sure. He seems bewildered by them, and yet
he is attracted by authority. Apparently the Sentani have
rigid organizational patterns, and he reacts to commands."

"Well, we had better be moving ice. Jos will be yelling at
us in a minute."

Winnt was already tiring, now that they were about
seven ayas west of Northwall, across the river. They were
following a fox track. He was glad when they had found a
kill, and he could stand while Ursa exclaimed and examined it. Winnt read the tracks for her, as easily as if they
had been language. "No," he said, "he first smelled the
hare over there, back of the rise."

"How can you tell?"

"Did you not see where he stopped? Then he no longer
trotted. The marks are closer and have no scuff of snow.
Then he stopped again by the oak tree, and for a longer
time, because the snow shows a hint of melting under his
paws. The hare was not alarmed until he reached that
point, and I expect that was after the fox took those first
two leaps. The snow was with him. What I don't understand is why he reached that ridge there and suddenly
turned aside. There must be something over there. Are
your people up here?"

"No. None of us, I think." Ursa heard a whisk as
Winnt's short sword was out. He suddenly seemed hard
and alien. "Do not go. You are not well yet. Let us go
back."

"We will just look," he said.

From the top ridge, she said, "You see. There is nothing. Now we may go back."

"There are the tracks of a man."

"Where?"

"Down there. Look between the two sycamores."

"I see something. Let us go back."

"No. We will go look."

"You are always contradicting. Well, before we go, do you see more than one?"

Winnt scanned the whole bowl-shaped valley before them. "No. Only one," he said, and sheathed his short sword.

When the pair reached the tracks, Winnt said, "It is one man, a Shumai, and he is weak."

"How can you tell that?"

"Here. See here where he is using the base of his spear as a cane. See the oval tip? That is made to fit a spear-thrower." He began to follow the tracks up the slope toward a hill overlooking the river.

"Wait," said Ursa. "Come back. At least return for Jestak."

Winnt was already far ahead, and she had to start after him. "See here where he leaned against this tree," he said, "and up there he fell and lay for a time. Come."

From the hilltop they could see him, sitting against a tree far below, and Winnt started down the hill before Ursa could say anything. They had not gone far before the Shumai saw them and stood, his spear at ready. Winnt brought up about twenty arms away. Ursa soon reached his side. "Wait," she said. "He is a Shumai savage. Let us get away from here before this has gone too far."

At that the Shumai laughed. He did not fully understand it, but could not mistake the tone. "Come," he said. "Spit yourself on a Shumai spear." He was gaunt to the point of emaciation. Beneath his shock of light-blond hair, his blue eyes glinted hard. "A couple of wild onions to have with dinner," he said, and then fell in the snow. It took Winnt a few moments to reach him and step on his spear. His sword was out and he turned the young tribesman over to give him the stroke of death, but Ursa intervened, pushing him aside.

"You cannot kill him. He is weak as a baby. Is this Sentani courage?"

"They would serve us so, even killing the wounded, which we never do. Get out of the way." As he went to thrust her aside, they struggled a moment, and his full weight was thrown on his hurt leg, which gave a little under him. At that moment the Shumai made a weak thrust with his now uncovered spear, but only succeeded in going through Ursa's coat and slicing her side. She screamed and fell on him, and he was too weak to move her off. Winnt was standing, angry, panting, in pain.

"Now get away, woman," he shouted.

"No," she shrieked back. "Stop. Stop, stop, stop. Both of you stop!"

Winnt stopped. "Well, if you love him so much, at least stop bleeding on him."

She looked down and saw that indeed the blood from her side was dripping on the young tribesman's face and beard. "Ahhh," she said, taking snow and rubbing it away.

The Shumai looked up at her and laughed weakly. "At least," he panted, "use something besides snow."

She recognized the "snow" and using the heel of her mitten, brushed it away, and then sat back as the pain in her side made itself more evident. "Ahhh," she murmured. "Look at me, Winnt. How badly am I hurt?"

Winnt, moving quickly with his game cord, whipped the Shumai's hands behind him and tied them, then looked at Ursa. "Go ahead," she said. "Take aside all the clothes."

He looked a long moment, then turned to the Shumai. "Piece of dung," he spat.

"No, Winnt, do not hurt him," said Ursa from the snow.

"Sentani turd pusher," murmured the Shumai.

Winnt stood. "This is all madness," he shouted. "Madness. You cannot be merciful to them. They kill for recreation. He would kill us now even if it meant his own death."

"Come and be killed," came the hoarse voice of the Shumai.

"But many said that about you, Winnt," said Ursa, rising on her arm. "You never said how I was."

"Oh. It is ugly, but it was mostly the coat. I am afraid you will live. Lie down and I will do what I can to dress it." And, kneeling by the panting Shumai, he gently dressed her side, his hands trembling from the proximity to this Pelbar woman.

"Would you happen, swill of the river," said the Shumai, "to have anything to eat? I would just as soon die full as empty."

"You aren't going to die," said Ursa, from under her coat, catching his gist.

"Do not be too sure of that," said Winnt. Finally he finished and stood up on his snow sliders. Ursa sat up stiffly, saw the Shumai in the snow, and lifted him up against the tree again, brushing the snow from his head and neck.

"It is pretty hard to offend her, Shumai," remarked Winnt, slowly, so the westerner would be sure to understand. The emaciated man laughed.

"Here, eat this," said Ursa, taking some travel bread from her pack. Then the Shumai ate, while Ursa lay on her good side in the snow and Winnt squatted on his heels. "We have to take him back," she said.

"I was beginning to get that idea," said Winnt. "I suppose I am in no position to object."

"No, you most certainly are not. Now cut some poles and we will make a drag. You," she said slowly, "what is your name?"

"None of your affair, Crowbait," the Shumai rasped, but also slowly.

"Well," she returned, "no matter. Here is some more bread. Eat it slowly or it will just come back up."

Jestak was on the wall scanning the horizon. It was reddening with sunset when finally he saw a speck coming from the west. It parted into two. "It must be them," he said to the watchman, "but they seem to be bringing something. Perhaps it is game. I will go to meet them."

When Jestak arrived, Winnt was tired with the dragging and his still weakened leg, and Ursa, with her wound, was moving stiffly. Jestak turned and with three long hoots on the horn called the roving guard to help. Then he took the drag, talking to the Shumai in his own dialect, but getting mostly hostility in return.

When the four guardsmen arrived, the party was conducted to the walls. There they dropped the drag. Turning to the Shumai, the squad leader, who knew the dialect because of his duties at truceweeks, said, "Do you swear, by your god Sertine, that you will not attack or disrupt or circumvent or undermine or lie while you are under our care?"

The Shumai laughed. "I swear nothing. I owe nothing, wish nothing, swear nothing. Do you think a Shumai needs the help of swines' snouts? Give me my spear, and I will show you of swearing." He ended this statement in a short fit of coughing. The others stood silently.

"Well," said Jestak, "if you wish, but we would tell the Shumai at spring truceweek what your name was, and what happened to your party since you wish to die alone."

"What party? You found me alone, did you not?"

"We know that Shumai never hunt or travel alone. They go in packs like dogs. You are an outlaw then, and shunned by your own people?"

"Jestak," said Winnt. "Perhaps he is protecting his party because he thinks we are tricking him in order to kill them."

"Perhaps," said Jestak.

"Roar your garbage," murmured the Shumai.

After some conferring, the Pelbar built a small shelter outside Northwall and supplied the famished man with food. At first they had to feed him, but he recovered and began to feed himself soon. In the morning, they could see by the tracks that he had tried to leave but had fallen and then returned to the shelter, where a store of food was left for him. Jestak looked in on him soon after dawn.

"Where are you going, Pelbar? Aren't you afraid? Don't you think that you should lock yourself away?"

"No, Stiffneck. I am going to find those you left. Clearly they are in some kind of trouble. The herds have long left these lands and they must be in worse condition than you are." He carried a heavy pack.

"Pig. I am an outcast, as you said. There are no others. What Shumai would be here in winter? We would have no use for this bare ice and small deer."

"And yet you are here."

And Jestak slid away across the snow westward, as the anguished Shumai lay in the shelter, saying to himself, "Ah, Sertine, forgive me, Sertine."

"You idiot," the Mejana was saying to Winnt. "Why did you let her walk when she was hurt like that? And all to save a Shumai snake who does nothing but try to kill us."

"Is she all right?"

"All right! How could she be all right? Do you think we all run ourselves into the ground like the Sentani packs? No, she is not all right. She has lost much blood. Too much. She must be quiet, perfectly quiet, and rest and eat."

"She insisted . . ."

"She insisted. Bedbugs. She insisted. I thought you were the one who did not listen to women. Even a Pelbar man knows when women are simply not to be obeyed. Now get out of here and go about your business. And don't misuse that leg again or we will have to go back to where we were and start again, and we shall never be rid of you." And she turned her head and left him in the hallway.

Jestak had followed the track well beyond where he found those of Winnt and Ursa, so far he saw he would have to spend the night in the open. It was not until the western sky was brick red that he came upon the Shumai camp. It was pitiful. The Shumai, who despise permanent dwellings and feel the body must be tough enough to take anything, had made little provision for their present situation. Nineteen men lay on the ground and in small skin shelters. The first three he checked were dead. The fourth heard his entering rustle, and muttered, "Thro, are you back?"

"So that was his name—Thro."

The Shumai turned and reached for a knife, but he was weak as a puppy, and Jestak simply held his hand. "Your friend got as far as near Northwall. He would not tell us anything, not even his name, so he lies outside our walls now, in a small shelter, with food, recovering. I will help you, but I must know who is your leader."

"You speak . . . good Shumai . . . for a Pelbar."

"I have been among Shumai. Let that go. I will not help you unless I have your leader's oath that he will not kill me as soon as you are strong enough. Otherwise you will all die. Do you understand? I wish you no ill."

"Thro was the leader."

"He is not here. Who was next?"

"Inkon. He lies in the next tent."

Jestak departed. Soon he was back. "He is dead. Who next?"

"I am next."

"Good. Do you swear?"

"I have never sworn to other than a Shumai."

"Good Armon, man. Here some of you are dead and others near death, and you have reservations."

"A Shumai is not afraid to die. However, to save the others, I, Iley, assigned chief of the Stone Creek band, swear to you, Pelbar, by Sertine, that I will not harm you, nor will my men, if you help us in our present emergency. This swearing will end when we are parted and you have entered your own safety."

"Good. I accept your swearing. Now eat this," and he

thrust some soaked bread at the Shumai, who took it in one gulp.

"I will give you more soon, but not until your stomach has accepted this."

Jestak made the rounds of the still men. He found that of the nineteen, eleven remained alive. One was nearly gone. He fed each one, then returned to Iley and fed him again. He gathered the survivors together under one tent, which he enlarged, and built a large fire before the entrance. Feeding each in turn, he heated tea, added maple sweetness, and got each to drink. It was not long before they were beginning to move. He stayed up much of the night with them, then went to sleep between Iley and another man as if he had been in his own bed.

"This is a strange Pelbar, Iley. Look how the fool trusts us."

"Somewhat a fool, Ouwn. He made me swear by Sertine for us all that he would be safe."

"But you cannot swear for us. Irdban is now the chief. We may kill him, but we must wait until we are stronger."

"It weighs on me, Ouwn. I cannot do that nor can I allow it. It is not proper."

"We will do it for you. You need not even see. We are not bound."

"Sertine knows that I am bound. I will kill the man who touches him."

"And if you do not know who touched him?"

"Then I will start at one end and kill until I am killed."

"And I will help him," said a voice from the shadows. "This is no good thing to talk of killing a man who has aided us, and when the name of Sertine has been brought into the matter."

Ouwn was silent a long time. "Then he was no fool at all."

"No. He knows how and when he can trust the Shumai. Now let us sleep."

And the whole band, except for Iley, slept until the dawn. He, taking the responsibility, watched the sinking fire.

Two days later, Thro, with a pack of Pelbar food, met the shaggy and weary party near the river. All were somewhat recovered. There were now ten, and the others had been buried as well as possible, awaiting warm weather and a return to give them proper interment. Jestak led them, but somewhat apart, and when he saw Thro coming, he moved even farther away, finally calling back, "We will leave further food at the message stone." He then slid across the snow well ahead of them and left for Northwall, but no one made any hostile move toward him.

"I do not understand this, Iley," said Thro, when they were joined.

"He has lived with a Shumai far in the eastern city of Innanigan, so he says. He is not hostile, yet not very afraid. How are you?"

"I am better, but I do not like this obligation to the Pelbar. What of the Sentani? They seem to have made an alliance."

"No. Jestak, that one, has said that he has also lived with the Sentani. It is he alone. He brought the thin one to Northwall, and it is only by his influence and their mercy that he is with them. Yet it may be the beginning of an alliance. I do not like it."

"Nor I. What can we do? How is the girl?"

"What girl?"

"Did he not tell you? When they met me—the Sentani and the woman—I in thrusting at him cut the woman."

"You cut a woman?"

"I was weakened and unable to guide the spear. She was preventing the Sentani from killing me and came between."

"He did not mention it," said Irdban.

Stopping at the doorway of the small room that Winnt shared with Jestak, the young man said, "She wants to see you."

"Oh, hello, Essar. Who?"

"Ursa."

"Ursa? How is she?" But the other had left.

As he entered the room where she was, he saw a very old woman sitting in the corner. He went to the bed. Ursa looked very white. "Winnt," she said softly. "They say I might die. I do not think so, because it was mostly blood, and blood can be replaced."

Winnt said nothing.

"But I wanted, in any case, for you to know . . . to take the precaution that . . . that you do not blame yourself for my trouble."

"But I was the one who insisted on following the tracks."

"Yes, but you are a hunter. I got between you."

Winnt still said nothing.

"Besides," she continued, "it is all right. If you had killed him, we would not have saved the other ten, and all would have died. It is better to trade one life for eleven."

"They are the enemy. Do you not understand? One good life for eleven of the enemy? I do not understand that. It makes no sense at all."

"The word of Aven says to bless one's enemies. It is an ancient work and holy."

"I will bless them, with my sword's tip."

"No, Winnt. Do not say it. For me, please do not say it. I beg of you. Cleanse that dark place from your heart."

Winnt was silent, and soon he saw that she was asleep. With a surprising strength, the old woman was taking him by the arm and guiding him from the room. She said nothing, but her look was accusing.

"I do not understand, Jestak," Winnt continued.

"Aven, our God, does say to bless one's enemies, Winnt. Most of us do not take that too literally, and so we try not to kill or to be killed, and to do what we must to provide cohesiveness for the Heart River peoples. It is a deeply felt religion with the Pelbar. Unfortunately it has had little effect on the Sentani or Shumai, who kill us whenever opportunity offers, outside of truceweek, and for no real reason that I can see. And yet within their own groups, each tribe has as strict a sense of honor as does the Pelbar. We have tried missionary work but all our missionaries are killed. It is that one point, the mutual killing, that keeps all the peoples apart."

"Jestak," said a guard at the doorway. "The Shumai are at the message stone. They have their food and are waiting. Apparently they wish to talk."

"Thank you, Jod," said Jestak, and rose to leave.

From the wall he said to Manti, "I do not like so many there. They swore to me only until I reached safety, where I am. They are free of their swearing now and could kill me." Then he took the megaphone and called out that he would meet with one man only. After a minute the others withdrew a hundred arms toward the river.

Jestak went over the wall on a rope boom, which lowered him to the snow. The Shumai was Thro. "How is the woman?" he asked.

"That is what you wanted? To know how the woman is?"

"Yes. It goes against the grain to hurt a woman."

"She is very weak. They say she may not live. But she says to blame no one."

"Aiii. I did not aim at her but at the Sentani."

"She has made us all understand that."

"She is somewhat light and has a Shumai look."

"Her grandmother was found as an infant, here at the message stone, many years ago."

"Here?"

"Yes. She was taken in and eventually became a great and powerful Pelbar leader and did much good."

The two men faced each other, the cold wind blowing their hair, their breaths caught by it and whipped aside.

"She must have been, then," said Thro, "the one of the legend of the river child. We have a song about her, born to an axeman and his bride, taken by a jealous rival, and left on the stone at Northwall to die in autumn."

"Perhaps so. If you need anything more, we will give it to you. If you stop at Pelbarigan and call from the message stone, they will supply you if you give the name of Manti. Do not give my name."

"Do not give your name?"

"No, I am in exile here. I have too much to do with the outside tribes."

Thro seemed reluctant to go. Finally, he reached inside his coat and took from his neck a copper necklace, with a round pendant of bronze. "This is for the woman," he said. "What is her name?"

"Ursa."

"Good-bye, then." And they palmed hands as Jestak had with Waldura in Buckmonth. Thro turned quickly and left without looking back.

From the wall, Manti said to his guardsmen, "This is extraordinary. This is becoming a crossroads for the outsiders, and Jestak meets them all and parts friends."

"I am glad, Ursa, that you are better," Winnt was saying. The old woman was in the corner again, apparently, Winnt surmised, as a chaperone or guardian.

"I beg you, Ibar, if it is possible, to let me talk with Winnt alone," said Ursa.

Ibar rose without a word and left, flashing Winnt one look on her way out. "That glance," said Winnt, "would make me behave well even if I had any wrong inclinations."

"Any inclinations you had toward me I could not regard as wrong, Winnt."

"What?"

She made no reply. Finally Winnt put his head down to her and said, into her shoulder, "Little woman, I'm glad you are getting better. I have to leave for the north soon, but I could not go if you were in danger. And had you died I am unsure what I would have done."

"You could put your arm around me to say that."

"We must not let this turn into love, Ursa. I could never live in this city, all jailed in, subject to women, even you, and working at some tradesman's task."

"I could come with you."

"There is hardness and danger. It is no place for a woman. They age quickly and turn sour often. Otherwise they stay behind and we see them only when home from the hunt. You would not like it."

"We shall see."

"How shall we see? I must go. Mokil has commanded that I should go if I am well."

"You do not love me."

Winnt hesitated. There were many risks he would much rather take.

"I will stop to be with you in spring truceweek when I have spoken with Mokil," he said. "I will ask him."

"You have not said."

"It is a big thing to say. When a Sentani says it, it is forever."

"Then you do not. When you go, please tell Ibar that you have gone."

"Oh, Ursa. You do not see the difficulties. We even have different gods. How would the Sentani take you? How well could you understand them?"

She did not reply.

"All the starbands have rules, strict rules. I cannot simply marry whom I choose."

She still did not reply.

"It is not that I do not love you; it is that there is much to think out ahead of any commitment."

"What does that mean? 'It is not that I do not love you.' Does that mean, 'I love you'?"

Winnt did not answer. Then, "Before I say the words, outright, I want to know that I am not creating a disaster. But I will promise you this, that I will work it out, and if it is possible, I will say the words, and to you and to no one else. But you must wait for that, if you want me."

"I will wait then. I think I will. I have not even seen how you kiss yet."

Winnt remedied that and after a long moment, Ursa said, "Good."

"What?"

"You don't kiss very well."

"What? How can you treat a man like this? What do I know of kissing? I am a hunter."

"Yes. You have not had practice, but I will see that you will get it."

"Oh," he said, and sat by the bed staring at the wall.

It was not until Longmonth, as the Pelbar called the second month of the year, in which winter still held strong and seemed to be lasting forever, that Winnt left Northwall. Ursa was well again, and was watching from the wall, as Jestak, who was seeing him on his way as far as Skydeer River, accompanied Winnt on his long trip to join the Sentani starband.

That night they camped on the high ground overlooking the river junction. Winnt was whole and strong, and had mastered the snow sliders. They had made good time. They roasted a white hare he had killed with an arrow, and ate Pelbar dried fruit, which was tough but rich with sugary flavor.

"How did your council react to the news of Ursa and me?"

"As usual. Some do not like to see any change. Some will accept with caution. But everyone in the whole city has seen you, and most have talked with you, and they do not regard you as a barbarian. You have seen the reaction of the women. But they worry about Ursa and the hard life she will have. And yet the minister to Aven took it as a sign that the long period of hostility is breaking."

"And you?"

"I agree with him. Something is breaking. All the east is restless. Big changes are coming. Ursa is a very religious woman, and although the names are different, and some of the customs, I cannot get it from my mind that somehow, far back, Pelbar and Sentani religion had the same root. Do you know whose religion is the closest to ours that I know of, Winnt? It is that of the Saltstream prophets, over a thousand ayas overland eastward and then another thousand over the sea. Not only are many of the ideas the same. So are the wordings. It is clear to me that we were all one people, who were broken apart by some ancient disaster, which killed almost all. Now the numbers are such that we are beginning to come into contact again. There is much evil among all these peoples, but also much good and much kindness. There are those who would enslave, like the Tantal, and the irreligious and self-indulgent, like the eastern cities. And then there are those who are simply cruel. Now that all these ways of thinking are coming together, there will be many struggles that will last beyond our lifetimes.

"As to Ursa, you may be sure that she will always be devoted to you. The flower of love had never germinated in her at all until you came along. I could see something happen during those days she spent in your room questioning you about wild things. I think it was your encounter with the Shumai that suddenly made it bloom. But she will be as firm in her adherence to you as to anything. And you and I know the pleasures of the Sentani life that would be closed to her in Northwall."

"Sentani life is not always easy for a woman."

"How easy a thing is depends on the strength and love with which it is met. We all expend ourselves on something, whether we will it or not. The whole point is how worthwhile that thing is and how well we make our expenditure."

"You sound like Wilona."

"Who is Wilona?"

"My mother."

The two talked a while longer, then curled into their fursacks. Far to the west a Tanwolf barked and then howled, and was answered by another, but no human eyes saw the wink and flash of the flames, which sent their light over a wide wilderness with no men of any tribe nearby.

"Look, someone is coming."

"Where?"

"There, to the west of the willows."

"Is there only one?"

"I think so."

"It must be Winnt."

"And Dar?"

"If it were he, he would have come sooner."

"Aiii. We have lost one of them anyway."

"It would seem so. Juk, tell the starband. We must welcome him with a feast and hear his story. And whichever one is not here, we must mourn him."

"Jestak," said the Protector. "When you next bring your outside friends here, bring old and ugly ones. We cannot afford to weaken Northwall with the loss of the women to the outside."

"Perhaps, Protector, our women may have more children."

"As you well know, it interferes with their administrative work. No matter how we train the nurserymen, they work like sheep. The constant supervision they need is my distraction."

"They have not the proper equipment, Protector."

"Jestak, that line of argument has been gone over centuries before you or even I were born. It is all in the roll of Oson, as I am sure you have read. I still find the logic impeccable."

"But you have not seen the way a mother and child can become one. It is so even among the Tantal, whose indifference to human life is so great."

"Do you not see how you argue against yourself?"

"Perhaps you are right, Protector. I still find it anomalous that we Pelbar, in all the world, seem different."

"We are also less cruel, and do good to the other peoples."

"The people of the eastern islands are like us, yet their family structure is much more like that of all the other peoples. Except us."

"Protector."

"Ah, yes. I am sorry, Protector. I meant to say, Protector."

"Now that your friend has gone, and things have settled into a late-winter routine, perhaps it is time, Jestak, to reassemble the general council to tell us of these eastern islands."

"Yes, Protector. I am eager to do that, for of all my travels, that was the one most glorious experience—even though I enjoyed my stay with the lake Sentani. The eastern islands—"

"Tell us all together, Jestak," said the Protector, turning to the reports on her table. Seeing the interview was ended, Jestak bowed and retired.

 VI

IT was evening. The judgment room was filled with people, and unlike the previous questionings of Jestak, this one was treated more like an entertainment or information session, less like an inquisition. It was plain he had already made a mark on Northwall society, and he could see his hope of getting to Northwall to escape the strictures and rigidities of Pelbarigan had been a realizable one. Had he never taken the right of reticence in Pelbarigan, he still would have been scrubbing steps and hallways. The strict rules of mere answers to questions of the council, without further explanation or elaboration, had been used by the Sylves party to its own advantage, and the larger city was much more conservative than the smaller northern outpost.

"When we left your story, some time ago, Jestak, you had told us how you left Innanigan by ship as a result of the public reaction to your defense of the Shumai named Stantu. Is that correct?"

"Yes, Protector."

"Will you tell us, then, what happened subsequently?"

"Yes, Protector. As I may have mentioned, the trip by sea was difficult for me at first, because the constant tossing of the ship on the large waves, which often reach a height of four or five arms, though they are capable of much greater heights during storms, is a difficult thing for a landsman.

"For this reason I was overjoyed to see in the east the dim forms of the eastern islands looming in the mist. I had arranged with the shipmaster to stay until the next voyage, in their small trading quarters there, for a mere pittance as an agent. They made only one voyage a year, and it was hard to get a coaster to stay there, as they thought of it as a forsaken and lonely place.

"The voyages were so few because the products of the islands are not many either. In a sense, the eastern islands are much like the cities of the Pelbar. They live in part by manufactures and crafts. They have never been conquered by the eastern cities, or taken over, because of their remoteness, and because they do not represent a power—at least as far as the Innanigani or others know of power. Saltstream inlays and Midridge ceramic work are well known and highly prized on the east coast. So is their stone sculpture, in which they excel our work, and their metalwork, though not nearly like the sturdiness and clear hard design of Pelbar work, is skilled in fineness and decoration. Their jewelry is unmatched. I was able to obtain several pieces, which I intended to bring back for examination, but circumstances demanded that I give them to the lake Sentani, and they now are worn, I assume, by Igon's bride, Ildra.

"The islands themselves are very recent, and of volcanic origin."

"What do you mean, Jestak?"

"Our limestone, as we can tell by its fossil sea creatures, was laid down originally underwater, and somehow the water retreated from the Heart River lands. But you have seen the grainy rocks from the streams to the north. These somehow got there some other way. There are regions that have these rocks commonly. There are fires in the center of the Earth that throw these rocks up so hot as to be liquid, as if one were working molten metal. As they flow and cool, they form rock of a different kind. The eastern islands are all of this rock, and Midridge is still being built up, from a high conical mountain with a hole in the top, from which a cloud of smoke always rises. At times at night, one can see the glow of its interior fires, though this is not usual. I was told that this rock sometimes flows out, and a tongue of liquid and fiery rock runs down the cone and hardens. I believe this because I have seen the flows, which look like mud on the river bank in spring, melted in the sun, then refrozen in the evening—only of course many times larger.

"But to return. As we neared the islands, I saw a small harbor in a largely rocky and steep coastline, with many seabirds, quite like our winter gulls, but of great variety, coursing and wheeling in the air around the coast. We were to land on Saltstream, in the small town of Godspalm, so named because the people believe their deity provided the safe harbor by shaping it like a giant human hand.

"The first thing I noticed was that there were no soldiers, and only two guards, scantily armed. A large crowd was there, to see the rare visitors, and we were openly welcomed, though strangers whose motives were unknown, into houses for food and drink. It was exhilarating, but also very tiring, because they questioned us all at great length about the doings on the shore, and they were so frank and truthful that I had a hard time avoiding my own recent troubles in Innanigan. I thought it would be a dangerous thing to tell complete strangers of what had befallen me, and especially of what I had done in escaping. They were so charming and kind. It was as if we were to welcome a Shumai into this chamber, feed him, and question him, with no thought to his weapons—for I was wearing a short sword—and they acted with complete and ingenuous openness.

"I never changed my Pelbar dress, or my roundcut hair, so they knew I was not of the same society as the coasters, and when they got from me that I was from the far and unknown west, a sort of hush fell over the company. Their questioning became more quiet and selective, and probed me intently. I could not understand it. Only later was I to learn that their religion involved a prophet coming from the deep wilds of the west to Godspalm. Somehow they thought I was that prophet, even though I assured them that though I was a religious man, I was not a minister of Aven, nor even was I a devotee, but was a metalworker from a family of metalworkers.

"Soon they found me work in metal and insisted that I live not in the small building on the harborside, where I was to serve as agent, but with an old couple well up from the water, facing westward. Near sunset, we could look from their small, stone porch, over the fingers of the harbor, where the pelicans and cormorants flew in toward their rookeries and the high-circling albatross, which has wings that spread farther than a man is tall, flew with incredible grace and joy in the pink and orange sky. I will never forget it, the utter calm of it, sipping their bitter tea and eating fish cakes and arrowroot pudding, in air so mild and fresh that it seemed to wash away the work of the day like a spring shower.

"My host, Irec, always wore a brown tunic, belted, that hung below his knees, and sandals. He sat with crossed legs on a stone bench. He liked to talk of philosophy and religion, his particularly, of course. They call their deity God. Soon I discovered that this deity is so like Aven as to be recognizably the same. Many of the precepts were the same. I well remember when he said, one night, in their dialect, which is not far from that of the Innanigani, 'Loved one, love one another, for love comes from God.' "

"He used those words, Jestak?"

"Yes. And I returned, 'Beloved, love everyone, for love has its origin in Aven.' "

"Were there any other similarities?"

"Yes. That was the first. But as soon as we found it, we began to trace as many as we could. We finally decided that both of our religions must not only have come from a central source, but from the very same writings as well."

"We must question you further about these things in the temple, Jestak," said Ommu, the minister.

"Willingly, for it is a subject of vital interest to us all.

"Of course I spent much time at work, for the work was not an idle thing with them. They are devoted workers, perhaps for the sake of the work itself rather than for material rewards, which they have not great value for. They try to put simplicity and excellence in everything they do. Like the Pelbar, they have great discipline, but theirs is purely voluntary, not brought about by the necessities of hostile neighbors, for the sea is their high wall, and no one comes over it. The whole society rides on it as freely as we might, if we were small, on an eagle's back, far over the heads of all hostile spears and arrows. The sense of freedom was something I had never felt before, though I felt a bit of it on my way home because of the isolation of the wide landscape.

"We worked chiefly in silver, making fine work, such as jewelry, buttons, and trimmings for furniture and boxes. Most of it is exported. I learned much about metalwork which we do not know, though I have never had the opportunity of passing this on because in Pelbarigan I was kept in the most menial of tasks because of my reticence. I in turn taught them some of the skills of iron and steel work from our Pelbarigan foundry, and from what I had picked up in Innanigan, for the Innanigani have skills in making mechanical devices which are unknown to us.

"The master of our shop was Irec's wife, Iring, who had begun as a fine silver worker. This does not mean that women administered everything, as they do with the Pelbar, but rather that everyone works without regard to gender, and there are no clearly defined roles or levels of status. Only during the first years of the lives of children are the mothers primarily responsible for them. After that they genuinely have no distinctions of gender. Of course the men do the very heavy work, but women also do work which is physically very demanding. There are gender distinctions in sports, but their games tend to be designed so that as much as possible both genders participate equally."

"Hardly an ideal society, Jestak."

"Yes, Protector. But it seems to work well with them. Of course there is little military training, except in their love of wrestling and stick games. And they use the bow expertly in fishing and birding.

"I had been there several months, when, at the time of the long winter holiday, Irec and Iring took me on a long trip up to the high hills of Saltstream. I did not know why we were going, other than for a vacation and to see the hills, gardens, and islands. That is what we did for the first two days. Many of the places have poems associated with them, written on large stones set upright by the pathside, and it is a pleasure for the islanders to walk from poem to poem guessing what the writers meant, for they are very brief and enigmatic.

"We had been doing that for some time when we took a side path, very narrow and steep, up toward the highest hill on Saltstream. There, in a sort of cove under the brow of the cliff that rose to the summit, was a low stone house, wide in extent, with a temple associated with it. It was obviously different, and it was there I met the Saltstream prophets.

"They call them prophets, at least. Here is a tiny community of men and women, living in celibacy, devoting themselves to religious study and manufacturing small wooden objects to sell for their maintenance, which was scant enough. They lived with great discipline and rigor. Yet they were warm and kind. Plainly they had heard of me before I came to them.

"I was ushered into the temple where all twenty waited for me around a very large circular table. There were places at the table for Irec and Iring, as well as for me. It must have been midmorning when we arrived, and we talked for the rest of the day, mostly of the West, and of my experience. One of the prophets, Ord, took down all that was said, and often questioned me again and again so as to get everything correct.

"Toward evening, Irec and Iring withdrew, but all convinced me to stay with the prophets for fourteen days so that further converse might be held. It was clear to me that in part they wanted to see if I were that mythical prophet from the west that they had looked for. I think I convinced them that I was not, but really at that point a stray waif without much wisdom, entirely cast loose, and very far from his home society, which would afford him only a doubtful welcome when he returned. If he possibly could."

"We have given you welcome enough, Jestak. Look. Here you are, holding the center of attention."

"Yes, Protector. And I am grateful for it."

"Tell us more of these prophets."

"Yes, Protector. There is not that much, really, to tell. It was largely religious conversation, comparing their beliefs to ours, their hopes to ours, their mode of prayer to ours, and then explaining to me the nature and direction of their concepts of deity. I think you would find it tedious.

"One part may interest you, however. They felt, as I have told you, that after the time of fire mankind was nearly snuffed out. We are now beginning to reawaken. They see a testing time for the ideals of love and brotherhood they hold. They conceive that they will eventually be invaded and will have to match their ideal, and their prayers, against the steel of the invaders."

"If that happens, I feel for them."

"I, too, Uncle. But then I am not sure. Just as no one knows how we would repel an invader, or even the extent and training of the Pelbar guard, so no one, surely not me, knows of their inner defense, or of how effective it will be. One thing is certain. While we pray out of our great sense of duty, and hope our prayers will be answered, they pray as ones with full confidence that they will be answered. The depth of their trust is remarkable."

"Surely, Jestak, we pray, but a part of our actual prayer is the sharpness of our arrowpoints. That is as sure as prayer because it shows that we really mean what we hope for in safety, and mean to take those steps we can, relying on Aven to supply those needs and energies that lie beyond our abilities."

"That is true, Captain. I have been led to wonder, though, if the trueness and height of these walls around us are not more of our prayer than our weapons, in which we may be trained, but which we almost never use."

"The height of our training is our prayer, as well as our devotion to forbearance from using them."

"Yes, Leatch. Perhaps Jestak will tell us more of his islands, as the hour for our adjournment grows somewhat near."

"Yes, Protector."

"Yes, Protector, I will. Most of the rest of my encounter with the prophets was material of interest chiefly to the ministers. But I might summarize by saying that they visualize the reawakening of the world as a period of chaos and military clashes, but that they also anticipate a reuniting of all the peoples into a single society. Their prayer is that this society is one based on truth to law and justice, and on love and mercy, rather than on some tyranny. In this, from what I told them, they see the Pelbar way as a part of the great hope of the west. They do not hope for much from the eastern cities, which are self-centered and indulgent."

"Perhaps you may tell us more of this later, Jestak. Could you summarize for us how you got home?"

"Yes, Protector. I was ready with a fine cargo for the ship of next year. They were pleased with me and tried to get me to stay on as a crew member, as before, and dropped me at the northernmost of the eastern cities, the small town of Selegan, which lies deep in a river mouth in a country of rocks and evergreens. From there I made my way west to the Sentani and my old friend, Igon. I stayed with them for a time, and attended his marriage, at which time I gave up all the gold things I had intended to bring home. It was just as well, because the rest of the way was very arduous.

"Igon's people gave me a small boat, and since I was

now adept at the use of sail, I went far to the north of the Tantal country across the Bitter Sea. The Tantal have become more aggressive, though they have not done well with the Sentani, whose arrows cut down the invaders as a white-faced bull chews grass. I landed on the archipelago I mentioned before, and again met with the Rits, who also have experienced the invasions of the Tantal, though they are better able to handle them now. My old friends among them were very good to me, and sent me on my way west. I went far to the west to the northern headwaters of the Heart, which is some hundreds of ayas from here, and made my way down the Heart in an attempt to avoid the Shumai."

"Did you see any?"

"Yes. I saw some, though they are not that many when spread out in so great a country. I had only one slight encounter, but made my way downriver. I well remember the joy with which I passed Northwall at night, in the river, on my way home to Pelbarigan. I was received, but not welcomed, as you know."

"And that is the story of the journeys of Jestak, the great traveler of the Pelbar?" queried the Protector.

"Yes, Protector. That was it. It was a grand experience, I suppose. I do not understand it in the least. It is probably insignificant. But it has widened my world. I do fear one thing. If the Tantal continue to grow, and to invade, how long will it be before they begin to move into the west?"

"That is something the council will discuss. We thank you for your story. And now, since the work of tomorrow will not await our talk, we must retire." With this signal from the Protector, the group began to rise, murmur, and move to the doors.

"Jestak."

"Yes, Protector?"

"I would see you a moment in my chambers after I have had late tea."

"Yes, Protector."

Winnt was looking at the fire, his hands idly working a skin spade across the inner surface of a giant beaver pelt. Mokil was watching him.

"What is it, Winnt?"

"There is something I must talk with you about, Mokil."

"We may use my shelter, young one."

"No need, my leader. All must know of it soon enough. And they must think about it, too."

"We are listening."

"While I was at Northwall, I met a young woman. Her name is Ursa."

"Ah. I had thought you had not fully left behind the Pelbar. Ursa. We will listen, of course, but you realize what you are doing. There has never been any intermarriage among the western peoples. That has been our strength."

"The grandmother of Ursa, apparently, was a waif taken in as an infant by those of Northwall. She must have been Shumai."

"Suffering river toads, Winnt," exclaimed Juk. "Are you going to mongrelize the Sentani?"

"No, Juk. But I would indeed like to marry her."

"How could you stand a Pelbar city for always? You said how stifling it was."

"She has already agreed to come with us. She is not nearly as chatty and Northwall-centered as the others I met. And surely I met enough, because I was, it seemed, Jestak's pet coney to most of them. Or more. At any rate, I received enough attention."

"It is not often that they see a real man."

"Their men are real enough. It was there, among the metalworkers, that I saw the largest and strongest man I have ever seen—Jestak's cousin, Ut, who could hold Mokil up in one hand and Weldi in the other. He is a giant, and spends his days in pounding hot iron into shape."

"The girl, Winnt."

"Ursa administers their investigations into the plants and animals of the area. She knows the plants more intimately than I ever believed possible, but only the smaller and nearer furred creatures are known to her."

"Of what use would that be to us?"

"I don't know. She has agreed, as I said, to come with us. I do not anticipate the whole thing's being easy."

"But you love her and have told her so."

"Not precisely, Mokil. I told her that if I did, that would be forever. I did say that I would say it to none but her, though, but only if it were agreed to by the starband."

"Then, by your word, you will either have this woman or no woman. Is that not correct?" Mokil shook his head. "Well, we will call a general council. That is one sort of game that they of Koorb never anticipated our bringing home."

Comm ushered Jestak into the Protector's chamber, bowed, and departed. He stood before her while she sipped the last of her tea and put the cup aside.

"Sit down, Jestak. Bring that stool over there."

"Yes, Protector."

"Now. I have begun to believe your story, for there are things in it that it would be hard for the most inspired prevaricator to make up."

"Thank you. I suppose that is quite a compliment."

"Protector."

"Yes. Protector."

"I would question you on a few things. First, would not the Tantal, whom you say might push westward in their desire for conquest, run into much opposition before they reached us? Could they handle the central Sentani?"

"It is hard to say. There are two things that we must think of, though, Protector. One is that they themselves would not have to come all the way here for us to feel them, for when they exerted pressure, then that pressure would be exerted by the next people and the next until we felt it. The other thing is that they are very skillful in the use of large boats, and hence could navigate the upper waters of the Heart and come directly here. They are in a sense engineers. The Shumai and Sentani can melt back into the wilderness before them. We are right here behind our walls."

"That would not go easy on them. These are defenses that it would take a great deal to breach."

"Yes, Protector. That is true. But they certainly would be a great trouble to us. They are a determined and capable people, and if they were not being harassed by the outside tribes, they might even try to dig to Northwall from the river."

"That, as you know, would be impossible. Unless, of course, they have an easy way to cut rock."

"There is a way, Protector. In fact it might even be a way to remove our wall in one great puff of smoke. I heard of it in Innanigan. The Tantal do not know of it now, but it is surely possible that they may find out."

"You are an alarmist. But it is good to be aware of these things, I suppose. Now there is one other thing. You mentioned a 'slight' encounter with the Shumai. Your 'slight' events have a way of turning out larger than that. Would you care to tell me of it, please?"

"Yes, Protector. I was far north in grass country. It was hot weather, and thunderstorms were in the area. I was spending the day under some willows on a caving bank of a branch stream, fishing with a hand line, when a storm came of great violence, with torrential rain. The stream I was by experienced a quick flood. I heard it, then looked upstream and saw water about three arms high moving down toward me fast. I threw my pack back onto higher ground and started to move after it when I thought I saw an arm in the water. It was, I saw on looking again, and so by instinct I waded out, keeping hold of a willow limb, and grabbed it as it went by. The rest happened very fast. The water was roaring by, tearing at me. It was also rising. I heard faint shouts, and as I was about to be swept away, someone grabbed my arm. There were several Shumai there, forming a chain. I and the next man were taken off our feet, but we all held on, and so drew the person to shore. She was a young woman, very beautiful, especially with the clothes torn away."

"You may spare me, Jestak, the details."

"Details, Protector?" grinned Jestak. "That was the central part."

"Yes, yes. Go on."

"She was not breathing, Protector, and one of the Shumai put his head down to her and said that her spirit was gone from her, but I insisted on being allowed to bring her back, and so I used the way they have at Saltstream of blowing in the mouth at intervals, supplying breath, and after a time she revived."

"And so the Shumai savages, because of this, let you live?"

"Well, yes. They were not very happy about it, but they were also bewildered at finding, of all peoples, a stray Pelbar there, and then they did not know what to make of my saving the girl. You know the way they are. They told me that since I had done them a good turn, they might cut off only one of my arms. Then they asked me to name one favor they would give me. I said not to follow me until moonrise. They agreed, saying then that the killing of me would be better sport, because 'No one can outrun the Shumai.' I of course made no attempt to outrun them. I simply outswam them, for the Heart was not far, and it was already a large river. I ran the bank until nightfall and then swam quietly. Even their dogs never tracked me, and they had no conception of anyone's spending hours in the water."

"And that was all, Jestak?"

"That was just about it, Protector."

"What was the girl's name, Jestak?"

"Tia, Protector."

"So they told you."

"She told me, Protector."

"Tia." The Protector looked into her empty teacup. "Will she be coming to truceweek?"

"I do not know, Protector. I saw her brother, Mogan, at Pelbarigan, at the last fall truceweek, and even spoke with him, but she was not there. It was a great disappointment. Mogan said, upon my inquiring, that she was well."

"That was a great concession on his part."

"Yes, it was. I gathered that they had decided later that they should have shown a little gratitude. But as you know, Protector, they really do not know how. Their habit of bluster is too much for them sometimes."

"Then they do not know you are at Northwall?" she said, teasing. "Too bad for you, Jestak. You will not see your lady love again. But I have a good one chosen for you, you know, and I may command you to serve her for always."

"Alas, Protector. Would you do that? That was an outmoded way, I thought."

"No, Jestak, I would not do that. We have enough intrigues around here without my creating more. I will wait until some girl is fool enough to decide that a wild one like you should serve her."

"Perhaps there shall be no fool like that, Protector."

"Perhaps, but I doubt it. You are noticeable. Meanwhile, I want you to know that the last thing we want around here is a wild Shumai woman living here as your wife. So you must forget that romantic vagary."

"I only saw her for a matter of a half quarter of the sun, Protector."

"That long. And of course, you only rescued her from oblivion and blew her life's breath back into her lips—while, of course, she was lying there with hardly anything on. I am assuming that she had something on. Did she?"

"Of course, the Shumai immediately covered her, even though they are not so squeamish about such things as we. She was well tanned almost all over, as I saw it," he grinned.

"Indeed, I imagine so. Well, Jestak, you sometimes do my heart good. You remind me of a man I once knew. But you have come here with so much that is new. You seem to manage to make friends with the outside people and keep your blood in your skin, which is miracle enough."

"I have had the good fortune always to encounter them when they needed help, and I have been able to render it. They feel obligation, you know."

"Yes, I see that. We must exploit that tendency, though not too greatly, lest we overdo it. By the way, were you addressing me?"

"Protector. Yes, Protector, I am truly sorry."

"I imagine how much you are. Well, that is all," she said, rising. "You may embrace me before you go, for you are a good boy, however unwise."

"Yes, Protector," he said, putting his arms around the old woman and giving her a quick squeeze."

"I said 'embrace,' Jestak, not crush. No matter. Good night."

"Good night, Protector," he said, departing, smiling inside at the fact that she had not perceived that Tia might well appear at the Northwall truceweek, since the Shumai would not be expecting him to be there—unless of course she were already married, or dead, or some such thing.

The Protector summoned Comm and ordered another pot of tea. She sat a long time looking at the small coal fire in her iron stove, and thinking. She called Comm again and had him sit with her, but he was a servant, and a sleepy old man, and she said nothing at all to him.

VII

MOKIL'S starpoint stood on top of the hill to the north of Northwall, where the Pelbar bury their dead, who finally escape the walled city only to enter the ground. The grave of Dar was there, with those of the Jestan of Northwall. A new stone marker lay over the grave.

"What does it say, Jestak?"

"It says, 'Dar, of the Sentani of the Fastness of Koorb, member of the northern starband, whose courage was absolute, whose faithfulness to his friends was without measure, and who died at Northwall, calling on the name of Atou, in obedience to orders. May his name be praised wherever men value goodness.' "

Mokil wiped his eye. "It says that? Did you write that, Jestak?"

"No, Mokil. My uncle Manti, chief of the defenses of the city, wrote it, and it was approved by the Protector and cut into the stone by Sert, our engraver of stone. We hope that it is satisfactory."

"It is good, Jestak. You must write it all out for me in our spelling so that I may take it to his family in Koorb. Now let us go again to the message stone so that we may see about this matter of Ursa. The starband has approved the wishes of Winnt, though with reluctance."

At the message stone the horn was sounded, and soon Ursa appeared through the small door, as had been arranged, accompanied by Manti.

"Winnt," said Mokil, "you had not told me she was so beautiful. It is no wonder your head was turned."

"I did not realize it myself, to this extent," returned Winnt. "She is more beautiful than ever I remember."

"It is the winter and the absence of women," said Willton, the starband leader, who was the third in the meeting

83

party. "Yet I do concede that she is a lovely woman—though you can see the Shumai in her."

Despite the eagerness of the young people to see each other again, the meeting was conducted with due decorum, as always had been the case between these two hostile and suspicious groups. It became necessary to decide how the marriage ceremony was to be conducted. This took considerable negotiating.

"We have arranged a way, should you desire, for us to welcome your entire starband into our temple within the walls. You would have to leave your weapons in a room inside the wall, for our surety. But if you feel that violates your security, then you may want to choose a portion of your people to come into the temple," said Manti.

This was the final decision—that seven men from each pointband would enter the temple, the others to remain outside the walls with the winter goods. Then a second ceremony, more in the manner of the Sentani, would be conducted in the forefield near the message stone, with Pelbar attendants. Both groups realized that more than a marriage was at stake, and that they were really beginning the process of amnesty between the peoples. Many were suspicious. But put in the guise of a single wedding, this was the sort of gesture that could be later disavowed should it prove to be unworkable.

"We must," said Willton, "though I do not wish to rush the matter, proceed with these festivities as quickly as possible because a delay of days may mean that we would meet the northbound Shumai, and with our small numbers, and the encumbrance of our winter goods, we would not easily sustain a fight."

"Agreed. We are ready now and can conduct the ceremony in the morning if you wish."

"That is agreeable to us. How long, did you say, that your part in the affair will take?"

"One daylight quarter at the most, and it can be less."

"Then we will have our ceremony following that, and a general celebration can be held following. If it is agreeable to you, we have a few things that we might trade, though it is not yet truceweek, and then we can retire to prepare for an early departure the following morning. With the high water, we can push our skinboats as far as Pelbarigan, or Banner Island, below it, by nightfall. Then another hard day's paddling should take us to the Threerivers, and in a further day, we will be beyond the swath of main Shumai migration. They are no match for us on the river anyhow, with our bows, but I would rather not meet with them."

The meeting drew to a close, and as was the habit of the two peoples, both sides prepared to withdraw to their own groups. But this time Ursa, addressing Willton, asked, "Sir, if it is possible, might I spend some time in your camp with Winnt, since we have not seen each other?"

Willton looked at Manti. Then he shrugged. "Why not, since you will be there soon enough anyway? Is that all right, Pelbar?"

"Yes, but return before sunfall. You must begin your preparation and purification. We will watch for you."

So the Sentani hunters, who had been gathered near the river, were greeted by the unprecedented sight of a beautifully dressed and beautiful Pelbar woman wandering in their camp, being introduced by Winnt, and then meeting with his pointband. She wore a long, dark red robe, with rich black embroidery, specked with small leaves done in tiny metal beads. Her hair was long and roped behind her head with a black ribbon and clasped with a silver hinge clasp. On her shoulder she had a tooled leather bag in which she carried a small greeting present for each of the members of the northpoint band. Juk, looking in the small metal mirror at his heavily bearded, weathered face, simply said, "Huh." But he was pleased, and soon began to comb the winter out of his hair.

Even the Sentani sentinels turned their heads as Winnt and Ursa walked back across the forefield to the walls of Northwall and she entered the small door in the center. "What is this all going to mean, Mokil?" asked Chogtan. "It will be strange to paddle our way southward with such a woman in the boats."

"She will urge you on to your own woman, Chog."

"Yes. She will do that."

After the dawn fires had sent their smoke plumes up to mingle with the river haze, and the forty-nine chosen men had scrubbed and dressed themselves as well as they could, given the circumstances, they assembled near the message stone, with Winnt making the fiftieth. From the towers of Northwall came the sounds of horns, and the central door, which the Sentani had never seen opened, slowly grated up. From it issued twenty of the Pelbar guard, marching in

step. The Sentani had never seen this done, and it somewhat unnerved them, though they took it as like a dance.

Manti spoke first. "We of the Pelbar at Northwall greet
you on this occasion of the marriage of Winnt and Ursa,
and welcome you to our city and temple. We are unarmed.
You may leave your arms inside. Please accompany us to
the temple."

"We accept your offer with pleasure and trust in its honesty," returned Willton.

The group entered the city, which was a wholly new
experience to the Sentani, who saw now more of how the
stone was interlaced and fitted, so that it made a single
piece, and each stone itself could not be dislodged. They
took off their weapons with some trepidation, but the central door remained open, though guarded. They moved
down a long corridor, dimly lit, turned to the right, and
moved down another long corridor, then out into a court-
yard, and to the great bronze doors of the Pelbar temple.
The Sentani had never seen such carved stone, such a massive building, or such an extensive and dedicated attempt
to make something beautiful. Inside, they found that Pelbar
glass had been lavishly used, in many colors, to flood the
interior with daylight. The broad stone floor was covered
with woven rush mats, but the benches stacked along the
wall showed that this ceremony was to be conducted standing. On a balcony to the right were musicians and singers.
As the party entered, flute music played a song with harmonies very unfamiliar to the visitors. In a special high
compartment above the singers the visitors could see an
old woman sumptuously and ceremoniously dressed, with
her hair piled in three tiers. She inclined her head to them,
and Willton returned a salute, understanding that this must
be the Protector of Northwall. "Look at her. Ruled by a
woman, they are," he murmured to Mokil.

"She doesn't look like much," he whispered in return.

Meanwhile the Protector murmured to the westcouncil,
by her side, "Look down there, Nois, look at what we are
giving Ursa to. How could we have consented to do that?"

Ommu began the wedding by summoning the singers to
a hymn, which they rendered with many harmonies, dazzling the ears of the Sentani, who had never heard grouped
voices work in harmony before.

Ommu then greeted the visitors with a low bow, and
began, "We of Northwall on this unparalleled occasion

wish to welcome the Sentani of Koorb to our city. May the blessings of Aven be on you, conduct you well down the river to your families, give you good hunting, good fishing, many children, safety, and prosperity, with justice and mercy, all your days." Then, she turned to Cipi, the south-council, and said, "Are you willing that Ursa, who has been under your jurisdiction these many years, be given to Winnt, the Sentani of Koorb, and he to her, each to belong to the other?"

In silent reply, Cipi brought Ursa from a door to the right and conducted her to Winnt. She was dressed in much simpler fashion than on the previous day, surprisingly enough, in a long black robe without decoration, and bare-foot. The ceremony had been modified because Winnt was not a Pelbar, and the marriage was not a ceremony of his submission to her, and the placing of her foot on his back, as a public declaration of her administration of the family affairs, was omitted. Instead, Winnt was given a candle, which he lighted with stone and steel, then lighting one part of a central candle with two wicks. Then Ursa lit the other half. Then Ommu took a heated knife and separated the two candles so the wicks burned apart. Then she took the two and placed them over a small charcoal fire until the wax softened, and twisted the two together so they would not separate, and placed them in a central holder.

Winnt then took both of Ursa's hands, kissed her fore-head, closed eyes, mouth, and hands, and she did the same. Then an apple was brought, cut in half, and each took a bite from each half. Then the couple took hands, and Ommu intoned, "Here in the northern city of the Pelbar, on this day and forever, you are married. May Aven bless you, bring you happiness, bring you consolation in distress, an-swer your prayers, bring each patience with the other, bring to each the fullness of the reality of the goodness of the other. We of Northwall now give you, Ursa, to the Sentani, in hopes of seeing you again, and your husband, and your children, in joy and love. And now, Willton of the Sentani, we give Ursa into your charge, as chief of the band of which she is now a part. May a bond of love grow up between you."

"We accept her, Ommu the Pelbar," said Willton. The flute music resumed, and the party began to file once more through the same corridors, wondering indeed if they had ever been in so strange a place, or if it had been a dream, yet knowing its reality by the fact that nothing in their previous experience would ever have caused them to dream such a thing.

The ceremony of the Sentani was much simpler, especially since it was not being conducted at home, but rather on a hunting expedition, with men only. But it was not at all casual to the starband, who were arranged in order, and at rigid attention in their pointbands, as Willton nicked the right thumbs of Ursa and Winnt, mingled their blood, and then each took the thumb of the other into the mouth and removed the droplets of blood remaining with their lips. Then, since Ursa was not of the band, Willton squeezed the tiny wound, and himself took in a drop of her blood, making her one with the band. All married Sentani have the wedding scar on their right thumb as an instant identification of their marital status. Juk had three scars indicating that he had been twice widowed.

Following this, each starpoint leader filed by and kissed both the hands of Ursa, and she kissed both their cheeks. The slight smell of apples about her made some heartbeats race a little and reminded men of home. Following this every man in the starband filed by Ursa and placed hands on her shoulders, and she on theirs. After this, Mokil came once more, this time in a black fur sash, and placed hands with her. "This," he explained, "is for Dar."

When the ceremony was over, refreshments were brought from the city, out the central door, which was still open, and all drank the icy peach drink of the enclosed Northwall orchards, and ate small fruit cakes. The Sentani, after so many months on a heavy meat diet, returned again and again for cakes, but Jestak had warned the bakers, and plenty were on hand. This was to be an appetizer. Dancing would follow, then a more substantial feast.

The first dancers were those of the Pelbar guard, which was composed of both men and women, highly disciplined. These were not the general guards, which came from the populace as a whole, for the city was always under guard, but those whose specialty it was to deal with whatever emergencies might arise. They wore the familiar Pelbar tunic, but with breastplates and some leg armor, long gauntlets and a low-visored steel helmet. They carried not the familiar Pelbar short sword or small bow, but long swords, on this occasion, low slung in ornate scabbards.

They began their dance slowly, in two facing lines, to

the music of horns, pipes, drums, and pellutes, with ritual movements. Soon the swords were drawn, the dance speeded up, with leaps, sword clashings, and aerial flips. This continued for some time, until the audience began to wonder how they would sustain it.

"Frek," said Juk, aside, "I begin to wonder if these Pelbar are such prairie flowers after all. They might fight."

"Um. Maybe. I see some I would like to have other business with than fighting."

Finally, a long series of high kicks ended the dance, and a general applause of shouts and foot-stamping greeted the exhausted dancers. Their performance was followed by the male dance of the Sentani, a slow and formal hunters' dance performed by fifty men to flute and pellute, and in this instance, a borrowed drum. It was performed with hands held high, a straight trunk, and much footwork, with the men weaving among each other in ornate patterns. The idea was that the music alone should make a sound, emphasizing the quiet of the hunters, but with fifty moving in unison, a pleasing muffled tap and shuffle was the sound of the dance itself.

The dance had continued for some time when, almost in unison, the four horns of warning from the four corner towers of Northwall sounded a continuing blast. As was the custom, the high arrow of the side nearest danger was swung to point at it. All instantly stopped. The Pelbar guard formed, swords drawn, between the company and the direction pointed out. Manti had insisted, against some opposition from Willton, that the Sentani work out a defense plan in advance, for this was Pelbar routine. Consequently, all the Sentani and their equipment were near the wall. So there was no general rush.

Shading his arm, Jestak said, "Shumai. It is a small band, with women and some children," and all followed his gaze to the point of a hill to the south, a fourth of an ayas off. The Shumai made no attempt to move.

"It must be Thro, come back early to take care of the remains of his fellows. He said that he would. And who is that? It is Stantu, I think—my friend Stantu." And he took a horn and blew three short blasts, and then gave one of the chilling, quavering yells of the Shumai, surprising all there. Jestak then began to run toward the party, and one man detached himself there and ran toward him, and all stood while the two friends met and greeted each other with a long, muscular, boyish embrace. The Sentani were inclined to be angry, especially now with this interruption to the wedding dance, but Jestak was already beckoning the Shumai and moving toward them with a tall, light-haired man in Shumai clothing, both talking rapidly.

Winnt raised his hands. "My friends, if it is Thro, for my sake let us welcome him, for inadvertently he brought Ursa and me together in love, and without him, we may never have realized our need for each other."

The groom's request, made at this point in part out of regard for Jestak, eased the tension, for groom's requests are to be obeyed on a wedding day if it is possible. Jestak and Stantu were nearing the company, and Jestak called out, "Manti, all of you. Look. It is Stantu come back all the way from Innanigan. He is really here, and safe. It is our request that he may join our celebration in peace and harmony, as well as the others, who are the party of Thro come back to honor their dead."

It made a strange sight, the travel-worn Shumai moving into the company of a mixed group of Sentani and Pelbar celebrants, everyone suspicious. But the Northwallers, who had heard of Stantu, and seen Thro earlier, and were by now getting used to Jestak's wonders, were quick to rally and welcome the new party.

Thro himself had quickly seen where things lay. Once he had been seen, he had no hope either of running or fighting. His party was too small, and the women and children would have been quickly captured by pursuing Sentani, as well, in all probability, as himself and his men. A fight he could have accepted, with the typical gusto of the Shumai—but not the capture of the others.

Jestak had gone out to meet him, and Thro stepped out in front of the spears of his ten men to greet him. "Well, Pelbar, I see you have had the good fortune not to have been spitted on a Shumai spear up until now."

"Thro, for Aven, leave off the bragging. We have Sentani here, who have no cause to be kind to you. Mind yourself, or you and all of yours will get the worst of it. Come now. Make yourselves welcome to join our feast. You look tired and dusty. Take that section of the creek bank for your camp, upstream from that tree. But first, all of you come and meet the company."

"So the Pelbar and the Sentani are making an alliance

against us," remarked Kod, a young hunter even taller than Thro.

"I am not sure," returned Jestak. "At any rate there is a wedding today between the two people who found and rescued you last winter. There is that alliance at least."

"I do not like it," said Kod.

"Fish guts for what you like," said Jestak. "We are welcoming you, and you, with typical Shumai ill-breeding and stupidity, find fault. Stick your head in the river if you would prefer."

In one motion, Kod had raised his spear, Thro had broken its shaft in two, and Iley had kicked his legs from under him. Kod turned to rise, knife drawn, but found three spears at his neck.

"What will it be, Kod, do the spears go in or do you behave yourself?" asked Ouwn, quietly. "These are the people who saved us. None of us, they or us, care for your vomit."

"I will be quiet," said Kod, sullenly.

"Come," said Jestak, squatting down to him. "This is a wedding day. Do not be angry. Come with us, and for today be at peace. Tomorrow you may resume your opinions." And he held out his hands to the Shumai, who was truly embarrassed by this conciliation, and grinned and took his hand, using Jestak's grip to pull himself up.

"We will mend your spear," said Jestak. "Come."

So, for the first time in anyone's memory, the three peoples of the Heart River met, with suspicion, but in peace. The Pelbar struck up music once again, and Manti, Thro, and Willton met, a little apart, and conversed, pledging truce for the time.

The Pelbar were setting up trestle tables and benches, and bringing food, fresh meat, piles of vegetables, fruit pies, made from their store of dried fruits, and cauldrons of herb tea. Honey was available to sweeten the drinks to taste, which, in the case of the outside tribesmen, meant very sweet.

The Shumai women and children were invited to wash at large kettles of warm water brought outside the wall, and they were given scented soap and fresh towels, as well as a screen of cloth so they could undress. They were bewildered by this, since it was so unlike their outdoor nomadic life, but they agreed, in part out of intimidation, and the children, especially, who are usually fair and dark-eyed, emerged from their baths shining and with the feeling of being cleaner than since they had bathed during the last fall.

The Shumai at first insisted on sitting apart at their own tables at the feast, but the five children tended to wander, and seeing a young head worm its way among their elbows, and a small hand reach for some piece of food on another table, soon charmed even the Sentani, who took the children on their laps and made much of them.

The feast was followed by more Pelbar music, and the singers singing among them. As the sun waned, the amnesty seemed well established, and when Manti came to Willton, then to Thro, and invited them inside to the council room for tea, they went without much hesitation.

The Protector was an imposing figure, even to the outsiders, for her self-control, her rich dress, and her obvious valuing of herself. She well knew that the council room itself would be an advantageous meeting ground, because neither of the others would ever have seen any place so rich in artistry, with the exception of the Northwall temple.

"Jestak has told me," she began, after pleasantries, "of a people called the Tantal, who inhabit the south coast of the Bitter Sea, who enslave any people they can reach. He was their slave. It was there he first met Sentani and Shumai, and became their acquaintances, for they also were slaves. This led to his fluency in Shumai and his adoption into the Sentani of the lakes. This led, I assume, to our meeting today in a roundabout way."

Jestak translated for Thro so he would be sure to catch all of the Protector's words.

"Jestak fears," she continued, "that they will exert pressure westward, and perhaps even come to this region, to further their depredations, to the detriment of us all, even though we are hardly friends. I would like to ask if you have heard of these people and have felt any general movement westward."

The others sat in silence when this had been rendered for Thro. "I do not believe so," said Willton, "though we met a hunt of central Sentani this winter, and I do not remember this ever happening before."

"No," said Thro. "Our problems are from the west. We would not know about these Tantal, though the north bands of Shumai may. I do not think they need concern us. We can handle ourselves well enough."

"Yes," said the Protector. "I am sure that you can. And yet Jestak did meet four Shumai slaves on the Bitter Sea. Tell him about it, Jestak. And that was now seven years ago."

Jestak recounted the story. Thro did not reply.

"My feeling about it," said the Protector, "is that the western tribes have gotten along quite well with their own warfare. We have developed, though you do not acknowledge it, a workable interdependent economy, through the somewhat unsatisfactory means of truceweeks. However, if pressure from the east, or actual invaders, arrived in the area, our present system would be disrupted. I hope that you will at least remember this in case we may have to arrive at some agreement in the future."

Both men seemed doubtful. This was outlandish. They tended to regard the whole proposal as another example of the incredible cautiousness of the Pelbar. Conversation waned.

"I wonder if you would feel free to tell us about the trouble from the west that you mentioned, Thro," said the Protector.

"It is a problem. But we can handle it. It is why my party were winterbound and almost died last year. The Emeri, who live in the high mountains far to the west, made an eastward raid. They killed and carried off a number of our people. We fought back and killed some of them. But we were unable to recover the people and finally had to turn east and south to find the herds. We had lost many men, and when you found us, we were nearly spent. We owe you an obligation, much as I dislike admitting it; but I think perhaps I am paying it in being here."

"Do you render obligations so easily as that, Thro?" asked the Protector gently. "No matter. We are well able to stay out of your way, though we would rather that the peoples were at peace with one another. How many men did you lose?"

"More than enough, and women and children. They were taken. Almost the entire Rush Creek Band were taken or killed."

"Aiii," said Jestak.

All turned to him, surprised. His face was dead serious. "Tia," he said, "was she taken?"

"Tia?"

"When I was returning down the Heart, by chance I saved the life of a young woman, by name Tia, during a flash flood on what they called Rush Creek. They rewarded me by saying they would not chase and kill me until moonrise. Her brother's name was Mogan."

"Mogan I know. He was one of those who await a better burial a few miles from here. Did you not see him?"

"I did not really look. Then she was one. Was she killed?"

"I do not know. I will ask the others. Have you a claim on her?"

"No. No claim. But if she is taken, I wish to go west and release her."

The other three laughed. "Ah, Jestak," said the Protector. "You have no claim, but you will try to arrange one, I see. Well, perhaps we need to return to our other duties," and she stood and bowed, then retreated from the room.

Northwall lay to the south. The star of fires of the Sentani could be seen in the dark, and, to the east, the two Shumai fires near the creek.

"My name is Cise," she was saying.

"And mine is Zen."

"It is getting cold. You must put those furs around me. There. Now you may kiss me again. No. Not so fast. All things must have their measure and their time."

"What is this? Do you want love or philosophy?"

"Some of each, and both merged, Zen. Now, there, if you wish. No. Not there. Mmmm. You are a tall man. How is it you are so thin? You must have a hard life. No, remember, I said no."

Zen twisted free and stepped back. "What are you doing, woman! What is it you want?"

"Shhh. Someone will hear. Please. Please, I am sorry. No. Come back."

Zen stopped. "I will come back, if . . ."

"If what?"

"If I run things."

Cise sank to her knees and cried. Zen came back. "Stop now," he said. "Stop that."

"You may hold me, but you may not lie with me. It is not proper. What if I were to have a child?"

"I would come back for you and you could come with Ursa."

"No. No. I cannot. I am not made for that. My life is at Northwall."

"Then why did you lead me on?"

"I am sorry. I thought . . . I did not know you would want so much."

The anger drained out of Zen. "We had better go," he said, kindly.

From the ground she replied, "Yes, we had better go. But hold me once more."

"No," said Zen. "No, not now. I will hold you if I may have you, but not otherwise."

Cise rose, and he heard her footsteps retreating. He stood a long time looking at the city and the fires, then walked slowly toward the star of light.

The Sentani had moved their band near the river's edge so they could get an early start in the morning. The band was arranged in its typical star, but this time Willton was with the eastern point, and the wide central area was dark. There the bride and groom stayed in a small tent, surrounded by the whole band. As the murmuring of voices quieted, and the fires grew dimmer, occasionally hunters would look toward the tent, musing.

"Quiet there," said one.

"You are too far away," was the reply.

"I agree."

"Fona would have something to say about that."

"Fona. Fona will have nothing to say when I get home."

Inside the tent was all the bewilderment of the launching of a new ship in the eastern shipyards. It has been all prepared, examined, and checked, but it may not, after all, float true, and no one knows until the chocks have been knocked out and it slips down the way into the water.

"Ursa," Winnt was saying. "There will be difficulties at home. But no matter what they are, you may count on the fact that I will be with you."

"Yes. Now move closer. There is a little chill on this side."

"Closer than together?"

"Yes, closer than that."

Jestak was at the Shumai camp, talking to Stantu, for the Pelbar had declined to admit him for the night, except to a small by-room in the rear of the city, where the walled orchards adjoined the east wall, and Stantu had refused the offer.

"I much regret this," Jestak said.

"It is nothing. We are not precisely of friendly peoples, are we?"

"Yes, but after your coming so far. I will stay with you until the council decides otherwise."

"It is nothing, Jestak. Do not think of it."

"If you were hurt or in need, they would not hesitate."

"Do not worry, Jestak," put in Thro. "Remember, if you entered a Shumai camp, you would look like a net with the spear holes."

"Perhaps so."

"And besides, I was invited to have some tea with the old lady. That's about all she could stand of the unwashed."

"Please be patient with us, Stantu," said Jestak. "It all takes time."

"I really do not care, Jestak. I came here to see that you were safe, after you put yourself out for me. At Pelbarigan they would not answer the call to the message stone at first, but I waited a long time and finally an old man came, with a guard. I asked for you, and he would say nothing, but as they were going, the guard whispered that you were at Northwall."

"Ha. What did the guard look like? Was he short and dark, with a slight hook in his nose?"

"I cannot tell one Pelbar from another, Jestak."

"It must have been a Jestan, and probably Tanbar, my cousin. My exile was not met with unanimous enthusiasm throughout the city."

"You are just as well off, it would seem," said Thro.

"Far better. I engineered the exile, to speak the truth."

"That old lady who runs this place is no mother goose. She has it up here," said Thro, tapping his forehead. "She is a careful old bird."

Jestak laughed. The Shumai stood, hearing footsteps in the still dry grass of the spring. It was a Pelbar guard.

"Jestak," he said. "The Protector would speak with you."

"Thank you. I will come." Jestak turned to Thro. "It is about the matter of Tia, I expect."

"Tia?" said Stantu.

"Yes," said Thro, snorting. "Jestak thinks he is going all the way to Emeri country to free a Shumai girl he once met. He thinks it is like walking to the river and catching a frog."

"No matter how far . . ." Jestak began.

"Jestak," said the guard.

"Yes, I am coming. Good night. I will be back. Do not spear me."

"We will try not to."

Jestak followed the guard toward the still open central door of Northwall, while the two Shumai men watched him, each with his private smile on his face.

The Protector greeted Jestak, when Comm ushered him in, with a slight bow. She motioned him to take the bench, then motioned to Comm to bring her more tea. She sat looking at Jestak for a time.

"Well, Jestak, this has been quite an eventful day."

"Yes, Protector."

"It has cost Northwall a considerable sum in supplies and labor, not to mention the education of Ursa, whose work is now lost to us."

"Yes, that is true, Protector. But there may be gain as well if some future hostilities may be averted by the beginnings of an alliance."

"Do you think Ursa will be happy?"

"I do not know, Protector. I am sure that Winnt will care for her. I think she will have a grand adventure with the Sentani, and she will finally have a chance to observe her beloved wildlife."

"Yes, if they ever let her off from scrubbing pots and nursing babies."

"There is much leisure in a Sentani town. I have been there."

"I know that you are embarrassed by our declining to admit your friend, Stantu."

"Yes, Protector. But he seems to understand."

"Would he agree to come to the judgment room and tell us of his experience in the eastern cities?"

"I will ask him, Protector."

"Now, I am very tired from all of this, and having even

admitted the two barbarians for tea, but I—You are smiling?"

"It is nothing, Protector. I am sorry. Go on. I apologize."

She was silent a minute. "I am concerned," she continued, "with this matter of this Tia, the Shumai who was captured somewhere far to the west. I can perceive that you intend to get up some sort of wild and foolish expedition to go and rescue her. The events of this winter, and these of today, have made me think that perhaps there was something to you, Jestak. You have been instrumental in accomplishing much for Northwall, and we have now made more meaningful contact with the outside tribes than ever in memory.

"We cannot afford to let you waste yourself in a chase of a ghost. I can feel it that you fully intend to go. And perhaps with a few Shumai as your companions. I had thought better of you. You have seen this wild woman for only a day portion, and now you are ready to throw your life away on her behalf. I had thought you were a thinker. Now it would seem that you are only an idle dreamer, not a person of sense. What do you say to this?"

"You did not see her, Protector. She is more than any other woman I have ever seen. She is purely and simply dazzling. And—"

"I am really surprised. Dazzling. Have you thought? What of these people who captured her? Do you suppose that she is still dazzling? What would they do to a dazzling captive? Do not wince. These are considerations. And suppose she is dazzling. What then? How could you live with a dazzling savage, tearing the meat from the bones while squatting in the dirt? I am afraid I must forbid you outright from going on this ghost chase."

"Protector, may I say something?"

"Do not think to sway me."

"Protector, I would not go on my own account, though I am really not essential to Northwall. But you must have seen the way I have made contact with the outside peoples and survived. I have always managed to put them under obligation to me. Now I am in a unique position. With the few Shumai allies I have, I think I can traverse the whole Shumai country, and if we work together, I will, if I survive it, put a great many Shumai under obligation to me. I know of no other Pelbar who can do that. We need to ally ourselves to these people, and we can do it by being useful to them. I will admit that Tia is, or was, dazzling. But there is far greater opportunity here, a chance to unite the peoples even further. That is well worth my expending my life. Even if I were to die, some progress will have been made. Eventually most of the Shumai would know that a Pelbar died in an attempt to rescue one of their people. That will make a difference."

"Dandelion fluff."

"Well, Protector, I see that Thro was wrong. He said that the old lady was no mother goose."

"Protector."

"Yes, of course, I am sorry. Protector."

"Now, Jestak, if you think I will be insulted by you, you are quite mistaken. Now you may bow to me."

Jestak bowed somewhat. "I mean to the floor," she said firmly.

Jestak was so angry he almost could not comply. But the Pelbar habit was strong in him, and he knew that insubordination would mean a complete loss of Pelbar status at this time. So, slowly, he bowed, and knelt, until his forehead touched the floor. She moved a slipper forward and touched his head.

"You may get up now," she said, drily.

Jestak stood, flushed and grim.

"Now," she said, "you will return to Stantu, your friend, and ask him if he will speak to the company in the judgment room. Let us do one thing at a time. We have not even seen Ursa depart yet. Now go."

Jestak bowed and left.

"Jestak, what is wrong? Do not worry. I am not insulted that the Pelbar have not let me in their precious city."

"That's good. But that is not it."

"What?"

"Let it go for now. When you talk to the judgment room, Stantu, please try to emphasize a little that I was a help, not only to you, but to the Shumai. I am not saying this for myself, for I really do care nothing of that. But the Protector is beginning to draw back."

"She means to keep you here."

"Yes."

"I will do what I can, Jestak. It may not be much. If she

is as Thro says, she may be hard to influence. She seems to know her own mind."

"She let the girl marry a Sentani," muttered Thro.

"Ho, Thro. I didn't know that troubled you. Ha. Perhaps she should have married you."

Thro did not reply.

"It was Thro, Stantu, who really brought them together, by wounding Ursa in a thrust at Winnt. He is the matchmaker."

"Enough, Jestak."

"Ha. Then you are troubled by it all," said Stantu.

"No matter, Thro," said Jestak. "She is a good woman, but there are other good women. You will find one someday."

"This one has the fairness of a Shumai, and the courage. She saved me, and I owe her, and I repaid her badly."

"She does not think so, Thro."

"She is the grandchild of the legend, Dailda, the lost child. She should not have been given to a Sentani."

"Think of Winnt as your brother, Thro. He saved you, and was instrumental in saving the other men."

"My brother. No matter. Let us sleep."

The Sentani were up before daybreak, and the boats were nearly loaded when a party from the city came with travelbreads. Two older people accompanied the party and stood nearby. They were Ivel and Leta, Ursa's parents. They had little authority over her upbringing in Pelbar society, but the parental fondness remained. Leta was crying.

"Be happy, Father," said Ursa. "I will be back sometime. I will bring grandchildren for you to see."

"Good," he said, nodding, and with some effort.

Thro was taking the leave of truce with Willton, and came near the new couple.

"Thro," said Ursa. "Would you like your neck chain back?"

"No. You must keep it."

"You have blessed me, you know, though you may not have meant it."

"It is a strange way to bless."

"Blessing is often strange, and it is always returned on the one who blesses. So says Aven."

"The blessing was not meant, though now I would have meant to bless you."

"Thank you for that," said Ursa. "And good-bye to you. Perhaps we shall meet again sometime." She gave him a quick embrace and a kiss.

Thro did not know what to do at that, so merely stood, saying eventually, "Good-bye, then." And to Winnt, "You are a lucky man, Sentani. Good-bye to you, too."

"Good-bye, Thro. May the sun shine lightly on you and the rain make your life green from spring until fall."

"May the deer walk to you."

The herald's horn called all to the boats, and the clusters of starband boats began to lengthen on the river, the north-point first, with Ursa in their midst, waving and looking. By the time the last boats took up the formation, she was already a small dot far down the river, tan in her travel coat. The small group on the shore did not see her turn her back for the last time on her lifelong home.

One of the Shumai children put his hand in Thro's. "They are our enemies, Thro. Why did we not fight them?"

Thro picked up the child and walked slowly toward the Shumai camp.

 VIII

AGAIN the judgment room was crowded. Stantu was the center of attention. Unlike the previous meetings, at which Jestak was questioned, this time Stantu was seated on a raised dais, at equal level with that of the council. Jestak had insisted on this in advance, as what must be done so as not to insult the Shumai, though it had been entirely his own idea, and he and Stantu had had their own quiet laugh about it. But Jestak had done it seriously as well. He did not want to give the insular Northwallers a further opportunity for patronizing the Shumai, and the dais would remind them of their courtesy.

"Had it not been for Jestak," Stantu was saying, "I am sure that I would have waded into the Innanigani financiers with a short sword and eventually been killed. It is not like a Shumai to put up with such injustice, and to try to work it out in judgment, then to suffer even though the cause is just."

Cumven, a guardsman who dealt with the Shumai at truce-week, translated Stantu's comments every few sentences. The Protector had arranged that so Jestak would not render Stantu's story his own way.

"I was imprisoned," Stantu continued, "as Jestak has told you, and made to work at cleaning fish. After Jestak was attacked, and took care of some of the pigs—I wish I had been there—they tried to lengthen my sentence, but even then a few of the Innanigani saw that as unjust. I do not know if they were really sincere in their desire for justice, or if they were merely arguing, for they seem to love to wrangle at legal matters and never seem to arrive at any final decisions. So my sentence was not lengthened. I was kept cleaning fish for over a year. There was another full year of the sentence, but I managed to escape, finally. It was not easy, especially since I am not a swimmer, except as Jestak had taught me the stroke of the lake Sentani, but I made my way south until I was past Baligan and the great bay, and then I knew I was free of the eastern cities. So I then turned westward, and passed across a great length of empty land. Much of it receives good rainfall, but nothing grows there, and I was hard put to it to stay alive. It is all eroded and blasted. Finally I came to a range of mountains, like those of the north, but higher. Here there was forest again, across the first ridges, and game.

"Jestak had warned me about the Peshtak and the Coo, but I was apparently south of their country. I did meet with a people, the Siveri, who live in some of the deep valleys in these mountains. There life is very different from the way we live it in the west. They are quite peaceful. They are farmers and do some hunting, but they maintain cattle of their own, which are not wild.

"I found this out when I came out of the forest and killed a cow. They were angry about it, and surrounded me. I was not in a mood to fight, because I wanted to get home. They speak a slow dialect that I found very hard to understand, but with effort, I finally made it out. I have had nearly the practice that Jestak has now with dialects and have learned that the language is basically the same, but that one has to learn the keys of difference to pronunciation. Then of course each dialect has its words for some things. I am sure that Jestak will teach me enough Pelbar soon so that I can talk to you without a translator.

"At any rate, what the Siveri wanted was for me to pay for the animal by working on the farm. I agreed to this. They seemed sincere and did not want trouble with me, but wanted justice. It took me several months to pay for the animal, but they fed me well, and I learned a good deal about them. They had there among their possessions things that must have come from an ancient time, from before what Jestak calls the time of fire. They work hard at some times and not at all others. They make and drink much intoxicating liquid. These drinks are not like the wines of Innanigan, but are much more powerful. One cupful of them sets the head spinning. When they are drunk, they are often violent, getting into fights and breaking things. All of this must be paid for when they are themselves again. They seem to agree to this heartily enough, even when the payment is very time-consuming or expensive. They are a curious people.

"In appearance they are generally thin. Their hair varies from very light to very dark, and some have a very dark skin, almost black, with very curly hair, though intermarriage among all types has produced gradations from the dark to the light. The darkest have faces quite different from the light, with wider noses and broad lips.

"When I had paid my debt to satisfy them, they let me go on agreeably enough. In fact, they even had a party for me, at which four separate parents tried to induce me to marry one of their daughters, because I am taller and stronger than almost all of them, and have better teeth. They tried to get me intoxicated, and one even threatened violence, but I did not drink and made no trouble, because even though they live on farms, they are extraordinary trackers, and I wanted to go on without trouble.

"They inhabit quite a span of country, though in widely scattered and small groups. After a time I avoided their roads and villages, staying to the woods, because I did not want to become involved with them. But I saw nine villages in all.

"Then I passed through a great stretch of uninhabited woodland and came to an extrordinary thing—a great mass of artificial stone and dirt that had once spanned an entire valley. It was cracked and broken, but the water still backed up behind it. I spent some time there, looking at it.

I could see that at some time, long ago, the ancients had built a great lake behind the barrier, and even conducted the water down through conduits larger than this room is tall. In the upper parts of the structure, rooms now shattered held remains of glass windows far larger than Pelbar glass—larger even than that of Innanigan. But all was ruin, and the countryside nearby was quite bare and desolate.

"I moved downstream on the river that passed through the barrier, though cautiously, because, as I suspected, I was entering Sentani country, of which the river is apparently the southern border. I traveled at night, moving always farther south. I did not want to do this, but I thought that eventually it would flow into the Heart, which it did, but far south of where I wanted to be."

"How did you know it was the Heart?"

"There cannot be such another river in all the world. I have seen many and the Heart swallows all with its wide brown waters. I crossed the river, which is more than twice what it is here, and continued on up the west bank, still at night, often staying on river islands during the day, and fishing in the way Jestak had taught me, with a hook and line like the Pelbar.

"I saw a number of small Sentani encampments, most deserted, because they tend to gather together in the summer and spread out in the winter to hunt, though it was not yet winter. But as the season progressed, and I began to see signs of the grasslands, I struck westward up one of the other rivers, which I later found was the Ontex, and rejoiced to see the first of the south-migrating herds. Then I knew I was getting into Shumai country, and as the leaves turned, I met the first band of Shumai following the herds. You may imagine my pleasure. It was from them that I learned where my own people would be. I wintered with them, but anxiety for Jestak led me to come east looking for him, for he had been of great help to me in more ways than I can say, and so I struck the Heart again and joined with Thro's band, who were also come upriver earlier, to care for their dead. And that is how I arrived here."

"Stantu," said Hildre. "I am dizzy. Jestak has set the map of things on end, and now you have done it again. If you will, I would very much value a time with you to clarify some of these matters you have told us." The Pelbar geographer rubbed the handle of a fine-tipped pen in her graying hair and looked both troubled and eager.

"I will," said Stantu, through Cumven, "provided Jestak translates for me." The guard rendered it coolly.

There was a silence. Finally the Protector said, "Manti, see that Jestak is brought to translate for Hildre."

"Yes, Protector."

"And now," she said to Stantu, "perhaps you will join the council for a little refreshment."

"All right," said Stantu, smiling faintly, "if Jestak may join us."

Jestak was there, but Cumven still did the translating.

"One thing, Stantu," said the Protector. "If you are an expert in languages, how is it that you never learned Pelbar?"

"When Jestak and I were together, he was always trying to improve his Shumai, or we were mastering the quick speech of Innanigan. It never occurred to me that I would ever have dealings with the Pelbar. I do not want to be mistaken, and I am sure of Jestak's sympathies."

"I see," she said, smiling slightly at him. He grinned back ingenuously.

"Now that you have seen that Jestak is safe, what do you intend to do?"

"I am not sure. I have no special plans. I thought it might be possible to visit with Jestak for a time."

"Indeed you may, though we are unable to offer you the freedom of our city because you belong to a hostile tribe, and one of our best defenses is the fact that no attacker is sure what we will do to him."

"Yes, so Jestak has said."

"He, you know, must get to his metalwork, and he has duties in the orchards and elsewhere. His time will not be free."

"Yes, I understand."

"You know, too, that Sentani truceweek will come within a few weeks, after the Shumai spring migration."

"Yes. I will take care to stay out of their way. I may be gone by then anyhow."

"Will you rejoin your people?"

"I suppose that depends. Thro may go west again to see about retaking his people."

"Ah, Stantu, that is the sticking point. If you are thinking of inducing Jestak to go with you, I would like you to know that I have expressly forbidden it."

"That, you see," said Stantu, "is where a Shumai has a hard time understanding the Pelbar."

"Where?"

"A man, with a dedication to an idea that would benefit his people, being held back by a woman who has never ventured far beyond a stone box. She holding an absolute authority over him, managing him as a mother does her child, when his grasp of things is inevitably so much wider than hers."

Stantu had spoken in a quiet and courteous tone, and Cumven tried to render his words as gently as he could. Nonetheless, the council was shocked. A silence ensued. Finally the Protector motioned to Comm to refill Stantu's cup with tea.

"We cannot expect you to understand our customs. We have found they work very well, and have protected us from the ferocity of your people for hundreds of years. Are you aware, also, that Jestak is in exile from Pelbarigan?"

"Yes."

"What would you, if you were among the council at Pelbarigan, think if I, Protector of Northwall, let Jestak go on this ghost chase? He has already managed to have many things his way here. They had him scrubbing floors, you know. They will be astonished enough if they hear how things have gone here."

"I should think, ma'am, that they would be proud of him for accomplishments that are far beyond what any other Pelbar has done."

"That depends, of course, on how you measure accomplishments. The Pelbar have their own criteria."

"What, ma'am, would happen to Jestak if he went anyway?"

Cumven translated this reluctantly. Again there was a silence. Brin Brunag spoke up and said, "No Pelbar takes a step like that. It might be possible among the Shumai, but not among us."

"He would be," said the Protector, "no longer a Pelbar."

"Would you kill him upon his return?"

"We would not accept him unless he had been ordered to go."

"And yet here I am, and Winnt, the Sentani, both of us barbarians."

"I do not propose to argue the matter, Stantu, but merely to tell you what would happen. Jestak understands that well enough. Now might you tell us how far are these western mountains that lie beyond the grasslands—where you say that this girl has gone?"

"Tia? She is, I assume, in the southern part of the great west barrier. It lies perhaps twelve hundred ayas from here, though the way might be longer because of the land."

"Twelve hundred ayas. Have you been there?"

"No. I have never been nearly that far. But it would be enjoyable to go."

"Would it not take you over a month just to make the journey?"

"I expect it would, perhaps more if we took our time."

"And what would you find there?"

"I am not sure. I have heard from the horseriders that the Emeri live there, and that they are a sedentary people who live in stone cities in the hills. They farm, and when they can, they enslave the western Shumai to work on their farms."

"So that is what you expect might have happened to Tia?"

"I do not know. Perhaps. We will find out, perhaps."

"Then you intend to go with Thro."

"Perhaps. The Shumai do not allow anyone to treat us that way without a fight. A repeated fight. We will go back as long as it takes, as long as there are any of us to go back."

"It would seem that they are good fighters."

Stantu shrugged. "They have some good weapons. They hide behind their bows like the Sentani. They wear armor like your guards. They use long swords. But I think they must be cowardly. They often simply hide behind their walls."

Cumven snickered very slightly, but the whole council shot him hard looks, so he quickly changed his tone.

"Stantu," said the Protector. "What are horseriders?"

"Some of the western Shumai ride on the backs of animals. They got the idea, and the animals, from the Emeri. Now they ride themselves, and very well, I think. The practice is beginning to spread eastward, but it is still very far from here, and there still are very few horses. Many say that they are not nearly as good in the river brakes as a good runner."

"What then are horses? What are they like?"

"They are as big as a cow, about, but they have a solid

hoof, not a split one. They have long necks and long faces. They can become quite tame, and even love a man the way a dog will, and good riders can learn to control them and ride them at great speeds. But they need quite a bit of care. We prefer to be without them. I have seen them only once, when some of the horseriders came far to the east. They say the Emeri use them regularly to carry burdens too. They can carry as much as a number of men."

The Protector was very thoughtful. "Do you think we could use them here?"

"You would have to keep them inside and gather food for them outside. I do not see what good they would be unless you were more free of these walls. They eat a great deal of grass, and even grain."

"As a source of power."

"Well, I have heard that the Emeri use them to lift water from their wells, using a long rope. But you have plenty of water. And Jestak could teach you the use of the windwheel they have in Innanigan."

"Windwheel? Another novelty? Let us stick to the horses for now. If you can, you might draw us a picture of a horse. Is that possible?"

"I am not good at that, Protector, but I will do what I can."

"You can use the services of Oduc, and Jestak will take you to her, if you will. Jestak, perhaps you could do that now, and then, Jestak, return to me here immediately."

"Yes, Protector."

"Thank you, Stantu, for meeting with us." All the council bowed their thanks.

"It was good tea," said Stantu, and left with Jestak, the two straight-backed young men passsing out the door like bulky shadows in the hunters' way that always gave the Pelbar a certain unease.

"Protector," said the southcouncil. "What was all that about the horses? I do not understand."

"We have been in great need of power. Perhaps this will help us. It ties up many men at times, and wears them down in drudgery. We have heard from Jestak of wind-driven ships, and now Stantu has mentioned both these horses and the windwheel, already in use by other peoples. We cannot afford to be behind in such things as affect our safety. Now, if you would leave me, I have some things to say to Jestak when he returns. And if you, Comm, will get Manti, please."

Manti looked grave. "I do not know, Protector. Perhaps he will go anyway. Should we keep him under guard?"

"No, Manti. This is more complex than that. He is the first Pelbar friend of the Shumai. I can tell that Stantu does not take kindly to our treatment of his friend, and thinks it a great foolishness. If he goes west with Thro, then all the Shumai will know of our refusal to help them, when Jestak was willing to go. On the other hand, if we let Jestak go, the Pelbarigan council will not take it kindly, and of course we depend on them for many things, as you know. I have an idea, which may work. Then again, it may not. Of course, Jestak stands a good chance of getting killed if he goes, but that is his concern—if his heart is set on going. I do not wish to be called on to renounce him. That would produce all sorts of problems. He is coming back here soon. Perhaps Stantu has given us a way out. It is not much of one, in fact it is a transparent, almost childish, ruse. But it is a way."

Jestak was outside, and was announced. "Bring him in, Comm," said the Protector.

A moment later Comm returned with the young Jestan.

"Now, Jestak, remain standing if you please. Has Stantu told you about horses?"

"Yes, Protector. Some things. Not very much."

"Did they have them in the east?"

"No, Protector, but in one museum of ancient things, they had an ancient sculpture of a man on one. It appeared as Stantu described it, and the man sat on it, on a sort of chair that fit the animal's back, with apparent comfort, controlling the animal with ropes that went to its mouth."

"Then you would know one if you saw it."

"Yes, Protector. Without doubt."

"Do you think that horses would be of value to the Pelbar?"

"I have never thought of it, Protector. As Stantu said, they would be hard for us to feed."

"I have given the matter much thought—for some minutes. I think they might be of great value to us. I want you to go to the west with Thro and bring us back some horses—a male and a female—if you are willing to undertake so dangerous a piece of work. Of course I will not force you. We can put you to good use here, too. Do you think you will be able to do so dangerous a thing?"

Jestak was careful not to smile. "Yes, Protector. I am willing to undertake this assignment. I will try to do better with it than I did with the last one."

"You did not altogether fail with that one, Jestak, or I would not send you out again. We will give you gold to trade for the horses. You are not to get them by violence, Jestak. Except that you may defend yourself, of course. The Shumai are still with their dead, I believe."

"Yes, that is true, Protector."

"Will you be able to make yourself ready before they move farther westward?"

"Yes. I am nearly ready now, Protector."

"I was afraid of that. Remember now. You are buying horses. See if you can get them home without a Shumai spear in them. You had better learn something about them, too, since we know nothing at all of them."

"Yes, Protector, I will learn."

"You may go now. Come to see me again before you depart. And do not delay."

"Many thanks, Protector. Does the council know of this?"

"Leave the council to me, Jestak. That is my affair. Now go."

Jestak bowed and then left. Manti was smiling and frowning. "Do you think you can get away with this, Sima?"

"Yes. Perhaps not, though. They will be glad to get him out of their hair, I think, especially Brin, who resents him deeply. The means is not convincing, surely. But the gold will be my own. I have nothing to do with it anyway. Doesn't this make me a good friend to the Jestan?"

"Yes, Sima. It does indeed."

"Now, Manti, summon Comm to recall the council."

"Come," said Winnt, "keep stroking, Ursa. We are nearing the great ford of the Heart, where many herds cross. Come, sweet. Put your lovely back into it, and let us keep the boat level. We will have a rest soon. If the Shumai are there, and get close, pile those two bundles on the sword side and stroke on the other. If there is a fight, get behind them."

"Have you any gloves, Winnt?"

"Gloves? No. Here, Ursa. Use these skins."

"There, there it is," said Juk. "It looks clear from here. So far."

"You are letting him go, Protector?"

"To get us some horses, Brin. Perhaps we will make a new thing for the Pelbar."

"You are aware, Protector, that all will know the real reason—that you are favoring Jestak?"

"Have you considered the alternatives?"

"Yes. Put him to work. Do not pamper him. You know how he failed in his eastern mission. You know the death of my son, which he described."

"Is it your opinion that Jestak could have prevented that?"

"We know nothing of any Peshtak. All our reports have been different. We have nothing but the word of Jestak and of that riffraff friend of his. He could have killed the others himself."

"I think that hardly likely, Eastcouncil."

"What will Pelbarigan think?"

"Pelbarigan has been much in my thoughts. In giving us Jestak, they gave us a problem they could not handle. Undoubtedly, they would be angry if we let him go chasing a girl with the Shumai. They may be angry if we do as I propose. They may be pleased, on the whole, if we put him to scrubbing or digging, though I confess I do not know how they will feel when we send them some of his new-method metalwork and let them know it is his development. There are also the Jestan. They are not in control in Pelbarigan, but they still have much power.

"We have to remember that we will not break his spirit by menial labor. He may go anyway on his own. That would please no one in Pelbarigan. They would have lost him permanently. They would have failed. And we, I think, would have lost a man of great ability."

"A man, Protector."

"Yes, a man. But we have always used our men as our outside contacts. If these contacts grow distant, their responsibilities must grow greater."

"And they will make decisions without the judgment of women?"

"Ultimately, no, of course. We will make the policies.

We may even have to learn to go outside ourselves so we can direct them."

"We go outside? Protector, you go dangerously near altering basic Pelbar law and precedent as old as the roll of Digas."

"Perhaps, Southcouncil. But I hardly think so. Law allows much more latitude than our rigid usages. I see you are displeased. I am sorry for that. I do not think you have sufficiently weighed the effect of our relations with the outside tribes. Jestak has already changed them, and potentially for the better."

"As in the losing of Ursa?"

"Or the gaining of the Sentani of Koorb. It depends. I do not think they will so readily kill the Northwall Pelbar as they have tried to, given the opportunity."

"We will be sure that we do not give them the opportunity if we follow the established patterns."

"Perhaps. But since I am Protector, my will will carry in this matter. I see that the council begins to lose confidence in me. Do you all agree with Brin?"

"Yes, the southwall does."

"I am not sure, Protector, but I think that the north and orchard sector will, too."

"I am not sure at all right now," said the westcouncil.

"This is more serious, then. Well, in this issue, at least, I must insist on my judgment. I see a more general one arising, which we will handle as it comes. Now let us turn to the matter of the recent expenses and the reimbursement of the constituencies."

"Stantu, the Protector is backing my going west, but with a story of my going to bring a pair of horses back for the Pelbar. She has even given me gold. Will you come?"

"Ha. I am half gone already. You and I will be the most traveled people in the world. There may be a good fight, too."

"Perhaps. Maybe we should avoid it—at least at first. I dare not return with Tia and without the horses. The Protector would be wholly discredited. She is in trouble enough now. Without her backing, especially if Brin takes control of the council, I will have no place here."

"You can always live with the Bowbend Shumai and me. Tia would like that."

"Yes. That would be a pleasure. But there are larger

issues here. Now we must get going. There is much to do."

"I am ready now. Thro will have begun to move if we wait until tomorrow."

"All right, but I first must meet with the Protector. Here comes Manti. Ho, Uncle."

"Both of you please come. The Protector wishes to see you. I hope, Jestak, you see how far she has gone for you. She is now in danger of losing her position."

"I know, Uncle. I am sorry for that—and sorry for Northwall if that occurs, though perhaps they may learn from it what is valuable. She is much more responsive than I had at first thought. She is doing it for Northwall, you know."

"And for you, Jestak. Do not forget that. And for you."

"This will be our last tea for some time."

"Yes, Protector."

"Stantu, I have a present for you. It is old, but it has seen good service and will serve you well also."

"Thank you. What is it?"

"It is a Pelbar folding knife. Show him, Jestak."

Jestak snapped the blade open, then pressed the catch and shut it again. "Like that," he said.

Stantu worked the blade in and out several times, a smile growing on his face.

"Do not use it until you have to. Keep it in your pouch or the pocket of your tunic."

"Why do you say that?"

"Because few will know it is a knife. They will think it an amulet or some useless thing."

"I see. Good. I will do that."

"And now I must go. I wish you both to embrace me in parting. Yes, you too, Stantu. Jestak will show you how the Pelbar say a warm good-bye. But do not crush me, Jestak." She held out her arms to the nephew of Manti. "May Aven go with you both," she said. "Now do not delay."

Afterward, as they strode quickly down the corridor toward the small pivot gate in the west wall, Stantu said, "I do not understand. Why that last?"

"It worries me, Stantu. As does her insistence that we leave at once. I think her position is in immediate jeopardy."

"Then should we go? Why did she agree?"

"I don't know. I know she thinks that my desire for Tia

is a great foolishness. I know she simply would not indulge me. I do not know. Now let's be out the wall as fast as we can. We can be to Thro's group before moonrise if we really trot."

The northpoint was already beyond the ford when they heard a long horn from the shore, and shouts.

Instantly, Mokil shouted, "Front and back, take bows. Middle man, paddle." The lead boats of the Sentani slowed, while those behind raced on to move through the ford and close up ranks. More shouting from the shore indicated a number of Shumai on the bank.

"Do not worry, Ursa," said Winnt. "If they were ready for us, we could not have gotten this far. We have surprised them and will outdistance them before they can gather enough men to follow. I hope."

Ursa was looking at her hands.

The eastern starpoint had lined their boats to the shore side of the others, all of whom bent their backs to move through the broad ford as fast as they could. Here the river was almost a mile wide, too shallow for boats in the western seven-eighths, and the channel near the east shore was narrow. An animal, or a man, could wade most of the distance except in high water. The eastpoint men were quiet in their boats, all with arrows nocked. The shore was silent. Then one man appeared, with a spear mounted on a spear-thrower. He ran into the shallows and launched it high and far at the line of boats. From the nearest boat three arrows were on the way as he threw. He had known that would happen, and dove forward, but one took him in the back of the leg as he went under. He yelled, and when he came up, the stern man in the next boat alone took aim and put an arrow into him.

His spear had fallen true, though, into the center boat, and the middle man was bailing, holding a rag of beaver skin into the hole.

Another yell came from the bank, and Willton shouted, "All take bows." Immediately all the boats slowed, and as the line of Shumai appeared at the bank, running to throw, the Sentani were ready. Spears and arrows passed each other in the air. Seven Shumai fell, and all the boats of the eastern starpoint were holed. One man was pinned to the bottom of his craft by a spear, and as he struggled, it slowly rolled over, pitching his companions into the river.

The first line of Shumai was followed by another. They did not throw, but ran farther toward the boats, holding their spears ready, straining as the water deepened.

"All shoot," shouted Willton. The Shumai had miscalculated. They were hampered by deeper water and the next line was too far behind. Their spears could not reach. Meanwhile, the south starpoint had paddled up on the shore side of the struck boats, dangerously close in, and as the stern man worked the boat, the others aimed arrows at the struggling Shumai.

"Fools," said Compli. "They can never resist a fight." As he said it, a knife blade appeared just ahead of his knee, and sliced a long gash in the boat. Before it was withdrawn, he was in the frigid water, his short sword out, stabbing at the man who had swum underwater to the boat. There was a short struggle. He came up bleeding as the boat swamped. The other men abandoned it, swimming for midriver. Immediately the next boat had moved in on the hostile side of Compli, who sheathed his short sword and swam away slowly.

"Now quick," shouted Willton. "Ends paddle. Southwest, pick up the men. Center men, watch the water."

Three more Shumai had swum underwater to the boats, which swarmed underway, and when they finally came up for air, the arrows of the center men took them. Then a fourth appeared.

"Hold," shouted Willton. "West, throw a rope around him. All paddle." At that point a far-thrown spear took Willton in the thigh and went through the boat. He didn't make a sound, but hacked it off near the wound and then drew it through, catching the thwart in a near faint, recovering to stuff the hole in the boat.

"Luxi," shouted Willton, and sank in his boat.

Luxi, southeast pointband leader, took charge, shouting, "Southpoint, ends paddle. Southeast, rope that boat. South center, on the axeman."

On the shore stood an axeman, furred, legs apart, as the remaining Shumai struggled to the bank.

"Now, high, center men," shouted Luxi. An arcing flight of arrows lofted toward him, but he saw them in time and trotted a few steps upriver on the bank. As he began, Luxi said, "Near ends, level," and two more arrows came at him fast, one taking him through the midsection. He pitched down the bank and rolled into the water.

"All paddle," shouted Luxi. There were no more spears. The Sentani moved south and toward the west bank, but not too close, dragging their swamped boat, the body of Ocer, and the roped Shumai, who struggled in the icy water to stay up.

"Northpoint," Luxi shouted. "Examine that island." They had already passed two, for the sake of safety, and Luxi planned on landing for a short while on the next to repair damage and tend the wounded.

Two fires burned in the trees, and Stantu gave a short, quavering call as he and Jestak approached. It was answered. Soon they came upon Kod, standing guard.

"Here, Kod. We have hafted your spear for you—and sharpened it."

"You, Jestak. What do you want?"

"I am going with Stantu to bring Tia back to her people."

"And with us."

"You, too? But what of your wife and children?"

"They will stay at Black Bull Island. They will be all right until the main bands arrive."

"Is that far?"

"No. A hundred ayas."

"I hope you are not still hostile to me."

"It is all right. Thro says it is."

"I hope it is all right with you."

"Thro says it is."

"All right. I will be true to you anyway, Kod."

"Call to the others. They are not expecting me in from watch."

Ursa was crying softly as they cut away Willton's leg wraps.

"Take her away," he said, weakly.

"No," she said. "Here. Put your fist there. No, Winnt. Your whole fist. Now press. More weight. That will stop the blood. See? You must hold it there hard, but let up every few sun widths, to feed the leg. When the bleeding stops, then you may let it go, but watch." Ursa then turned to bandage another man.

Incor would not talk. The Sentani had roped him to a tree and were questioning him. He was shivering from the river.

"How many Shumai?" Zen asked. "Tell us or it will be hard for you."

Incor laughed, then coughed hard. He knew the Sentani aversion to torture, and he was Shumai enough to confront death without much fear.

"How many?" Zen repeated, taking out his short sword and sharpening it on a small, round stone. Then Ursa was there.

"Are you all right, Zen?"

"Yes. Go away now."

"The starpoint?"

"Yes," he said, sharpening the blade quietly, spitting on the stone.

"Is he all right?"

"He is a Shumai. He will not be all right soon. But he is now. He has swallowed a lot of the river."

"He is shivering."

"It is not summer."

"His neck," she said, reaching out. Incor winced, then his eyes went stoic.

"Let the wild pig alone, Ursa. You do not understand."

"It will not hurt if I wash it," said Ursa.

"So he will die with a clean wound? Let him be. Go away now."

"If Willton intended that he should die, why then did he bring him?"

"To get information, I suppose."

"You know Shumai never talk, even if they suffer. And you do not like to torture. Even the Pelbar know that."

"We may start now."

"No, Zen, do not say it," and she put her hands on his shoulders. He shrugged her off.

"Your hands," he said.

"They are not used to paddling. It is all right. Ask Willton before you do anything to him. Do it now. I will watch him. Do not worry. I will not do anything."

Zen paused, then sighed and went toward the men around Willton. He would act from authority.

Incor watched her. "You are Pelbar," he said.

"I am married to Winnt of this band now," she said, slowly. "Now hold still and I will wash the dirt from your neck. It is ugly where the skin is gone."

"Get away, Sentani rotpit," he spat.

"Shut up," she said, slapping his face hard, then wincing

and holding her hand. "Shut up," she said more quietly, "and hold still while I wash your neck. Are you afraid of a little pain?"

Incor was astonished. She had finished, and then was washing the dirt from his face, which was only bruised, when she sensed Zen standing behind her. His face was hard.

"What did Willton say?"

"He has died."

Ursa cried out, and covered her face with her hands, weeping.

"Now what do you say?" said Zen.

Ursa continued to cry, and got up, stumbling toward where Willton was. Some men were standing around him. She went through them and knelt by him and put her head on his chest, listening for a heartbeat. She looked into each eye. Then she put her head on him again and gave herself up to weeping. Winnt started toward her, but Luxi held his arm.

"She has not seen this, you know," he said.

"Do not kill the Shumai," cried Ursa, muffled, her head down. "Enough have died." The men looked at each other but said nothing. Munit came to Luxi.

"The boats are all repaired," he said.

"We must go," said Luxi. "Keep close formation. Put the wounded in the middle—and Willton and Ocer."

"You got the axeman for Willton," said Ursa, standing up as they took the limp body to the boat. He was tall and thin, but a dead weight.

"You must be a Sentani now," said Luxi.

"Yes," said Ursa. "But he will be under obligation to you."

Luxi shook his head. "Not when there was all that killing. We nearly wiped out his band. Come now. Winnt will take you to your boat. Look at your hands. Here. You go with Frek. He is hurt and a woman's touch will do him good."

"It has been decided, then," said Brin. "The council, upon consultation with the constituencies, has decided that your term as Protector is at an end."

"What was the vote?"

"Three to one."

"Which one?"

"The west."

"Large majorities?"

"The vote was three to one."

"Very well, Brin. You may take over now."

"Manti," said Brin. "You may go and tell Jestak to report at once to me in the Protector's room."

"He has already departed, Protector."

"Already?" She turned, startled.

"Yes, Protector. He left by the west wall a half-sun ago now. He wanted to join the Shumai before they moved on."

"Then we must send the guard to bring him back."

"That has never been done, Protector," said Sima Pall. "You will immediately jeopardize your position if you gained it by appeal to precedent and now your first command is to break precedent."

"And you care about my position? This is your plan, Sima. We will see about it."

"Perhaps we shall. I well knew that everything has a price. Now you are learning it as well. I fear for Northwall if you do not."

"Are you addressing me?"

"Yes, Protector."

"Go."

Chogtan, in the bow, kept looking back at the middle of the boat where Frek, his younger brother, lay with his head on Ursa's lap. She had arranged the skins around him and smoothed his hair. He lay slightly twisted so no weight would fall on his left side where the spear had gone through.

"It is all right, Chog," she said. "He is asleep only because he is exhausted and has lost blood. But I feel no fever."

Chogtan said nothing. Then, after another half-ayas of stroking, he turned again and said, "What are doing with your eyes shut?"

"I am praying."

"For Frek?"

"Yes. And for all of us."

Chogtan turned and put his back into the stroking. Winnt, in the stern, could see his shoulders working on both sides of his wife's narrow body between. He had to put muscle into it to keep pace with his bowman, who did not turn around anymore but paddled as if the next bend of the river would bring his brother to Koorb.

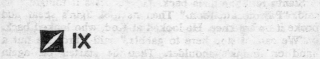

IX

AFTER the reinterment of the Shumai men, a grisly task conducted ceremoniously, the small party began to run southwestward, moving toward the Isso River, which flowed southeast toward the Heart. The Shumai usually traveled light, even with families, and even with small ones they moved fast, running when they could. Fairly young children made good runners, and infants were subjected to long periods of jogging on their mothers' backs. The Shumai were moving at what they called the "family pace," not nearly that of the men alone, who, unencumbered, could quickly cover an astonishing amount of ground.

Jestak was glad for the warm-up, because he was not in shape for the running he would get after they left the family at Black Bull Island. He knew he was in for a real test, and that suspicious Shumai like Kod would like to see him run into the ground. But he thought he could keep up or catch up. The lake Sentani, who had really trained him for running, lived in a rougher country. They moved slower than the Shumai, but they could run forever. The saying was, "Nobody can outrun a Shumai." Jestak thought privately, "Nobody could run as long as a lake Sentani."

Kod's wife, Iben, was something of a slattern, and extremely hard-bodied, as were Shumai women. But she loved her children dearly. Ary, her girl, was ten years old, freckled and short, and her boy, Igin, was eight. All the others had died from the hard life and lack of cleanness and care that inhere in Shumai culture. Igin already carried a small spear, sharpened though without a steel point, and showed his Shumai instincts on the second day by hurling it lightly at Jestak's pack. It struck below the pack and made a gash. What surprised the boy was the instant reaction. He hadn't been thinking, really. Jestak whirled, short sword out, and hacked the spear on the first bounce. All stopped.

"What's this?" said Jestak.

Kod looked back. "You won't last long if a boy can spear you," he remarked.

"No, I won't, if it is one I trusted. But I know better now."

Stantu looked at his back. "I will dress it tonight," he said. "Pay no attention." Then he took Igin's spear and broke it on his knee. He looked at Kod, who looked back.

"We cannot stop here to gabble," said Thro. He put a hand on Jestak's shoulder. Then he started off again through the tall grass.

That evening, Iben was worried. She didn't want trouble, and she saw that Jestak had true friends, though her husband seemed not one. Igin was peeling a sapling for another spear when she encountered him by the stream bank where they had camped. She shoved him and stepped on the peeled shaft.

"Do you want this?"

"Get away, Mother. It is mine. I am making it."

"No more trouble."

"He is only a Pelbar."

"He is Thro's friend. And the Bow Bender, Stantu. He would die for him."

"What of Father?"

"They will get along. Igin. I beg you not to make trouble. And more than that, if you do, you will have to deal with me. It will not be easy on your fanny."

Igin said no more. When she returned to the fire, she saw Ary sitting with Jestak. He was playing a small musical instrument for her. It was composed of steel pieces mounted on a small, hollow box so as to give a different note when each was sprung. Ary tried it, while Jestak lay at ease, watching, occasionally instructing her. She began to catch on, though it was not tuned for typical Shumai usage. He played another tune for her, and she copied it, looking earnestly at it as she sprung the notes. When Igin returned, with his new spear, she was asleep by Jestak, the springbox in her hand.

"Jestak, come here," said Stantu.

"Not now. I do not want to wake her."

Stantu looked surprised, but then Iben came over and

took the girl to her roll of furs. Kod saw all this with a slight frown, but then said nothing.

"Why did you want the water boiled if you were only going to cool it off later—and the cloth, Jestak?"

"It keeps the wound from getting angry."

"That makes no sense."

"I do not know why, but we have found that if a wound is washed with river water, it gives much trouble. Spring water is much better. The cleaner the water, the better the results. That makes sense, doesn't it?"

"But boiling."

"We have found that boiling the water tends to cleanse whatever in it will cause the trouble. The healing is clean."

"They did not do that in the east."

"No, but they always used clean water. And they did it at Saltstream."

"The Innanigani were always afraid of a little dirt."

"And of us western barbarians." They both laughed.

"Thro," said Stantu. "In the east, Jestak and I were both alike to them. We were the dangerous western barbarians."

"They must be stupid," said Thro, arranging his fur roll for the night. "Nove, you take first watch," he added. "Then Stantu, then Iley, then Ouwn."

Two days later they heard the distant barking of Shumai dogs, and Thro blew a long call on his horn. It was answered in a short while.

"We hit it just right," he said. "Both the river and Black Bull."

Not long after, they arrived at the bank, and a small skin boat brought them over in three trips to the island. There were about two dozen people there, living in crude rush mat shelters, but mostly in the open. Thro knew them, greeted them in a circle of agitated dogs, and made explanations, especially for Jestak, who stood apart with Stantu until welcomed by the old man, Cwan, who was in charge of the mixed group of travelers.

They stayed there all the next day. Two of the men agreed to go westward with the party. They were young and eager for the adventure. The taller, Reor, had a touch of red in his hair, while the other, Olor, was a typical Shumai blond. As might be expected, they did not take to Jestak readily, but when he retempered and trimmed up Reor's battered spear point, they accepted him.

This brought all kinds of other metal equipment out, and Jestak saw he would be at least another day in fixing it. Cwan produced an old Pelbar trade hammer, and after trimming it up, Jestak set to work. He always had an audience. It must have made a strange sight to the nine Shumai men who trotted in at evening. Five of them had wounds. Three hours after they arrived, another straggled in. He was more seriously hurt in the side, and only Shumai hardihood could have carried him that far.

That evening, around Jestak's forge, the group was talking idly, and Stantu found out that they had attacked a large party of Sentani in boats at the great ford. They had lost nineteen men, including their leader, the axeman Nox.

Thro, Stantu, and Jestak were looking at each other. Kod remarked, "We just were at their wedding party at Northwall a few days ago." They explained.

"The girl," said Jestak. "Did you see a girl?"

"She was in the lead boats and was beyond us. She was the bride?"

"Yes. She was not hurt?"

"No, but we got their leader through the leg, right here."

"There?"

"Yes."

Jestak winced. Thro shook his head. "I just had tea with him in the judgment room of Northwall, with the old lady, their Protector." He walked away, then turned. "Did you kill him?"

"He died later," said one of the newcomers.

"How do you know?"

"I was roped by the Sentani and dragged down the river to an island where they landed for a while."

"Why did they not kill you?"

"It was the woman, I think. Her name is Ursa. I was tied to a tree. They wanted information from me, but I never gave them any. They were going to kill me, I am sure. The woman begged them not to. Then she went away when the leader died. I could hear her crying. The man they sent back to kill me was her husband. He looked at me a long while, with his sword in his hand, but for some reason he did not kill me. He cut my ropes partway through and told me to hang on them as if I was dead. He said it very slowly so I could understand. They were calling him from the boats. And then he left."

"It was for Ursa," said Jestak.

"Ursa," said Thro. "She did the same for me, you know. She saved me, too, last winter. Do you know who she is?"

"No."

"She is the granddaughter of Dailda of the song, the axeman's child left at Northwall."

"She?"

"Yes. I do not understand what power she has."

"It is the love of Aven," said Jestak. "Winnt will have told her when they were together, so her hurt would be eased. I suspect that Mokil knew enough to send Winnt."

"Mokil?"

"The leader of the north starpoint. He would have killed you in a fight without winking, but the Sentani have no use for killing the helpless. Now you tell me something."

"What?"

"Why did you attack them in the first place? They were no threat to you. Your whole party would be here, and the axeman, all alive and hale, and Willton would be on his way home. What was the use of it?"

"We always fight the Sentani. We always have. They are the enemy."

"It makes no sense."

"You would understand if you were a Shumai."

"Maybe, but I doubt it."

All of this was strange and new, and that night there were many silent faces staring at the fire. Incor began humming the song of Dailda, but Thro told him to be quiet, looking at him hard. There was no argument.

In the morning, Incor had joined Thro's band, as had three others. The man with the wounded side was very weak. They had put him in a mat shelter, where he lay, breathing hard.

"It is the bows. They will not fight like men. They use bows. What are you doing?"

"I am praying for you," said Jestak.

"We do not even have the same deity."

"He is the same, but we call him different names."

"He will not help a man who has fought through his own will."

"I am glad that you realize it isn't such a good idea. But He will help you. He will see you as a misguided child. You do not kill your children even though you may punish them—or they themselves."

"I do not understand it that way. But when I get better, I shall follow you and join you."

"Good. May Aven protect you."

"Sertine go with you," said the wounded man.

It was midmorning when the line of thirty men left Black Bull Island and began to run up the south river bank. They would follow it for ease of passage for a day, then as it turned northerly, strike out across the groves and grasslands. The pace was fast, even though all the men had packs. There was a short noon stop, and then the group started again. Jestak was tired already, and began to fall back. The pace was too fast for him. Stantu looked back at him, and thought to slow, but did not. Jestak would have to keep up if he were going all the way to the mountains.

Finally, Jestak decided to fall into the easy Sentani pace, and after that the ache slowly went out of his side. The others went ahead out of sight, but he could follow the swath of bent grass easily enough. When he arrived at the evening camp a fire was already burning. Kod had expected Jestak to limp in and fall exhausted, but was surprised when he strode in easily and began to skin the two rabbits he had shot with his Pelbar short bow. The others were eating dried meat, and were glad for the smell of the fresh, and for a taste.

As the party turned westerly, away from the river, Jestak saw a country broader and flatter than any he had ever seen, with shortening grass. A few cattle herds grazed there, mostly the wild blacks, but they were small and widely scattered. The sky burned hard, even though the spring was still not advanced, and the prairie was full of flowers. He ran now at his own pace, and the others, for the time, did not worry about him, knowing he would show up. He was different, but they increasingly grew used to him. They were taking some time to hunt now, so fresh meat was available. When they wanted to, they would take a day or two off to mend their soft leather shoes, dry more meat, and talk. Jestak thought the grassland would never end, especially when Thro told him they had not really gotten deep into it even yet. It was like the eastern ocean, with grass for water. When spring rains found them without shelter, except what they could hurriedly construct, the Shumai took it as a matter of course, but Jestak found it difficult. Stantu was a help.

"It is not like Pelbar comfort," he said.

"No."

"But you will get used to it. It is a great life here. There is a freedom to it that I could never get east of the Heart, even in the open, because of the trees. And Innanigan. And worst of all, the prison there. Faugh. It is a great blessing to be home again."

"Yes, but could you not build a shelter, so it would be waiting for you the next year?"

"We usually follow herds. Suppose they do not go near the shelter. They don't fill the whole landscape. We must be where they are."

"I am glad to be here, Stantu, but I would not have it for always."

"I hope Tia will see things your way."

"I hope we find Tia so she can choose."

"We will find her, Jes, and if you give her back her life twice, she may very well choose for you, even if she is as free as we are, and even if you are as serious always as you look now."

As they moved farther west, the grass became shorter, water scarcer. The Shumai never carried it unless they had to, and they could endure privations that were hard on Jestak, even though he had been deprived before.

He was beginning to do better at keeping up the pace, though he still came in to camp later than the others. Stantu was beginning to be worried because there were a few scattered groups of Shumai who overwintered, and he was afraid that if they came on Jestak alone, they would kill him. Thro's band was wholly isolated from everyone but other Shumai, never traveling far, or for long periods.

Jestak was seeing a country he had known nothing of. Long lines of migratory ducks and geese he was used to from the Heart River area, but not the thin white-winged hawks, not the great cranes that flew north in large flocks, crying down from the sky like lost creatures. Occasionally there were deer with branched antlers, and small deer with white rumps, called Zi by the Shumai. The sky seemed larger without trees, and overarched a world that seemed wider and more empty than he could have imagined. The flatness and sameness of the land seemed at times unutterably endless, but so much of it was new to him that his attention, when it could be called from the running, was alive with excitement.

Nevertheless, Jestak was grateful when Olor turned his ankle one day descending a hill to a small stream and could not go on. Thro called a rest day to give the stocky spearman a chance to heal. No one could throw a spear like Olor. One day, when he was running second, he had suddenly fitted his spear, sped past Thro, and launched it high and far. All stopped and watched it drop cleanly through the side of a yearling black bull. When they reached him, the bull was already lying on its side. This was welcome meat, for they had been nearly out, though Jestak, when he could, had furnished rabbits with his bow. It takes a lot of rabbits to fill thirty men. Nonetheless, they were already showing interest in his technique. This worried Jestak. If they were to become bowmen, it might go hard with the Sentani, though it would be a long time before they reached the skill of the eastern people, and without a great cultural shift, they could never match the Sentani's superb military organization.

But as Jestak began to fit more into the group, he found, to his astonishment, that there was much more to Shumai culture than he had known. They were a curious blend of practical simplicity and hardihood and a rich mental life. They loved games, many of which involved keen memory and quick reaction.

Lying under the stars at night, Jestak listened to them play the star games. Every principal star in the sky had a name, and all of the Shumai seemed to know these names. One would call out "Mu," and then the next, perhaps "Caro," a third, "Lide." Jestak was bewildered, knowing many stars himself, and all the main groups, but not nearly so many names.

"It is not hard," said Stantu one night. "For example, if I say 'Setts,' you will see that that is the third star from the south in the group 'Histo,' the mat weaver. What I am doing is setting up a pattern. At this point, though, the pattern can take other forms. For example, if Kod were to answer 'Okli,' he would be saying that my star was to alternate with the third star from the north in the next group, in this case 'Lace,' the horn. Then you would see that Histo lies in the south, Lace in the north. So the next man would have two choices. If he called out 'Lecta,' he would be moving the pattern to the east, and the next star called would have to be 'Essa,' moving it to the west. But if he said 'Eddo,' he would be moving it back to the south, and the next man would call out either 'Evek,' if he wanted it to be opposite the summit of the sky but to the north, or 'Ounek' if he wanted it to be the east of 'Okliu,' as Eddo is."

Jestak remained bewildered, though he began to catch on a little. They would all lie at night, with the prairie wolves barking in the distance, and one would call out "Vertha," then almost immediately another "Spear." A third would say "Arly," and then a fourth, a little slower, "Skig." A fifth would eventually say, perhaps, "Ilat," and so it would continue, more and more slowly, until one man would announce a star, and all the others would break into a laugh at his expense, usually with a few in the lead, and then the others. Sometimes an argument would arise as to which stars should be counted, and which were incidental to the groups, but it was all in good humor, and every band, so Stantu said, always had an arbiter of such things just as they had a leader. The advantage of the game to the Shumai was that they could see a few stars through the clouds at any time of year, and their vast knowledge of the skies would tell them directions immediately. They also knew where the wandering stars ought to be, and in the hill of Kan they had a smooth place made with a great chart of stones, carefully marked to predict the positions of the wanderers. Jestak had a great argument with them one evening about the nature of the sky, and after laughing at him, they built a large fire, for the sun, then all got up and they showed him how they knew that the moon went around the earth, with various men standing at various positions for different things. Kod was the principal star, Essa, and was stationed far out into the brush, from which place he called periodically trying to find out what was going on. Jestak eventually saw that they were right, and felt the chagrin of seeing all the science of Pelbar astronomy disproved by the wild runners of the west. Stantu saw his feeling and laughed, swatting him on the rump.

"What of the eastern cities, Stantu?" Thro asked. "Didn't they even know the star patterns?"

"No, I think not. They are indoor people. Their ocean travelers know them, don't they, Jes?"

"Only to use. Like the Pelbar, they regard them as on a great dome or roof around the whole earth."

Reor and Olor, who were cousins, loved to play "Na, na." Jestak had assumed that this too was a childish game because of the rollicking, boisterous spirit of the young men, but on the evening they rested by the river, the two were chanting variations on the four words, slapping hands, and laughing, and the Pelbar took the time to watch them closely. Again he was bewildered.

Reor was saying, "Na, na, na, ta, ga, in, ta, ga, na, ga, ta." As he did this, he picked up or put down four small cylinders, each painted a different color. Olor then repeated the words and the rhythm in which they were said, picking up and putting down cylinders from his own set. In this round, Jestak saw that the rhythm was full note, full, half, half, half, then a rest, while Reor put his hands on his knees, then four halfs and two fulls.

Then Reor said again, "Na, na, na, ta, in, ta, na, ga," and Olor repeated it perfectly, though this time the rhythm gave each syllable a full count.

Usually the game started slowly and simply, with a count like "Na, na, na, ta, ga, ta, na," all with full counts. Then it picked up rhythm with the leader chanting more rapidly and adding variations in rhythm to his movements. When finally either he broke the rule of variations or the follower failed to recall or execute exactly what he did, all those watching would laugh, and a small pebble would be added to the pile of the one who won the point.

"It is not easy, but children learn it early, and everyone is good at it," said Stantu. "You see, each of the four cylinders has a color and a name. There is na, in, ta, and ga. When you call a name, you pick up that cylinder. If you call it again, you must put it down, and in its proper order. You can use the spaces between the fingers if you are really good. And you have to follow the rhythms exactly. We all know the possible rhythms. There are forty-two legal ones. That way, if you start a rhythm, you cannot break into one not in the forty-two if you get confused.

"Harder than 'Na, na' is 'na, ta, ga,' a game you play using the same pieces. I have already found out that Thro is unbeatable at it, but I can play it with others here. What you do is assign a numerical value to each of the four pieces. Then, when the one picks it up, he mentally adds the number. When he puts it down, he subtracts the number. So he goes through his pattern while he and his partner calculate the numbers. Either you can play it by alternative leaders, with each one giving the pattern, and the other announcing the resulting number, or you can do it the hard way, in which the leader goes through his pattern, while the follower calculates, and then the follower does a different pattern to come out with the same number at the end. He can use any of the forty-two rhythms, and even continue from one to another if he sees he cannot come out with the right number. He can do this until he gets it. It is hard enough when the numbers are small, but Thro can play it with numbers like forty-one and twenty-nine. Fifty is the highest you can go. Here, Thro, show him."

Thro sat down with Stantu, who was good, but no match for the leader. They went through a simple game, which Stantu then explained, and then Thro "skinned his bull" as the Shumai put it. Jestak was bewildered at the rapidity with which the Shumai leader calculated, at the same time chanting in rhythm.

Eventually Thro said, "Do not the Pelbar have games?"

"None like those. We sing a good deal. We have sports we play, mostly with balls or long swords, and we do have some calculation games or strategy games. One is played on a board of squares with sixteen pieces on each side. It can take a quarter sun or more to play, or in some cases it can be over in a sun width. It is much like a game they had in Innanigan. Perhaps they had one root. But we have no calculation games anything like this."

"What of 'tati'?" Stantu asked.

"Oh, yes. But that is really a simple game. Here, I will show you." Jestak drew out the board of squares and got pebbles to play it with. Thro picked it up quickly, and soon Jestak saw that he was beginning to calculate several moves ahead. He was still no match for Jestak, who had had long practice, but the Pelbar saw that Thro could already beat some average players in Northwall.

"Thro," he finally said. "I do not understand why you do not use these amazing mental powers to give more ease to your life instead of living constantly in the open and running for days on end."

"How would I do that?"

"We, for instance, employ our mathematics for careful measurement, engineering, calculation, and building. You use it for your play."

Thro looked at him, smiling. "It is all play," he said. "When I am running through the grass, with all their blades beautiful, reaching for the sunlight, and the wild cattle are ahead of me, and the birds above, soaring, and the grasshoppers flying from my path, I could want nothing else. It is that way with us. We have no use or need of cities, walls, the shutting off of the sky. This is exactly the life I want. It is all I have known and I am satisfied with it."

"Come in," said Sima Pall, from the depth of her small, dark, inner ground-floor room. Manti entered. "Manti. Where is your cape? Has she retired you? Who now has the job?"

"Her nephew. Monar."

"He is not bad. Perhaps inexperienced. What do you think?"

"He is inexperienced. He has not worked his way up through the positions, surely," Manti mused. "I am not sure how he would handle an emergency."

"But that is not what you wanted with me, is it?"

"No." Manti hesitated, running his heavy finger around the edge of a bowl on the table.

"I think I know, Manti. It is really too late for that. We would be two old herons together."

"We could get you better quarters."

"She would find something just as miserable. Besides, I am not dead yet. I still have a lot of support. I only hope she shows her incompetence before she does something truly disastrous for Northwall."

"She does show a certain inclination for ceremony and display which are not what we are used to."

"Yes. I went to the council and reminded them that they had not tested and regreased the trap table by the river after high water. Do you know what she said?"

"That it had been there for over three hundred years and had never yet been used for anything else than a landing platform. That she doubted whether it would work anyway if much weight of enemies were on it."

"She told you as well."

"Yes, but I think the real reason is that she wanted to use the credits to redecorate the Protector's room. She described it as an old stone apple shed."

"I wonder if Monar will go along with the ending of other special defenses?"

"He surely does not know the importance or operation of some of them—of the creek dam, the forefield ditch trap, the steam thruster."

"Well, Manti, we will have to make it our duty to know so anything neglected can be restored as quickly as possible when the need arises. We must build up our party and keep a record of these things. If they add up to too long a list, we will simply call a general judgment. Then they will be forced to maintain some defense order."

"It is not the same, all this wrangling."

"No, Manti, but it is the best we can do, is it not?"

"Sometimes I wish Jestak had never come."

"He had to come, Manti. I did not see it at first, but he had to come."

The second day, they walked. Olor was better, but Thro did not want to test his ankle severely the first day after the rest.

"It is all right. We are not far from Oldtree, and we will spend the night there. Let us try to kill a couple of big animals on the way," Thro remarked.

"What is Oldtree, Stantu?"

"It is a small settlement of Shumai too old to run. They stay there all year. Of course many of them die there and so it is a revered place. They get on well enough, though winter is hard for them. We all contribute what meat we can, and they dry it. They also gather seeds from the surrounding countryside, and fish some, so they do all right. I expect I shall see my last days there—or someplace like that."

"Why do they not winter in the south, east of the Heart?"

"It is too close to Sentani country."

"I am sure that some truce agreement could be drawn up so that the Sentani would leave them alone. They are not aggressive."

"But what if the Shumai wanted to raid the Sentani? Then they would retaliate, and it would go hard with the old ones. We would rather they stay here, out in the long grass."

"Rather than renounce the right to raid?"

"You still do not understand the Shumai, Jestak. Besides, are you not on a raid right now?"

"But only to right a wrong."

"Do you think we feel no wrongs from the Sentani? And what of all these men? They are on a raid for the fun of it as much as anything."

"All of them?"

"No, but many. And it is natural to all of us."

"That is bad."

"Why?"

"Because if they go at it in the Shumai way, with spears flying, we shall never get anywhere. The whole situation must be studied if we hope to succeed. We would be much more likely to get away if we simply took back the prisoners than if we tried to burn down whatever it is we will meet."

"Where is the courage in that? Where is the poetry?"

"In being with Tia."

"You hope, but perhaps she will not agree."

"That will be a poem, too, in a minor key."

"A what? Look, there is Oldtree."

The village of the old Shumai was located on another river island, but it spilled over onto the north bank, which was steep with rock outcrops and out of the reach of flood waters. The river was the Enfac, a sluggish prairie stream that shrank to a mere trickle in late summer. But there was always water.

For the old, the Shumai had gone against their usual custom of hardihood and built large communal houses of logs, covered with earth, to make them warm in winter, cool in summer, but most of the old people there retained the Shumai custom of living outdoors except in severe weather. Some of the rock outcrop was also used as shelter where it overhung, or where loose strata had made it easy to dig into.

Over two hundred people lived in the village, almost all of them ambulatory, but many of the number were quite old and physically beaten by the Shumai life. They seemed happy, though, and as many of the wrinkles on their faces followed lines of laughter as of squinting against the weather. A few racks of meat were drying over small, smoky fires tended by a few old men who were playing games, though not vigorous ones like "Na, na."

The villagers were poorly clad, but their clothing, mostly skin, was richly decorated because they had plenty of time and spent much of it in slowly working on finer handicrafts than were usually seen in Shumai camps. Jestak realized that places like Oldtree were the source of the elaborately carved drinking noggins that the Shumai carried. Not only was the wood sturdier than the Pelbar trade ceramics, but it was a tribal craft of which the Shumai were proud. All the figures on the carvings had meaning, but many of these meanings were rather fanciful or obscure and not strictly religious or philosophical. The Shumai took the reckless side of poetry as their approach to meaning, rather than its ordering side.

Oldtree also had its memorization circle, where the priests of Sertine and the old learners passed down the stories of the deity and His precepts, and preserved some semblance of the literacy for which the Shumai had very little use but did not want entirely to forget.

Naturally the settlement was curious about Jestak, who still wore his maroon Pelbar tunic. Many had never been to the cities on the Heart and had never seen anyone but Shumai, except perhaps for hostile Sentani.

The old ones had no leader, not needing one among themselves because they lived so communally and agreeably together, and all genuinely helped each other when help was needed. But naturally one individual did emerge as spokesman, in this case a tall, thin man named Urthu. He was still straight, though somewhat slow and enfeebled. His wife, Lest, companioned constantly with him and voiced her decided opinions on everything. There was a jocular and affectionate relationship between them.

Thro's party was the first of the spring, and so had to stay four days helping the older people gather wild bulbs and onions, kill more meat, and bring heavy wood, which often had to be gathered at a distance. Jestak set up his forge again, and there seemed no end to the repairs to be made on metal things, all Pelbar trade items. Thro and his men would have to leave long before Jestak could finish.

"Urthu," he said on the second day. "You ought to send some Shumai men to one of the Pelbar cities to learn metalwork. You could do a lot of this for yourself. I could be here over a week and still just be doing the worst of it. Or else you could allow the Pelbar to come out here and do it for you. There could be a central point, like our truceweek, and all could bring their broken tools to be fixed. The Pelbar could even teach you to do your own out here."

"Hmmm," said Urthu.

"What is that you have?"

"An old spear point. Now it is so worn it is a skinning knife. But it wears quickly now."

"Yes, that is because of the way we tempered it. We

gave it a hard surface so it would keep an edge. Then we gave it a soft center and shaft so it would not shatter."

"It is magic."

"No. It is simply the way you cool it from red heat. I could show you, but to do it the way you want takes much practice." Here Jestak reached out for the old spear point, and saw on it the familiar Jestan mark, a very old date, and "Wella."

"Wella," he said. "Wella. She was my mother's great-aunt."

Lest laughed. "Your mother's great-aunt made this?"

"No. She headed the family shop in Pelbarigan. More likely it was made by one of the workers. But she may have had a hand in it. You got it at Pelbarigan?"

"My father must have. It has been good and cut the heart of many animals."

"I am glad we have done true work for you—even though you have sometimes thrown our own spear points back at us."

"Yes," said Urthu. "But I never have. I have always lived in the west, and wintered directly south."

"Have you seen horses?"

"Horses? A few. The Emeri had them, though I have heard that the western Shumai now have them too. Though not many."

"I am going to bring back a pair of horses, so when they go by here, don't spear them for supper."

"All right," said Urthu, laughing. "As long as you bring us a bull. Stantu tells me that you can fish in the winter. You must show us how. We can neither net like the Sentani then nor spear."

Jestak showed a small crowd of the Oldtree people how to fish with a hook and line, and how to put out a set line for the night. The catfish were not long in biting, because the old men usually fished only in summer when the water cleared enough so they could see their quarry. They were skeptical until a large catfish flopped on the bank, and then, with much laughing and shouting, they clubbed it and took it to cook.

The old were great storytellers, and naturally had to hear all about the travels of Stantu and Jestak, with many interruptions and questions. One man, Olum, had lived with the northern Shumai and had even seen the western-most Tantal city, Cwilgan. He knew the Shumai as a cruel and aggressive society and was surprised at how they had multiplied.

They played a poem game at night, with a group of as many as forty. It demanded knowing by heart about three hundred short Shumai poems. One would state a line, and the next would have to add a line from another poem that would fit. They tapped softly and slowly, and the next person had ten taps in which to give the line. If he didn't, or if he gave one that really did not fit, much hilarity resulted, and one of his five straws was put into the small pot in the center near the fire. When he lost all five straws, he was out, though he stayed in the circle. One was allowed to make up a line, too, as long as it preserved the prescribed meter and rimed with the previous line, though the known lines did not have to rime. Jestak could see that many of the combinations were so well known they were formulas, but new combinations showed another side of the active mentality of the Shumai.

Toward the end of the fourth day, the old people gave Thro's band two racks of dried meat to take with them. Each had a hundred narrow strips on it.

The band was sitting around a fire in the evening, and Jestak was to divide it up and hand it around. He immediately gave Thro six strips, and, moving on to the next man, gave him six, remarking, "I will divide the last eight." They all looked at him in surprise. As he had announced, there were eight, and he nonchalantly cut them into fourths and gave each man one piece. Urthur, who was watching, shook his head and said, "More Pelbar magic."

"What?" said Jestak.

"Jestak, how did you do that?" Thro asked.

Stantu, who knew the simple process from his stay in Innanigan, laughed. "It is not magic, Urthu. It is simply division. We share and have never learned multiplication and division, but other peoples know them."

An immediate flurry of interest arose, the fire was built up, and Jestak and Stantu had to teach everyone the basics of multiplication and division in the dust with sticks. Jestak was a skilled mathematician from his Pelbar engineering training, though he was no match for the average Shumai "Na, na" player in speed of calculation. Interest was so great that the Oldtree people wanted them to stay another day, but to Jestak's relief, Thro said, "The nights are warming already. We have a long run, and we must be going."

They started the next morning, very early, but all at Oldtree, except those confined to their mats, were on hand, with much smiling. Jestak even was given an odorous hug by Lest, and he had to stoop into all the dark earth houses to say good-bye to the invalids inside, as did all the men. One old woman, lying on a dirty mat, held his hand a little long, and murmured, "Tia is my great-grandchild."

Jestak looked at her sturdy, bony face and shuddered inwardly at the thought of Tia herself arriving at such a place and condition. "We will bring her to see you," he said.

"Do not wait. I may be over there," she said, gesturing in the direction of the cemetery across the river.

"Stay alive to see her."

"She is beautiful, is she not?"

"Yes. In all my travels, she is the most beautiful woman I have ever seen."

The old woman smiled, showing dark gums. "My name is Riadin. Good-bye. Sertine will help you."

"Yes. Good-bye. Stay well."

She closed her eyes.

They ran for another week, the land getting drier and the brush sparser all the time. One afternoon, Jestak said, "Kod, what are those clouds?"

"They are not clouds. They are mountains. That is the snow."

"Are we nearly there, then?"

"Closer. We are now in the country of the horseriders. They hold the plains up to the foothills. The Emeri are well back in the higher ground. But we must watch out for them even now. Sometimes they come down onto the plains on their horses."

It was late afternoon when the party saw the curls of a group of campfires ahead, and at evening, Thro halted and blew his horn about an ayas from the site. In a short while he was answered, and as they moved toward the camp, Jestak heard the thudding of heavy hooves, and was startled and thrilled to see fifteen men, long beards in the wind, riding horses out to see them. The riders drew rein abreast across the path.

"Thro of the Highbluff Shumai with a party to retake our people from the Emeri," said the leader.

"Is that you, Thro? Welcome. Welcome, all. And what is that one?"

"That is Jestak, the Pelbar, of Northwall on the Heart, Ottan. He is come with us to buy a pair of horses, and to fight the Emeri with us and regain Tia of the Rush Creek Band, whom he has met."

"Tia?" said Ottan, and then laughed. "Tia? Her tongue will rattle his moustache off. A Pelbar, huh. I have heard of them. I thought you lived behind walls."

"We do, except for me," said Jestak.

"Come then, come eat. We have a whiteface cow on the fire—the whole thing—for there are a hundred or so of us. Come."

The riders turned and trotted on ahead, with occasional glances back, especially at Jestak, who was a novelty. The camp was typical of the Shumai, arranged in a random manner, mostly in the open, with large, low skin tents and cooking fires in the open. The smell of drying meat, rotten entrails, curing hides, wood smoke, and spitted meat was oppressive, even with a slight breeze, but the camp dwellers did not seem to notice it.

The party found itself surrounded with dogs, especially Jestak, who was noticeably different. They were large hounds, blotched with white, black, and brown, and they barked continually at Jestak from about two or three feet away, making his trunk reverberate. But Jestak bent down to their level and let them smell his hands, and they soon accepted him, wagging tails held up like a circle of banners. He petted each with care, smoothing their hair and pulling burrs from their ears, talking softly. So when he entered the circle where the Shumai were all talking and greeting each other, he was surrounded by dogs and children.

Ottan laughed again. "Come, Jestak the Pelbar. You are welcome here and must tell us of yourself and the east when we have eaten."

"Thank you," Jestak replied. "I am glad to be here with you and finally near the mountains."

There was a general laugh. "They are not as near as you may think," said Whin, Ottan's wife. "The air is clear and they are still many ayas. They are very high. It is winter at the top all year. People from the east always mistake them."

The party sat around soon, eating, Jestak receiving many stares, with his maroon tunic and square-cropped hair. He also shaved his facial hair, all except the moustache, while it was usual with the Shumai to grow beards. The eastern bands kept them fairly short-cropped, but these westerners let them grow freely, and some of the older men's were long and flowing.

"Jestak," said Stantu. "You had better get out your spring box and amuse the children the way you did Ary."

"Ah, I gave it to her. You will find her an expert when we get back. But I do have a small flute." And soon Jestak was playing for a circle of youngsters. The horseriders also had flutes, which were tuned differently, but the children seemed unoffended by the strange Pelbar notes, and soon he and they were exchanging songs as the group relaxed. They talked until very late at night, both Stantu and Jestak summarizing their travel stories. The horseriders were willing to help supply the party, and two men joined it, but they were not willing to do more than defend their own land from the Emeri, who had bested them numerous times. Again the difference was strategy and bows, as Jestak saw it.

In the morning, Ottan nudged Jestak, who was still asleep, with one foot. The Pelbar was awake and on his feet in an instant, startling the westerner. "Oh," he said. "It is you. I must have been dreaming. I am sorry. I was trained that way. I am far from home."

"No matter. I understand you want to buy a pair of horses. Have you ever ridden one?"

"No, until just now I had not so much as seen one."

"Come, then. We must show you how to ride." A large black horse, ready bridled, was standing nearby. Ottan walked to it, spoke softly, and then lightly vaulted to its back. It plunged and whirled a little, but soon settled down under Ottan's expert hand.

"You see? It is easy. To make him go, you touch your heels like this, and let loose the lines." The horse began to trot slowly. "You turn him like this," Ottan shouted over his shoulder, and he expertly pivoted the horse around back toward Jestak.

After further explanations and assurances, Ottan said, "Now you get on. I will hold him."

"No jokes, please, Ottan. I do not want to be trampled on before we go to the mountains. I don't want any broken ribs now." By this time there was an audience, most of them grinning.

"You have to start sometime. True?"

"Yes, I suppose so. All right. I put myself here?"

"Good. Now up." Jestak sprung to the horse's back. The horse objected, but Ottan had its head.

"Down, Gerontal, down," he murmured, scratching its ear. Then, to Jestak, "Here now, take the lines." Jestak took them, and the horse just stood there.

"Dig him. Just a little." Jestak touched his heels to the horse's rib cage, and Gerontal began to walk, but the unfamiliarity of the man on his back made him nervous, and he nickered and tossed his head, then began to trot. Jestak bounced on his back, jarring his crotch, but then the horse reared, and Jestak would have slid off, but he caught the horse's neck. Gerontal came down hard, and while Jestak was still out flat, neatly bucked him off into a thorny bush. By the time he had climbed out, the Shumai had caught the animal, with much hooting, and Jestak knew he would have to get on again. After a dozen tries, either Gerontal was tired of misbehaving or Jestak was gaining a feel for what he was doing, for he could ride the horse slowly in a circle. Naturally everyone was watching. And naturally Reor had to try, with results like Jestak's.

Finally, Thro said, "Well, before we cripple all my men, let us quit this for now. There will be time later. Jestak, these people have some iron to mend, if you are of a mind to. The rest of you, we have shoes to repair and trade for, and much work to do."

As Jestak, his scratched arms tingling, prepared a rude forge, he was handed the first tool, a curved knife for hides. One look told him it was not of Pelbar manufacture.

"Where did this come from?"

"From the northwest, in the mountains, where we trade with the Forman metalsmiths."

"Is it far?"

"Three hundred ayas. Why do you ask?"

"It is much different from our work. This is the first I knew that anyone in the west worked metal."

"The Emeri do, too, and better, but we are hostile to them."

Jestak found the Forman work of sturdy but somewhat

inferior quality. It was internally uneven, often poorly tempered, and not made to close tolerances. Late in the afternoon of his second day at the forge, though, a young Shumai handed him a long, curved knife with a broken guard on the handle. It was of finer workmanship than any but the best Pelbar work, and its intricate metal etching, of a stylized lizard, was superior to anything he had ever seen.

"Aiii."

"What?"

"Where did you get this?"

"I took it from the Emeri. In a fight."

"Is it their work?"

He looked puzzled. "I suppose it is. They have enough of it with them."

"How many of them are there?"

He held out his arms. "Oh, around six thousand or so, I suppose. They are almost all together in one city, with surrounding farms and small dwellings."

Jestak knew that his task would not be easy. What was it that the Saltstream prophet had said?

> To win the hawk,
> To lose the dove,
> To lose small praise,
> To gain great love.

Was that he? Was Tia the dove he would then lose? Perhaps it was only a poem. That was the trouble with enigmatic prophecies. They seemed a game to amuse the troubled and idle. He began to disassemble the Emeri knife.

At that moment, Escripti was walking down the long stone corridor of Emerta's largest building, the palace of the Krugistoran, rubbing his arm. He passed Shaffermi.

"Ah, Escripti. What has befallen your limb, Escripti?"

"It is the girl again, Shaffermi. The wild one from the east, Shaffermi."

"Did she scratch you, Escripti?"

"No, Shaffermi. She twisted my arm. She is as strong as a horse and twice as hard, and her tongue is like a long sword. I think we would be much better off to hamstring her and put her back in the fields shackled, Shaffermi."

"But, Escripti, the Krugistoran is convinced that she can

be tamed, like the others, and she certainly is beautiful—a fine addition to his other two, Escripti."

"I wish he would try to tame her himself, Shaffermi."

"Ah, Escripti. Then you would have toppled from your position, and perhaps might be found toiling in the fields yourself, Escripti."

"I might, indeed, Shaffermi, live longer at that. She refuses to put on weight. We cannot force-feed her without her struggling so hard she will mar herself, and then my back will be as good as without skin. She is, strangely enough, very willing to learn to read script, to sew fine needle pictures, and at playing mathematical games she is already superior to anyone but Fountagorist, and he can best her only in problems involving calculus. She is a strange one, with the tastes of a clod of dirt and the mind of Unsettomati, the astronomer. I think the Krugistoran is asking for much trouble with her. She would perhaps be meek as a pet rat, with pink paws held up for a seed, then leap at the throat, Shaffermi." Escripti adjusted his long blue robe in dignity.

"That, though, is your job, Escripti. To see that she does not do that, Escripti."

"It is the worst possible position, Shaffermi. She is not normal. How many Emeri women would give a limb or two to be in her position? But she scorns it. She says she belongs to no one, except that she owes her life to a Jestak the Pelbar. What is a Pelbar? A savage of some variety, Shaffermi?"

"A Pelbar? I have heard of them, I think, Escripti. They are a people far to the east, all the way across the great flatlands to the land of trees by the large river into which all the country drains. I have heard they are dwarves who can charm metal into whatever shape they choose. They are very ugly, so ugly they come out only at night, and they are cowards and live in great cubes of stone, Escripti."

"Who told you of that, Shaffermi?"

"It is written in the reports of the cartographers, from the material of interrogations from the Shumai savages, Escripti."

"It sounds like a fairy story, Shaffermi."

"Yes, it does, Escripti. But so do your stories of what Tio the Shumai can do. But you assert them to be true, and I suppose they are, Escripti."

"That is true, Shaffermi. Suppose you insist on taking

over my position. I am sure that the Krugistoran would allow it, so anxious is he to have that lovely form against his, his form. He has great faith in your abilities, Shaffermi."

"No, Escripti. I think this position is well suited to your talents, Escripti," the other said and departed, laughing drily.

Escripti continued down the hallway, turned right, down a series of archways, coming to a great carved oaken door, flanked with guards dressed in wide flaring blue pants and well-polished cuirasses and carrying long swords. As he came near, they opened the doors, closing them behind him. The floor inside was of polished stone squares of alternating black and white. A group of women were standing on the squares, and from a divan the Krugistoran himself was directing them to move according to the calculations of a game he was playing with a tall and very thin man. As Escripti came near, the Krugistoran laughed throatily, calling out, "Now, Acco, one up and two over, Acco. There now, I have beaten you as always, Pristiginagi."

"Yes, Krugistoran. As always, Krugistoran," said Pristiginagi, bowing deeply and standing aside.

Escripti went down on his knees and shuffled forward, hands behind him.

"Bend, Escripti," bellowed the Krugistoran. The servant then crawled forward, nose to the floor. "Acco, come here, Acco. Look, there is your teacher. Put your foot on his neck, Acco." She did, with evident pleasure. Escripti grunted from the pressure. "There, Escripti. What do you think of the way you have trained her? Is she not obedient? Ha, ha. Now give me your report on the new savage, Tio. Is she nearly ready for my bed?"

"May I look up, Krugistoran?"

"Of course, fool. There now, let him go, Acco." She released him, stepping back. She was a heavy girl, with drooping lids. Evidently, from her light coloring, she was Shumai in background, but her life now had so erased that wild spirit that she looked like a painted doll.

Escripti looked up. The Krugistoran regarded him sourly. Escripti saw a man of enormous proportions, his bare stomach making the red couch sag greatly, and drooping over it like a skinful of apple wine. His arms showed wide gold bands, intricately inscribed, biting into the swelling flesh. He was nearly bald, but what hair he had was a deep, curly black, as were his heavy brows. His lower lip fell open and was slightly wet with saliva. All his thick fingers had heavy rings, with large stones of several clashing colors. His feet were bare, and on the large toes were similar rings. Around his middle was a rich blue cloth, and above his hairy knees protruded a pair of bright red shorts, clinging to his widening thighs. He evidently enjoyed seeing Escripti so subdued.

"Krugistoran," said Escripti. "Tio the beautiful is making wonderful progress, but we feel she is still not ready for so august a presence as yours. We have felt, for security, that your importance and generosity have not been yet sufficiently instilled on her spirit. Your value to us is so great that we wish only the most polished of jewels to be added to your crown, Krugistoran."

"What you are saying is that you are making a botch of it, Escripti."

Escripti said nothing, but again bowed his face to the polished floor.

"Acco—subdue him again, Acco," said the Krugistoran, throatily, and, with a slight smile, she again placed her foot on his neck and pressed until Escripti involuntarily grunted. This seemed to excite the ruler, who clapped once and bellowed, "Leave us, all of you. Now. Come here, Acco." As he hurried out the door among the women he had trained as attendants to the Krugistoran, Escripti saw a flashed reflection in the armor of the door guards, a grotesquely bulbous view of the Krugistoran reaching for Acco. Then the doors thundered shut.

At the horserider camp, the party was nearly ready to continue. In a final gathering around the great roasting fire, Jestak was counseling strategy. "You say," he remarked, "that they have bows. Only I among us carry one. We must go stealthily. Surprise will be our best weapon. We must have an avenue of attack planned, and not only that, a route of escape afterward. Or several. They have horses. They will not take our attack lightly, I fear. We must best them with our intelligence in every encounter. I see by their metalwork that they have real capabilities. We must match them and beat them. We must cut across their habits of thought so they cannot anticipate what we do."

"They are beasts," said Ottan. "They are no match for a

Shumai, except for the bows and long swords. We stay out of each other's way pretty much, but we do well enough when we meet. We can throw spears as far as they can shoot, and on foot they are nearly helpless."

From other remarks, Jestak saw that they were not listening. He shot a look at Stantu, who returned it with a slight frown. To the Shumai fighting was not a game to be played with brilliance, but a matter of instant reaction and unremitting courage, of attack the same way one went after a herd of wild cattle. Jestak was worried.

Finally, Stantu said, "Jestak is right. We must go in quietly, plan our whole attack, hit hard but quietly, and get away with the captives before the Emeri are ready for us." The others looked at him.

"Well," said Thro, "we will try it then, once we get to the mountains. We will stalk them and hit them at night, and be gone before they wake up." Jestak saw that Thro really didn't grasp what he had in mind, but was grateful for the support.

Later, Ottan said to Thro in a low voice, "This Jestak. Can you trust him? How will he be in a fight? He seems to want to sneak around like a weasel." They looked over to where Jestak was playing a slow game of "Na, na" with a small, tow-headed girl, Indy. There was a crowd of children around, gleeful at how well Indy was doing against the grown-up stranger. Two dogs lay at ease among the group, one with a head on Jestak's thigh. It did not look promising to Ottan.

Just then, Stantu, who was working on a hard knot in a cord about ten arms away, called, "Yaah, Jes, lend me your knife." Jestak stood and flipped his short sword over, sticking it in a log five spans from Stantu's hand. He took it and nonchalantly cut the cord, then pitched it back in a high, gentle arc, and Jestak caught it by the handle, sheathing it in the same motion.

"I think he will be all right," said Thro.

X

As Whin had said, the mountains were not as close as they appeared. A day's run brought them into the wooded foothills, but these were gently rolling hills, and the mountain peaks still were far away.

"Thro," said Reor. "Are we now into Emeri country?"

As if in answer, they heard hooves and crowded for cover. A band of fifteen riders swept across their rear, heading north. They had almost passed when the last man slowed. "Ho," he said, studying the ground. As the other riders wheeled, Olor's spear hissed out and took the last man through the shoulders. Instantly the Emeri had out their longbows and the air flashed with arrows and spears. It was just what Jestak had feared, but he stood behind a tree and put arrows through four men in quick succession, firing as quickly as he could aim, as in Pelbar guard training.

The Emeri wheeled away, and Jestak hit one more, toppling him. A horse was screaming where a Shumai spear had pierced him, and the rider's comrades, in an attempt to save him, turned back again and came on, waving their long swords and yelling in a hoarse quaver. Jestak took two more off their horses, and one more spear found a man, but the swords swept aside the others, as the five remaining Emeri horsemen hit the Shumai hard, slashing aside the short swords and downing the men who could not stay out of their way. Reor leaped on a horse and took off another man, receiving a sharp, glancing blow with a sword across the left arm in the process. He went down. Thro's spear, which he had held, went through the swordsman's belly and Jestak put his remaining two arrows through two more men. The two men still mounted rode off hard eastward, but Stantu, taking a long throw, pierced one, and Jestak, running for an Emeri longbow, quickly

146

got off an arcing shot that hit the horse in the neck, throwing the remaining rider. Five Shumai went after him.

"Jes," Stantu shouted, and whirling, Jestak saw the first man thrown coming at him with a long sword. Jestak just had time to run aside and pick up one of the fallen men's swords. The Emer laughed cruelly, desperately, expecting to cut him down, but the Pelbar parried every swing, striking at the swordsman's weapon near the base. The Emer was a skillful fighter, and was driving Jestak back, slashing and hacking, when one parry shocked his blade near the hilt, and it snapped, singing off into the dirt. Stantu had fitted an arrow awkwardly into one of the longbows, and drawing for the first time, sent an arrow into the Emer as he stood there momentarily with the sword hilt.

It was a short fight, but expensive for both sides. All the Emeri were dead, nine killed by Jestak's arrows. Thro saw this with some strange feelings. Olor was jubilant at his first kill, but was also upset over Reor, who lay bleeding and twisting. The cousins could not help remembering the survivors of the fight at the great ford, not many weeks before, and the deadliness of the Sentani arrows. Nine Shumai were dead, six to Emeri arrows. Kod had been shot through the arm and was sitting stoically while his comrades worked it free. Jestak saw this with some feeling of relief, for if Kod went home now, at least Ary would have her father. But this reduced their band from thirty-four to twenty-five, assuming the wounded men would make their way back to Ottan's camp. It was decided that one of Ottan's men should go with them, reducing the number one more.

The Shumai went over the bodies of the Emeri. Thro said, "Bring all the bows." Several men looked at him. "It is plain," he added, "that we will have to learn to use them." Once the wounds were bound as well as possible, the two groups parted, for it was important to leave the area. Those going home were going to try to leave a wide path, suggesting that they had been defeated and were going home with the six Emeri horses they had caught. Those going west picked a path from rock to rock for some distance. But before going they hastily dug graves, not only nine true ones for the Shumai dead, but several false ones as well. Jestak had odd feelings lowering Iley into one of the graves. He took a long sword with him.

"Jes," said Stantu. "You were very good with that sword. Where did you learn that?"

"The Pelbar guard all have daily training in it for years. But that Emer was at least a match for me."

"I don't understand what you were doing. I thought he had you."

"Like that knife I mended, these swords have a lizard motif on them. See? It looks nice, but it makes a weak point near the hilt. He gave me no openings. I saw I might break the sword, though, by shocking it repeatedly just there. It is remarkable art, but poor metalwork."

Stantu grinned. "I felt odd with the bow, but as Thro says, it is clear we will have to adopt it."

It was already night when they left, but they pressed their advance another twelve ayas or so before camping. They made a tiny fire in a hidden gully, well shrouded with trees and brush, and posted guards. Thro made his way to Jestak and asked in a low voice, "Well, what do you think?"

"I don't know. We may have warned them that we are in the area, and our success may truly alarm them, but the patrol may also show that they were expecting Shumai anyway. They may increase the guard at their farmsteads. We ought, I think, to work by stealth. I don't blame Olor, though. The tail man had surely seen something, and it was probably the best thing that he killed the man when he did. At least they had no time to make a planned approach. As you well know, I would much rather glide in at night, free the Shumai, and glide back out without touching a hair of the Emeri. It always arouses a people to have its men killed."

"We learned that in Innanigan, didn't we," said Stantu.

"Yes. Of course now we have already drawn blood. But if we somehow could get into the farmstead, get our people out, and disappear, that might even strike them with awe. It would be something new. The Shumai never avoid fights but look for them. The Emeri would not know what to make of it, and so would be cautious, especially after losing an entire mounted patrol, which must be rare enough."

"We have done it before, but only with many men," said Ottan's man, Engil.

"Your bow did it, Jestak," said Thro. "We cannot but acknowledge that."

"Maybe so, but I do not think you all should rely on the

Emeri bows for this fight. It is an untried weapon for you. I can show you the rudiments of its use tomorrow, but count on your spears instead. I imagine, though, that a first flight of arrows would soften them up, no matter how aimed, and it would be sure to make them keep their heads down. We are taught to get off the first shot and then aim with the second in a surprise. The Sentani never shoot unless they think they will hit something, but they are cooler than we, perhaps."

"Let us talk about it in the morning," said Thro. "It is time for some sleep." Touching Jestak's arm, he laughed lightly. "Ottan asked me how you would be in a fight. I imagine Reor will tell him."

"It is hard to lose Reor," said Jestak. "And the others."

Soon he could hear Thro's measured breathing, as the Shumai went to sleep as gently as a full baby, though a fight was just behind him and nine of his men newly buried. Jestak watched the fire turn into embers, then a slight blue smoke floating upward in the moonlight. He could not keep his mind off the Emeri, and seemed to see the patrol as children, with their mothers holding and nursing them, they tucking small heads in against their mothers' arms. Yet he was in it. They were not children anymore. Was this what had made the time of fire, this on a large scale? He felt a chill.

He thought of Saltstream, and of Oi the prophet, smiling at tea, his face all gentleness, and wondered what he would think, and what Aven, whom he called God, could think of this raid. Of course the enslavement of a people is wrong, and must be opposed. But could there be no better way? He had not resolved it when Ogta touched him. "Your watch," he said, and as Jestak got up, he took the warm spot the Pelbar had left.

In the morning the Emerta guards saw a lone horseman coming from the north, cantering easily but rapidly toward the city wall. From the highest tower of Emerta a gong struck. The city gate was opened to the horseman, who proved to be a cavalryman from Wildakibernipati, a small outpost to northeast.

The captain of the guard met him as he dismounted. "What is it, Tenoran?"

"Our east patrol of yesterday, Captain. They were due in before sunfall, but they never came. I waited until high night, took the eastern path, but never saw nor heard them. Then I came here to report, Captain."

"Perhaps they were chasing Shumai, Tenoran. It is getting to be the season of raids, Tenoran."

"Yes, perhaps, Captain. But the hunneran thought it best to send me on the route I followed and then report here, Captain."

"Yes, that is good, Tenoran. Report to the barracks and have some breakfast, then return. If nothing is heard from them today, or if you find that they have been in a fight, send a man tonight. We will warn the farmsteads now. They will not have any trouble with the Shumai. They always come yelling like madmen. Perhaps we can shackle a few to replace those who have died this winter, Tenoran."

"Thank you, Captain. It shall be done as you have ordered it, Captain," said the tenoran, saluting, hand up, palm flat, then leaving for his food. The captain watched him go, musing.

"Captain?" asked the young guard by him.

"Take this horse to be fed, watered, and stabled. Prepare the tackle on a fresh one for the tenoran, Experienti. A whole patrol is missing. This is something new on our own land. Perhaps there are a great number of them."

"What, Captain?"

"Nothing. Go now, Experienti," and he patted the young man's shoulder lightly, turning to report the matter to the guardcore.

The Krugistoran had barely awakened, and was still indulging himself in the caressing and washing of three young womanservants when Prestiginagi entered, marching stiffly, never looking at him, facing at right angles.

"I trust, Prestiginagi, this is some great emergency. Otherwise you would never enter so and endanger your back. My dear, now the towel. So, Prestiginagi?"

"Krugistoran, a tenoran has just ridden in from Wildaki-bernipati to say that an entire patrol on the eastern route never returned last night."

Instantly the fat man's demeanor changed. The women withdrew. He stood, flapping and swaying slightly, then moved to a bench. "How many men?"

"Fifteen, Krugistoran."

"When due?"

"By sunfall, Krugistoran."

"How long did he wait?"

"Till high night, Krugistoran. And then he rode on their route for some time before turning to come here, Krugistoran."

"How many quarters then?"

"Nearly three night quarters, Krugistoran."

"Is this precedented? Do they sometimes chase the Shumai eastward and so become benighted?"

"No, it is against orders, Krugistoran. They may follow a trail, but they always send two men to report, Krugistoran."

"Get the thousoran, Prestiginagi."

The old man spun away from the fat ruler and left rapidly, never having looked at him. The fat man took a heavy robe and put it on, and put his feet, with their heavy rings, into soft shoes, clapping once, so a young attendant came and laced them for him. He motioned her away. She had no more than disappeared behind a drape when the thousoran appeared, briskly, in the precise manner that Prestiginagi had.

"Look at me, Dependiandi."

"Yes, Krugistoran," replied the rigid man, spinning at attention to face his leader. He was middle-aged, but well preserved and well tanned.

"You have heard the report?"

"Yes, Krugistoran."

"What do you think?"

"I think there has been some Shumai contact, Krugistoran. We have already sent word of that to the farmsteads and outposts. It is the season for their nuisance raids, Krugistoran."

"You think that is enough, then?"

"Yes, Krugistoran, unless we may, as I have suggested, mount a full attack on them and clean out the whole of the western plains, Krugistoran."

"Pah. We have not the men for that. They move on the plains like cottonwood fluff ahead of us. The plains would eat us up. Besides, they are a source of labor. Are we to clear out our source of slaves? They even come to us, asking to be enslaved."

"If I may venture it, Krugistoran, they make indifferent slaves, quarrelsome and resentful. They are never trustworthy. Freedom is at the center of their system of values. I think we expend nearly the same labor in getting them to work that we would doing the work ourselves. And then we incur the danger of their presence among us and the resentment of their fellows on the plains, Krugistoran."

"And we gain the beauty of their best women," returned the other, eyes narrowing. "But what I think is that this is a new thing. We have never lost a patrol before, except well onto the plains. Therefore there is a reason. The Shumai have been thinking. They have come up with something new. We cannot defend against it unless we know what it is. Judging by their nature, I conjecture it may be the use of large forces. Therefore, please send word to the farmsteads and outposts to look out for large forces and defend themselves accordingly. However, this is merely a conjecture. I want you to see to it that we discover precisely what this new thing is. Now go."

"Yes, Krugistoran," said the thousoran, spinning as had Prestiginagi and leaving the room rapidly.

The Krugistoran clapped. Immediately his coterie returned. He pointed a fat forefinger at one. "Hot tea." Then, to Acco, "You stay. All of you go." They were troubled. Here was something different. But nonetheless, they left.

"Acco, tell me how likely it is that your people would band together in a large force to regain those we have rescued from their barbarity on our farms, Acco."

"They are not my people anymore, Krugistoran. You are, Krugistoran."

"Yes, yes. But what do you think of that possibility?"

"I do not know, Krugistoran. Perhaps they might do that, though I do not remember any tendency that would make it likely. But everyone changes, Krugistoran."

"Have they any principal weapons other than the spear, Acco? Could they have gained any from neighboring peoples?"

"You are their neighbors, Krugistoran. If they gained it, they would have gained it from you, Krugistoran."

He tossed his great arms. "Krugistoran, Krugistoran," he muttered. "Leave."

"Yes, Krugistoran," Acco said, bowing very low, turning, and running softly from the room. He watched her go, but did not see the slight smile on her face as she gained the drapery.

The Emeri patrolled widely, so there was still a good distance from the point of encounter to the farmsteads. But the Shumai walked, for stealth and wariness. Twice they saw small patrols, always on horse paths.

"They are warned," said Thro.

"Yes," said Jestak, "but of what? They are warned of a typical Shumai attack. So we must be sure that this is not one. This one has to be different. They must not be able to imagine what is going to happen."

"But not so different that we cannot execute it," said Thro.

It was past sunfall when they reached the eastern farmstead and lay high among the trees looking down on it. "There's a fat one," said Olor.

"What do you say, Jestak?" asked Thro.

"Perhaps we might do this: move through it tonight to the west side and see tomorrow if our people are there if we are unable to tell tonight. On our way, we will see what their defenses are. But we must not let them know we are there. I imagine this is the one you usually hit."

"Yes, as I am told."

"You see? It is the nearest. They probably expect you. And I conjecture that they may have moved the Shumai to some other location, probably the farthest west, so that if we do retake them, we then have to come back through all this to regain our territory. Is there any other way home?"

"We could go north, but that would take much time."

"Thro, I suggest this. Let us assume that they are in the westernmost farmstead. There are four large ones, are there not? Let us spy this one out on the way through, but go all night to reach the land around the western one, then watch it tomorrow and hit it tomorrow night. I would rather sweep around the north than fight my way back through. We will have others with us."

"What if you are wrong? What if they are all here?"

"Then we will learn that by watching and come back, farmstead by farmstead. We rested a day when Olor turned his ankle. This is worth such a day or two."

"Agreed," said Thro, and divided his forces for the move through the farmstead.

It was past high night when they met on the other side, well back up the far slope.

"What did you see, Enta?" said Thro.

"Not much. But there were a number of horses, so I assume their riders were there, too."

"Agana?"

"The same. I could not go close on the south because dogs were there. The whole farmstead was dark, though, with no lights even in the main house. I think they are expecting us."

"I did not hear any singing from the slave houses, or any games," said Olor.

"Perhaps the Emeri prevented it."

"If so, only because they expected us," said Stantu.

"Let us then move on to Ilet, the westernmost farmstead," said Thro. "If we arc north, we can run in this moonlight."

The Krugistoran was still up, though it was late. He was talking to a young cavalry tenoran.

"You found all the bodies, then."

"Yes, Krugistoran. All fifteen of them, Krugistoran."

"And the enemy?"

"They were gone, Krugistoran. We found fourteen graves. We dug one up and found a Shumai in it."

"Then the force was large. It took fourteen losses and still had men to bury them. What else?"

"There was a trail leading back east which we followed for some ayas, but it suddenly disappeared, Krugistoran."

"Have you no trackers?"

"Good ones, Krugistoran, but the Shumai can move like breezes when they want to, Krugistoran."

"With a loss of fourteen, they may have given up. There were no tracks leading on?"

"We found none, Krugistoran."

"But you then suspect some?"

"I do not know, Krugistoran, but we did warn the eastern people at Elonginikaniwaki, Krugistoran."

"Why is it," said the Krugistoran, "that the smaller the hamlet the bigger the name?" He threw his hands in the air, fat flopping. "I think I shall issue an order cutting all the names to no more than six letters. Have you anything else to report?"

"No, Krugistoran."

"Very well. Maintain the vigilance at Elonginikaniwaki. Have the slaves go out as usual. What is the matter?"

"The thousoran moved them all, Krugistoran."

"Where?"

"To Ilet, Krugistoran."

The hulk of the Krugistoran was very still for a long time. "Have the Shumai ever attacked Ilet?"

"No, Krugistoran."

"I do not like this at all. Well, go now."

"Yes, Krugistoran."

"Wait."

"Yes, Krugistoran?"

"How is Ilet defended? With all the slaves there, it should be well defended."

"The thousoran has doubled the garrison, Krugistoran. We have fires burning all night so that when the Shumai run across the open ground, if they come, we can drop them with arrows, Krugistoran."

"And what if they do not do that this time?"

"They are creatures of habit, Krugistoran. They have always done that, Krugistoran."

"But have they ever killed an entire patrol before, Tenoran?"

"No, Krugistoran."

"Then perhaps they have broken their habits. This gnaws on me. How were my men killed?"

"All were pierced, Krugistoran. No sign of an axe, Krugistoran."

"Spears, then."

"We think so, Krugistoran, though some of the wounds looked small for spears, Krugistoran."

"Arrows, then!"

"There was no sign of arrows, Krugistoran. But they did take all our bows and all the arrows, Krugistoran."

"Ah, now I have got the detail I need. I do not like this at all. Send in the guard-corps captain."

"Yes, Krugistoran," and bowing the tenoran walked rapidly out.

Soon, when the guard-corps captain arrived, bowing, the Krugistoran said, "I have given this anomalous attack much thought. I think that since Elonginikaniwaki has not been attacked, as is the habit, and the patrol was wiped out, as has not happened, and the bows were taken, as has never happened before, the plan may be to attack Emerta itself. Plan your guard accordingly."

"Emerta, Krugistoran? How could they do that, Krugistoran?"

The leader glared. "If I must explain. We see that new and effective elements are a part of their attack. We must assume that they have reached the logical conclusion. Where is the seat of their troubles? Here." He gestured a forefinger at his own rounded chest. "Here," he repeated. "Send out the word. Maintain the garrisons at the two eastern farmsteads, especially Elonginikaniwaki. But let us assume that the attack will be here."

"Yes, Krugistoran. May I ask, then, if there has been further evidence of Shumai presence after the encounter with the patrol, Krugistoran?"

"No, fool. I am taking that itself as evidence. This is something I feel. Now go. Do it."

"Yes, Krugistoran."

At Ilet, the small band lay above and west of the farmstead. It was broad day, and the Shumai slaves were already in the fields, shackled, working at hoeing the young rows of beans, while men on horses watched them.

"How many do you count?"

"Two hundred forty and more, Thro."

"Women?"

"I see seventeen. There is Maate, my cousin. The swine. She looks thin and weary."

"Yes. Well, you may comfort her soon. Tonight, perhaps. But off there behind that hill," returned Thro, gesturing northward.

"Do you see Tia, Stantu?" Jestak asked.

"Tia? No one fitting your description. No. She is not there, I think."

Escripti entered the richly brocaded but barricaded room of Tia. He was startled, and looked around. "Guard," he called. The man rushed in, dove under the bed, looked, and rushed to the window drapes, then turned and grinned sheepishly. Escripti turned.

Tia laughed. She was standing on the top of the door molding, bracing her arms up against the ceiling. "What is this, Tio? Come down this instant or I shall get the wet towels. The Krugistoran will never see their marks."

"Do that," said Tia, but she nonetheless leaned out, and leaped lightly toward the bed, landing with legs outstretched, splitting the whole thing down the middle.

The guard laughed. "Out, out, out," screamed Escripti—then, "No, him, him, him. Not you. Look, you barbarian, what you have done. That will come from my salary again. A perfect bed."

"What is wrong with your neck? Has Acco been standing on it again?" Then, turning to the guard, who was still staring in at the door, Tia pointed and added, "Out, lout, take your snout, go and pout."

"Stop, stop, stop, *stop*!" said Escripti. Then he sat unexpectedly on the floor and wept.

Tia sat cross-legged on the ruined bed. She bent over. "Escripti?" she asked.

He looked up. "Please, I beg you. You think it is funny, but do you not see I will die because of this? I will really die? There will be no help for it. The Krugistoran makes demands, and when they are not, cannot, be met, he is as cruel as a man can be."

"Crueler than stealing a person's freedom and trying to fatten her up to nurse a gigantic tub of sweat like him?"

"No, no, no. I am not a bad man. Please, do you not see what you are doing? I am begging you." Escripti began again to cry in an abject and disheveled heap.

Tia reached a leg down from the bed and gripped his hair with her toes, giving a yank. "Escripti? Where is your verve? You've lost your nerve. You'll never serve. I observe you've no reserve."

Escripti jumped up. "Stop. Is this all I have for teaching you the Emeri art of poetry? Lakes full of doggerel. You pervert everything you have learned from us."

"Here is a quandary. To pervert perversion. What does one get? Perhaps normality, Escripti. Surely you do not consider the culture of the great lard pot to be anything but perversion."

Escripti leaped at her with all the force of his aging and thin body, but only succeeded in splitting the bed further, for she had tumbled over its foot. He stopped again, head into the bedclothes, totally frustrated. "Tio, I beg you. If he hears you or of you calling him a lard pot, he will not be swerved even by your beauty from killing you for it. And it will not be an easy death."

"You just said it."

"I? What?"

Tia screamed her loudest, *"Lard pot!"*

Escripti did not react, but the guard put his head into the door.

"It is all right, Mr. Guard," said Tia, grandly. "He is not

trying to force me. I am intended for the lard pot." Escripti only rolled back off the bed and sat on the floor with his head in his hands. The guard disappeared quickly so as not to have heard officially. Soon he was followed by Escripti, who began to leave without a word more. But Tia blocked his way. "There is another way, Escripti. Get me out. Come with me. If you bring me to the Shumai, they will not hurt you."

Escripti put his hands over his ears and tried to get by. She held him with her tough Shumai hands. "I mean it, Escripti." She shook him. "If he kills me, you will not survive it. Do not think you will. You know what a great gut he is. You have no other choice. Where is your intellect? Think, man." He would not answer. She shook him lightly again.

"There is no life but what is here for me, and you have destroyed it."

"Not so. Please? Go and think about it." She kissed him on the cheek and pushed him out the door. He went without expression, and she turned and sat on the ruined bed for a long time, musing. Then she methodically began to do the exercises with which she had remained hard for her entire captivity, to the frustration of Escripti, whose job included softening the body and rounding the curves of his pupils.

Brin the Protector had her council about her in the judgment room. "But where will we get the men to do the work, Protector?" the eastcouncil asked. "We have drawn so many workmen from the orchards and crafts, and from gathering and mining, for what are less essential things, that we have had to weaken the guard."

The Protector frowned. "Less essential? What need of so many guards now? Are they essential? This is not a high-danger season."

"And yet there are Sentani about occasionally in the summer, and even a few passing Shumai, Protector."

The Protector sighed, then stood, throwing her arms up. "And can they climb these walls?" she asked grandly.

At that point, the guardcaptain appeared in the doorway, bowed, and stood.

"Yes? I do not recall requesting you."

"A petition, Protector."

"Which of the guard?"

"All of the guard, inside and outside, Protector."

"This," she said, addressing the council, "is what comes of giving men any authority."

"The signatures of all the guard, including the women, and the leader, the inside captain, are subscribed, Protector."

"I declare this meeting over," she returned, and pivoted to retire by her private door. It was barred by the person of the inside captain.

"The petition, Protector," said the inside captain, Appro.

"I will not receive it."

"You will receive it or eat it, Protector," came the level reply.

Brin the Brunag stopped, then turned, grandly, and took the petition.

"Wait," said the guardcaptain. "Know this before the whole council. The guard has determined that if you destroy this petition, or do other than read it to the council, we, the guard, will leave this city in a body, all of us, and go to Pelbarigan."

Brin was stunned. She sat, handing the petition to the eastcouncil, who began to read, "We, the entire guard of Northwall, in the light of recent events, request that the entire voting city refer themselves to the competency of their present Protector in a general election. Our concerns include the failure to maintain the platform trap by the river; the diversion of essential guard personnel to nonessential functions; the dilution of guard training; the refusal to recruit new guard personnel for training; the refusal to replace broken power bows with new ones; the—"

 XI

THE band had worked its way down close to the westernmost field, in which two dozen Shumai were hoeing beans, shackled.

"I have to get a closer look at those shackles," said Jes-

tak. "If we can get them off easily, we can free the whole
bunch. If they are hard steel, and thick, we will have to
leave with only a few, or all die here."

Thro scratched his beard. "We cannot leave with only a
few," he said.

"Yes," said Jestak. "Come, Thro, Stantu." The three
worked their way down to the edge of the field. "Come.
Down there."

"Why?"

"I think that is where the Emeri will let them go to re-
lieve themselves. There is an open place beyond. Escape
would be more difficult." They crawled and stooped down
into a narrow tongue of woods, a gully too steep to culti-
vate. After a time one of the Shumai called to a guard and
requested permission to go to the woods. He was allowed.

He had shuffled well into the trees when Thro called to
him in a whisper, "Shumai." The man turned, saw the
men, then casually kept going, getting behind a tree. They
worked their way over.

"How many men have you?" the man whispered.

"Not enough for a general attack. We will try to free
you tonight. We will have some plan. Here, let the Pelbar
look at your shackles. Be sure that everyone knows. Try to
sing or play games in the slave houses, but not so noisily
that anyone suspects. I am Thro. That is Stantu, and this is
Jestak the Pelbar."

"I am Irth. Good. Now I must go." They touched hands
lightly, and the man hobbled back to the field. They
watched him jerk his head lightly to the man next, and saw
them slowly hoe more closely together. The Emeri guard
was watching a high hawk and not paying attention to the
slow song they began. Nor did he notice occasional heads
begin to turn in their direction, then turn away again.

Back on the ridge, the three studied the setup of the
farmstead again.

"What of the shackles, Jestak?"

"They are soft iron. If there is a good shears in the
blacksmith shed, I can cut them quite quickly. So could
anyone. That is a lot of cutting, of course—more than five
hundred cuts for all of them, just to rid them of the links
so they can run. When we get to the mountains, we can
drive the pins out. We could do that here, but it may take
more time than we can afford in an attack. Of course, as

we free men, they can drive pins or cut shackles as well as handle weapons. Did no one see Tia?"

"No. Do you have a plan of attack?"

Jestak sketched on the ground. "Here are the slave houses. Here are the guard posts. Here are the horses. All this is open ground. They must expect that a typical Shumai attack will come across the open ground, judging by the way the posts are set up, and these barricades, and the bonfires. Look, though. Here is a drainage ditch."

"It will stink."

"Not like a dead body. Look. We can pick it up at the base of the south field and advance up it quite rapidly. We can enter their perimeter here. It is scarcely any problem. We must reach the horses first. Hatch, you are our only horseman. You must lead out a good horse. While we take these men from the back, on a signal, you must get the horse to the door and loop a heavy rope through the door bars. Two men must go with you to kill the door guards if there are any. They will make the signal so these guards are the first to go. Those on the inside will have to work on the bars with you and the horse. Then you must work on the next house, in this pattern. The freed men must then hold off these guards, there, and those of the next house must reinforce them. In that pattern we can work through the houses, and as we go down—for we will, we cannot help that—we will be reinforced by new men. Now—"

"Thro, Jestak, look there," said Olor. Five horsemen were cantering in from the south. Soon they entered the guard perimeter and slowed to a walk, stopping when met by the guardsmen already there. Those on the hill held very still. Far below, they saw the mounted leader swing his arm and point south. Plainly the other man was arguing with him. The man on the horse held out his arms in the Emeri gesture of resignation. The other looked angry, but spun and marched off to the center guardpost. Soon other men were coming out and moving toward the corral of horses.

"Aven, they are leaving," said Jestak.

"Maybe, it is a trap. Maybe they know we are here."

"Maybe. But I do not think so. It looked like a genuine argument to me. If they go, then our plan will have to shift."

"Why? Will it not work?"

"Now maybe we will be able to do the whole thing without killing anybody."

"What? Not kill the weasels? What for? No, Jestak, not that. Look what they have done. This is not a Pelbar dance."

Jestak squinted at him. "Well, Thro, I like you all, and I have observed that when people get in fights, some on both sides die. Which ones do you want to die among us?"

"That is cunning, Jes, but you know that is what every fighter accepts. Look. All are going but five. And then there are about twenty farm overseers. They do not look like fighting men."

Far below the luxurious rooms of the Krugistoran, a guard was strapped against a steel grating. Another man was plying the whip on his bare back. Two others stood at ease, one counting the strokes. The man on the grating grunted, then screamed aloud.

"Nine, enough," said the counter.

"The sentence was twelve," said the man with the whip.

"Do you like your work?" asked the other, drily.

"If the Krugistoran finds out this disobedience, you will get a hundred."

"Who will tell him? You?" said the second observer. "If you do, you may not like the consequences."

"This is treason."

"Look at his back. Do you know what he did? He turned his head when one of the Krugistoran's near-nude beauties went by."

"He never should have done that."

"Look at his back. Has he not paid?"

"Not the full amount."

The first man took out his sword. "This will be for giving him thirteen. Remember. There are more swords than this one, and you will never know whose will get you. Now. Take him down. And remember—mouth shut."

The two observers turned and left when the victim was laid out on the floor. The jailer looked, and then said to the other, "Now. I will give you the other three." He hesitated. Then he touched the whip three times to the man's back. "Now, the sentence has been carried out. I will get you the orderly."

* * *

All afternoon, small parties of Emeri soldiers rode in from the hills or marched on foot from nearby stations. "What do we need this many for?" one officer asked. "There could not be more than a couple of hundred of them at the outside—if they are coming, which I doubt. We have nearly seven hundred men here, practically the whole fighting force."

"We are protecting the seat of government," said the other. The first man flashed a look at him. He appeared to be serious.

"Yeah," said the first. "The seat of government. Quite a seat."

Prestiginagi found Tia standing on a table which she had pushed over near the high, barred window. She was straining to see. He coughed lightly. She turned. "Presti, what is it? What are you doing?"

"I? I am here to proceed with your studies, girl. Come down here. So you did break the bed. Escripti is nearly destroyed with you. You are going too far. I will order the wet towels for you."

"I?" she mocked. "I cannot go too far. I have decided—I—that I will have no part of the lard pot, and I do not fear consequences."

"They can be painful if he rejects you. Very. We are protecting you, you know."

"Wrong, Presti. You are protecting yourself. Perhaps in a former condition you would have been protecting me. I hear he has grown worse. Now he punishes his own people. That is where I have you. If I fall, you fall. And I am willing to fall because becoming another Acco is as painful as whips and fire, and it lacks self-respect."

Prestiginagi came to the table and looked up at her. "Escripti has told me what you said. Your alternative. That is dangerous talk. You near the breaking point." She put out her foot to pinch his nose, but he struck it away. "I am not Escripti, Tio. I have self-respect, too."

"You? Self-respect? And you serve him?"

"I am an Emer. What choice have I? Were you one, you would be glad to serve the Krugistoran."

"In the abstract, perhaps," she replied, leaning down and putting her hands on his shoulders to jump down. "But in person you know as well as I that he is a monster of self-indulgence. No people could possibly be proud to own him."

"Don't underestimate him. He is an extremely penetrating man."

"He couldn't penetrate his own suet—it is so thick. He has turned in onto himself so far that he doesn't even see his people and their needs. Why do you argue? You see that. Any fool would. Do not give me any official line of talk. I am not going to tell on you."

Prestiginagi did not answer but turned his back, hands clasped behind him. She ran in front of him and took his shoulders again. "You come, too. You must help me. I could never get out of here with only Escripti to help. And I can help you survive in the mountains."

"Do not try your charms on me," said Prestiganigi, taking her wrists to remove them. He found he could not. She was too strong and he too old.

"I am not trying to charm you. Who would want to? You are an old man anyway, and I am not yours or any man's. Well, I am owed, but I may never pay that debt. Never mind. Do you not see? You are the only sensible person anywhere around, and even you are so full of your parochialisms that you will not see clearly. Come. We do not have all the time in the earth." He said nothing. "What are all those men doing here? Protecting the lard pot against a fly or two?"

"If it concerns you, it is because some of your friends killed a patrol a while ago and are not yet eradicated." Tia shrieked lightly and leaped back up onto the table.

"The whole patrol? How many?"

Prestiginagi shook his head. "It is a new thing," he said. "It grows serious. Before long there may be a clash of major proportions."

She sat down. "How? The Shumai ask nothing but to be left alone. We never enslaved anyone. How can you call that just, with all your talk of law and justice? By the way, where is Operistiani? Have I learned enough law now? He has not been here lately."

"He is in prison."

"He? That dodderer? Why?"

"He defied the Krugistoran."

"He? He never defied anyone. Look at him. He chews his cud as he talks. Ah, I know. He reminded the lard pot of some point of law that said lard pot had heretofore and whereas violated. And the lard pot forthwith shut him up, because, to wit, said lard pot is law to himself, and is his own legislator, judge, and board of justice, having forgotten the former tradition of the Emeri, the light of the west."

Prestiginagi made no reply. "Then," she continued, "beware, Presti. If his guards are whipped, his legal advisor jailed, his army called in to protect him, where are you? You are only a strategist and advisor. I judge that you would not meet an invasion this way. Are you going to betray him by disagreeing? Where do you stand?"

"Or you, Tio. You are only a slave being trained for concubinage. You have not yet been fully healed of the shackle scars. Much worse could happen."

"Not me. It has already happened, Presti. You cannot hurt. I am beyond hurt. I have had the ultimate and am now proof to it. But you can help. Both me and yourself. Come . . ."

But he had turned and was leaving. "I see you are in no mood to learn now," he said at the door.

Once again Sima Pall sat in the seat of the Protector. The judgment hall was full. "I am gratified, but concerned," she was saying. "Pelbar society depends on the guard. Yet it cannot be controlled by the guard. If we grow, as we must, there must be checks here, just as you have put checks on the council by your petition."

"But Protector," said the captain of the inner guard.

"Yes?"

"Protector, the guard comes from every family in Northwall. We are not a separate or elite group. Our judgment reflects the judgment of all. And we did not force the issue any more than did Brin, who resisted the normal procedures of the law—as you did not when you lost office."

"Yes. That is what I meant when I said 'if we grow.' We cannot afford a separate group with its own interests. We must think this out carefully. I feel we cannot allow the Protector as much power as Brin showed us the Protector in reality has. I have been thinking, down in my damp room, and realizing that I, too, exercised an excessive power, though I never saw it until Brin used it in ways that seemed to me wrong."

"But Protector," said the captain of the inner guard again.

"Yes, Appro."

"Our defense, Protector, demands that quick decisions be made. They cannot be referred to the council."

"True, Appro. But many of these decisions affect our defense only very indirectly. They are economic matters. I think we need, when we have recovered our former balance, to convene a special council to study these matters out."

"Will you ask the advice of Pelbarigan, Protector, before changing our government?" asked the eastcouncil.

"I see no need of it. They have evolved away from the original model themselves and are steeped in factionalism. Perhaps our model will help bring them back to Pelbar harmony. Now we have work. Please remember that Brin is to be accorded all courtesy, and her backers, which will include some of you, as well. Now we must adjourn." All rose in a murmur of voices, and the room slowly emptied, except for Brin the Brunag and Sima Pall. They looked at each other in silence. Finally, the Protector said, "Let us part in love, Brin."

"You can say that because you won," returned Brin.

"Protector."

"If you must. Protector."

Esis was a farmer who had lived all his life at Ilet. He particularly loved horses and had always rejoiced in riding in the rich cold of the morning, especially in early spring, when the high flights of plovers went north, sending their sharp cries down through the clear air. Since the Krugistoran had instituted the slave policies, things had not been nearly so good. For nearly fifteen years now Ilet had had slaves for some time during the year, and there was always an edge of fear and danger in the air. Nor did Esis like oppressing people, and the Shumai, being quarrelsome and unwilling workers, had to be oppressed if they were to work hard enough to pay for their scant food and clothing. Secretly, he enjoyed them. They shared his love of freedom, and he was inwardly anguished at their condition. So were many of the farmers. But now that the Krugistoran had stationed guards, even the camaraderie that he had managed to approximate with the Shumai was hardly possible. He knew some of them, but under the hard conditions of farm slavery, they did not last long. That is, none except Veel.

Like Esis, Veel was rather an old man. He was gentle by

nature, and Esis had privately decided that he would at least take care of this man. He had managed it, and Veel had been at Ilet now, off and on, for the slaves were moved around, for nearly seven years. He understood well enough that Esis favored him, and he returned the feeling by various considerations, and by doing what he could to establish a bond between the white-haired farmer and the herd hunters, some of whom would have killed Esis if he got within reach of a shovel or hoe.

It was past nightfall. The Shumai were playing singing games in the slave houses. Esis thought this rather odd, though his easy nature did not make him ask why. He went to the southmost house and looked in at the barred door. "Hey. What is it? Hey. Better get some sleep. Plenty of beans for tomorrow."

Veel appeared at the bars. "We are hungry. That stew had no meat. Old potatoes mostly. Come on, Esis. There are new peaches. Give us some."

"We are lucky to send any to Emerta, the way you eat them when you pick them. No peaches."

"Come on, Esis. There are forty-five of us in here. How about ten peaches? That will be a bite each—if we give Ibem his the last." There was a protest from inside. "The Krugistoran can spare ten."

Esis grinned. "If I bring them, will you quiet down?"

"Yes, surely, by all means, Esis. We would be indeed very grateful, most grateful, as you say."

When Esis returned with a double armload of peaches, he went to the door and said, "Veel?"

"Here. Got them? Thanks very much. We will each do an extra row tomorrow, perhaps. And chop none off. A promise."

When Esis had finished handing in the fruit, he said, "I hope that is all."

"No," said a whisper by his ear. "Keep silent. Now, open the door."

"Who is this?"

He felt a knife in his back. "Open the door."

"I cannot. The guards have the keys."

"Do not kill him," said Veel, softly. "He is not the worst of them. Get the guardpost over there. If you are quiet, the others will not know."

At that moment, Olor appeared with the keys, fumbling through them.

"Here," said Esis. "That one. Let me go. I want no—"

"Quiet," said the voice by his ear.

The Shumai crowded to the door. Thro put his face to the bars, and said, "Keep playing, keep singing. You may have alarmed the rest already. The door is free but we have five more houses. Jestak is coming in to work on the shackles."

They could hardly be contained, but Thro insisted. Jestak slipped in. "What is he?" said a voice.

"Blue snakes, a Pelbar!" said another.

"Sing, for Aven, sing," said Jestak, "and clap in time, but not hard." Jestak knocked pins from the shackles in time with the clapping, moving in the dark with fumbling unsureness. "Here, you," he said. "Line the others up. I want to move through without hesitation." They caught on, and Veel arranged them in rows.

Before he was half through, Thro looked in the door again. "How many are free? Never mind. All free men come quietly." A number of men left so quietly that the straw on the floor rustled only a little. "Here, three of you . . ." Jestak heard, but then they were all gone.

Jestak was tiring, but there were fewer now. Veel, according to instructions, held the freed men by the door until Thro called. As he worked, Jestak asked one man, "Do you know Tia?"

"Who?"

"Tia."

"No."

But the next man said, "She is not here. She was taken to Emerta for the Krugistoran. The bastard." Jestak's heart jumped, but he kept working. He said nothing more, but his eyes smarted.

Finally he was done, and all went outside, though they stayed by the wall until Igka came back. "Jestak, Jestak," he called.

"Here."

"Come to the next house. You all. We are going to try to get out of here without awakening anyone."

"Kill them," said a voice in the dark.

"No. We need to get north. Some are weak. We need all the start we can get. The soldiers are at Emerta, but they can follow fast enough on horses. Do what you are told. No fires, no killing. Can any of you ride?"

"Yes," said several voices.

Another said, "Polla. She is in that house with the farmers."

Igka looked. "Stay here," he said, and left.

Later he got to Thro and told him. "That one?" asked Thro. "Then we will kill the men in there, but with absolute silence. How many?"

"Five," said one of the freed men.

Olor reappeared. "The guards are dead," he said.

Thro explained the situation to him. "Take ten men," he said. "You must be perfectly quiet. If one escapes, that gives us less time to reach the mountains."

"But Veel, take us all," Esis was saying. "The Krugistoran will only have us killed for letting you escape."

"I have no say," replied Veel. "I will ask him, the leader. They call him Thro."

Thro was busy, but to get rid of Veel, he agreed. "Let him come. The others will have to get away themselves."

Esis was disappointed, but Veel said, "Let it go. They will have to hide. Most of them are worth only killing. I am with you, and remember, I will have to kill you, too, if you try anything."

Esis was crying quietly. "I will do nothing," he said. "I am only a farmer." The two old men went off together to where the others were gathering to the north beyond all the houses.

It was afternoon before a mounted soldier cantered into the south field of Ilet. He stopped his horse and looked. No one was in sight. He flicked out his sword and moved forward at a trot, then a walk. Still nothing. The slave houses were open, and reaching the south guardpost, he glanced in the open door. He saw an arm and blood. Then he turned and galloped back in the direction of Emerta.

The thousoran strode into the Krugistoran's chamber, finding him sitting in a wide chair, with no attendants anywhere.

"Yes?"

"Krugistoran, the slaves have all escaped from Ilet. Sometime last night, Krugistoran."

"What? Where was the guard?"

"All dead, Krugistoran. Most of them were here, at your request, Krugistoran."

"The farmers, too?"

"No, Krugistoran. They are gone. Except for one house. *They* are killed. They were in with a woman. May we pursue, Krugistoran?"

"Send fifty mounted men. It may be a feint. So they took the farmers."

"It would appear by the tracks, it is reported, Krugistoran, that the farmers fled by themselves westward. The Shumai did not kill them, Krugistoran."

"They fled? They were driven, you mean."

"No, Krugistoran. The Shumai went north. It would appear, as you have said, that they are thinking in a wholly different manner, Krugistoran."

"The farmers fled, you say, rather than sending the alarm?"

"I imagine, Krugistoran, that they feared that you would have them killed for allowing the escape, Krugistoran."

The Krugistoran heaved himself to his feet. "You imagine? You imagine treason. Is that what you would have done? They were obviously driven. You will send a force west to retake the farmers. Ten men in addition to the fifty."

The thousoran bowed low. "Krugistoran?"

"Go."

The thousoran turned, then turned back. "Krugistoran, there are about two hundred and fifty slaves, in addition to those that freed them. May we not have more men? With fifty we will have little chance, Krugistoran."

"Guards," shouted the gross leader, sinking back to his chair. As they came running, he pointed a heavy hand at the thousoran. "Take him, take him. He wishes to leave the seat of government defenseless when this may be only a feint. Fifty strokes, one for each man. Send me Ertat. He will lead. What? Are you hesitating?"

"No, Krugistoran," said a guard, bowing low. They led the thousoran out, their heels clicking smartly on the polished stone.

The Shumai were not making good headway northward. The freed people had been so long in shackles and so poorly treated that some could not run at all and had trouble keeping up a fast walk in the rugged forest.

"Perhaps we should turn eastward," said Stantu. Jestak said nothing. "What is the matter? Oh. It is Tia. Yes, we must . . . I hear she is in Emerta with the Krugistoran, Jestak. You must forget her. You cannot—"

"I am going to get her."

"Alone? When? I will come. We will die, you know—or become the first slaves of the new lot."

"You stay. You have found Anset, and he needs help. No man should leave family for me and my ideas."

"You stay, too. It is too late for her, Jes."

"I have come too far now, Stantu. Besides, it seems right. I mean no one harm. How could I turn back now?"

"You can't, I suppose."

"Thro," Jestak called, and loped up to the leader, who waited. "Have you been here before?"

"No, never, but some have. Here, what do you want to know? Ask Pilon."

"It is this. If we are being followed by a large number of horsemen, then we need to get them into some place where they have to spread out, preferably in single file. If we can find a stream in a ravine, especially a steep one, we can make a dam trap."

"Do you know a place like that, Pilon?"

The stooped former slave eyed Jestak suspiciously. "It is all right," said Thro. "It was his plan that saved you. Did you not see him knock your own shackles off?"

"There is a place like that," said Pilon. "But we must bear west from here, farther from home."

"Have you been there?"

"Yes, where the water comes down from the mountain. You cannot see it now. We had to carry ice from there in summer several years ago, to cool drinks for the Krugistoran."

"No ice storage?" said Jestak. "Huh. How far, Pilon?"

"From here about ten ayas. It is hard walking, though. I would rather turn east."

"They will patrol that. They may send their whole army against us," said Thro.

"Then this is the way. We had better turn here before we get any higher."

Thro called the signal to halt. He then explained to all what they were doing. There was a murmur of disagreement from many, who were eager to get home. But then one young man, Idia, said loudly, "That is all right, Thro. There are many goats up there we can hunt."

"Come," said Thro. "Let us move some legs." All fell slowly into line.

Prestiginagi stood by the window of his room in the palace gazing out at the soldiers standing outside the walls. They were idling, hardly working at the extra fortifications the Krugistoran had called for. It was plain they did not see the point. He heard a slight sound behind him, as a young guard entered the room unannounced.

"Uncle," he said. "Forgive me. The thousoran, Acetorani, is dead."

"Dead? How?"

"He could not sustain the fifty strokes given him for disagreeing with the Krugistoran." Prestiginagi shook his head. "Uncle, I fear to say it, but I think you should leave Emerta. I will come with you. He will try to throw this whole foolish business onto you. There was only a small band. They are not coming here. They were after slaves, as usual, and we as well as handed them over when we pulled all the soldiers in here. There are fifty horsemen following them, and ten following the farmers who fled west into the mountains."

"The farmers fled? Were they afraid of punishment, too? And the Shumai did not kill them?"

"The Shumai killed all who were in a house with one of their women. The others they did not touch. The farmers were probably afraid. That is what the thousoran suggested to the Krugistoran. Then he asked for more than fifty men to follow the fugitives. After all, there are over two hundred slaves alone. That is when the Krugistoran ordered that he be whipped."

"It is truly terrible. He was the best commander we have had in some years and a good man."

"Remember Operistiani, too, Uncle. Come. We must get you away before it is too late for you, especially if the Shumai wipe out the mounted men."

"Well they might, Noti. I hardly know how I can do what you suggest. It is so unlike my whole character. But even the girl, Tia, suggested it yesterday, and offered to help me to survive in the mountains."

"Good. Then we must bring her. Come." He tugged the old man's arm. "Come. Do not delay."

Prestiginagi thought a long moment. He started to

speak, then hesitated. "If we bring Tia, we will have to bring Escripti as well. All right. I will come."

The door to the jail section rasped open, and the jailer idly looked up from cleaning his whip. "Yes?" he said. "What now? No, no!" He slashed out with the whip, only to find it sliced off three spans from the handle. He turned to run, and took three steps before the sword bit into the side of his neck, and he fell with only a murmur.

The horsemen could not trot in the moutains, but they kept up a brisk walk. "Look," the lead scout said. "They have turned west. What a trail. They surely cannot hope to evade us. They do not even know the area. Look how some are dragging."

"Some of them know the land," said the hunneran. "Some have been sent up there to get snow and ice for the Krugistoran's summer drinks."

"Ice for his drinks?" smiled the scout.

"Enough. You follow the tracks." They turned their horses and began walking westward.

The Krugistoran remained unreconciled. No amount of soothing could now mollify him. Acco watched him warily, and seemed to him not to respond to his wishes as she had. He thought it was fear, and smiled to himself that perhaps that was a good thing after all. He wanted grapes, but even in the south grapes were not yet in season. He would soon send horsemen to inquire, but perhaps not now when the defense of Emerta was of utmost importance. Then he could plan a wholesale attack on the Shumai to recover slaves. It might be costly. But it could be done. He saw how he could play on the ambitions of the hunneran, Hist. He heard footsteps coming to the great doors, and so composed his face toward the window, with a heavy-lidded expression. He liked to see them request notice. It was a tenoran of his inner guard who marched smartly across the floor and stood, then bowed, and said, "Krugistoran?"

"Well?"

"The jailer has been killed, Krugistoran."

"Killed? How?" He stood, his jaws trembling with anger. "A sword, Krugistoran."

The Krugistoran reeled in his anger. This was the first

open defiance of him. He would deal with it so harshly that no one would think again of even quibbling with him. Had he not proven himself in the reorganization of Emeri society? How could they question his abilities and judgment? "Some accomplice of the traitorous thousoran. Give him twenty more."

"He is dead, also, Krugistoran."

"Dead? How?"

"Of the beating, Krugistoran."

"Well, do not just stand there. Dead or not, I expect my orders to be carried out—unless you want his whipping."

"You mean, the body, Krugistoran?"

"That was plain enough. Can you not understand? Now, out! I have the defense of Emerta to think about."

The tenoran fled. When the doors closed behind him, he said to the two men in attendance, "He wants the dead body of the thousoran given twenty more lashes." They looked at each other.

Jestak was making a model with large twigs. "See? Like this. Here is the key log, which holds the whole weight of water. It will hold, unless this pry is applied here. Then the whole thing will give way. This looks like a good place, with all this down timber. We need to dig across there, bring timber, bring plenty of branches to lay in this cribbing to hold water and build a pool."

"The men are tired as spring cattle, Jes," said Stantu.

"I, too. But we must do it. It is better than fighting mounted men with this infirmary," he said, gesturing at the exhausted Shumai.

There was a shout from far up the hill. "Olor is bringing a deer," said Igka. Many stood back up and looked.

"A fire. Here, make a fire," said Veel. The tired people began to rouse.

"We will get the timber," said a young Shumai with ankles still raw from the shackles. "Come on, up, up. You, too, Esis. We want to see a little work out of you. There now, how did you do it? Like this?" And he kicked the old Emer into the dirt.

"I never did that," said Esis from the ground, amid general laughter. "But I will help." He got up and kept out of everyone's way.

Prestiginagi opened the small door in the wall softly. Several soldiers were outside, but they only turned idly when he and Escripti appeared with two guards. "Huh," said one. "They are taking on guards young now." But then they went back to their gambling. The four walked purposefully out into the city, turning down a side street toward the west wall, eventually dodging into a low house.

The larger guard emerged and continued. Soon he returned, entered, and said, "There are no horses, Uncle. They are all commandeered for the defense. The defense against clouds and smoke."

"No matter of that," said Prestiginagi. "We are committed now. We must walk, then. We will never be safe here. The woods westward are the safest. If necessary, we can make our way north. They will look for Tio in the east. If we get there, we will have to go around northward."

"If we get there?" said Tia. "If? I fully intend to go, even if I go myself."

"You do as you are told," said Noti.

"Stick your arm in your ear," said Tia.

"Please," said Escripti. "Let us do our arguing somewhere else."

The group left the house again and walked smartly to the west gate. Here Noti gave papers to the guardsmen and saluted, then the four continued out the gate beyond the town, making their way toward the hamlet of Ammusini. A freckled guardsman said, "That young one would make a good woman. Look at that behind." They laughed and idly watched the four out of sight around a bend in the road.

The guards had learned the fate of the thousoran, news of which spread through the soldiers across Emerta like a mist. When their watch was nearly over, two horsemen appeared, shouting, "Prestiginagi! Have you seen him? He is with his nephew and perhaps a girl. Were they here?"

"Here?" said the oldest. "No. We have not seen them. Only soldiers and a few old women." The guards looked at each other and held arms out. The horsemen turned and galloped away toward the north gate. The oldest guard looked at the others and said, "I trust none of you wants to slit your own throats."

"We must tell him about Prestiginagi."

"You tell him."

"Me? You outrank me."

"Correct. Therefore I am ordering you."

"Perhaps we could get Acco to tell him."

"She? Where is she? You do it."

"I will, on one condition. If he decides to flog me, let me escape, too."

"Then I would get it."

"No. You come, too. This cannot last. He is offending everyone. Where is his base of power when he punishes the army and his guard? Who is left for him?"

"We will see. Now. You tell him."

"How is it holding water?"

"It is good, Jestak. Look how it fills up."

"There. Put the two braces there. We do not want it to go before they get in position. Thro, do you think we should send most of the people farther on, so if it fails, they can get away?"

"No," said Hongu, an older man. "We have gone far enough. Look. We have spears now. We will have two apiece by morning. We will stay."

"They stay," said Thro.

Across three rises, about five ayas eastward, the Emeri horsemen lost the trail in the dark. "Here," said the scout. "Here is a good place to camp for the night. We will pick it up easily enough in the morning. We are plainly getting closer."

The Krugistoran awoke, but it was still dark. The lamp against the far wall had gone out. He reached out a foot. Where was Acco? Rolling his bulk over the edge of his bed, he bellowed, "Guard! Guard!" There was no answer. He walked across the room, swaying in the dark. Reaching out, he punched at the doors, expecting them to clang aside and reveal sleeping guards. He would show them. The doors would not move. He put his shoulder against them and shoved. They gave a little. Backing up, he ran three steps at them, then plowed his massive shoulder against them. They burst open, projecting him into an empty corridor. "Guards, guards!" he shouted again. Soon he heard running. A tenoran and three soldiers appeared. "Where are the guards?"

The tenoran put out his arms. "I do not know, Krugisto-ran."

"Find them. Find them now, or it will go hard with you. Leave two men to guard the doors. Now go."

"You and you," said the tenoran. The two stood by the sides of the great doors at attention, while the tenoran and the other man ran away down the hall. Breathing heavily, the Krugistoran heaved himself back into the room.

He turned. "Shut the doors, louts!" he shouted. The doors shut behind him. Before he had reached his bed again, the two left behind had walked quietly away.

The scout led the horsemen into a gorge. "You see," he said. "They came up here and are following this gorge up into the mountain."

"When?"

"Last night. They must be hoping to get across the pass into Atten country. Fools. They must have rested. We will catch up with them today. They cannot be too far. You can see where the slaves have been dragging and falling."

The hunneran looked up the gorge. He had little stomach for what he was commanded to do—chase down a bunch of scarecrows, led by wild Shumai, here in the high mountains where the horses could not move. "Look sharp to your weapons, men," he said over his shoulder. By the first half-quarter of the sun they were well up the gorge. The sides were steep and the men growing uneasy. Ahead there was a long, quavering shout. The scout stopped, holding up his hand. Then there was a strange, distant rushing sound, growing into a rumble.

"Weapons ready," shouted the hunneran. "Odds, take swords, dismount. Evens, nock your arrows." Then he turned and saw a tower of rushing water rounding the curve of the gorge ahead. A man screamed and ran for the steep bank.

In a few minutes, the whole body of the Shumai stood above on the hillside, looking down.

"There were only fifty," said Olor. "Why? Were they so confident?"

"I don't know," said Thro. "Let us go home. Jestak?"

"You go. I am going to find Tia." Thro started to dissuade him, then decided against it. Jestak and Thro exchanged the formal Shumai good-bye, then Thro gave the Pelbar a family embrace, after which Stantu also embraced him briefly.

"Good trip," he said. "We will see you at Ottan's. If we have to move camp, or start east, we will leave some sign—an Innanigani road marker. That would puzzle an Emeri patrol."

Jestak laughed. Then he turned and started off southward at a slow Sentani trot. Thro watched him go. "We will see you at Ottan's. Huh. Well, perhaps so. Look there," he added, pointing down at the ruined gorge.

To the south and west the tenoran blew his horn again and again. As the nine horsemen came in, they all had the same answer. No farmers. They had scattered, and knowing the country, had vanished into it.

"What now, Tenoran?"

"I do not know. The farmers fled because they feared the Krugistoran. If we fail, what then?"

"I will go out again," said one man.

"No," returned the tenoran. "If we flee, let us flee together. Let us turn north to the primitives. We will not have that long to wait. This sort of oppression cannot continue forever. How many are with me?"

Six agreed. The others, fearing for their families, decided to return. "You must tell them that we took your weapons and tricked you when you were asleep," said the tenoran. "Perhaps your punishment will be lighter because we have been so treacherous."

"I am not counting on that," said one. "I am getting my family and leaving."

It was late that evening. Watchfires flickered around the city, especially on the north and east, and soldiers idled around them. From the distance some could hear the faint clumping of horse hooves.

"Quiet there," said one to some soldiers at a game. "Listen."

They paused a moment, turned to their game again, then heard it themselves and stood. Soon a single man cantered into the firelight by the main gate. His horse was lathered and weary. The hunneran was called, and came out to the man, who had dismounted and was leaning on the horse in a circle of soldiers.

"Yes?" said the hunneran.

The man never came to attention. He said, softly, "Hunneran. They are all lost. I alone am escaped."

"Who, man? Who? Not the whole fifty under Utteri."

The rider nodded. "It was water, in a gorge. We were tracking them up a gorge far to the north, on the eastern slopes of Taffinani Mountain. They must have picked it with great care, as we could follow them only there, and the slopes were steep. I was behind the rest because a stone had lodged in my mount's left foreshoe, and I was getting it out. That is why I am still here. They never saw me. I was gone by the time they got down the mountain."

"A large force?"

"No, Hunneran, only a few and the slaves."

The new thousoran, now that Acetorani was dead, had strode up and heard the last part of the report. "Have you seen any sign of the invasion we are preparing for? Did you ride alone directly here?"

"I saw no invasion. Yes, Thousoran, I came directly here. Had we two hundred men—"

"Never mind that. You have done well. Go and get some food. Here, you, take the horse. Iamigi, assist this man. He is tired." As the rider walked out of the firelight, Thousoran Eadini turned to the hunneran and said, softly, "The men are deserting. Prestiginagi, Escripti, and the Shumai girl, Tio, are gone. No one can even find the concubine, Acco. We must put a stop to this. Will you back me?"

"Willingly. Between you and me, we are long overdue for a new Krugistoran."

"That is a big step. But I agree. Who?"

"You. Or Prestiginagi, if we can find him."

"Not me, Aptani, not me. I am a military man. Then Prestiginagi. Aptani, call your men. Let us assemble here and feel out the army. I think they are with us, and will be even more when we tell them of the disaster which befell the cavalry in the north. Now go, and I will see that this place is prepared for my speech."

The Krugistoran could not lull himself to sleep, even with beer, which he had laced with sleepweed. He would let the situation go until morning. Then things would be righted. What had gone wrong? His old habits of power had become stupefied. Even he had realized that, but somehow he had always put off the consolidation of power. He saw now how he should have done it. He had relied on the Emeri habit of loyalty, but he should have built a system of informers so it would have been backed up by fear.

The light from the windows was brighter now, though it was far from morning. He could hear shouts far off below. Rolling to his feet, he groped to the window. It seemed that the whole army was gathered before fires at the main gate. Who was that on the plank table addressing them? Good Alliki, it was Eadini. He would see to the traitor in the morning. No, now. He would find his robe of office and go down to confront them all. Now, where was it? He had not robed himself without help for years. They brought it from that room there. Feeling his way, the Krugistoran fell over a stool, very heavily, and lay breathing there for a time, rubbing his shin. He would have to remember to have even the servant girls' stools upholstered.

Again a shout from outside. Another. Good Alliki, they were going to overthrow him. He would barricade the door. He crawled toward it, then stood, found the oak bar, and slipped it into place. Now the windows. He had seen that his room was impregnable, and, if necessary, he would slip out the hidden door behind his couch. A fear flickered across his mind. No. He had not used it in years. It was narrow—far too narrow for him now. Well, he would meet them armed and robed.

As the shouts continued, the Krugistoran prepared himself. He even lit three lamps, so when they finally battered down the door, he would be sitting, sword in hand, to meet them as a leader and a man should.

Below, Eadini was finishing his speech. "Finally, as to our present Krugistoran. Let us not kill him. From the unanimity among us, I think he can safely be ignored. Completely ignored. He will never gain power again. No one owes him anything. He served us well in the old days, before he changed. Let him go. Let us then return to our own homes and villages, set the guard, and find Prestiginagi. He has the experience and the selflessness to put things right again. Perhaps, and I hope it, he will leave this foolishness about enslaving the wildmen. It has never been effective, and it has turned Emerta and the farmsteads into armed camps. Perhaps we can arrange a truce with the Shumai. They seldom raid this way by themselves. The herds avoid the mountains. The Shumai have learned military strategy in some way. We would do well not to encourage its use, because if they ever were to gather their people from across the plains, we, with our few numbers, would never stop them. But that is for Prestiginagi. Do you agree?"

A general cheer rang out. It was heard by the Krugistoran in his chamber. He took it as a signal for the general rush to kill him, and so steeled himself. But no rush came. He continued to sit there for the rest of the night, slowly growing sleepy, as the fires died outside and the noises of departure ceased.

Sparrows began to chirp on the ledges outside his windows, and the light grew. The Krugistoran grew hungry. Again he went to the window. Outside it looked like an ordinary dawn. The early risers were on their way to the gardens, tools on their shoulders. Only a few soldiers remained at the main gate. He could hear no noises in the palace. Going to the door, he unbarred it and walked out into the principal hallway. No one. He continued downstairs. Still no one. The palace was deserted. He was enraged, but knew now how powerless he was. He would confront them in due time. But he knew where the kitchen was, and would first get something to eat. He could manage that by himself.

 XII

JESTAK was weary with running southward in the mountains, watching for Emeri, trying to keep moving even though he had had little rest since the preparations for the raid on Ilet. By evening, though, he knew he would have to stop. Two rabbits swung on his belt, for he still had his short Pelbar bow, and he found a sheltered place among the granite rocks and built a small fire to cook his game.

There was a lot of meat, but he finished it all. Yet he was too tired to be sleepy, utterly bone-weary, and so he lay at ease in his fur roll watching the embers lose their power to temper the chill mountain air. It was a time of strangeness, even more strange than his periods alone on the eastward journey. So much had happened. He had succeeded in finding a place among the Shumai, as he had among the Sentani. In fact, here he had a much greater importance. Although Thro had been the leader of the expedition, Jestak had supplied the ideas. And the whole thing would have collapsed at that first encounter with the patrol had it not been for Jestak's bow.

As he lay back and watched the stars, he thought of the Shumai games at Black Bull Island. Perhaps they were playing them now, gleefully shouting star after star, weaving a pattern more complex with each move. Jestak felt alone.

"When alone," they said at Saltstream, "pray." For what? Could he pray for Tia? Was that not a personal prayer? What was it about Tia, whom he had seen for so short a time? She was dark for a Shumai, and reminded him of Arthil, the young prophet, who had sensed Jestak's growing attraction, and had said, "One must separate the demands of the species, which are not always in one's real interests, from those of God, which are. The species, even that within, tells one what it wants, namely its continuity, at the cost of any or all human happiness and progress. When the voice of the species speaks within, it speaks with strong words. But they weaken when one recognizes what it is that is speaking. Then one may set aside those words, and ask what has God to say about that?"

"How can one tell?" Jestak had asked.

"It is often hard," she had replied. "But one may line up the qualities one knows are Godlike, and compare to them what one wants. Then one seems to hear, in silence, the voice of God telling him what His nature would say about a situation."

"That seems very difficult. There are so few like you," Jestak had replied.

"That," she had said, smiling, "is a mixed voice. There are many, and you will find one. Perhaps between you and me there are indeed some of the requisites for happiness. But you are even now preparing to leave, to go home, to satisfy those distant ones who are wondering about you and what you have done. You could not stay here. So there is no rightness there, is there?"

"I could come back."

"The water in the stream never comes back. When the fish, who have swum away as tiny ones, finally return from their travels to lay their eggs, they are different. They are tired with all their life and have come to die. You must lift your intentions above all that, Jestak. Put it on a plane above the intellectual, put it on a metaphysical plane. Then you may give forever, because you are not giving of yourself, but only of the qualities that pour out from God forever. Perhaps you will find a right woman, but it will be another manner of giving for you, a radiance of goodness, not a craving and needing, a wanting and not having, and having to have, then having to have again and again, until one is so fattened with having that he has wholly forgotten the habit of giving, the good of giving, the glory of giving, and the ease of giving."

Jestak had sighed. "The ease of giving," he had replied. "The ease of giving is hard."

She had laughed and patted his arm. Then she had said, "Then you must be in silence in your thoughts until the hardness becomes easy because you have united your sense of how things should be with God's. Searching for happiness among humans only, one is always disappointed. The merging of that human life with whatever one understands of God amounts to the bringing of goodness to the life of the earth."

He had said nothing. Now he wondered what that had to do with his recent experience. It seemed like nothing but murderousness. And yet he knew that the cause itself was a just one. The giving of freedom is a good thing, is it not? What of the killing of the guards and the cavalry? That was not a good thing. But they had, after all, allied themselves to a force of oppression. Of course, they had not seen it that way. Given the society into which they were born, they had little chance for another view.

Jestak had seen raccoons and badgers so defend themselves that prairie wolves and wild dogs had eventually left them unmolested, even though the predators had all the advantage in a fight. Perhaps the small western bands of Ottan and his like could now be like that. It would be too costly for the Emeri to attack them, so perhaps they would leave them alone. That would be a good thing. Comparatively good.

"The merging of all these separate peoples into one people, without divisions, without cruelties, is a great thing."

So Arthil had said. If she were right, he had had some small part in that, so that good had come at least.

But now what of Tia? She the concubine of the Krugistoran? So the slaves had said. She was clearly loved by them, and yet Jestak sensed that none of them would ever accept her on equal terms again, unless the circumstances were very unusual, or only after a long, long time. She would be tested in the fire. He himself felt loathing for the whole thing. But it was a force, like the stream he had reached into and pulled her from, that she had nothing to do with. Would he not reach in again? He had had help then. Perhaps he would have it now. He would pray for that help. Aven had led him this far. His rescue of Tia could be seen in the light of a further purpose. She looked like Arthil, even. That was strange enough. That, he smiled to himself, is the species getting in its word. Well, he was of the species, was he not? Surely the world needed more men.

"But not you, Jestak. You are different. You are more than the average man. You have already proved that and will have to accept the burden of continuing to prove it, though you will find it less of a burden and more of a joy as you work at it." Arthil had said that, too. Arthil. Go away, Arthil, he thought. It was easy to think such things on a mountain in the middle of the ocean. I have sleep to think about, and Tia, and the foolishness of this whole venture, and the sharpness of my arrow points. "And praying about it," said the Arthil inside him. Or was it Arthil? Was it rather what she had taught him in that short time? Or what Adai had taught him, and Arley, and the Pelbarigan worship classes?.

No. How could it be? This was all too far from that. His recent actions lay in another world. Arley would have said, "Think about it as Aven would think about it, bringing good without harm, protecting oneself to bring more good. Oppression is not good, and the oppressors have placed themselves on the side opposite that of human fulfillment— except in their own warped view of things. Therefore they should be opposed." But is it that easy?

When finally he grew drowsy, he found himself praying, trying to resolve the complexities of the situation seen close. Then he slowly fell asleep, his slight breath lost in the insect sounds of the cool summer night in the mountains.

So Annut had said, it you were right, he had said some
small part in that, so that pnud had come at least.
But now what of Tisu Like the concubine of the Kneigis-
toran? So the slave had said. She was clearly loved by
them, and yet Jestak also felt none of the haracid eye

◪ XIII

WHEN Jestak awoke, the thoughts of the previous
night seemed very dim. He tried to recall them, but then
the clear morning air sharpened his sense of danger and
wariness so that that was all he could think of. He prepared to run south again, wishing he had saved a little of
the rabbit. Then he resigned himself to his task, and began
a slow trot along the shoulder of the high ground. Sometimes he slowed to a walk. He had to think, to watch, and
he was still strained with fatigue.

At that time, the Krugistoran finally opened the palace
door, the side kitchen entrance, a little bit. People were
outside, going about their business. He stepped out into the
street and walked to confront the soldiers at the gate. They
stepped around the corner and were gone when he had
finally panted his way that far. He shouted. A few heads
turned, and he heard one laugh. A man was coming down
the road pushing a cart loaded with stones. The Krugistoran stood in his way. The man calmly tried to go around
him. The Krugistoran moved over in front of him. The
man stopped, looked at him, then set the cart down and
walked back up the street. The Krugistoran stiffened, then
took a stone from the cart and threw it at the man's back,
but it went wide. He tipped the cart over, scattering the
stones, but the man continued to walk. The Krugistoran
screamed at him.

"Lippini," said a familiar voice behind him. No one had
called the Krugistoran that for many years. He turned
around slowly. It was Acco, in a plain farm dress, with a
bundle. "Lippini, they have told me that there are some
empty slave houses at Ilet, and that we may live and work
there undisturbed."

"Slave houses!" he bellowed.

"Don't shout," she said quietly. "It is all over. You had

better do what they say, or I will go on without you. I am not very popular here, as you may imagine, though I cannot say my fate has been my doing, entirely. You must be happy with your life."

"I will never go," said Lippini, breathing hard from his round, florid face.

"Then I will go alone," said Acco. She started up the road.

Lippini watched her go, then said "Wait, wait," and followed her, slowly and ponderously, to where she regarded him with a level and unsmiling look.

Tia and the others had been turned northward because snow remained deep in the higher country. This Prestiginagi resisted, but finally realized that the only refuge he could be at all sure of was among the primitives in the north, the Forman villagers. He kept an eye on Tia, and instructed his nephew not to let her go. And yet they all relied on her. She sat on any rock with the same comfort that she had on her table below the high window, in a room softened by the crafts of the best Emeri working people. She caught trout and snared a rabbit. Unused to a bow, she was unable to bring down any game with it, but she had led the guardsman to a den of coneys as if she had a map.

The previous evening she had amazed Prestiginagi with her knowledge of astronomy, and only laughed at him when he tried to contradict her. Then, by the light of the small fire, she had diagrammed for him the movements of the wandering bodies with a natural insight and precision of detail that he recognized as far beyond any knowledge the Emeri had. She had shown them how to sleep together in the cool night, being careful to place herself between Presti and Escripti, keeping the young man in front. Prestiginagi felt ambiguous toward her. He was deeply an Emer. She was from an enemy tribe. She was wily and troublesome, knew her mind, and had no thought of submitting in spirit. But her goodwill, her personal beauty, and flashing mind attracted the old man, and when he felt her shiver in the night, he put his arm around her, and she took his hand and held it there as innocently as a child. Prestiginagi himself was cold, but he would not have thought of moving, even though he laughed at himself for acting that way.

It was not really coincidence that Jestak was coming south by roughly their route north. The valleys cutting into the mountain rises were cultivated near Emerta, or else they offered deep obstructions to travel. It was easiest to travel above the valleys in the sloping forest and parkland that lay east of the steep rise of the mountains.

It was nearly evening. Tia was deep in the grass, with Noti by her. She was pointing out a rabbit for his bow when it suddenly leaped and flopped over, a short arrow protruding from it. Noti stood and turned to shoot at a figure suddenly seen, but he disappeared, and the Emeri arrow went overhead. As Jestak pulled to snap another shot, Tia leaped up and grabbed the guardsman, yanking him to the ground, yelling, "Down. What a target. Stand when you can shoot only."

Jestak could not believe his eyes. He was deep in the grasses again. Was it Tia? Impossible. They knew where he was anyhow, and he could still see those two old scarecrows standing bewildered farther off. This was no patrol. Only two old men, a girl, and a soldier. Perhaps some others. He thought he would risk it, and called, "Tia, Tia. Is that you?"

She stood. It was. He stood, and said again, "Tia?"

She put her hand to her mouth, then laughed. "It is the Pelbar. It is Jestak," she said to Noti, and ran to him, grinning like a child, taking his hands in hers. "What? You came all the way from the Heart? What are you doing here?"

"I came for you," said Jestak, still bewildered, his eyes filling as he tried to watch Noti.

"Come," she said. "You stink. What have you been doing? Come and meet my Emeri. Were you all alone? Where did you get that sword? You came for me? Do you always travel around getting into trouble?"

He was smiling at her. He knew already that it had been worth it. Noti had wandered up to them and was standing, suspicious but nonplussed. "Noti, this is Jestak the Pelbar, all the way from the Heart River, about twelve hundred ayas east of here. He is the one I kept telling Presti I am owed to. Really. It is the same man. He breathed my life back into me. Jestak, this is Noti, and that there is Presti— Prestiginagi, that is, and the other one, the dry twig, is Escripti." She hugged him, then ran down the hill to get the others. The two young men stood eying one another.

"What is a Pelbar?" said Noti.

Jestak didn't answer. The other man still had his arrow nocked. Finally he said, "Are you going to put that away, or shall I kill you?"

Noti looked down and said, "Oh. I had forgotten." He slipped his arrow into its quiver. Jestak put him down as inexperienced, but he still kept an eye on him.

When Prestiginagi and Escripti finally had come up, the latter limping and tugged by Tia, Jestak was introduced with a gleeful formality, by the whimsical Shumai.

"So there is a Jestak," said Escripti, tiredly.

"We have heard of you almost daily," said Prestiginagi, drily. "You were one of the reasons why Tio was never quite ready for the Krugistoran."

Jestak felt a wave of relief. "I am glad to hear that," he said. "I cannot imagine, though, what sort of dog would prepare a free human for any glutton. It would take somebody enormously degraded, some carrion bird."

Noti made the mistake of being outraged and half drew his long sword as a threat, but with one sudden swipe of Jestak's it was snapped off near the hilt. Noti found himself looking at a sword point. Tia interceded, stepping between and saying, "It is all right, Jestak. They haven't manners. They are used to tyrannizing everybody and haven't yet been broken of it. He will behave—won't you?"

Noti murmured assent, holding his shocked hand.

"You see," said Tia, "these are the carrion birds who were readying me for the Krugistoran. But he has grown too dangerous and frightened, and is striking out at everybody around him, so we had to flee. There have been a couple of small Shumai attacks. He has been beating people to death. Now, why don't we bleed that rabbit before he gets stiff on us. I see you have two more. Good. I think we may find a campsite down there, Jestak. I will go ahead. Here, give me that knife." She took Jestak's short sword, leaving him with the others.

"You make her nervous, Pelbar," said Prestiginagi, as they turned to follow. He made no reply.

"You must have been involved in the Shumai attacks," added Prestiginagi. Jestak still said nothing.

"You must be a warlike people," ventured Escripti, who was leaning on Noti as they walked.

Jestak laughed. "Warlike? Cowlike is more like. The Pelbar live much of their lives behind high walls simply to avoid the attacks of the Shumai and Sentani. Until me. Nor am I warlike. I only came out here after Tia, and now we will go home, and I hope never to come within five hundred ayas of Emeri territory again. Let the Shumai deal with you, since they enjoy a fight, and you seem to go out of your way to provoke one."

"Then you were with them."

"I came for Tia—and for horses."

"Horses?"

"They are unknown in the east—except I saw a statue of one in Innanigan—which is over two thousand ayas east of here. It seems to have been from before the time of fire, many centuries ago. We would like horses. They would ease the burdens that our men now carry."

"You do not know of horses? Innanigan? Over two thousand ayas to the east? What would you have us believe? What time of fire?" complained Escripti.

"Be quiet," said Prestiginagi.

Tia was returning to borrow flint and steel. "I have found a brook, and sheltering rocks," she said. "I hope you are friends now."

"Friends?" said Jestak. "They have made no further attempts to kill me." As he said this, he undid his short-sword sheath and handed it to Tia. "Keep this," he said.

"You are the stranger in our country," said Noti. "You are the one declaring yourself dangerous."

"Only because you steal people to enslave. I will leave as soon as I can. While we are together, though, we might as well get along. Unless you want a fight. But you must admit that two old men and a boy are no match for a man and a Shumai woman."

Tia laughed, and led them to the spot she had picked, saying, "They are all right, Jestak. They do not even know how they are. We will leave soon, so we should try to get along."

After they had eaten, Escripti went to sleep, tired to the bone. Jestak put his fur roll over him. Noti, who truly was inexperienced, eyed Jestak with suspicion somewhat mixed with admiration. He seemed to know what he was talking about. Prestiginagi's intellect was so aroused by all the new things that Jestak casually dropped into his conversation that he was kept alert and awake. Tia washed herself carefully, downstream, in the darkness, then returned, fresh, and took Jestak's fur roll from the sleeping Escripti, curl-

ing up in it next to the old man. Noti brought wood, and
sat listening to the two men talking.

"And this time of fire?" said Prestiginagi.

"It is an idea partly my own, partly from things I have
seen, partly from old ideas in all the peoples I have met.
Here tonight I have found a further confirmation of it.
Your dialect is closer to my own than is the Shumai
speech. We both depend on writing, which is not of great
importance to a herd follower. In fact there may have been
a time when they were without it. But they teach it now as
a matter of ritual, almost.

"How, then, could two peoples, of no great numbers, so
separated, speak more or less alike? Only if they were once
one great people inhabiting the whole mass of land. In
Saltstream, far in the eastern ocean, they also speak the
same, more or less. At least one can comprehend with a
little practice. Only the Rits, to the west and north of the
Bitter Sea, speak differently. And even there, some words
are somewhat alike."

Jestak went on to describe the various ruins he knew of,
and how the writing on them that had survived showed a
common alphabet and some common words. "I have seen
two tumbled piles of artificial stone with the word,
C-O-U-R-T-H-O-U-S-E, on them. One was in Sentani country, one near the city of Innanigan, several
hundred ayas apart, with hostile peoples between."

"What, then, was this time of fire?"

"I do not know, except that it seems to have destroyed
nearly everyone then alive. Then scattered groups of survivors slowly formed our present tribal groups, and out of
one people have been created a number of warring peoples.
It must have been a colossal tragedy. I have seen the pillars
of bridges too large to be imagined, standing or fallen,
across stretches of great watercourses. The Sentani have
told me of two across the Heart to the south of Pelbar
country, and Stantu saw one in the blasted land south of
the seven eastern cities. It must have been vaster than any
I saw. Have you no ruins here?"

"Only one that I know of, and it has been forbidden
territory from the depths of our history. It lies to the south
of Emerta."

"That is often the case that these places are forbidden
territory. It is as if some danger or some memory of danger
is connected with them."

"Our writings say that Mamtugali, enemy of Ison, our deity, lives there, and all who go there become the enemies of Ison and are eaten by Mamtugali."

"If you will forgive me, it sounds like a superstition."

"Perhaps," said Prestiginagi.

The two men talked far into the night. Prestiginagi recognized that Jestak was a young man of much brilliance, and an extraordinary breadth of experience, though somewhat blunt, and lacking in a knowledge of mathematics as the Emeri understood and valued it. He had a keen sense of poetry, and in his comparison of the literature of his own culture with that of the Sentani, Innanigani, Saltstreamers, and Shumai, Jestak dizzied him with four approaches to poetry and story that were far beyond the tame and mannered efforts of the Emeri. He noticed that Jestak was particularly reticent, though, about the location of the Pelbar cities, except to say that they were on the Heart River.

On his own part, Jestak came to admire the insight of Presti, as he called him, since Tia did, and the depth of his political insight and commitment to his own people. But he also did not trust him. The Emeri had built a habit of tyranny around the structure set up by the Krugistoran that left them blind to the rights of others. He told Presti as much, but got no real reply. There were freedoms, he saw, that the old man was not even aware of, no more than were the Pelbar of other freedoms.

Finally, Jestak said, "Well, I have already offended Tia with my travel dirt, so if you don't mind, I will go and wash." He rose and disappeared into the dark, leaving the old courtier to his thoughts, which were many and mixed.

When Jestak finally returned, he said, "Jestak, we are depending on Tia to get us to the north in our trouble."

Jestak only looked and grunted, then curled up next to Tia, who was in the fur roll, though not really asleep.

"I wish you could have your roll," she whispered. "With me."

"That is all right. You know I could not do that. I am glad you are in it."

It was shortly after dawn that Prestiginagi was awakened by his nephew, who heard horses. As they stood, they saw a body of mounted Emeri coming directly toward them at a trot. Prestiginagi turned, and only then saw that Jestak and Tia were gone. He felt a moment of panic. But there was no help for it. He would have to face what he would have to face. There were fifteen men, and they were following the trail, largely of Escripti, as easily as a road. The old man sighed and walked to meet them. A tenoran was at their head, and when he saw the fugitives, he cantered slowly forward.

Prestiginagi was surprised when he dismounted, respectfully, and asked, "Are you all right? We have food here. Greetings from the army of the Emeri. You, Prestiginagi, have been appointed Krugistoran. We are here for you to command."

The old man took hold of his nephew. He did not know how to control his feelings until he took a moment to steel himself. But then he snapped back and said, "Tenoran, you must find the girl Tio and an eastern tribesman who has left with her. I believe that this man has been the master thought behind the Shumai raids. We must take him before he causes us more trouble."

The trackers in the patrol followed the trail as far as the brook, but then after nearly a quarter sun of looking, they had to give it up.

"I am beginning my rule with a failure," remarked Prestiginagi. The tenoran looked crestfallen. "That is all right," the new Krugistoran added. "I did not mean to criticize you. He is a man of great resource. We must return now, but we must send soldiers out here to comb the area. I do not think he will cause us further trouble. But I would like to be sure."

As they turned to the southeast, toward Emerta, Jestak said to Tia, from where they watched from the high slopes to the southwest, "There has been some change of events. Presti is clearly not now out of favor. He is giving the orders. And I am sure that they would have taken us back with them."

"Or died trying," said Tia.

Jestak looked at her. "Not much chance of that. Look at all of them. Come, Tia. The Shumai direct charge is really not the only way to do things."

"Maybe," she returned. "But it was my Shumai directness that saved me in Emerta."

Jestak had awakened Tia shortly before dawn. She had instantly been of his mind, and he never had to explain why they walked to the stream, backed far up the trail of

Escripti, which could still be seen in the bent grass, as far as a high rock, which they could climb and leave by rocks above.

"You must admit that they do not track like Shumai," she added.

"No," he laughed. "Now we had better do some running." They turned north and went at an easy trot and walk all day, only toward evening beginning an easy northeast swing toward the plains.

"It is good to be going home," said Tia.

 XIV

THAT night they camped against a huge boulder. Jestak had shot a small deer, and they feasted, though because they did not dare make a large fire, they had to cook it in small portions. Jestak informed Tia of his adventures, and she, in her turn, told of the life of the Emeri, and the great lard pot, as she called the Krugistoran, Lippini.

"My guess is," said Jestak, "that they finally got too much of him and deposed him, and that Presti is to take his place."

Tia thought. "Perhaps so. He is a much better man. He has some kindness to him. But he is also much more intelligent and so more dangerous. Ottan had better watch out. But there was a considerable sentiment against Shumai slavery in Emerta. I think Presti himself felt it, though he never would confess to a traitorous thought like that to me."

"Even to you? I thought you were his confidante."

"Not really. He would say some things to me, but with the lard pot in charge, Presti knew that I could repeat his expressions, and then there would be trouble. He knew I would not do that, though. I had told him that my honor extended even to him."

"In a sense, Tia, you were the stone that would not fit into the wall. I wonder if you really helped bring it down."

"I doubt it. It was a rotten wall, and a pigeon flying against it would have toppled it."

Jestak was silent for a time, roasting a strip of vension. "Tia," he said, "if Presti is as you say he is, then he will wait for us out on the plains with mounted men. Can you ride?"

"Only a little."

"I can barely ride, too. A horse they put me on at Ottan's nearly killed me. But we will have either to ride or to make the run from the mountains all at night."

"I don't see why you think he will do that."

"We are loose ends in the net. He will want them tied up. Any politician must anticipate. You know the court. By this time he has figured out my responsibility in the Shumai victories. These are things he will not want to allow."

"This Jestak, I am certain of it, was behind the Shumai raids. There were not many men at all. He would not talk of it, but I could see a mind of much strength at work. He is too dangerous, in league with the Shumai, to be let to go. We must either take or kill him."

"I thought you said he was peaceable, Krugistoran."

"Perhaps peaceable, Thousoran, but certainly deadly. I would rather have Shumai spearmen."

"What do you propose?"

"He will think, as I see it, that we will wait for him on the plains with horses, since he must cross to the western Shumai camps. Of course he is right. We must do that, and it is our best chance. But I also think we should patrol the foothills just east of the western edge of the prairies. If I were he, I would make the run at night, and I would prepare for it in the foothills during the day. That will probably be two days from now. What do you think?"

"It will be a help with the people to capture him."

"Or kill him," said Prestiginagi. "I have nothing against him, personally. I would enjoy a two weeks' talk with him. The quarter night we talked expanded my world more than anything else ever has. But it is for just that reason that we cannot have him loose. Yet he is resourceful. It will be, in any case, a good contest."

The thousoran smiled. "Well, we could use one, now that we have had three such poor ones."

"Yes," said the Krugistoran. "Because of him."

* * *

Tia was in the fur roll, and Jestak lay with his back against it, in front of her, toward the fire. She had her arm around him. Neither was asleep. "Jestak, what is to become of me now?" she asked.

"That is up to you, Tia. You know I would not have come all this way after you for nothing. I would hope you would stay with me always as my wife. But I would not have you feel you owed me."

"You are a strange man. You are the opposite of the lard pot, who did nothing but demanded all."

"What do you say?"

"Jestak, I will stay with you. You were a dream to me when I was in Emerta. I remember the arm coming into the water and catching me, and I knew right then, by the way you held, that I was saved. There is a sureness to you. But——"

"But what?"

"Jestak, if they examine me, as is the custom, if they think I was the Krugistoran's . . . Well, the Shumai are strict about such things. It would hamper you with them."

"You weren't his, were you?"

"No, but I was a slave on the farms, Jestak. I was in shackles. You cannot think—Did you suppose they would let me alone?"

"Are you all right now?"

"Yes," she said very quietly. "I am all right. But not all all right."

"Well, then let us not talk about it anymore. If the Shumai are so benighted, that is their business. I care nothing about their theories. You have an entire spirit and an entire body."

"What does that mean?"

"If a cloud passes in front of the moon, does that affect the moon? Only to the viewer."

"Oh. Jestak?"

"Yes?"

"What if I were not all right?"

"Tia, the custom of the Pelbar is for the men to be the servants to their women. It is a curious one, I see, now that I have been in other societies, and now I think it is foolish. In practice, there in the cities, of course, things tend to operate as partnerships. I am still enough of a Pelbar to have a high regard for women, their judgment, their warmth. They can, as I have seen, be unutterably cruel. But I am not a predator. What if there were something wrong with you? I see nothing. I am glad there is nothing. But even when you lay in the mud when I first saw you, I knew an innocent spirit and a keen mind—not to mention a lovely body. That has not changed. If there were something wrong, we would do what we could to make it right. And if there were nothing we could do, we could still survive it. I gave my loyalty a long time ago, and to a Pelbar, once that is given only the unworthy ask for it back." He paused a few moments. "Tia, do you think my coming to you was a matter of accident?"

"What else was it? It was your doing."

"I am not sure," Jestak mused. "I am confused on that point. It seems too miraculous."

"We are not yet home, Jestak. And I fear things we will meet there."

"No. What worries me is that I am assuming that we will make it. I do not want to be unwary. If Aven helps us, I must see that it is in the matter of our abilities, not in the simple sweeping away of all obstructions. If we think that way, then we may not see one until too late."

"I think we will make it because we are careful and strong."

"I have never done anything, I think, with that alone. But I am confused by how a peaceful spirit can help one in warlike matters. It makes no sense."

"Well, you will not be enlightened by me. It is imponderable to me. Now I think you had better kiss me lest I think I have been carried off by one of Escripti's texts of philosophy."

Jestak turned and kissed her. "Where did you get so good at that?" she whispered.

"Imagining you." He cradled her head in one hand, smoothing her hair with the other.

"I think," she said, "that we had better go to sleep. It is not that I am unwilling. But I have really had enough of doing things outside the customs of good people."

Jestak was again confused—disappointed but glad. He kissed her again. "I will make up for it," she said.

The next morning they began a slow run eastward, traveling all day on a long declivity that was taking them to the foothills. Through an opening in the tall pines they saw the flat plains stretching eastward, and decided to run into the night, after another supper of rabbits, this time flavored and stuffed with seeds and bulbs.

"Good," said Jestak. "I was getting awfully tired of meat."

"You have gotten outside of enough of it."

"True. But I will be glad to get into blackberry country, or a good cattail swamp. The roots will make the meat mild. Well, I suppose we had better go. Let us walk at first. I am heavy in the stomach."

They had walked and run until past high night, when finally Tia said, "Jes, I am so weary I do not see how I can continue." They stopped, and only then, in the utter silence, did they hear a distant horse.

"It cannot be the Shumai. It must be an Emeri patrol. I see. Presti is not only patrolling the plains. He plans to patrol the foothills as well. He must want us badly. They must be in camp. You wait here. I am going down to see. The moon is bright enough."

"Be careful."

"I will. Don't run away."

"I am too tired to crawl away."

Jestak worked his way down the hill until he could see a small fire, and several men sleeping. He knew there would be guards, so he did not go closer, but watched for a time. Meanwhile, Tia waited, then sat at the edge of an old mud slide by a steep ravine. The ground felt funny, almost spongy. She bounced a little on it, and it gave way beneath her, carrying her downward on a slant into a deep hole. She hit finally on a flat floor. Feeling outward, she found it was strangely smooth. She was in some sort of cavern, and it was unutterably dark. Faintly, she heard Jestak calling above.

"Here," she called, "down here." He could not hear her. She risked a loud call in the note of the mountain owl. Above, Jestak stopped. He repeated the call, as well as he could, but more softly. Then it came again. He was sure of the direction now, and walked cautiously that way. It came again, as if from the ground. He felt forward and found a hole.

"Tia? Where are you?"

"Down here. I am in some sort of hole. The ground gave way under me. Be careful."

"Can I get down?"

"I think so. It is not far. But be careful."

"Wait. I will cover the hole as I come down." Carefully dragging a broken branch, Jestak laid it across the hole and let himself down into the darkness.

"It is some sort of cave," she said.

"No," he returned, feeling the floor and wall. "It is a ruin."

They decided to stay the night, and slept together on the dark floor, among old earth smells and great dryness. Tia woke first after the sun sent a filtered light down through the dry pine needles above them. She stood and looked around, then drew her breath in a little shriek that brought Jestak instantly upright. She pointed. They were in a room, now dimly lit, made of the ancient artificial stone. It was very dry inside. Even the ceiling was the same artificial stone, though caved in at the corner into which Tia had fallen. A table with drawers stood at the far end of the room. Tumbled across the table lay a skeleton, with a few rags of dull cloth hanging from it.

Their eyes ranged around the room, where they saw a number of skeletons of children, scattered around, also with rags of clothing. Smaller tables, evidently for them, lay tumbled, or still standing in place. Jestak put his hand on one, but it crumbled beneath his weight. He took from it a square object and laid it gently on the floor, then opened it slowly. It too crumbled.

"A book,"said Tia. "Like those in Emerta. Rather more old, though."

"Look. We are in a ruin from before the great fire. Look. They were children. See? Look at the lettering there on the black wall. You can see that children wrote it. I think this must have been a place of learning, but somehow they all died in it together."

Tia drew in her breath. "Jes, let us get out of here."

"No, Tia. We can't now. The Emeri are around. And besides, this is the best chance I have ever had to see remains of the ancient people. I have seen their ruins from here to the eastern ocean. We have to be still all day. We might as well do it here while we rest and look around."

"But the dead, Jes."

"They are beyond dishonor, Tia. Look how long they have been here. This must have been buried very deep by something, and erosion has only now brought it near the surface. I have never had this chance. Come, help me look. Here. See this cloth. Amazing. No Pelbar weaver could have done it. It is knit, but so finely that a mouse could not have held the needles."

Tia laughed nervously, but Jestak's lack of fear, and her own curiosity, helped her overcome her Shumai feeling about the places of the dead and brought her to help him. They spent much of the day examining the room. Jestak grew more and more amazed. Not only was the desk made of metal, but molded as if by enormous force, which no man, or hand brake, could possibly have exerted. There were no weapons anywhere. They found writing implements, both for ink, for the dark wall, in white and yellow, and of wood, encasing something that made a gray line. Crumbling paper was everywhere. Opening the books, very carefully, they saw pictures reproduced, of a world that was wholly strange to them.

"How did they ever do that?" said Jestak. "Look. Look at their glass. What is that light metal? I have never seen it. It has not rusted at all through all this time." He was almost overcome with the wonder of it. "Tia, now we absolutely must get out and get back. This is a wonder that few have seen. A whole world must have been destroyed at the time of fire, and few people have ever seen or known of it. We must take some things—this glass bottle, this strange metal, and what is that on the wall?"

He reached out and took an object, fastened to the wall. It came loose in his hand. Sitting on the floor, he worked with it for a long time. Part of it gave in his hands. "There is wood inside," he said. "Tiny flakes. And black powder." After a time, he said, "It is like those writing tools, even some paint. See? It is yellow." He studied it further. With some working, he found the crank at the end would turn, though reluctantly because of rust. "Look at the fasteners," he said. "I have seen some like them in Innanigan. But what labor to make them—unless they know some way of cutting those grooves that we have not learned."

The couple went on to other things, but, at last, pausing, Jestak looked back at the strange implement he had found. Scrambling up into the hole, he snapped off a small twig of dead pine, came down, and put it into the hole. Then he turned the crank. It ground, stuck, moved again. He took out the twig, and said to Tia, "Look. This is the way they sharpened their writing sticks when they wore down. See?"

Tia was uncomfortable, looking at the small, scattered skeletons. "Jestak, this is too unutterably sad. Look at them. Did this happen, then, all across the whole country-side, with everyone, and all their dreams and promises, simply blotted away like cow's blood sinking into the sand? How can that be? It is too evil. How could Sertine allow it?"

"They must have known so many things," he replied, "that they found a way to destroy everything all at once. But what they did is no different from what the Krugistoran did, and the Emeri are still doing. They are forcing their wills on other people. Maybe men do not outgrow that."

Jestak wanted to stay longer, perhaps two days, but they knew their situation was too precarious to allow them to do that. "We must make the run tonight," he said. "Perhaps we could get a couple of horses."

"It would be too great a risk, Jestak. Perhaps not if we knew how to ride them well. Come on and sleep now so we will be ready. There is still some meat." They ate and lay down again, but neither could sleep in the presence of all the silence, and the pitiful bones of the ancient young, who had been robbed of not only the promise of their own lives, but of all the world that then was. "They are our people, then, Jes. Look at them. They are us. I believe you now. There is no Pelbar, no Emeri, no Shumai. There is only the ancient people, now destroyed—except for us few. Can you read on that dark wall?"

"It says,

> though I take the wings of the morning
> and dwell in the uttermost parts of the sea . . .

The rest is blurred."

"What does it mean?"

"I am not sure. It is only a fragment. 'Even . . . there' . . . It looks scrawled, as if it were written by someone who couldn't see. Why are you crying?"

"It is too sad."

While the two were deep in the entombed schoolroom, the hunneran was restless. No sign of the fugitives had been found. Surely they would have been seen by now. A message said a dead fire, surely theirs, had been struck back in the mountains, a day's run to the west. Perhaps they had made it across the plain undetected. A horseman cantered in with a message from Emerta, and leaning down, handed it to the hunneran. "From the Krugistoran," he said, dismounting.

The hunneran broke the seal and read it. "If you have not found them yet," it read, "you must attack the nearest Shumai camp. They may have made it there." The hunneran sighed. It had been a weary time, and now he must call in his men and make an attack. That would be tonight. He beckoned his assistant.

Ottan had moved his camp northward about eight ayas after the nearby Emeri patrol had seen where it lay. He was nervous with all the freed slaves there, still unfit, eating hugely of his supplies. The hunters were bringing in new meat, drying it, and the old people were gathering the first seeds of the season. But he still did not trust the Emeri.

Stantu was with them, but very restless, spending much of his time looking westward. The party had a full twenty-seven Emeri bows, and many arrows, and he insisted that the younger men practice with them. Thro was willing, though Ottan scoffed. "You should have seen Jestak pierce them, Ottan. So fast you would not believe it. One, two, three, four. We must gain skill in these."

"Give me a spear," said Ottan. "Not those grass straws."

"I will take a spear, too," said Reor, who was mending well. "But you should have seen it, Ottan."

Stantu and Thro held endless discussions about how the position could be defended. Ottan had chosen a good location, with high ground, a deep stream bed that would impede a charge with horses, trees along the stream to shield defenders from arrows, and a narrow enough perimeter to be defended. Yet the western leader was impatient with discussions of strategy. It was enough, for him as for other Shumai, to stand up with a spear and short sword against any attacker.

At dusk, Jestak slowly lifted the dry pine branch and looked out. There was no fire down in the direction of the Emeri patrol camp. After a long look in all directions, he lifted Tia out of the hole. Finding branches, he carefully added them to make a natural-looking thatch for the hole. Then the couple worked their way slowly down to the patrol camp, finding it deserted.

"It would seem," said Jestak, "that they do not intend to come back."

"Perhaps they called off their search."

"Maybe. But we cannot assume it. I think perhaps they are surmising that we are on the plains, perhaps in Ottan's camp. Perhaps they need all their men to attack it."

"He would have moved it, Jes."

"Where?"

"To the south it is all flat country. Perhaps, with the freed people, north only as far as Alder Creek. That is not ten ayas."

"We should be careful. If we go there, we may arrive at the same time they do. Being on foot would be dangerous. How many soldiers would the Krugistoran, or Presti, have to spare for something like this?"

"I do not know. They would have had to be mounted. It could not be more than four hundred. It would be more likely two hundred to two hundred and fifty."

Jestak whistled softly. "With their bows, that would be a great many. Can we make Alder Creek tonight?"

"If we run hard. I am weary and hungry, Jes, but if we have to, we will have to."

"Can you find the way?"

Tia laughed. "Of course." She turned and began a slow trot down through the darkening trees. Slowly, the tall growth turned into scrub, as they emerged onto the rain shadow of the mountains. Soon they were into bunches of grass and shrubs. The land began to flatten as night advanced. Occasionally they stopped, as much to listen as to rest. "We will be there," said Tia, "before Iox rises in the southeast."

"When is that?"

Again she laughed. "Shortly before morning, barbarian. Where is your astronomy?"

"About where Shumai architecture is."

The hunneran had brought his only son, for whom he had planned a career as an officer. The mounted force, over two hundred strong, rode out across the western edge of the plains to the former site of Ottan's camp.

"It was here, Hunneran," said a scout.

"Are you sure?"

"Yes, of course. Look here. It is an old fire. See the pegs for hides? They have moved."

"How long ago?"

"It is hard to tell in the dark. All the fires are cold, even the deep ones."

"Suffering centipedes. Can you find a trail?"

"We will have to have light, but if we get the direction, we will probably be able to follow it."

"That is bad. At least the old Krugistoran is not in power. He would have flogged us all for not bringing them in on a plate the same day as his orders. Let us hope that Prestiginagi is more reasonable."

"He will be, Hunneran. He has just gained power."

"Yes. Well, get your fires so we can find the trail."

Eventually the scout returned. "It leads east, Hunneran."

"Where would they be headed for?"

"That means they went either north or south. They would know that a half-mile of eastward travel would be well rewarded if we came at night."

"All right. Divide your scouts into two parties. Have each make a large arc, one two miles to the north, the other to the south. Then return here where we will await you."

"Yes, Hunneran."

This tactic took some time. Finally the riders returned. "They have gone north, Hunneran," said the scout. "We found their trail to the northeast and followed it a distance."

"Where would they have gone?"

"There is a stream some distance north, with higher ground. If they are still in the vicinity, they are likely to be there."

"Do you think that likely?"

"Yes, Hunneran. They are not sure of attack. A long move would not have been worth their while."

"Then let us get moving. Tenorans, mount your men. Go by patrols."

Jestak and Tia were running, though both were tired and famished.

"How soon?" Jestak said.

"It is taking longer than I thought, Jes. We are too tired. We will not be there before dawn."

"Is there anywhere to hide?"

"Not much, no. Listen. What is that?"

"Is it horses?"

"It is the Emeri, coming north. How will we warn Ottan?"

"I imagine he expects them."

"Look, there is Iox. Soon it will be light. Should we make a run?"

"No, Tia. We had better stay where we are, or work around toward the north. Perhaps we should follow them. How near are we?"

"Very close, I judge. Surely the Emeri came from the old camp northward. We are converging on Alder Creek."

Dawn came slowly, revealing an arc of mounted men facing the bend of the creek and the rise beyond. Behind them, on slightly higher ground, was the observation point of the hunneran. And behind this party of five were Jestak and Tia. There was no sign of life at all from the Alder Creek campsite.

"Good," whispered Jestak. "That means they know the Emeri are here. It also means that they are not charging out with spears, ready to get cut down."

A man cantered out from the hunneran's post to a patrol in the center. They lined up and nocked arrows, moving forward at a trot. The others filled in behind them, also nocking, and unlatching their long swords.

"Hold, hold," Jestak muttered.

"What?"

"If they let those men in, they can finish them. If they meet them at the stream, then the others will follow and cut them down, opening a gap."

The rest of the long line started forward at a walk. The front patrol had reached the ravine of the stream, and angled down out of sight, then appeared at the far side. They were having trouble getting their horses up the slope.

"Good," said Jestak. "Look, Tia. They are all watching the hill. I am going behind and will take the hunneran. You stay here."

"No, Jestak. I am coming."

"Please, Tia. For Aven. Stay."

"No. I am coming. I am not a Pelbar woman. After all, I am Shumai."

"We haven't time to argue. Very well. Look, there is a little boy. I imagine it is the hunneran's. If we take him, and the hunneran as well, we may bargain with them."

As the two worked up close to the observation post, the patrol had made it out of the stream bed and were on their way up the hill. The hunneran ordered a single note on the horn, indicating that they should charge. The others moved into a trot, then a slow canter. Before the blast had echoed from the hill, the lead patrol was full of long arrows, falling from their horses, and the other men had begun a charge. The hunneran did not even see the first two of his own men go down. His son had turned and screamed, as the third fell, and the hunneran, turning, faced Jestak's drawn bow. Tia ran to the boy and held her short sword to his throat.

"Call them back," said Jestak.

The hunneran turned and saw his men stopping horses to get down the stream bank. Spears began coming from the far shore, and the men returned arrows. Through the shouts and screams, Jestak again shouted, "Call them back now or the boy dies. Now."

The hunneran looked at his screaming and weeping son, turned, stooped, and taking the horn, blew three blasts on it. The mounted men turned. Many were already in the stream bed, and were having a hard time of it, but soon they began a galloping retreat, converging on the hunneran, now that they saw the situation.

"Hold tight, Tia," said Jestak, moving to the hunneran and holding his own sword to the man's neck. To himself he murmured, "Stay, Ottan, stay there." But he could see already that the Shumai were emerging from the near side of the stream, some on foot, some mounted on their own or Emeri horses, and advancing.

"All hold," shouted Jestak.

"You are the Pelbar," said the hunneran. "You are in it now."

"Maybe. We can stop it now, if you want. You know we would have won. You are getting off easily. You are even going to get your son alive—if you all leave and let us alone. Otherwise neither you nor he will get out alive."

"It has gone too far."

"No, not yet. We must stop the killing now. With me now. Tell your men to hold."

The hunneran reluctantly blew four short blasts on his horn. Seeing the pursuing Shumai, the riders turned and galloped out beyond the hunneran, turning in a line some fifty arms behind him.

Ottan was the first to reach the group, riding a big white

horse. "Can you hold them?" Jestak called. "Get them to stop."

Ottan looked angry. But he turned and held up his hands, yelling, "Thro, Stantu, get them to hold. Here, here." With some reluctance, they stopped, clustering around the hunneran and his son, until Stantu spread them out in a line of defense, kneeling, bowmen first.

"All right, Emer," said Jestak. "It is your choice. Do you go home with your men and the boy, or do you die?"

The hunneran was crestfallen. He would have not minded dying, but he had a responsibility to the boy, who had not, after all, asked to come. He also could see that he had already lost a full quarter of his men, and any further fight would not have been conclusive. And he was the only senior officer to command them.

"Kill the snake, Jestak," said Ottan. "We would have cut them into wolf bait back there had the fight gone on. We are being kind, and the bastard hesitates."

"We will go," said the hunneran. "Come, release the boy."

"Hold him awhile, Tia. We will let him go, but we need some guarantees. Send your men on ahead. We will send twenty mounted men behind them. When they reach the far hills, and our men have returned, then we will let you go. Leave ten men to accompany you."

"What guarantees have we?"

"We did not kill you, did we? Maybe the Krugistoran will, but he is less kind than we."

"Prestiginagi said you were dangerous. He will not kill us."

"Presti? Then he *is* in favor again. And Krugistoran."

Tia was outraged. "Presti? After all the help I gave him, he has come to kill us. How could he do that, the string of dried cow gut!" The boy began to cry again. She held him, but leaned down and talked softly to him.

"Enough," said Jestak. "Call your ten men forward— without weapons. Ottan, get some of your men to bring his wounded. They may take them home. We will keep their horses. We will take all the bows and the arrows. You may keep the swords. While they are gone, perhaps we can work out a more permanent peace."

"Not with me. I am only a hunneran."

"You aren't much, but the best we have right now. You can talk, can't you? You can take our terms to Presti. All the Shumai want is to be let alone. Are you people so puny that you cannot do your own farming?"

"That is over now. I do not think the new Krugistoran will reinstitute slavery."

"He had better not, or we will gather all the Shumai, with bows—with bows now, I said—and we will come and burn you to the ground."

"The Krugistoran said you were peaceable but dangerous. He was too kind."

"I am indeed peaceable until made dangerous. It is your choice. Or his."

Arrangements were made for the transfer of the wounded, the burial of the dead, and the retreat of the Emeri. As they left, the boy, Affani, cried more bitterly. Tia had sheathed her short sword, and now she comforted him, wiping his face and tickling him. He had seen too much horror, though, and the haunted look remained on his face. At last he finally relinquished himself to Tia's comforts and held himself to her.

"Emer," said Stantu to the hunneran, "look. You thought you would bring him to a picnic, eh? The slaughter of the wild men?"

The other did not answer.

Eight Shumai had been killed, all by Emer arrows. One was Olor, and when Jestak heard it, all the tightness he could bring to his face could not prevent him from crying. Reor put an arm on his shoulder. "It is all right," he said. "We found his spear in one of them." Jestak just shook his head.

Stantu had set up much of the defense, and insisted on putting the men behind brush, with small holes through which to shoot. It had proven effective.

Finally, as the sun began to set, the Shumai horsemen could be seen in the distance, returning. "Well?" said the hunneran. "Now will you keep your bargain?"

"Of course," said Jestak. "Now, Affani, I have a present for you. I found it on your land a day ago, in a secret place of the ancient ones. If there is a peace between us, I will someday let Presti know where he may look for it. Here, give me your hand." The boy reluctantly held out his hand, and Jestak slipped on his finger a gold ring which he had taken from one of the skeletons in the schoolroom. "It has writing inside it. It says, 'To Billy with love.'"

"To what?"

"To Billy. That was the name of an ancient boy."

"That is a funny name," said Affani.

"You found it?" asked the hunneran.

"Yes. It belonged to a boy many centuries ago. A boy about his size, it would seem."

"That is not a good thing for him to have."

"It was originally made for love, and given for love. What is bad about that? Look what you would have given him. A life of weapons. This was a good start, wasn't it."

The hunneran looked at him, but saw only a frank smile. "You are a puzzling man," he said. "Now with your permission, we will go."

"Go," said Jestak. "May Aven go with you."

"And do not come back," said Ottan, waving a new Emeri bow.

 XV

AFTER it was all over, and the Shumai had crossed the stream to their camp, Jestak remarked, "Where is Tia?"

"She is asleep—in my shelter," said Whin, smiling, snaggletoothed. With her was Veel, also smiling vaguely, and his bewildered and frightened Emer friend, Esis. Veel was her cousin, and his endorsement of the Emeri farmer had given him the freedom of the camp.

"Come, Jes, you can sleep with Reor and me," said Stantu. "You look tired."

"I am," he said, looking toward Whin's shelter. "Show me where." He was aware of many eyes following him as he went with Stantu to the primitive mat shelter. He wondered why? Did it have something to do with the fight? Or was it Tia? The Shumai did not approve of unmarried couples wandering around alone. But how could it have been helped? Would that make a difference? And what of Tia's current status? She had made some worried comments on that. But he was too tired to think more about it, and fell asleep with the talk of the Shumai camp around him.

It was late the next afternoon that the hunneran, Ereni, reported to the Krugistoran. He was deeply embarrassed, but Prestiginagi listened with a grave gentleness and courtesy.

"I am deeply chagrined," Ereni concluded, "and will resign my military career and enter something else, Krugistoran."

"First, Ereni, let us drop the courtly speech and talk to each other as normal men of business. We must not get ourselves quickly frozen in the same ice that Lippini did. I can remember when he was a hard-headed leader, before he found he liked leading too much, and the power it brought him.

"Now, I do not want you to resign. First, you have experience with the Pelbar already. Second, you have done no worse than the rest of us, and it would seem that he arrived on the scene fortuitously behind you. Of course you might have put sentries out behind, but you had no real way of predicting that event. Third, his arrival, and the way he handled things, probably saved us many soldiers, and horses as well. Perhaps it stopped a total rout. Perhaps it saved your life and your son's as well. Fourth, all the Shumai seem to want, if we can believe the Pelbar, is peace. To be left alone. We can give them that. Perhaps we can even make it work to our advantage. From what little I know of the Pelbar, he is from a people more like ours than like the Shumai.

"They are town dwellers and craftsmen, though much more rigorous in certain disciplines than we. They appear to be deeply religious. They are, as a whole, apparently enemies of the Shumai, except for this Jestak. Perhaps they became enemies for the same reason we did originally— out of fear of the typical Shumai love of action, which spills over from the hunting of the big animals to warfare.

"Now, is your son here?"

"No, Krugis—No, Prestiginagi. He is sleeping."

"You told me of a ring. Do you have it?"

"It is here, Prestiginagi." The hunneran took it from his pocket and handed it to the old politician, who hefted it and studied it carefully.

"What is that stone? Do you know?"

"No, Prestiginagi. See how the light shifts in it when you move it? I have never seen anything like it."

"And this inside. You said the Pelbar read it? I cannot make it out."

"Yes. He said that it was an inscription to a little boy. He said it read, 'To Billy with love.' "

"The writing is strange, though I can make out the letters. They are ours. I wonder where the Pelbar learned to read that?"

"It would seem, Prestiginagi, that he knows a great many things."

"Billy? Billy. An odd name. Here it also says something else—a craftsman's mark?"

"I made that out as *one eight K*, Prestiginagi."

"What does that mean?"

"I do not know."

"You say Jestak said he found it in a ruin well preserved?"

"Yes, Prestiginagi. He said he would direct us to it if peace were made and proved to hold. He said it is on our land."

"Then at least he recognizes our territory. Perhaps we should have let him go. I do not plan to mount any major military campaigns. We are too few a people. The Pelbar threatened to gather all the Shumai and destroy us if we did, did he not?"

"Yes, Prestiginagi."

"I wonder if he could really do that. They are a numerous people, but widely scattered. Still, we have seen enough of his abilities not to want to find out. Escripti."

"Yes, Krugistoran."

"Escripti, I wish to send you to the Shumai, with a patrol, to discuss matters with them and with the Pelbar. No, no. Do not shrink back. I cannot go. The Pelbar knows you. So does Tio. It is sure that she does not regard you as a threat. Try to arrange a truce with them. There is no reason why we should not have a peace. We will arrange the details later. See if we can hire an astronomer from among them. If they are at all like Tio, and she says they are, they can teach us much. Now, Eadini."

"Yes," said the thousoran, who had watched the whole conference in silence from a side chair.

"To be safe, you must begin the design of a defense system now that the Shumai have the bow. You must also supply support for the truce party.

"Escripti. Be sure that you convey my sympathies to Tio, whom I would not have hurt further but for the demands of politics. And see if the Shumai are willing to trade with us or supply labor in summer for our farms. Is that not the way the Pelbar saw it? I recall his talking of the fusing together of all the peoples. He saw trade as the first step. I am not sure that I have the slightest desire to fuse together with the Shumai, but we have lost many men in the past week, and we cannot afford to let that go on much longer.

"Now, Ereni. You must go and rest. We will talk further of this whole matter later."

The same afternoon Jestak and Stantu were bathing in the creek. "Jes," said the Shumai.

"Yes?"

"There is a matter we must bring up."

"It is Tia."

"Yes. How did you know?"

"How did I know?" Jestak laughed. "Where has she gone? She would not have kept herself from me like this. I have not so much as seen her since the fight. If I have done something wrong, I am heartily sorry for it."

"No. It is not exactly that you have done wrong. But some things contrary to our custom have happened. No one is blaming you. We are well aware of what you have done for us. In fact, some people almost look to you as a special evocation sent from Sertine. But you have been with her on some nights. We will not mention the Emeri. By our custom, you must marry her before three-quarters moon or else never see her again. You see the moon's aging is symbolic of the—"

"When is that?"

"Well, it is tonight."

Jestak sat down in the water and laughed. Then he let out a long, delighted howl, a very poor imitation of the prairie wolf, went under, and came up sputtering.

Stantu was smiling slightly. "I take it," he said, quizzically, "that you wish to be married." Jestak leaped on him and carried them both into the center of the pool.

* * *

The Shumai ceremony, conducted in the second quarter of the night, to get it in before the height of the three-quarter moon, was simple but lengthy. Most of the time was taken up by the couple's kneeling together while two old people, first a man, then a woman, chanted a long poem expressing the duties of marriage, its hopes, its fears, its sadness and joy, its function in the spread of life and preservation of human happiness. Plainly it was not the work of a poet, but rather of groups anxious to promote duty and virtue, though it did rime the beginning words of lines, as was the custom in very formal Shumai verse. Some seemed the work of a midwife, and its frankness embarrassed Jestak until he took it as part of the open and wholehearted Shumai approach to things. The old man, Engla might chant a quatrain,

> When the sunflowers, always turning,
> take the sun into each core,
> then the seeds grow fat and healthy,
> break, send roots into the earth.

Gyna then replied,

> So, responding to her beauty,
> which in faithfulness he sees,
> grow husband's yearnings for his lover,
> rich he finds the soil of her.

Engla would then continue,

> As the rootlets of desire
> reach the waters of her earth,
> grasses of their fruiting kernels
> each lift heads in turn to light.

Then Gyna again,

> May the symbols of their fondness
> Also symbolize their search;
> Obey then worthy manhood's conduct,
> show then womanhood's great worth.

In the long run, it was highly moral. Like most men, Jestak did not relish the ceremony so much as he endured it to gain the condition it would bring about. Finally it was over—or so he thought. But this just began the celebration, which lasted the rest of the night. Much of this centered on an exchange of presents, but since the Shumai were not gatherers of many possessions, this was largely a ceremonial function, combined with a vast trading of things. Reor would give Jestak a wooden drinking cup, with a speech. Then Igka would give him a long, braided rope of cowhide, also with a speech. Jestak would give Igka Reor's drinking cup and perhaps Calla the rope. Calla's gift might eventually go to Reor. All enjoyed the gifting, with much laughter, to see who got what, and this was one of the few ceremonious occasions on which the Shumai drank their fermented honey drink, called Rotha, and much relished it.

There was only one exchange of gifts that was at all seriously made. Ottan gave Jestak a fine pair of horses to take to the Pelbar, and in turn Jestak gave him the gold things from Sima Pall. They were of a fineness that the Shumai had never seen before, a twisted armband, with animal heads on either end, and jeweled eyes, a running-deer pin for Whin, with inlaid enamel work. She was a clean and simple woman, and the gold deer showed up against her plain, Pelbarcloth tunic and beaten leather apron with extraordinary beauty. Her eyes glowed with it, knowing its preciousness. "May you have the happiness of the horses," she said. "May they be as fruitful as you are. I think you will find them gentle, even the male. He has been raised almost as a member of the family. His name is Heng. The other, the mare, is Loo."

Time went slowly in the Shumai camp. It was not until the next evening that Jestak and Tia were alone. Outside the shelter prepared for them, they could hear the old people playing the star game. "There," said Tia. "Hear Ivot. He is so happy now that he is free again. Oh, Jes, we all owe you so much."

Eventually the game subsided, and the camp gave itself to sleep. The couple could hear the prairie wolves in the distance, and a short fox bark far down the creek. Once there was a querulous bird stirred to wakefulness. They heard the three-quarter night guard change, in quiet stirrings of the new men and the nearly silent return of the ones relieved. The morning sun came up with a fullness they felt themselves. It was a moment that seemed to tremble like a feather on the point of a knife. Jestak knew it would not balance there, but he wanted to see it so clearly that for him it would always be clear.

They spent the day in preparation for departure. Stantu was coming with them, as were Reor and some others. Even Reor looked at the place of Olor's grave, on the hill above the creek, with welling eyes. Life would not be the same. Something of late boyhood had been taken from him. He would have to look for a wife and begin a family of his own.

It was toward evening that a horn from the western guard called their attention to a party of Emeri horsemen approaching. They wore their long swords, but carried no bows. A crowd from the hill watched, the men armed and tense. But finally, Tia said, "Look, it is Escripti. They have come to talk."

The horsemen camped a quarter-mile west of the creek, with a heavy watch of Shumai by the creekside. They were nervous, and kept their fire up all night, as requested. Escripti spent the evening in the center of Ottan's camp, negotiating nervously, surrounded by the blond people, with their knives and spears, stared at by children, smelled by dogs, offended by the odors, but, as expected, bowing, polite, never revealing his feelings in the slightest, except, of course, that all the Shumai could sense them plainly, and chuckled quietly to themselves. Finally Escripti retired to the Emeri camp for the night. The tenoran had prepared a bed for him on the ground.

"How does it look?" he asked.

"Oh, Gemigani. I will never get used to this sleeping on the ground. I have done more of it this past two weeks than in the last forty years. It looks all right. They are astonishingly easygoing. I must return in the morning. The former slaves are there, and they are the most hostile. But I can see why, now that I see them. They must have been frightfully mistreated. I did not know. I never saw them on the farms. It would not have been so easy for me to think that our society included that sort of thing."

"Yes, I know," said Gemigani. "I saw them. Many times. Too many."

In the morning Escripti returned to the camp, and talk continued. It was agreed that the border of the plains was to be the boundary between the two peoples. The Shumai were not to raid. Ottan made it clear that he could not speak for the whole of the Shumai, but he would try to get word around and hope that they would agree. The Emeri would not enslave. On Jestak's suggestion, there would be a truceweek in the spring, when the Shumai had returned, at the border, in order to see if the two societies had anything to exchange. Engla was to go to Emerta with the group as an astronomer for the winter. He was happy with that. The strenuous life of the open plains was getting to be difficult for him. Toward noon, Jestak had completed a long note to Prestiginagi concerning the ancient schoolroom, and gave it to Escripti, showing him the things he had taken from the place. He did not locate it for them yet. There was still a chance that the Emeri would learn something from the study of the place that would give them an advantage over their neighbors.

"It is a proof to me," Jestak emphasized, "that we are really the remnants of one people, and that in fighting each other, we are fighting the survivors of our own ancient selves."

The couple came out onto the prairie to say good-bye to Escripti. Tia was still amused by him, and could hardly refrain from giving him a hug. He almost expected it, and kept a man or a horse between them.

Finally Veel and Esis came out to the group. Esis wanted to go home, but since there was no horse for him, he said, "I will walk."

"I will go with you," said Veel, "as far as the border."

"May he visit?" asked Esis.

Escripti shrugged. "I do not see why he should not. You are returning to Ilet, then?"

"Yes," said Esis.

"Then you will probably be directing the work of the old Krugistoran, Lippini. He is there—as a worker."

"Perhaps I shall stay."

"No. Come. It is all right. He is no threat to anyone. He has even married his concubine, Acco, who is apparently resigned to helping him."

Tia was saddened by this. Acco had been robbed of her place as a Shumai, and was making the best of it. She ran to the camp and got a small bundle of things for Esis to take to Acco. Then, with the small group, she watched the Emeri ride away slowly, growing smaller, with Veel and Esis walking along in their trail.

XVI

REMING knew horses. He was also footloose. He belonged to the western Shumai, Ottan's band, who did not follow the big herds in their southeastern sweep in the winter, but rode straight south with their families to the southern herds of curve-horned cattle, and wintered near them, in the dry lands, near the great river canyons.

As Jestak's party prepared to leave, he volunteered to go with them. "I am young and have no family," he said. "I have never been east. It will be good for me, and I can show you about the horses. There is much to know about horses. They are pets if you treat them right. Otherwise, they are nothing but trouble."

Jestak immediately agreed. In addition to Reming, Stantu, Reor, and Thro's men, several others were going along. With the horses of the Emeri who had been killed, all were mounted, and Ottan had gained horses as well. Already swallows were gathering on the trees when they departed. Jestak exchanged the formal Shumai good-bye with Ottan, and there were general partings. Jestak and Tia both were tightly hugged by Whin, who cackled her dry, rich laughter into their shoulders. As they wound eastward at a walk, Reor sounded the long blast of departure roundly back across the dry plains. A return blast came, faintly, from Alder Creek. It seemed to last and last.

Reming laughed. "That must be Rux," he said.

The trip eastward was leisurely. Naturally they had to stop and talk with every Shumai band they encountered, and hear their adventures magnified and transformed in the telling, though never really falsified, and never told in anything but straight truth by Thro. Thro was genuinely fond of Jestak now. "Jes," he said, "now that Winnt has Ursa, and you have Tia, I am condemned to a life of bachelorhood."

Tia laughed. "I see how they look at you. That dark one

at Feather Bluff. She almost scooped you up and ran off with you."

"Aiii," said Thro. "That one. She gave me a seed cake. A grease cake, I should say. It sat in my stomach like a stone."

"That proves it," Tia returned. "She needs a good teacher. For the good of the people, you must go back to her. What if she got some lesser man? He would go humping around all his life, his stomach hanging down more and more, unable to convince her to change her cooking. One word from you—'My love, perhaps you could use a little less grease, and borrow some rich old dough for it'—and from then on, her cakes would be as light as clouds."

"And I would belch so much, I would stampede the herds."

But all this time, Jestak was worried. He had, after all, in essence given the Shumai the bow. Thro now used his Emeri bow almost exclusively. So did Stantu, who was learning how to make them from Jestak. Reor was beginning to convert. The shock of Olor was not lost on him. In the evening, especially, he missed his cousin, and was silent and restless. Tia tended to mother him inconspicuously. Had he suspected, he would have been much embarrassed.

What would happen when they met the Sentani? The eastern people had survived the Shumai attacks by their discipline and their superb use of the bow, but already the Shumai were gaining skill, and Jestak could not refuse to teach them the techniques that made the weapons so deadly—except for the rapid-fire method of the Pelbar short bow. He had never even told them about the Pelbar guard bows, which made even the Emeri bows look like toys, or the power-bow complexes of the Pelbar walls, special weapons kept in reserve against an all-out attack on the Pelbar cities.

Jestak had grown to love both peoples, and his sense of the foolishness and futility of their combats had deepened to a sort of anguish. There was so much bad blood between them that only a long process of integration could truly bring them together as Jestak had become convinced they were at one time.

But he had also seen how easily he had fit into both societies, and he also perceived how much closer they were to each other, at least in mode of life, than either was to the Pelbar custom of living within walls. He would have to make up to the Sentani the advantage of having given the bow to the Shumai by introducing some Pelbar armoring techniques—if he could get the permission of the council.

Curiously, neither people held grudges, unlike the Innanigani who seemed to enjoy lifelong embroilments in the law. If there could be a breakthrough, somehow, to bring a truce, then a start would be made. Jestak doubted that the Sentani from Koorb would ever attack the Pelbar anymore. A way had been opened for future interchange. But the Pelbar did not kill many Sentani, and when they did, it was always a clear and desperate case of self-defense.

They were over halfway home, when they met Kod and the Goose Lake Shumai at the Brask River. As usual, the whole band clustered around the newcomers and their horses.

"Well, Jes," said Kod. "I didn't think you would make it. Here she is, eh. I see why you did. So you are Tia. I have seen you a number of times, but only as a look in Jestak's eyes. Ha. Sometimes I thought they would catch fire. Did he burn the Emeri?"

When the story was told, Kod was even more surprised than he had been at the encounter with the patrol. Clearly Jestak was a man of resource, intelligence, and goodwill. And yet at the moment he was sitting by the fire, listening to Ary play the springbox, at which she had become really expert. As usual, several other children would reach for the box, for their turns, and Jestak was arbitrating masterfully. All Pelbar men had some nursery experience when they were young. It was a part of the old custom of making them gentler through understanding the domestic life. This was not the case with the Shumai, though the men were generally good with their children, never hitting them, and were careful teachers of the boys. They took little responsibility for domestic chores, and the constant toils of the camp turned the Tias into worn and sagging women, leathery-tough and hard-minded, before middle age.

Tia knew this. Unlike so many Shumai, whose addiction to the wild, outdoor life is absolute, she had seen enough of the settled life of the Emeri to be grateful even for the roof of a slave house when a hard rain turned cold. And her treatment in the Krugistoran's palace, though degenerate and luxurious, was also civilized. She had come to realize that the Shumai camps did indeed tend to smell, even though the people were as personally clean as their mode of life allowed them to be.

She saw that Jestak had a way of washing himself, and his clothing, that was so habitual that even on the dry plains, as the others of the party gradually grew more grimy with the journey, he maintained himself reasonably well. For Tia, though she was unutterably happy, the primitive life had become a little oppressive. Clearly the Shumai would benefit from more permanent buildings, even if they were only ones that were turned to periodically.

Already, Iam, who had been an Emeri slave, had left the party to go south. But he did not intend to resume his former way of life. He would rejoin his band, he said, and then go with them to the bend of the Root River, which he knew. "I've seen how the Emeri farmed and raised cattle," he said. "It is not a bad idea. I know a place where I can settle down and stay. I will build a good shelter. Then I will grow things and catch some wild cattle to keep for myself the way the Emeri do. Then when the blizzards come, I will be in my house, with plenty of wood to burn, and the cattle will be right there when I need them. It is all empty land there, except when my relatives come. Look at my legs. They aren't much good for running anymore."

Jestak wondered if this would catch on. If so, then the Shumai would become a different people. But it was plain that most of them were thoroughly pleased with their mode of life, and would have it no other way.

On the evening before they left the Brask River camp, Ary was sitting with Jestak and Tia. She was disturbed at how backward Jestak was with a simple game of "Na, na." "You must stay with us," she said. "It will be good for your mind. We will teach you."

"I would like to stay, but I must go home to Northwall. Will you come and see us?"

"If we do go near there. Will you let me in to see the inside?"

"I would like to, Ary. It is up to the council."

"Why would they keep me out?"

"We are not always friendly, your people and mine. My people think it is safer to stay inside."

"Well, we would not hurt you. You know that."

"Yes, but you know me. Almost all the Shumai and Pelbar do not know each other. Now lend me your springbox

and I will sing you a song." Jestak's song was a familiar
Pelbar lullaby, altered slightly to fit Ary's dialect:

> The owl is hooting on the strong rock walls.
> They lock together as a single stone.
> Aven, keep us safe within these halls.
>
> The walls are silent. Now the owl has flown.
> And now the mouse must crouch and hide in fear
> down in the woods and grass he runs alone.
>
> Aven keep us all together here,
> safe from Shumai spears, Sentani bows,
> peaceful, quiet, sheltered from their war.
>
> Fierce they are, but our strong walls enclose
> us, guardsmen watch, and Aven's love forestalls
> them, bless the children in their safe repose.

"That is one of the things sung to children when they go
to sleep," said Jestak.

"Oh," Ary murmured. "Are the children afraid?"

"Sometimes. But they are sure of the Pelbar defenses,
and they soon learn about them and how to make them
work. Everyone is involved in it."

"Surely, Jes," said Kod, "the Pelbar did not build all
that just to keep away from us."

"I think that was one of the main reasons, Kod. Our
records show that Shumai attacks formerly killed a great
many of us. But there was also a prophecy. It said that
there would be a great time of testing. But it never came."

"A time of testing?"

"Yes, when the Pelbar would be instrumental in saving
all the Heart River people, even their enemies."

"We can save ourselves, all right," said Kod.

"Yes," said Tia. "But Jestak saved me. That, for me, was
a time of testing. And I am a Heart River person. I never
could understand, Kod, why we took such delight in at-
tacking the Pelbar—though I never heard of us getting any
good by it."

"They are always behind walls. We make sport of them
because they are there. They amuse us by their hiding."

"Are you aware," said Jestak, "that any Shumai on the
Northwall forefield could have been killed at any time?

And a crowd of fifty could have been cut in half in a few sun widths?"

Kod looked at him. "I do not believe it," he said. Jestak did not reply.

In the morning, before they left, Jestak took from his pack a small gold heart on a tiny chain, and, stooping down, put it around Ary's neck. "Here," he said. "It is from the ancient children I told your father about. It is what the Innanigani call a heart. Take care of it. It is gold. See how fine the chain is? No one can make them like that anymore, not even the Pelbar, or the Emeri, or the Innanigani. See how tiny? Do not pull on it. It is too fine, like a spider's web."

Ary blushed and smiled. She fingered the heart, and touching it just right, caused it to spring open. She thought she had broken it, and hid it in her hand, but Jestak had seen and stooped, gently taking it and looking.

"I am amazed," he said. "I hadn't known it would open. Look. See the hinge inside? Be careful? See? It is a tiny picture of someone."

Very faintly, a child's face looked at them. All crowded down to see, but even as they looked, the breeze turned the picture to dust, and the powder scattered. "Look," said Ary. "There are scratches under it. Are they letters? Does it say anything?"

Jestak looked a long time. "I do not understand it," he said. "All it says is 'Ru.1.' Then two dots, one over the other, then '16.' And like the ring, it says '18 K.' "

Iorta was an old man, but sturdy. He was one of those peaceful, self-contained old men who are beyond desire, and who look at the world with a benign tolerance and goodwill, ready to endure if need be, willing to please if he can, but entirely beyond jealousy, beyond self-promotion, beyond selfishness. He could get up from the campsite, put on his belt, and walk out to his death with perfect calm if it were necessary. But he loved life too much to do that if it were not. Everything interested and amused him. He had seen most of the Shumai territory during his long life. His grandchildren were grown. He was long widowed. Unlike most of the Shumai, he would take long journeys entirely by himself, perfectly content, whether one of the camp dogs came with him or whether he was by himself. He seemed to have such a rapport with everything that even the tall grass kept him company.

He was only about sixty ayas west of the Heart, walking alone, the leaves red with fall and blowing down in the wind, when he saw a lone Sentani coming toward him, at a trot. Clearly the man saw him, but somehow seemed to have no hostile intent. Iorta swung his spear around, but when the Sentani approached, he held both hands straight up, slowed, and stopped by the old man. In all his long life, this was the first time Iorta had seen a Sentani except in combat. He was not frightened. It interested him. He stood his spear up and leaned on it.

The Sentani stood, getting his breath. It was clear he had come a long way. "You must help," he said.

"I do not understand," said Iorta. The Sentani repeated it very slowly and distinctly.

"Help? You? How? Why? What are you talking about?"

"Listen carefully. There are many large boats on the Heart. Very large, with many people, and oars as long as small trees. There is a strange people on them."

Iorta nodded. "I understand. Go even more slowly." He sat down, and motioned the Sentani to sit down, too. The man did, though impatiently.

"Now," said Iorta. "Slowly. The slower we go, the faster we will get there."

The man sighed. "My name is Epart. I am a Sentani of the Fastness of Koorb. I came north early this fall, ahead of the starband in order to gather rushes at the junction of the Gray Bog River to dry for spring trading. I was one of twelve.

"We were over halfway between Northwall and the Gray Bog when we saw a great number of very large boats, with tall poles and great pieces of cloth. . . ."

"I saw them on the Bitter Sea many years ago. They are ships. On the Heart? The Tantal make them."

"Who?"

"The Tantal," Iorta said. "A cruel people living on the south of the Bitter Sea."

"I do not know this Bitter Sea. They are in the Heart."

"Yes. I understand. Go on."

"We watched them for some time. They have long paddles, like trees almost, and many on a side. There were several men to each paddle. Looking from close up, I could see there were both Sentani and Shumai paddling."

"Uh," said Iorta. "How did they keep them apart?"

"They were chained, and there was a man to beat them."

"How many Shumai?"

"I do not know. There are forty of these boats. I am sure there are over a hundred Shumai, and nearly that many Sentani. Some of my party were careless in camping one night, and now they too have been captured."

"How many?"

"Eight of the twelve."

"Where are the other three?"

"One has gone to the Peibar, to tell them. One has gone south to meet the starband from Koorb. And one has run north and west to try to talk to the Shumai near Stone Creek."

"Huh. He will be lucky if he finds them—and if they do not kill him."

"Yes. So will I. But we do not have the people needed to stop these enemies, who are very numerous."

"How many?"

"There are forty boats, and on each of the four we were able to count people on, we saw about forty-five to fifty."

"Aiii, that is eighteen hundred to two thousand," said Iorta. "And they have a hundred Shumai?"

"Yes, it looked to be that."

"What were they doing?"

"They were slowly going downriver, taking game and fish as they went."

"Then they will soon be at Northwall."

"Yes."

"Then we will see if those walls will continue to stand. Come with me. We will go to Weasel Bend to talk to the axeman there."

"How far?"

"Only eight ayas or so."

A while later Direk looked up from his skinning and stretched. He looked eastward. Achi was entertaining the skinners with the silver skyrider section of The Epic of the Dust, a long recitation, all of the sections of which took four people's memories and about twelve sun quarters to recite.

"What is this?" said Direk, interrupting Achi in the middle of the skyaxe section. This was unheard of. But the others, seeing his earnestness, stood, looked.

"It is Iorta with a Sentani," said Direk. There was a general rush to look and the dogs went out, barking wildly.

Iorta came up at a slow trot, with the Sentani behind, Iorta beating the dogs aside with his spear shaft.

"Hey, Iorta. Driving them home to kill them now, are you? Here, let me help," said Direk.

"Old man, you are in bad company," said Ompu. "Turn around. Look what followed you."

"Did you not hear him?"

"You lured him in the right direction."

"We are drying meat. He is just in time to get on the rack."

Iorta held up his hands. "Quiet," he said, in so loud a voice that all stilled. "He is tired. Get him some food and water. Get the axeman. The rest of you, come here and listen." He led the way to the clear space at the middle of the camp. A horn was sounded, and soon others were coming, the axeman among them.

Iorta summarized the Sentani's story. The others were silent or disbelieving, thinking it some trick. But the axeman regarded him, finally saying, "Do you know Jestak?"

"The Pelbar?" asked Epart. "Yes. He met the starband last fall north of Pelbarigan, and started north. Then he and Dar took Winnt, who was hurt, to Northwall. The next spring I saw him again when Winnt married Ursa of Northwall."

The axeman was silent awhile. "Did Jestak send you?" he finally asked.

"No. I have not seen Jestak. He was going to go west with some Shumai to rescue a girl, so it was said."

"What Shumai?"

"I do not know. The leader's name was Thro. He is a tall man, taller even than you, with reddish hair and many freckles."

"You met Thro and he did not kill you?" asked a man from the crowd.

Epart slowly recounted the story of the encounter at the wedding, and then of how Jestak had come to rescue Thro the previous winter.

"What is your name?" the axeman asked.

"Epart."

"I am Waldura. I was chasing your starband and ran across the trail of Jestak and your men. We chased them into Northwall. I talked to him when he gave back our dead. I believe you. The men among us will go with you. We might as well go to Northwall. We will send runners to other bands, but we cannot promise what they will do. They may think me a fool. It sounds like the story of the skyhammer."

"We were just coming to that," Achi grumbled.

Waldura grinned at him. "I thought you would be near it by now. Now, Epart, eat and rest, while we get ready. Iorta, take care of him and see that the dogs do not chew him up. One thing—what if we meet Sentani? Will they agree to a truce?"

"I do not know. I will be there, and I think we will be able to stop a fight. We generally try to avoid you, as you may have noticed."

"Yes," said Direk. "We have noticed." He walked away laughing.

"Do not mind him," said Waldura. "He is a good man."

Direk was saying, in the background, "Trying to understand a Sentani is like listening to a toothless old man talking with his mouth full of raw meat." There was another laugh.

Hardo was worried. He commanded the forty ships of the Tantal. Things were not going quite as he had hoped. Neither the Sentani nor the Shumai were behaving well. While they tended at first to fight with one another, and the new ones always did after capture, they soon sank into a sullen silence, and then eventually some sort of bond seemed to grow between them. All of them were hunters. They seemed to understand each other even though they were enemies. He needed more slaves but he did not much want to take more of these people.

He had heard of the Pelbar of the Heart, a frightened people who lived behind high walls. He had hoped to get to their cities earlier in the season, but with the recalcitrance of his slaves and the way the ships tended to run aground on hidden bars, he was far behind his projected progress. He thought he might take one of the Pelbar cities and stay the winter there, then continue south.

This was to have been an exploration. The lake Sentani, tired of Tantal pressure, had begun organizing. In the last raid, in which they wiped out two Tantal farm villages near Mistan, some Peshtak were even allied with the Sentani. The Tantal were thinking of migrating as a whole. So far he had seen some good empty land, but these tribes would keep it unsafe, and the Shumai seemed more numerous than the Sentani at home. Perhaps the Pelbar would be the Tantal's solution. From a prisoner they had beaten, Hardo had learned that the nearest Pelbar city was called Northwall. It would be no match for their new weapon. But they were getting rather low on the charging dust, and he had no good way of making more here.

There was a good deal of restlessness, too, among his own people, especially the women, who did not feel safe anywhere but on the ships, and felt the cramped quarters after so long in them. The children with them were not doing well, either. No exploration is easy, he thought to himself. But we may have gotten into this one too deeply. Perhaps a smaller party on a trip down to the mouth of the Heart would have been a better first step. They even could have made an agreement there to come back to the eastern cities by ship, on the salt water, and then make their way, somehow, northwest to home, if things were too hard.

Well, they were here now, and would have to make the best of it. The Pelbar were the solution. The Shumai and Sentani seemed to laugh at the way they hid. And yet they all had Pelbar metalwork and textiles—even some ceramics. It was good work, better than the Tantal themselves could do. He must exercise caution. He would even try to save a few of them from slaughter in order to put them to work for the Tantal.

It was afternoon. The lead ship was stuck again, for a full quarter of the sun. But they finally got it loose, found the channel, and started on. As they came near a bend, and the lead boat got into the crossing, Hardo heard a distant horn sound, again and again.

"What is that dog howling, Tort?"

"I do not know, Commander. Listen. The frigging prisoners have heard it. It is something to them."

"Find out."

"Yes, Commander." He scuttled off, and after a time returned. "It is the Pelbar city, Northwall. The fish-gutted prisoners are laughing and saying it will stop us."

"They are slaves, Tort. Frigging slaves. Remember that." He brought down his stick on the hand of his aide.

"Yes, Commander, yes. I will remember," said Tort, saluting and then holding his hand.

The Tantal ships began rounding the bend, and saw,

about three ayas down the river, what appeared to be a large block of stone, incorporating the limestone river bluffs, on higher ground separated from the river by a broad field. It appeared to have no openings.

The prisoners were cheering and had to be silenced with whips. For once they seemed eager to row, and the armada moved more rapidly down the river toward the city. Hardo ordered a small boat and had twelve of his own men row him downstream ahead of the ships. He neared the city a full ayas in front of the rest, and hovered there in midstream, regarding the structure with some misgivings. Here would be a test. He had the advantage of mobility. He had no idea at all of their strength—only the reports of the slaves, which seemed to agree on Pelbar secretiveness. Well, this would do for the winter. He might have to kill some of the slaves if it became necessary to ration supplies. He had his boat turned to return to the others and direct the deployment of the ships.

"Virell spoke the truth, it would seem," said Sima Pall, from her vantage on the roof.

"Yes, Protector," said Manti.

"How many are there?"

"Thirty-two so far, Protector. But they are still coming."

"Call the council and the defense. We will want the river maps so we may know exactly where each of the ships stands. Manti, do they look to you like Jestak's sketches of the ships on the Bitter Sea?"

"Yes, Protector. They seem to be the same."

"I wonder," she began. Then, "No matter. Call the council. I wish Jestak were here."

"I, too, Protector," said Manti, as he bowed and left.

As Jestak's party entered the Shumai camp, there seemed to be an argument. Even the wonder of horses, a Pelbar with Shumai, and so many strangers, did not seem to take precedence. As soon as they could, the newcomers joined the debate. Orto, the runner from Waldura's camp, was telling what the axeman said, but the Green Hollow Band, where they were now, did not trust the whole thing.

"But Iorta knew of them," said Orto. "He said they were called the Tantal, from the Bitter Sea."

"What is this about the Tantal?" said Jestak.

"They are in the Heart River," said Orto. "Or so a Sentani came and told us. He said they had enslaved a hundred or so Shumai, as well as some Sentani."

"In ships? With tall poles and sails?"

"Yes, how did you know?"

Jestak shucked off his tunic shirt and showed them his back. "They did that," he said. "I too was their prisoner, now nearly eight years ago. So they are in the Heart. Are they near Northwall?"

"Waldura has taken his men to Northwall and wants us to follow. They will not come."

"Waldura? I met him last fall at Northwall. Who was the Sentani?"

"He was a member of the Koorb band. His name is Epart."

"I have met him. He is in the starband. Thro, you have met him too—at the wedding."

Thro shook his head. "I may have, but I do not remember. Now, explain to us what is going on, from the beginning."

Orto repeated his story. Thro looked grave. "With one thing and another," he said, "I shall never sit at my own campfire for three days straight. It is obvious we must go. So must you, Aug, and your men. If you want Pelbar metal, or cloth for your children, or even soap. I could use some good Pelbar soap right now. My skin is near gone with what Iben gave us. You could use some too, Aug," he said, smiling. "And there are a hundred Shumai to be saved."

Aug was sour. He was drying meat for the fall journey, and gathering herbs to dry. Finally, he said, "The men who want to can go with Orto." A heavyset man was first to come forward. Then two other young men joined him, joking and bumping each other. Soon every young man in the camp had agreed to go. Finally, disgustedly, Aug picked his spear up and stood with the others.

It was agreed that those on horses would go ahead of the others, while the runners would come as they could. It was a full two days of hard riding, but the horses were in good condition with the ease of their journey so far, and they were well able to take it. On the way, they met two other small parties of Shumai and finally caught up with Waldura. Epart was glad to see Jestak, and when their story was told, he was awed and amazed. Even Waldura said he had done well, and, looking at Tia, he said, "Well, Jestak,

I imagine it was worth it. As a sensible man, you would have to come to the Shumai to get a good woman."

Jestak laughed. Shumai frankness tended to embarrass him, especially in the first flush of his marriage, which tended to dazzle him. Tia was a continual delight, prattling as they rode, full of insight and fun.

They were near the Heart when they met their first Sentani band. Evidently these people had not heard of the Tantal, for they immediately formed up in a defense perimeter, chosen well for location even on such short warning. Epart ran forward to them, and Jestak followed shortly, on his horse, holding up his Sentani tattoo.

It was a strange meeting, full of suspicion, but the two groups did come together, standing not far apart, while the leaders talked. Jestak was the melding point. A Pelbar with a Sentani tattoo and a Shumai wife made the Sentani men shake their heads. The world was falling apart when such a thing could be allowed to continue.

The Sentani leader was named Ajeron. He was an older man, scarred and wary, but he had heard of Jestak from the people of Koorb, and he had seen Ursa. With Jestak easing their understanding, he and Waldura formed an agreement. They would go in unmixed parties, but together, to prevent any other Shumai bands from fighting with Ajeron's Sentani. Now, since it was afternoon, they would camp in adjacent groups. Ajeron had women and children with him. They were returning from rice gathering in the north, and were heavily loaded.

A gift of rice to the Shumai, and instructions on how to cook it, were welcomed when one of the Sentani women—an old one, the Shumai noticed, to their amusement—brought it over. The children remained behind, though if they were Shumai, they would have soon been wandering over among the Sentani.

Hardo had drawn up his ships in order on the shore at Northwall. There was still no sign from within. He sent his chief officer, Jell, to the message stone, having been informed by the prisoners that this was the way to communicate with the Pelbar. Jell stood there, with two of his men, for a long time, but nothing happened. Finally a messenger came from the shore and told him he would have to withdraw the two men, who carried bows. He had them withdraw about fifty arms off, flanking him. Here, alone, before the tall, bland wall, he was a little frightened. Finally, though, a small door swung in the wall, and a single man appeared, walking up to him. He was short and dark but well built and apparently without fear. He came and stood silently on the rock facing Jell.

"Have you no tongue?" said Jell.

"We have no need to speak to you," said Manti. "It is you who seem to want to communicate."

"We have come to demand your surrender and that of this harzas village in the name of the Tantal."

"We decline," said Manti.

"Do not be so hasty. It would be better for you to do it now, rather than have us knock that cow-turd wall down. Look behind me. There is a weapon that can do it from the river shore."

"Don't be ridiculous," said Manti.

Jell was angry. He turned, and raised his arm. On the trap stone by the river the Tantal had erected a machine with a great hollow tube, aimed at the wall. At Jell's direction, fire was brought to it. A great flash emerged from it, then a boom, and a large projectile arched up, out, and exploded against the front wall of the city. Manti winced. The facing of the wall cracked and slid, tumbling into a heap. But it was only the facing. The wall itself remained intact. Jell smiled. "Now do you see?" he said in a level voice.

Manti raised his right hand and turned his finger in a small circle. The guards saw it and shouted a command below. The trap stone, which had stood on the shore for over three hundred years, never used before, was put into operation. It had been a platform for trade, had been used by countless bands of the outside peoples in their visits, hostile and otherwise, to Northwall. It seemed to be a large, low stone surface put there for the convenience of those on the shore. It was natural that the Tantal should have put their cannon on it.

As the guards in the basement level of Northwall grunted, turning the great screw, the crowd on the platform was laughing and cheering, reloading, and one of the officers asked, "What is that grating noise?" Several stopped, but they were not alarmed until it was too late, and the heavy weapon and they themselves swung, tipped, and dropped down into a pit. At the last moment they glimpsed the water and the spikes.

Manti smiled. "Where is your weapon?" he asked.

Jell turned, amazed, but recomposed himself, and behind his back made a signal to the two bowmen, who quickly nocked and drew. As Jell stepped back quickly, Manti went flat. Four arrows from each side of the Pelbar wall flicked out toward each man, and they dropped before they could shoot.

"One of them missed," said Manti. "We will have to give him some extra practice."

Jell had no more to say. "You will hear from us, and you will not like it, fish suckers," he finally remarked, and turning, he walked back toward the shore as calmly as he could, his spine prickling.

It was dark. From Northwall no lights showed, but in the dim sky light, its bulk loomed, square and tall, almost like one of the bluffs past which the Tantal had been cruising for some time.

"Now, perhaps, is our chance to go right to the walls, if we had a plan. We could put some of that harzas-charging dust right under the frigging wall and explode it."

"We do not have that frigging much. Maybe you are right. But we better coordinate that with some other cursed plan, or else we will have wasted the fish-sucking dust. It is plain they are well defended. Pood, how are the harzas men doing with the tube weapon? Have they dismantled the frigging pit yet?"

"No, Commander. It is not that frigging easy. All the stones seem to be locked together into one. We are breaking them with our pig-sweating hammers, but it is taking too cursed much time."

Hardo slammed down his fist. "Nineteen men lost, including the four harzas subalterns, and a first harzas orderly. They will pay for that with triple when we take them."

"And the bowmen," said Jell.

"Only two," said Hardo. "What report have the patrols brought back? How is their harzas rear defended, Tapi?"

"The patrols have not returned, Commander," said Tapi, as gently as possible.

"Not frigging returned! When were they due?"

"A quarter of the night ago, Commander."

"How many men?"

"Twenty-six in all, Commander."

"Then we must execute twenty-six of the fish-sucking slaves before their eyes tomorrow morning."

"Pardon, Commander," said Jell.

"Yes?"

"Apparently these frigging Pelbar care nothing for the other tribesmen, and all that would be lost is their frigging arms at the oars."

"Would it not provoke enmity among them, preventing them from joining forces?" smiled Hardo.

"Have you been eating dog vomit? Has it ever done that?" Melo cried. "Is that what happened at frigging home? Did the eastern Shumai not even join with the fish-sucking Peshtak? Are they not in communication with the cow-faced Rits, even as dangerous as that trip on the frigging Bitter Sea is? You must have sprung a leak!"

Even the Tantal were shocked. Hardo turned slowly and looked at Melo, who was the chief expert in the new weapon. A quiet man, usually, inclined to be studious, no politician, he was on the expedition to keep the tube weapon and the smaller shot weapons in order. An officer, from a prominent family, he was nearly untouchable, but Hardo would not allow this affront. He snapped his fingers at a guard. "Take him," he said. "Leg and arm shackles will do. In the morning he will take a place at the oars."

"But the slaves will kill him," said Jell.

"And then we will kill that whole oar," returned Hardo. "We will not have done it." From his voice, they knew he would not be crossed. "Now go!" he shouted at the guard.

"I beg your pardon, Commander," said Pood. "We now have word of a light on the west shore. A fire."

"Evidently some fish-sucking straggler watching. These peoples are scattered. When we take this city, that will cause us no frigging harm."

"And if we don't?"

"We must, Pood. We must. Now here is what we will do in the frigging morning. Four of the smaller ships will go up that creek to the frigging south there, taking two of the smaller shot weapons with them. Two on each. We will work on that harzas wall from that side. The slaves will row, not our men. We will get the tube weapon out of the frigging pit and reassemble it. The slaves will be executed on the field in front of the frigging city. We will send out two more cursed patrols, this time with fifty-two men each, one frigging south, one north. Four ships will investigate

the dog-mothering fire on the west bank. We will also prepare battering equipment, to be manned by the frigging
slaves. We . . ."

A sentry had entered the cabin, looking frightened.
Hardo paused and looked up. He was in no mood to be
interrupted. "There are now eight fires," the man said and
ducked out.

"Send word," said Pood. "See that the cursed slaves are
kept below all the ships and do not see these fires." A subaltern left rapidly, but returned almost as soon as he could
have reached the deck.

"They have seen already, Commander. They were sleeping chained to the deck. Now they are all cheering."

Hardo leaped up in a rage. He dashed his quill down,
spilling the ink, some of it splashing on his leggings. This
made him even more enraged. "Have them all put below,"
he shouted. "Have one man on each of the ships killed as
an example to the others. Harzas fish suckers. They will
learn."

The subaltern slipped out, but Jell followed, stopping the
man on deck. "Have them put below," he whispered. "But
do not have any killed."

"But Hardo . . ."

"He is mad. That would cost us twenty-six men at the
oars and would cause that much more harzas rage among
them. He would not do that if he was in a level mood.
Now. Mouth shut, and do it. I will take the responsibility."

"Yes, then I will do it." The other turned back below.
He had a sinking feeling about the expedition. This Northwall, silent and imposing in the night, uncaring, without
apparent concern, frightened him.

The band of Shumai and Sentani had reached the west
shore at dusk, but all had kept out of sight. It was the
Shumai's idea to build the eight fires—one for each section
of the night sky, one for each division of the whole day, to
tell their comrades on the ships that all would be well. The
star game was completed only when all eight sections of
sky had been covered at least once. Hence eight was the
number of winning.

Jestak wanted to get to Northwall with the horses at
once, but no one knew what forces the Tantal had de-
ployed. But toward high night, he and Stantu decided to
cross the river themselves. Thus, as Hardo was finishing

his deliberations, the two men slipped silently by, in the chill water, touching the anchor rope not five arms from him, and continuing on toward the north end of the fore-field.

"There," Jestak whispered. "There should be a guards-man there if they hold the field. We must not get too close or we will be dead. I will call him." From the water, then, came the call of a sleepy waterfowl, as if a puddle duck had been stirred to wakefulness in the reeds.

On shore, Owat touched his fellow. He pointed. The call came again, but shorter. "Reat," he said. "It is a signal."

"But the Pelbar are all inside."

Owat grinned in the dark. "All but Jestak." He cupped his hands, made the call of a screech owl. Soon two men waded silently ashore, both standing, hands up, in the dark.

"Come, Jestak," said Owat. The two went to the guards-men, and knelt down so the four heads were close together.

"You remember Stantu," Jestak began. "We have Shu-mai and Sentani together on the west shore. More Shumai will be coming. We must get into Northwall. What is the guard pattern?"

"It is six squares, Jestak. We are glad to see you."

Owat explained the pass code to him. "One thing," he added. "Did you find the girl?"

"She is my wife," said Jestak. "Over there."

"I suppose you got the horses, too," said Reat.

"How could I come back to the Protector without horses?" Jestak whispered.

Reat simply swatted his behind, though gently.

"Hush," said Stantu.

"I am glad you are back, too, Stantu," said Owat, grip-ping his hand. The two silently left through the guard pat-tern, using the pass code Owat had described. It was a simple system. No more signals were necessary until they reached the wall. They only had to stay in certain corri-dors, and follow a certain pattern of movement. The guards would observe them, and, knowing that no hostile party would follow so strange a path, would understand they were friendly. It was not long before they stood at the westwall itself and whistled softly. The pivot stone turned, and Jestak was home.

*　*　*

Before noon Adai the Jestan again toiled slowly up the curving stone steps to the highest tower of Pelbarigan. As she reached the post, Tanbar turned to her and again said, "Not yet, Jestana." She sighed and leaned against the tower wall.

"Look, what is that?" said Dindani. It was a white bird, flying from the north straight toward Pelbarigan. From the north tower came the three ascending notes of a horn announcing the message bird. The dovecote was near the highest tower, and Tanbar was there to meet the bird. Soothing it, he gently took the capsule from its leg and put it into its cage, petting and feeding it.

By then four others were there. Adai was calling from the tower, "Tanbar, bring it here. Tanbar . . ."

He went to her, followed by a growing crowd, which occupied the whole central tower, as Tanbar carefully unrolled the thin paper on the tower wall, and held his hand up for silence. "Under attack," he began. "Forty large ships of Tantal from Bitter Sea. Maybe two thousand. Many Shu. and Sent. capt. to paddle ships. Shu. and Sen. gathering with us. Jestak back from west mountains with horses, wife. Send Sent. starband from Koorb. Supply them. Talk to Mokil, Winnt. Send guardsmen if poss. Tell starband to come by orchard—Tantal weapon danger. Enemy has women, child. Seem cruel. Sima P., Protector."

In the middle of the murmur and shouting, Adai was shouting, "Give it to me, Tanbar. Give me that," but he had already started down the stairs to deliver it to the council.

Later the message was reread to the council. Imeo, the Protector, raised her hand. "We must have silence," she said. "We must read this a little at a time, and deliberate. First, has anyone ever heard of the Tantal? Who are they?" There was a silence.

Finally Adai, "Jestak spoke to me of them once."

"Jestak? What did he say?"

"Not much, Protector. We were alone. I saw some scars. On his back. He would not speak. You know he had taken the right of reticence. I appealed to him as a mother. He said it was all right, but that he had been a slave of a cruel people by the Bitter Sea called the Tantal, but that he had escaped."

"What else did he say?"

"Nothing, Protector, except that he had escaped on a

ship. He made me swear to protect his reticence. Now I
am breaking it."

"Well, Adai, perhaps he will not condemn you," said the
Protector, drily. "Now, what of this next? That is just information, about the Shumai and Sentani. It is like Sima Pall
to drop that in—Shumai and Sentani. How could they be
cooperating? Let us assume they are, since a Protector has
written it. I do not know why she put in 'Jestak back from
west mountains with horses, wife,' except to torment me. I
have had enough about Jestak from her this year."

All raised their eyes at this, for it was the first they had
heard of it. "When Brin the Brunag was Protector," said
Imeo, "she gave a very different picture. Well, anyway,
what are horses? H-O-R-S-E-S, very clearly." No one
knew.

"We will see, Protector. Perhaps we should go on," said
Lothin.

The Protector raised her eyebrows. "They want us to
supply the Sentani. What is a starband?"

"That is their hunting organization, Protector," said the
chief of defenses. "Seven groups of seven sevens, totaling
343 men. Jestak described it to me once. He never explained how he knew about it. It would be the northern
hunt we are expecting."

"Very well. What is this, 'Talk to Mokil, Winnt.' Are
they men on the hunt?"

"Winnt," said Umid, ruefully, "is now my cousin's son-
in-law, Protector. You may recall that a passing band of
Sentani hunters left a message at the stone for me last
spring. It was greetings, you may remember, from Ursa,
and her new husband, this Winnt, a Sentani."

"Yes," said the Protector, rolling her eyes. "Evidently
Sima Pall expects them to return. I recall a description in
the spring floater by Brin the Brunag, who wrote about a
great mob scene in which all of Northwall entertained the
enemy at a wedding."

"Perhaps, Protector, if they are entertained, then they
are not the enemy,'" said the chief of defenses. Again she
raised her eyebrows. He was a Jestan, and the most influ-
ential man in Pelbarigan, though of course he had little to
say in the discussions of the ruling women. She made up
her mind at that moment that she would replace him—if
somehow she could get the Jestan faction to bend to that.

"What of sending guardsmen?" she asked.

"We could send fifty, perhaps, Protector," said the chief of defenses, "or even four or five times that, but that, of course, is up to the council. We could easily spare them. Sima Pall seems to assume they would be safe with the Sentani. But I would not want to be responsible for that."

"No," returned the Protector. "No, you would not. The council will decide that, but I would advise against it. We have had no evidence of friendliness from the Sentani."

A guardsman entered. "Yes?" said the Protector.

He bowed low. "Protector, there is a Sentani here. He came from Northwall with a Northwall guardsman, warning of a group of hostile ships in the north, coming down-river."

There was a silence. "They came south together, then?" said the chief of defenses.

"Yes, Okangain. They came in an arrowboat together."

"Thank you, Rial," said the chief of defenses. "We have just had a message from Northwall by bird. They are there now."

Rial bowed and left. A discussion ensued that lasted some time, but Imeo held firm. She would supply the Sentani, but she would send no guardsmen with them. She could not trust them. The fact that this was a refusal to aid Northwall in its hour of need meant less to her than did the safety of the guardsmen. The council broke up bitterly divided on that point, but the authority of the Protector and her party held.

Before nightfall the guardhorns again sounded. The star-band was coming from the south, preparing to spend the night at Pelbar Island.

It was well into the night when a horn sounded from the shore near Pelbarigan, and two guardsmen, with the Sentani, waded across the narrow channel to Pelbar Island, south of the city. They were met by seven men.

"I am Okangain," said one. "This is Ram, and, as you know, he is Teei."

"Teei. So you have talked to the Pelbar. Inek has met us and told us of the ships," said one of the shadows on the island.

"It is a long story now," said Teei. "Call the whole star-band."

XVII

BEFORE sending the message bird, Sima Pall and the council had talked long with Jestak and Stantu. The Shumai force gathering on the west shore, she had learned, was growing, but it was not of a known or dependable size. Ajeron's Sentani would not make that much difference.

Without their saying it, the Protector had caught Jestak's meaning that this was a chance to unite the Heart River people. They would have to fight together or else risk the continuing threat of Tantal pressures and the loss of people that would entail. This engagement must be a decisive one.

From Manti's brief meeting with Jell, as well as the force, the season, and the relative desperation of the Tantal situation, they surmised correctly that the armada would put all their power into taking Northwall, if only as a refuge for the winter. With such a base, they would be in a position to invade the Heart River country on a large scale.

It was not long before dawn that three men slipped into the chill river again and glided across to the west shore, greeting the Shumai outposts as they had on their trip across. Jestak and Stantu had brought a Pelbar guardsman.

Waldura was awakened, and when Thro had been brought, the five talked briefly. Jestak explained about the message bird. This was a new fact to the Shumai, and it caused Waldura to look at Thro with some amazement. Thro only said, "There is much about the Pelbar we do not know. Jestak enjoys continually surprising us."

"I am sure the starband will help," said Jestak. "I am not sure at all that Pelbarigan will release some guardsmen to go with them."

"Not even for their own people?"

"For their own people they would all come. They will fear that the Sentani would kill them in the forest somewhere."

"Would they?"

"No," said Jestak. "Not if they had agreed, and certainly not if they knew of the Sentani prisoners."

"Then we can expect no help from Pelbarigan."

"We must not depend on it. At Northwall they are expecting some sort of coordinated attack in the morning," said Jestak. "They are hoping that the Shumai will hold the west shore, to keep the Tantal on the river. They are also hoping that if you have any spare men, you will send some to Northwall to guard the approaches and the walls. If you will, you will be admitted by the west gate, if that is safe—otherwise by the orchard."

"Orchard?"

"To the north, behind the lower wall. That is all orchard and garden."

"What of our attack?"

"We hope to wait for more Sentani before beginning our own attack, but we have devised a series of harassing operations that may prove decisive in the long run."

"The Pelbar have stressed to me, Waldura," said Stantu, "that they want to see the prisoners liberated without harm. They are fearful that an attack on our part on the whole of the Tantal might bring them harm. Unless we have a way of drawing away a boat with prisoners, or a group of boats. The Pelbar swim fairly well, but we are poor in general in the water, as you know. We need to separate out our swimmers. I agree that it would help to wait for the Sentani, if it is possible, but the Tantal may force the issue."

"I am not accustomed to waiting," said Waldura.

"I was not, either," said Thro, "but I saw in the west how effective some of Jestak's methods are. I would probably be there now, with weeds growing through my ribs, if we had not used them."

"What are these harassing operations, as you call them?" said Waldura, resignedly.

"There is a long list of possibilities, including fire rafts, underwater drilling of ships, loosing of anchors, attacks on barricaded rafts, cutting out the ships with their women and children, taking the leader's ship, guarding the creek, allowing them to force the orchard, then trapping them there, using flights of power-bow darts to keep them back, catapulting from Northwall or catapulting their ships from this bank—we brought Flandoro, here, to direct the construction of catapults if you will do that—and the firing of the river itself, with floating oils. But we—"

Thro whistled. "All of that? That will keep them busy."

"Yes," said Stantu, "but they also hold hostages, and we do not want to cause their destruction."

"At Northwall, most of our defenses are responsive rather than aggressive. We are afraid that the Tantal may use the prisoners to their advantage. We are not helpless in the face of that, but some people are going to get killed."

"Obviously," said Waldura.

"Tomorrow we expect further patrols," said Jestak. "They sent two around the city yesterday, of thirteen men each. The guardsmen eliminated them. We expect they will send larger forces. They should be harassed, of course, though the Pelbar have not enough men to wage a full-size opposition outside the walls. We could use Shumai on that. And Ajeron's men. The Tantal are good with their bows, and we do not want to cost you men, Waldura. If you can stalk and fight along with the guardsmen, we can hurt them heavily without even being seen. This tends to demoralize an enemy."

"Yes," said Waldura. "I remember chasing you, Jestak. All right, have your man here explain this thing, what was it?"

"A catapult."

"Yes. And I will send half the bowmen and twenty-five spearmen across to fight with your guardsmen. We will also hold this shore. I will send twenty men upstream to begin work on these rafts. You must send another guardsman upstream, to the Bend of Tall Rocks, to direct them. Now, Jestak, you and Stantu must get some sleep. We need your minds tomorrow, and not in a fog of fatigue. I will get this started and sleep some more myself. I am not young anymore, and I fight better on a full belly and a good night of dreams. Now go."

It was not long after, when five Shumai were standing at their ease on the shore, in the first light of morning, that out across the misting river a puff of smoke came from a Tantal ship; and as they turned, a roar, and four of the men, looking, fell riddled with shot. There was a rush to the spot. Another puff from the ship brought panic, and two more were killed. The Shumai did not show themselves after that. But they worked on the catapult with the eagerness of the vengeful.

Jestak finally crawled into the mat shelter Tia had put up. She was awake, and reached out for him. "What did she say?" was the first thing Tia murmured into his ear.

"What? Who?"

"The Protector."

"Her? About us? She asked if I had brought the horses. I said I had. She said, 'And?' I only smiled. There were others there, and much business. But she smiled back."

"Is that good?"

"A smile from Sima Pall is very good, Tia. She will love you."

"Will I love her?"

"She is hard to love. She is a politician. But you will love her."

"What of Northwall? Will we be able to hold out?"

"I don't know, Tia. I don't know."

In earliest light the Tantal had occupied the shore of the forefield and brought men to raise the cannon. They had finally broken enough of the trap stone to see it, and the tangle of bodies, in the pit.

Manti stood on the wall with Tag. He shaded his eyes. "Prepare the power bows. I think they are going to bring prisoners to help with the hauling. We don't want to kill any. We will have to shoot now."

Tag shouted the order, and the massive apparatus of the power bows were prepared, loaded, screwed back, and aimed at the prescribed trajectory for the trap stone.

"Test the wind," Tag called.

"Look," said a man on the shore. "They are sending up a flag." It was a long banner, which took the lazy wind, slowly flapping outward to the south, then flying back inside the wall. Then the flag was hauled down.

"Now what was that all about?" said a man holding a maul and chisel.

"Never frigging mind," returned Tort, who directed the operation. "Keep on this. Lower a man to that filthy tube weapon."

They turned to their work again, and did not notice at first when the massive flight of long darts came over the wall and arced toward them. As they began to turn downward, one man looked up and screamed. Forty slammed into the stone area, killing seventeen, wounding four more. Tort lay with a dart in his stomach, saying, "Ah, ah. Luid.

Get this filthy . . . get this," but then he turned his head and saw his aide face down in the mud.

"It is as I feared," said Manti from the wall. "They are bringing up prisoners. A wall of them, to recover their dead, and set up barricades. Now they will get that machine again. Look, prepare the creek. There are three ships coming. Are the guardsmen on the south shore?"

"Yes, Manti. But they are using prisoners to row."

"Sound the horn to the dam, Tag. Tell them to hold the dam trap. Look, large patrols. Tag, come back. Sound the south and north warning horns to the guardsmen in the woods. Look upriver. There are Shumai crossing. Can you see? How many?"

"Quite a group, Manti, with some Sentani. I hope they are far enough off. Look. One of the Tantal ships is giving pursuit."

"They will make it. Look, they are swinging to use their weapon. The ship is still swinging. There must be prisoners at the oars. Is that a fight on board? The Shumai are turning. Oh, Aven. Can they not contain themselves?"

On the Tantal ship the prisoners had seized that moment to revolt, but the chains held them, and the Tantal guards were slashing at them. The gunners were shouting, "Hold the ship, hold it. We can't frigging aim." The Shumai soon came into bow range, and those who had learned the bow began exchanging arrows with the Tantal guards.

Reor was with them, shouting, "Aim, remember, aim. No shot unless you have a man." The one Pelbar guardsman with them was powerless to stop them, so eager they were for a fight, and the Tantal arrows began taking a toll. The Pelbar had a guardsman's longbow, though, which took a very strong man to bend, and had extreme range. Standing in the boat, aiming carefully, he sent out a shaft nearly level that took the helmsman through the middle. He went over the side, screaming, and the Tantal ship began to list, toppling three archers off the masts into the river.

"Good, good," said Reor, turning to the guardsman, only then seeing him gritting his teeth and pushing the Tantal arrow through his arm and out. "Give me that," said Reor, taking the bow. He could hardly draw it.

"Aim right at your target," the guardsman muttered. "No arc." Reor did that, and the arrow flashed out, spinning a man off the bow of the ship and into the water. Three more Tantal ships now set out in pursuit.

A horn sounded from the west bank, sending long and shorter blasts. It was Jestak, signaling in Sentani horn talk, to row for the east bank. The prisoners who were still able began rowing. The horn sounded again, saying, "To the trees."

The pursuing Tantal ships, also rowed by prisoners, somehow could not make much headway. As the Shumai approached, arrows began coming out of the trees also, and the Tantal clearly were going to lose the ship. The patrol that had landed to the north of the city had begun running toward the action when it started, but it was a long run. They came to a small bridge over a creek, and after the first ten men had made it across, the bridge suddenly tilted up, dropping eight more men into the creekbed, where spikes were set. Arrows came out of the brush beyond, downing the ten who had crossed. The others tried to wade the creek, but the position was too exposed, and they lost five more to the unseen attackers. Retreating, they formed up and sent a flight of arrows into the brush, hearing a couple of shouts in response. They then turned and raced upstream to cross safely.

By now the ship had grounded and the Shumai were boarding it. The first three men tumbled back into the river with arrows in them, but one oar of prisoners was now loose from the chains, and all six men swarmed freely over the bowmen. Eight Pelbar guardsmen waded, leaping, out from shore and climbed into the ship.

One, with a black band around his arm, shouted, "Quick, free those men. Larc. Fire the ship. In the stern." Pelbar swords hacked at chain and wood, and oar after oar of the prisoners was freed. They tumbled off into the shallow water on the north side and made their way to shore. By now the Tantal ships were coming into range, and sending scattershot out at the men, but they were largely protected, and the guardsmen's longbows began sending out flights of arrows at them.

Almost all were free. "Come," said the guardsman with the black band. "Over the side. Now. Come."

The thin Sentani who was fooling with the gun turned and grinned. "One moment," he said, and touched a flame to the hole. It erupted in an explosion, and the mainmast of the lead ship broke off near the top, the sail sagging.

The man clapped his hands and leaped up to follow the guardsman, but by the time he reached the water, he had an arrow in his shoulder.

The Tantal patrol had crossed the creek and ran north to intercept the escaping men and their allies. There were twenty-seven now, and only the presence of their own ships nearby kept them going. They themselves were outnumbered, but if they could gain the trees, they would have the enemy between them and the force on the ships. The first man into the woods suddenly vanished, screaming, into a trap. The others then went very cautiously, feeling the ground with their bows ahead of them. Shouts from the shore indicated that the other Tantal had reached the ship, which was now burning hard. Soldiers from the ship, and the patrol, joined up and moved through the woods on the edge of the river, but no one was there. All had vanished.

At the edge of the river, a Tantal turned over the body of a guardsman and remarked, "So that is what a Pelbar looks like. They cut their hair like a bowl, almost. We had a prisoner like that once. At the Bitter Sea. Ath, how I wish I were frigging there right now."

Through the far end of the tunnel into which the guardsmen had led them, the mixture of Shumai, Sentani, and Pelbar had reached the woods at the edge of the bluffs.

The guardleader was conducting all of them well into the woods, posting his own men at the edge of the shorefield. He had learned enough Sentani dialect from Winnt to communicate. The Sentani escapees would repeat for the Shumai, with whom they had conversed on the ships, until all was understood. "Now, we have to separate well men from wounded," he began. "The freed men must go to the city to have those irons cut off. Wounded men go with them. The rest of us have to prepare to meet the patrol the Tantal are sure to send around the city. I suppose they will reinforce it now. We cannot have any fighting at initiative. We do not have the men, and we do not want to lose anybody anyhow. Do it our way, and we will kill them off or drive them back without even being seen. Now, let us take only five sunwidths to organize, and then we have to get going."

Hardo, at this time, was cursing again. He had seen the action from his ship. This was the first effective opposition they had met on the river, and he had lost his first ship since the overland portage to the Cog River from the Bitter

Sea. He had been able to see the bridge go from under his patrol, and some of the fighting. He was pacing the deck waiting for a report.

Finally the small boat came up to the side of the lead ship, and a tired Tantal squad leader stumped down the deck to report.

"Well?" said Hardo.

"Commander, we have lost the whole filthy ship, and all the harzas men on it. Thirty-six. Nineteen of the prisoners were killed. I mean, slaves. And nine of the filthy attackers that we know of. They were Shumai. And one was a fish-sucking Pelbar. We wounded some. Three men are dead on the lead relief ship, and seven wounded. Of the patrol onshore, twenty-three were killed at the small frigging bridge, and one later."

"What is that, then?"

"That is, that is a filthy sixty-three, Commander."

Hardo stamped in anger, turned, brought his fist against the cabin wall. Then, nursing his hand, he turned again and said, "Are they in pursuit of the frigging enemy? What is going on?"

The squad leader paused and rubbed his eye. Then, looking at the floor, he said, "They have disappeared, Commander. The filthy men cannot find them."

Hardo turned his back. Over his shoulder he said, "Have them break off. We have a city to take. Reinforce the frigging patrol. I want a hundred filthy men on it. Send Captain Norto to me."

"Yes, Commander," said the squad leader, returning to his boat, and rolling his eyes at the helmsman as he clambered down into it.

"Cast off," said the helmsman. "Now, you pig snouts, pull together, pull."

Manti and his aide watched the three small ships row up into the mouth of Arkan Creek. "Will the barrier stones hold against them?" Tag asked.

Manti laughed. "Yes, they will hold. Watch."

About halfway up the length of the creek to the city, the lead ship suddenly stopped, sending men toppling onto the deck. Then it slowly settled into the creekbed. "You see," said Manti. There was a puff of smoke from the side of the lead ship, which sat in only five feet of water.

"Look out," said Tag. An explosion on the city wall scaled off some of the facing again.

"If they keep that up," said Manti, "we will have lost all our wall trap." Another puff came from the lead ship, from another gun further aft. This one hit near the first, and more facing came down. Then the third gun took its turn, again hitting nearby, dropping more stone.

"They are concentrating on one spot," said Tag. "They will put a hole in it eventually."

"It is too high up to do them any good," said Manti. "But we must see about a repair crew."

The second ship now joined in, but it was farther downstream and at a bad angle, and the shell fell short. Tag laughed. "They will find the range," said Manti. "I wonder where the guardsmen on the south are?"

As if in answer, scattered arrows flashed out of the trees to the south of the creek and pierced four men on the ships. A gun was turned, and a scattershot sent out in the direction of the woods. Two of the gunners went down. The other put up a wooden shield and reloaded.

The lead ship continued to batter away at the wall, but they were distracted by a slow, random fire from the woods. None of the crew dared show himself. The prisoners sat at the oars. They were not allowed to turn their heads, or a lash from the slave guard would sting their backs. The pain was not worth the view, so the prisoners sat and watched the slow, muddy current of the creek sift its way through their holed boat, eddying back, floating objects in the craft.

On the wall, Manti said, "We might take those prisoners, but losses would be heavy with two ships so close, and the Tantal at the trap stone too near. Tag, could you hit the gunners from here?"

"It is too long a shot, Manti. It might go wide and hit a prisoner."

"It is a tie, then. Well, we must have patience." Turning, he took a report from the action to the north. He frowned and shook his head. "That was too costly," he said. "Tag, keep me informed. I am going down to see the freed prisoners."

"Yes, Manti," she replied.

Hardo was again enraged. The lead boat had been holed, and thus effectively lost. He was losing men there again. The slaves would have to be unchained in order that they could be put to further use, and that meant further risk.

Behind Hardo's back, Pood was saying to Jell, "He doesn't know what he is doing. He is costing us all these fish-sucking men and getting nowhere. This is a foolish, filthy operation. We must break off and go south."

On the west shore, back in the woods, the catapult was being assembled. "There," Flandoro was saying, sweating in the cold wind. "Now we need to double-brace that piece. The swinging arm will hit it every time it comes around."

"Pelbar," Waldura said, "let us make two more while we are at it."

"Waldura," a man called from the shore. "Here. The Pelbar have sent another man by the south with shields. They want us to make shields against the missiles and arrows."

"The arrows are nothing to those things that roar."

"We know nothing about those," said the Pelbar. "Except how dangerous they are. The big ones no shield would stand against. They are already damaging our wall."

The Tantal patrol going around Northwall from the north was cautious and wary. The men went in twos, but spaced quite widely. They kept their arrows nocked. Nothing happened at first, then stray arrows came from the woods, almost every one finding a soldier. The Tantal never saw the source. When they came to a small stream, they avoided the bridge, the lead men fording. Looking up, they said, "It is all right. There are no traps in that one." Gingerly, the next pair of men went across. They were safe. Then, ten arms beyond the bridge, they fell into a ground trap. The others, peering down, saw a pit filled with impaled bodies.

Eventually, they decided to form up and go at a trot, staying off anything like a path. This brought them to the rear of the city. "Look," said the captain. "The wall is lower here."

"But probably just as thick," remarked the squad leader with him.

"A good charge of the frigging dust would take it down," said the captain. "We could do it now if we had it."

"And if the swine didn't try something else," said the squad leader. Down the way, another man cried and went down with an arrow in him. The city itself was silent.

Hardo signaled the holed ship to keep up the firing at the wall. From shore they signaled back that some progress was being made in breaching the wall about twenty feet up.

"Why so high?" Jell asked.

"We are assuming it is thinner there," returned Hardo. "If we widen the filthy breach, then all the frigging wall above it will fall down, and we will have something to climb on in storming the frigging city. Now, I want another hundred filthy men to sweep the woods south of that creek. The filthy arrows from there are hampering the fish-sucking ships in the creek. I want to occupy all the surrounding woods."

"What of the tribemen outside, Hardo? They seem to roam freely. Look at the west bank. Look now, what is that," said Jell, as the catapult was rolled to the bank. It was faced with logs, and a scattershot from the nearest ship simply slammed into it and rattled off.

"Signal them to use a single shell," said Hardo. The signal was sent, and the return came.

"The dogs' mothers have no more filthy charging dust," said Jell. "We'll send some filthy more over to them."

At that point they saw a rock from the catapult launch high into the air and fall harmless off the bow of the nearest ship. Then men on the ship jeered, but already the catapult sling was disappearing backward to be reloaded. The captain called out to move the ship, and the anchor was being hauled up. Hardo lashed his thigh with his stick.

Eventually, the sweep Hardo had ordered met the patrol coming around from the north. "What have you seen?" said the captain.

"Not much, except arrows," the other returned. "The wall is lower in the rear section, and the creek is dammed up to form a pond. Perhaps that is their water supply. We could cut that off."

"Not without destroying the ships in the frigging lower end," was the reply. "We have been all through the swinish woods to the south and met nothing at frigging all. But the filthy arrows have been coming from those woods for some time."

"We lost fourteen men coming around, and we never saw a single enemy."

"I am afraid, Wainig. We are losing too many swine-snouted men."

"We have no frigging choice," was the reply.

"The filthy men are unhappy. They are scared and mad. There seems nothing to fight."

Meanwhile, Manti was talking to the freed men, who had been admitted through the west tunnel from the woods entrance. As they talked, a door opened, and, turning, the freed men saw the most powerful man most of them had ever met. He was carrying a hammer, tongs, a punch, and chisels. Two men behind him were wheeling in a large block with an anvil on it.

"Here," said Manti. "He will remove the irons. Now, is there a Sentani here who knows how to talk with a horn?"

Once they understood, all the men responded that they could. Manti picked one. "Good," he said. "Free this man first. Bring him to the walls. We will talk to the prisoners on the boats in the creek." The man's name was Rawn. He had his arm around a Shumai woman whose ankles were bleeding.

Once the sweep south of the creek had passed, a Tantal in the lead boat put his head up to watch. An arrow promptly pierced his neck and he slumped back into the boat.

Across the river, the catapult was loaded and loosed for the fifth time, without effect. The Tantal were laughing and shouting derision from the water, keeping their vessels out of range, largely by rowing upriver. Then from over the trees, two large stones arced up, the first falling short, the other hitting a Tantal ship squarely, holing it. It settled rapidly to the bottom, the people in it struggling up, as other boats came to their rescue.

From the opposite shore a cheer went up, though, as the tube weapon finally was lifted from the trap stone. It was barricaded by logs and prisoners, so protected from another flight of arrows from the power bows. But south of the city, the patrol was conferring with the sweeping probe of Tantal from around the north, and a cluster of men, standing at their ease, never noticed another flight of arrows from the power bow until it was too late. But the flight had gone rather wide, and only four men were hit. On the wall, a guardsman shouted down, "Went west. Reload. Allow for more wind." But the Tantal were soon out of range.

The tube weapon needed repair. But as Hardo had predicted, the expert who had spoken up and been put with the prisoners had been killed. In reprisal the six on his oar were executed. No one else knew so much about the tube weapon, and repair was going slowly.

Another cheer went up, though, as the lead boat in the creek finally put a hole through the wall of the city. Plainly they had punched their way into some sort of living quarters. They began to widen the hole with repeated shots, but by the third quarter of the day, they had run out of charging dust.

In his cabin, Hardo was angry and worried. The wall was plainly tied together in some way. It was not tumbling. He was afraid for his supply of the explosive dust. He had lost men and had made little headway. He could tell that the other leaders were restless, and his severities had made them more so. Added up, his losses that day were 112, with 19 wounded. Plainly the expedition could not sustain such punishment for long. The Tantal had to stay well away from the west bank because of the catapults, of which there were now six. The woods were not safe. The tube weapon was out of order. Hardo had only one more idea to try that might be costly, but this time it would cost slaves. There was a door, out of which the Pelbar had come to talk to Jell. The Tantal knew well what part of the wall it was in. It was a small target, but he ordered it shelled.

Supplying charging dust to the ships in the creek cost him two more men, but then he used a shield of slaves, and made it all right. The tube weapons were successful, and soon the door area was breached, the door swinging open.

Hardo decided on an attack force of two hundred men sent across the forefield behind a shield of slaves, forty in all, to form a human wall. Four hundred more men, and another human shield, were poised at the river's edge. But both shields were thin. There weren't enough slaves. Experimental firing along the base of the wall had brought no further results. He had to concentrate on the one door.

It was the fourth quarter of the day when the advance began, at a walk. On the wall, Manti was with Rawn the Sentani, talking to the prisoners on the ships with the horn. The Tantal commander had opened the door in the wall, but it led nowhere, and the whole corridor had been sealed off. It was well protected by the inside guard.

"Look, Manti," said Tag. "What shall we do? The prisoners are roped together in a line."

Manti was silent for a time. Then he told Rawn, "I think they mean to use the prisoners for shields right to the wall, then perhaps kill them. See the drawn swords? We must tell them to run for the door when they get close to it. If any fall, the others must drag them in. We will take care of the Tantal behind them if we can. Tag, send the word. All bowmen ready for the Tantal. No prisoners to be shot."

Rawn began sending horn blasts. The men on the ships in the stream involuntarily stood, and had to be lashed back to their seats. In the moving line of men, the Sentani muttered to the Shumai among them, "It is a signal. Follow us when we run."

"Silence, you," said the Tantal behind them, jabbing them with swords. Soon the Tantal had stirred the prisoners into a trot, but at a long blast from the wall, they began to run in earnest, separating themselves from the Tantal. Arrows began falling from the wall and the Tantal were trying to keep up, slashing at the prisoners, who made for the door in a rush. A tangle of men made it in, then a door slid down, blocking the entrance. The Tantal on the outside began running, and those on the shore quickly brought up prisoners to shield them, but the prisoners fell repeatedly. The retreating Tantal took arrows halfway to shore.

Inside, the prisoners and those few Tantal who had made it were in complete darkness, shouting and milling around in total confusion. Then a single light was seen overhead, very slight, and a voice shouted, "Silence."

A Tantal aimed an arrow at the light, which went out. Utter silence followed, and darkness, with the groaning of wounded men. Eventually, the light reappeared, lowered on a small platform. "Now," a voice said. "All Tantal throw down your weapons."

They hesitated. "That is a woman," one said.

"Now," the voice said. Some did. "All of you." The rest slowly complied. "Now," the voice shouted. "No prisoners may touch the weapons. Now. Shumai and Sentani walk down the hallway. You will find a corner. Any Tantal who follow will be killed. Now walk."

The prisoners shuffled slowly down the hallway, bringing with them their wounded men. After they turned the corner, they watched a stone slide out from the wall and block the way back. Then a wall ahead opened, light poured in, and their freed fellows greeted them, along with Pelbar, with litters for the wounded.

The Tantal were left in the dark for a long time. They shouted against the walls in vain. They picked up weapons and beat on the walls. Again the light appeared, and they were allowed, one at a time, around the corner, squeezing through a narrow slit in the stone, to be shackled and led down to the Pelbar ice caves.

On the shore by the trap stone Jell was counting. There were sixty-two men dead on the forefield, and nineteen had been taken prisoner. As if to add insult, the door opened once more in the Pelbar wall. They had lost a full seventh of their fighting force. Hardo's methods might be all right against tribesmen and barbarians, but they plainly were not working against the Pelbar. Tort was dead. Pood wanted to leave, but that was no solution either. Jell himself would have to find a way to take over. Plainly Hardo must go. It would be tonight.

The patrol had brought word of a lower wall in the rear. He would send a force of five hundred there, with a charge of the explosive dust, and they would breach the wall in the dark. Working at night, secretly, they would not be hampered by arrows from the woods. No one, not even a Pelbar, could aim an arrow in the dark.

As darkness grew, the two ships in Arkan Creek began to withdraw. A shield of prisoners was brought to cover the withdrawal of the men in the lead ship, including the prisoners there. Again Northwall was shrouded in darkness. The door in the wall had closed again. On the west shore the eight fires were burning.

Hardo was angry. Jell and Pood looked at him with level eyes. He wanted an armed attack on the west shore. "We can put out those cursed fires. Look. They are only filthy barbarians. I do not like that kind of filthy tongue sticking from those I enslave. We can use a shield of fish-sucking prisoners and sweep the filthy shore, destroying those frigging catapults. Then we can turn to frigging Northwall again tomorrow."

"What makes you think that they will stay quiet tonight? Now we are at our most frigging vulnerable. And what frigging good will it do to take the west shore when we want filthy Northwall?" said Jell. "This is plainly swine-snouted."

Hardo rose, livid. "I said I do not like fish-sucking defiance," he said, drawing a knife. Then a startled look crossed his face, turning to agony, as Pood had put a dagger in him from behind. He slumped to the table.

"Now," said Jell, "throw that grease pit over the side. Order lights on all the frigging ships, and a watch, and we will mount our attack on that harzas rear wall."

The Tantal were very quiet. They had settled on an attack of four hundred men, with charging dust enough for the wall and for any obstructions they met inside. There was no sign of opposition. The force stayed well away from the city until directly east of it, coming in as silently as possible.

"I do not like this. It is too filthy easy," said a squad leader.

"Quiet," whispered another.

They made it all the way to the wall. Dust was placed under a large charge, and another, five arms south. Fuses were lit, and the sappers retreated with the main force. A flash and roar went up, then another, and the force rushed forward, lighting torches. The wall had not come down, but there were two ample holes, and Tantal began pouring through both of them. They were among trees. Lights appeared on the walls.

"We are in an orchard," one man yelled. Then arrows flicked out, and from the high city walls to the south, shadows appeared, enormously shrouded, and hurled large cubes down among them, which burst. The men nearest began yelling and running, shouting, "Bees, bees." The attack turned into a rout, and the way out through the holes in the wall became clogged with bodies, as arrows and some Shumai spears came from figures on the wall. The survivors made for the woods and the river. As they came over the final rise, one man in the lead looked upriver and yelled, "What is that?"

"Fire ships," said the man behind him.

They were not ships, but rafts, twenty of them, that the Shumai had built upstream with the help of five Pelbar guardsmen. By afternoon, Stantu and Jestak had plotted the position of every ship in the river, noting which held women and children, which had prisoners, and which were manned only by Tantal soldiers. Thirty-seven ships were left. Of these, twenty had some prisoners. About two hundred fifty women and children occupied six ships midstream, surrounded by other ships. Of the twenty with prisoners, fourteen appeared to have substantial numbers, though of their nearly two hundred some were ashore as laborers and shields. Fifty-three prisoners had been freed and were in Northwall. There appeared to be about thirteen hundred Tantal fighting men in all, after all their casualties of the day. Eleven ships, lined up down the eastshore side of the armada, apparently were manned solely by Tantal men.

These were the ships that were to be attacked with the fire rafts, especially if a night attack was made against Northwall. From the muffled sounds on the river, the Shumai could tell that these ships were being moved, and the men leaving. Then they took up moorings near the east shore, guarded, apparently, by small crews.

The Shumai and Jestak had had quite a discussion about the best means of freeing the prisoners. Some had thought that an attack on the ships crewed only by Tantal should be coordinated by attacks on ships with prisoners. Others had thought it easier and less costly to the prisoners to capture women and children, then trade for the prisoners.

The conclusion was a compromise. They would send fire rafts to attack the ships near the east shore. Then they would single out four downstream ships with prisoners and would also cut the anchor ropes of all those with women and children. That would be done before the rafts, which had been brought downriver, were fired. It was a sketchy operation, because not that many Shumai were good swimmers. At the last moment they decided to rescue only two ships with prisoners.

The night was dark, as the Tantal themselves had wished. At Jell's direction, lights had been placed on all the ships, so that no attackers could swim right up to them in the dark. That hampered the whole Shumai plan. It was decided that the fire rafts would have to be lighted first, to distract attention.

Jestak and Stantu were in the water under the counters of two ships with Tantal dependents when the fires were lighted. They swam underwater and cut the lines, sawing through the thick, tough fiber with short swords, then moving back to the sides of the ships as the current began to tug them slowly downstream. Then they silently moved to other ships. It was a dangerous operation, because there were still a full seven hundred fighting men on and around the ships, and all were ready to join the raid at the rear of Northwall if it got into the city.

The whole strategy was to move quietly and then get away. Five ships had been cut loose before anyone cried out. All eyes had been on the fire rafts, which floated down the river in twos, each one tied to the one at its side by a rope. The plan was to catch the rope on the bows of the vessels so the rafts would swing in, one on each side. As the rafts caught, the men guiding them would dive and get away. All were to swim to the west bank. It was a dangerous task.

Jestak and Stantu were moving west across the river, ship by ship, mostly underwater. The Tantal were alarmed, and several ships were getting underway either to intercept the fire rafts or to catch the drifting ships of dependents. All the ships were alerted, and the Tantal on those with prisoners were standing, ready to defend themselves or kill the prisoners if necessary.

The first fire raft hit a ship perfectly, and as the two rafts closed on it, burning furiously, it went up like tinder. Those aboard began jumping into the cold river, swimming for the east bank, where their own sentries were pulling them out.

The ships on the west shore expected some attack, but none anticipated the fury of the Shumai, swarming over the sides and fighting hand to hand in the semidarkness. The prisoners, standing at their oars, fought as well, and the defenders were too distracted to kill them. The Shumai shouted to them, "Pull, pull downstream." They sat back and gave way at the oars, pulling the ships away from those behind, who could not send arrows indiscriminately into them because their own men were on board.

Concentrating on just two ships of prisoners made the Shumai plan work, and soon they turned the craft west and ran them aground. The others dared not come near because of the Shumai still on the shore with the catapults. All but nine of the prisoners made the shore. The Tantal on board were all slaughtered by the Shumai, but they fought hard, and killed nineteen of the attackers.

On the east side, three ships were on fire. The Tantal had caught all but one of the ships of dependents, and that one was now underway under the command of men on

board. All the other fire rafts were avoided, and several of
the men guiding them were killed. It was clearly not an
unmixed victory, but it had shown the Tantal that the river
itself was not a sanctuary.

Jestak and Stantu had not swum ashore, but had made
their way to the upriver ship on the west shore, swimming
quietly and carefully. Jestak had a large drill strapped to
his back, and Stantu a small bag of wooden pegs.

The prisoners were confined to the hold during the fighting, watched by guards. One Sentani, leaning at his ease
against the hull, whispered, "What is that noise?"

"What? The fighting?"

"No. A chewing of wood." Then he jumped with a
squeal.

The guard above called down, "All right, swine. Quiet."

"Water. Water is coming in," said the Sentani, quietly,
putting his hand over the place. "Feel here."

"Hush now," said another.

The Sentani's hand was forced back by a wooden peg.
All the men there heard the tamping. Word was passed
quietly along. Then the sound was again heard further aft,
and the men there stopped the hole with a cloth until it
was pegged. In all, two holes on each side were drilled,
each one marked and hidden by the prisoners.

Working for several hours, the two men treated the four
ships in the upper west line the same way. Each time the
men inside understood. Things were quiet near morning,
when those ships were cut loose, and they drifted down
toward shoal water before anyone aboard realized it. A
horn from the west shore signaled the men inside to tap out
the pegs. They silently moved above the rising water until
the ships were beyond saving and were sitting on the bottom
in five feet of water.

The fight for them was long and sharp, but the fact that
the Shumai now had eight catapults, which Waldura commanded with gusto and pleasure, kept the other ships off.
In the end, about half the prisoners had been liberated, the
rest being killed by the Tantal. The Tantal crews had either been killed or had swum out to other ships for safety.

Now the Shumai had their first of the new weapon.
They examined it carefully, but could not make out how it
worked.

As the day dawned, the clouds smelled of snow, and a
cold wind blew from the north. Things had reached a stand-

off. The Tantal stayed in their ships, riding at anchor. The workers at Northwall repaired the breaches in the orchard wall and nursed what wounded they had, including some of the Tantal. Jestak and Stantu, completely chilled, lay in fur rolls to the west, shivering. Jestak was vomiting with the cold and the river he had swallowed.

Deep in the ice caves of Northwall, now largely empty, the Tantal prisoners lay chained. One young man kept saying to the woman who was washing his bleeding arm, "Why are you doing this? Filthy Pelbar! Why are you doing this?"

"Quiet," said Sendi. "Here is the Mejana to look at your wound."

The young man looked up at the severe woman who said nothing, but removed the dressing and peered, in the dim light, at the hole the arrow had made. She frowned. Then she touched the young man's hand, tapping it.

"Do you feel this?"

"Yes. A little," he said.

"Here, do you feel it here?"

"No. I feel nothing there."

"Do you ever pray?"

"Pray? What in the whole swinish, filthy world for?"

"You had better learn how." Viret the Mejan turned to Sendi and said, "Put a fresh dressing on it." She looked down the line of sullen men for the next with a wound. A guardsman stood by her.

On board the lead ship there was a deep discussion among the leaders.

"Plainly," said Pood, "we should leave this filthy place. Many think so. We should make a truce and leave. All we have succeeded in doing is uniting former frigging enemies and losing an incredible cursed number of our men. How many last night? One hundred and twenty? We cannot go on like this much longer. If we leave now, we can make it out of this filthy territory."

"To where?" said Jell. "It is hostile country all the way to the filthy mouth. And there where would we be? Would they have use for this large a frigging force, in frigging semihelplessness? And could we make it before the cursed winter? The water is already chilly, and frosts are nearly nightly."

"The tube weapon. What of the filthy tube weapon? I hear it cannot be fixed."

"We haven't much charge for it anyhow. Not for very long."

"I think we must try something frigging else," said Jell. "We have been fooling around with frigging minor efforts. We should mount one all-out filthy attack, with our charging dust, to blow down that filthy wall. We did it in the orchard. We put a hole in it. Why not a frontal attack, using prisoners, shields, and rolling shields? Once we are frigging inside, we will have them. They are not cowardly. If they had the frigging men, they would come out and fight us. Every day, these swinish Shumai seem to grow in numbers. We will have to mount an attack that will get us into the city and then we can shut out the filthy Shumai. They are nothing without the fish-sucking Pelbar. That filthy attack last night would never have been planned by the frigging Shumai—or even the Sentani. We have to plan today, and prepare, and then tomorrow, at first light, we will mount the filthy attack."

There was much argument, and disagreement, but they all saw the desperateness of their situation. Hatred for them was now general along the river. The enemy was growing in strength. Preparations would be careful. They would rely on their numbers and carry the fight into Northwall with their one effective weapon—the charging dust. The sun had arisen nearly a quarter ago, and the silence from the Tantal ships was watched with some anxiety by the people on both shores. They had not even moved when the freed prisoners were ferried across the river to the north and taken to Northwall for care.

About that time, the starband, running northward at full pace, came on a Pelbar guardsman. He was limping.

"Ho, Sentani," he said. "I cannot run like you. But the others are up ahead."

"We thought you could not come because of your Protector," said Mokil. "But we have seen the mob of your tracks."

"We decided to go anyhow."

"That will cause you trouble."

"Not at Northwall. Now do not let me hold you up. I will follow." As the last man passed him, he whacked him gently on the behind. The guardsman lifted a hand and called, "Ho."

Inside Northwall, there was order, but much concern. The Pelbar had never had more than five hundred men, and of these a number were either very young or old. The inside guard was almost all women, and some of the wall guard. They were well trained, and very effective, but it went against the grain of Pelbar society to expose them to the hazards of war. Already a number of the men, and some of the inside guard, had been killed. In spite of all their military training, the deaths had caused a wave of shock to go through people of a basically gentle culture.

A large gathering had met in the judgment room. Jestak came across the river again, and this time Tia was with him. He was still dazed with his time in the cold water. Many of the Pelbar looked at Tia rather overlong in their curiosity. She was embarrassed and flushed, and this simply brought out her beauty more and caused the North-wallers to see what a prize Jestak had gone west for.

"So you brought your wife but left the horses on the west shore where they would be safe," said the Protector.

"He is a doting husband," said Waldura. "He leaves her with me and spends the night bathing in the river."

"He has been busy," said Tia, smoothing Jestak's hair. "So have I. We have built catapults. Carried rocks. I have bent my bones pulling back the slinging arm. I am becoming a horse myself."

"Not quite, my dear," said the Protector.

"Well," said Tia, "if they do not do something to us soon, they will be working in the rain. The wind has turned south."

"True," said Thro. "You can smell it."

"Perhaps they will go," said the eastcouncil.

"No," said the Protector. "Perhaps they are deciding. But I doubt that they will go. Where would they go now? Everyone is against them. If they had decided to go, they would have. We must prepare. There are many prisoners still in their hands, and Northwall itself, which is our concern, has been more damaged than since it was built centuries ago. It is their weapon. What do you know of it?"

A brief report was given, and explanation from a Shumai who had been imprisoned on a ship with the smaller tube weapons. He did not understand it. "It is a dust they put in, a gray dust, that disappears with a roar in fire, and sends out the missile."

Jestak roused. "We examined the one we captured last night. They have discovered the secret of the eastern cities, the reason they are never attacked by the Peshtak and Coo. They have these weapons. They are a remnant of the ancient times."

"We saw pictures of them, Jestak and I, in the place of learning of the ancient children," said Tia. "In Emeri country."

"Can we make them?" asked the Protector.

"I am sure we can," said Jestak, "if we can find out how, and how, especially, to get the dust. That seems the secret."

"Yes," Manti put in. "They apparently used it up yesterday in throwing things at our wall, and they had to bring more. From the ships."

"Have the Tantal prisoners been questioned?"

"Yes, Protector. But they either know nothing or will not tell."

"We could make them tell," said Waldura.

"If possible, we would prefer not to do anything violent to prisoners," the Protector returned.

"Well," said Waldura, "that has nothing to do with our retaking the prisoners. If you find out, I trust you will not use it on us, anyhow. I do wonder, though, how many times I have stood on the trap by the river."

"I have stood on it, too, many times," said Manti. "It is safe enough. I almost wonder if those who had it built could foresee its use. The large weapon might have pierced these walls eventually."

A guardsman entered, bowed, and said, "The Tantal have begun building something on shore, Protector. And it is beginning to rain."

The high windows of the judgment hall overlooked the forefield, but they were narrow, and those who wanted to look had to take turns. None could make it out. But some work had begun on numerous structures. Plainly they were connected with further attack on Northwall. The rain had begun to grow heavier.

"I pity the prisoners in those ships," said Waldura. "It will not be a good night for fire rafts."

"Or for runners, either," said the Protector. "But I hope the Sentani are coming."

"And some guardsmen from Pelbarigan," said Manti.
"What do you think, Jestak?" But Jestak was asleep on the
floor, his fingers curled around Tia's thumb.

Pood was dead. He had opposed Jell too steadily, so Jell
had served him as they had Hardo. This weakened Pood's
party considerably, since he was the only spokesman for
departure from a first family. They were a less belligerent
group anyway. Jell had things his way for the time. He was
even more determined than Hardo, and benefited from
Hardo's various feints and scratches. He dismissed the obvious fact that the single most costly attack mounted so far
was his against the orchard wall. They had at least
breached the wall.

On shore he was making preparations to advance across
the forefield behind a row of prisoners and a roofed barrier
on wheels. He was sure that he could put a large hole in
the wall and then get his men inside. Calculating numbers,
he saw that he still had the advantage, especially with the
Shumai on the west shore. He preferred to be inside for the
winter, even if their losses were heavy. He trusted that they
could hold the city against any number of Shumai that
could gather. The Shumai were no good except in a quick
and fierce assault.

The Shumai were not responding in great numbers to
the call sent out by Waldura. Jell could see there weren't
that many. It was too late in the season, and preparations
for following the herds were too far advanced. The whole
thing seemed vague and far off. They were not concerned
with Northwall, and rumors of Shumai prisoners of a
strange and unknown people were to them perhaps only
that. Nonetheless, those that came had stayed. They had
fought bravely and effectively, and a number had died.

The Tantal were used to winning in a long fight involving the advanced weapons they had been learning, especially, of course, the redevelopment of gunpowder and explosive weapons.

They worked into the night on the rolling barriers, and
it was apparent to those inside the city what was underway
now. Northwall's only addition to their present defenses
was to activate the forefield ditch trap. It was not very
effective, but might help some.

In the morning it was still raining. The Tantal had
roofed over certain sections of their barrier wall. Those in-

side Northwall assumed, correctly, that these were the sections which would contain explosives. Rocks were prepared on the wall to drop on them, but even from where they watched, the Pelbar could see that these sections were heavily reinforced.

"I cannot understand. They look like straps on the top," said Manti from the wall. He did not have long to wait to learn. The Tantal were roofing those sections of the attack barrier with prisoners.

"The bastards," said Stantu from the wall. "The cowgutted bastards." Tag was with him. She blushed and turned away.

Even some of the Tantal themselves did not like this. Though accustomed to misusing prisoners and enslaving them, this struck some of the regular line soldiers as going too far. They could do nothing about it, though, and tended to try to dissociate themselves from the whole action only by expressions of sympathy when they strapped the men—and some women—to the barrier roofs.

It was into the second quarter of the day that the whole assemblage started across the field. Halfway, the ground tilted forward and the whole complex rushed downward into the ditch trap. The prisoners on the roof were yelling and screaming in fear, but they were comparatively unhurt. There was nothing the Tantal could do but haul the whole thing out and retreat. A steady pecking of arrows from the walls began to tell. The Tantal had shields, but the arrows from the heavy guardsmen's longbows went right through. Other sections of wall were rushed forward and placed over the ruined complex. They were the rest of the day getting it back in the rain.

Plainly, though, they were still determined, and the evening saw them building further structures meant to bridge the ditch trap. They had lost, in all, sixty-two more men. The prisoners on the roof were suffering in the cold rain and were finally taken down.

The Sentani starband had stopped for the night, after passing the Pelbar guardsmen. They were camped several ayas north of Highkill, when, quite late, they heard the Pelbar coming.

Mokil stood and went to greet them. "Ho, Pelbar. We thought you would have stopped. Come and have some hot tea."

"Thank you," said the guard chief. He was the nephew of the Protector, but he had come anyway. The only family not represented were the Jestan. It was agreed by all the guard, privately, that they should stay. It was an expression of solidarity, for the Jestan had most of all wanted to go. The Protector would have no complaints about their party.

The Pelbar were tired and sore, but it was plain to the Sentani that although they were not runners, they were superbly trained, disciplined, and very determined.

"When will we get there?" the guard chief finally asked, speaking very slowly, a mug of tea in his hand.

"Tomorrow, before high sun," said Mokil. "Or high rain, I should say." The rain was bogging down the runners, but it was warm enough not to chill them when they kept going. That night the starpoint and the Pelbar slept together under a great overhang of rock. Both shared the guard. For some of the guardsmen, it was the first night they had ever spent outside Pelbarigan, and that, with their extreme fatigue, gave them a surrealistic experience. They tossed much in their sleep, and when the Sentani were getting ready to run again at dawn, they could not move as quickly.

"You will catch us," said Orther, as they left. The guardsmen were ashamed, but they could make their bodies do only what the bodies could do. Soon they were running again. It was a nightmare experience for them, but they were determined with all their Pelbar loyalty and training not to let Northwall face its crisis alone.

That night the whole river was filled with fire rafts. The Shumai tried a new technique. They had put many men to building them. They came behind in skin boats. The first rafts were in fours, spread out, and the Shumai guiding them stayed out of range of the Tantal while releasing them.

The Tantal sent small boats upriver to cut the joining ropes and rendered most of the rafts ineffectual, spinning downriver separately, to be poled aside when they neared a ship. The second group, though, were doubly tied, and men on each bank ran, towing them as a whole band across the river. It was a frightening spectacle. Here, too, there were some problems, because the men on the east bank had to drop their lines when the Tantal soldiers ran up the bank toward them. Even then, some guardsmen from the city sent arrows into the soldiers, killing twelve. These rafts were cut, too, by the small Tantal boats, under a shower of arrows from upriver, but they still did not separate. Only then did the Tantal realize that there was a deep-water rope. They sent men over to cut it. It was made of thick grapevine, and by the time it was cut, three ships were burning. In the light of those tall fires, it could be seen that two of the ships of dependents had slipped away and were moving downstream, being rowed by Tantal. Here was a defection. They were nearly an ayas away, and Jell, after cursing, decided not to give chase. It would be too protracted and distracting.

"Let the dog mothers go," he said. "They have chosen their own fish-sucking fate. Tomorrow we will take this filthy city."

In the morning, the whole assemblage again moved across the forefield. The ditch trap was bridged, and fire arrows from the walls caused only a small disruption. Two hundred soldiers walked with the moving wall, and behind them six hundred more with another. The wall halted twenty arms from the city wall, too far for heavy rocks to damage them. The roofed sections moved forward, and then the attackers withdrew. Plainly the Tantal had studied the wall carefully, and then had chosen door areas, but ones so related that they could not, they thought, be trapped inside.

The guardsmen made a valiant attempt to save the prisoners on the roofs. Forty of them came around the corner of Northwall, running to the roofed sheds, behind shields, some cutting prisoners loose, under a rain of arrows from the moving wall. Almost all were down, and the guards moving away, when a heavy explosion thundered all along the wall. Guardsmen fell, and men fell off all along the wall. Much of the wall held, but there was a breach, a good twelve arms wide, and yelling, the Tantal rushed ahead toward it.

Liquid fire fell from the wall, but the roofs held much of it, and unburned, unscathed men ran into the opening. A row of Northwall guardsmen stood across their way inside, with shields, another behind it with longbows, along with Shumai and Sentani, mostly ex-prisoners. It was a costly breach, but the whole force of Tantal struggled toward it. Many were now by the guard and fanning out into the small city. They kept running into closed, blank walls, but enough were open so that they thought they would take the whole complex. The fighting was sharp and chaotic. Tantal were everywhere, killing whatever they found in their way. But they were dying, too.

The starpoint had heard the explosion as a muffled roar. They were now not three ayas south. "What . . .?" said the lead man.

"Don't talk, run," said Zen, behind him, spurting up and passing him. The Sentani were tired, but they kept on. In Northwall, they saw fire coming from the city in rolls of smoke. At Arkan Creek was a sunken boat larger than any they had ever seen, and the river was full of ships like it. They waded the creek and ran out onto the forefield.

"Hold," said Mokil. "In starpoints, by numbers. Fan out. One and two, hold those men by the shore. Three and four, through the wall and left, five and six, through and right. Seven, come with me down the center. We will go to the judgment room."

Those still on the wall saw the Sentani and set up a cheer. From the ships came a weaker cheer, though short-lived, as remaining prisoners were beaten by the slavekeepers. The Shumai from the west bank could be seen crossing above. The Tantal fighting in the city did not expect behind them the new force of over 340 men, disciplined as a fighting unit. They began to waver, running in small groups through the city halls, and up stairways. They were opposed wherever they went.

The council guard stood firm at the door of the judgment room, but over seventy Tantal came up the stairs, and even the wall of shields could not hold them. The inside guard was mostly women, well trained and disciplined, but few had fought before except in training. They were wavering and falling. The door was breached, and the Tantal yelled, knowing that this was some place of importance, but then arrows began thudding into the back men, and turning, they saw Mokil's Sentani. The survivors fled down a hallway, followed by Mokil. They didn't know that the hall led directly to an overlook onto the orchard. It was a dead end. As they emerged out onto the overlook, they were met by ten old people, all holding drawn bows, who shot the ten lead men. The rest turned on them with swords, and the brave old ones were no match, but Mokil was on them, and after a short fight, the survivors surrendered. Mokil's men tied them fast and left them, running back down the hallway. The judgment room was open. Only four of the guard remained in front of it. They let him through, and he turned and told his men to hold the stairs.

The Protector was on the floor, holding her side, which was bleeding. Tia was with her. Mokil knelt down by her. She smiled faintly. "Thank you, Mokil," she said. "I knew you would come. We have saved some of your people, but others are out on those ships. And many have died."

Mokil patted her shoulder. He looked at Tia, who smiled faintly. "I will be back for a talk," said Mokil, going out through the door.

"Cise, Cise," Zen was calling, running down the hall in the part of the city she had pointed out the last spring. "Cise." He stepped over a dead Tantal. She was back from the open doorway, holding a drawn bow. "Cise, it is Zen," he said.

"Get down," she yelled. He did, instantly, and her arrow whisked over into a Tantal who had been in the alcove behind him.

He looked at her and said, "I will be back." Then he turned and ran down the hall toward the shouting.

The Tantal were demoralized by the arrival of the Sentani, and soon began trying to get out of the breached walls. It was hard. They had not taken the high walls, which were completely blocked off. "This place is a filthy labyrinth," one shouted, as they ran. Soon Shumai began arriving from the west bank, and the first of the Pelbarigan guard from the south. The Tantal who turned from the Shumai faced a wall of new Pelbar guardsmen. They began surrendering, throwing down weapons and holding up their hands.

"Lie face down," said the Pelbarigan guard chief. They began to lie down in the mud. Inside the fighting was slowing, as Tantal there began to surrender as well. The ships, seeing what was happening, began hauling up their anchors and leaving, with skeleton crews on board, but with prisoners as well. The Tantal soldiers could not believe they were being deserted.

But one by one the Tantal ships with prisoners let them go, sending them over the side toward the west bank, still in their chains, in shallow water, realizing that the prisoners were the real cause of the aid of the outside peoples, and knowing that they would be pursued as long as they had any. They exchanged jibes and curses with the prisoners as they left. But they now knew better than to kill any more.

By sunset the wind was cold and dry, and the ground freezing. The freed men had all been brought to Northwall. Of the Tantal force, only a hundred and forty remained, with forty-seven more wounded.

Northwall was a shambles, and they had lost over three hundred of their people. The Sentani had lost sixty-one of the starband. But ninety-two Sentani had been freed, including some from the central bands and three from the lakes. Eighty-one Shumai had also been freed. The rest of the prisoners had lost their lives.

"There will be no northern hunt this year, I am afraid," said Mokil.

"Stay with us, stay as long as you like. We have food and shelter," said Tag. She was smiling sadly.

He looked back. "Do you have the authority?"

"I am chief of defenses now. I do not, but I know. You saved us. We are open to you now."

"You did rather well yourself," he returned. "But thank you. We shall see. We do have people to take care of. Look at them. They have been mistreated. Brutally."

Waldura walked up to him. He had a bandage around his leg and was limping badly. He took hold of Mokil's arm. He didn't know quite what to say, so he looked and said nothing. Then, finally, he said, "We will have to be peaceful with one another."

"That will be a relief to us," said Mokil.

Thro was there. "Where is Winnt?" he said. "Where is Ursa?"

"Ursa? She is having a baby so she stayed in Koorb. Winnt is with her. What is it now—nearly Buckmonth? It should be born by now," he said, grinning. Then he added, "Look, Zen has found himself a Pelbar. You can find one, I am sure."

Thro then said, "Where is Jestak?" No one knew. An inquiry started and a call went out for him. The Mejana was asked. She was busy, as usual, and sterner than usual. "He is over there," she said, "with Tia and that Sentani."

Thro and Mokil went to him. Jestak had taken an arrow in the leg and a sword thrust across the back. He had lost much blood. His head was also still ringing from the explosion. He smiled up at them weakly. "Look," he said. "This is Mers, all the way from the Bitter Sea. Look at him. He is the brother of my friend, Igon. We got him off that roof just in time." Mers held up his hand in the Sentani greeting, which did not differ much from the Pelbar sign of blessing.

◪ XVIII

ADAI could not climb the flight of stairs to the high tower. She was now the Protector of Pelbarigan, as an aftermath of the uproar over the departure of a hundred of the guard. She was in the judgment room when they brought the next message from the bird.

She read it aloud to the crowded room. "Wall breached, 321 North. killed. Also sixty-one starband, two your guard, Gagen, Rive. Thank you for them. They helped stop fight. Shu. also killed. I too hurt. We have won. Jest. hurt. Tia beaut. Have horses. Look out for Tantal ships. Undermanned. Beware of them. Very treacherous. Do not help. Do *not* help. Let go. Tell Threeriv. Many Tant. prisoners. May send some. S. Pall, Protector."

Rive's mother was there and crying. They were comforting her. "He did well," Opy said. "Think of it. They lost 321. All of us would have been there." But Uppor continued to cry.

Adai silenced the group with a raised hand. "This is a momentous time," she said. "Perhaps this was really the time for which the Pelbar cities were built and intended. Now we must make ready for the Tantal ships and prisoners, if they are sent. We will welcome the guardsmen back, and special honors will go to Gagen and Rive. With the council's consent I now name the two foretowers in their honor. They shall no longer be north and south, but Gagen and Rive towers. When the guardsmen return, we shall see about what relief shall be sent to Northwall. As to the surviving Tantal, I will leave them to the chief of defense. But Sima Pall's words are to be taken seriously. 'Beware of them. Very treacherous. Do not help.' We must think this out."

It was the second quarter of the next day, when the two ships of dependents came into view of Pelbarigan. They sent some women, and their children, ashore to the message stone. Pelbarigan remained closed.

Inside, many were shaking their heads with the cruelty of it. Finally, another crowd of dependents was put ashore. From the city it looked as if they were unwilling. They numbered forty-two in all. The ships then pushed off and started downstream, with the women running along the shore. But it was no use, and finally they returned to stand before Pelbarigan. When it was seen that the ships did not intend to return, five guardsmen were let out the small door and came forward to the group at the message stone. The guardsmen said nothing. The Tantal were crying for food and shelter.

Finally, the guard chief said, "What of them?" pointing at the now distant ships.

An older woman said, slowly enough to be understood, "They have abandoned us. None of our men is on board. All are back at your other city."

"Do not expect to be bargained for," said the guard chief. "Northwall has held. Most of the attackers are dead or captured. Some are following you in the remaining ships. Tuss, go ask the council what we may do. You, wait here. Tace, you and Essal build a fire for them. We will wait."

Word came from the council that food would be sent, and tents, but that the Tantal would have to remain outside the walls to await the other ships.

"How can you be so cruel to the helpless?" the older woman jeered.

The guard chief looked at her. "Northwall lost over three hundred defending against your people. We understand that you held prisoners as slaves and that many died. Do you talk of cruelty to us?"

"We did not do that."

The guard chief said nothing.

It was nearly sunset when the rest of the Tantal ships hove in sight. There were only seven. The others had been emptied of valuables and left to burn upriver. The seven dropped anchor near the west shore, and the cries of the dependents went unanswered for some time, until finally a small boat put out from one and came across, standing off the bank about twenty arms.

"What do you want?" a man called.

"It is Arga," said one of the women. "Arga, come and save us. We have been abandoned. The Pelbar will do nothing for us."

"You left us. Deserted. Why should we take you in?"

"We could do nothing," the older woman called. "It was the men, and now they have left us behind. We were helpless."

The man in the boat laughed. "We saw you at the oars," he said.

"What of you?" the older woman screamed. "We did not hear of your remaining behind to be killed or captured. You are like us. Do not be so easy on yourselves."

"Parg, you and your children come to the bank. You, too, Heth. Your husbands are on board. The rest keep back. We will shoot if you try to join us."

There was much screaming and shoving, and the women abandoned clung to the ones to go. Those from the boat waded ashore with swords drawn to separate the mass. Most retreated, but two women's arms were hacked severely to force them to let go. Then the men ran to the boat with those dependents chosen, and put off as mud and dirt was hurled at them from the bank.

From a high window the Protector was watching. "Should we put a few holes in that boat?" the chief of defenses asked.

"No," said Adai. "They are working out their own desperation. I see that they will be enemies enough to themselves. It has been a lesson to me. I understand Sima Pall better now. We can be merciful without admitting those people—or rather the servants of that way of thinking—into our city. Let them go. Go bring the two hurt women in. We will build shelters outside for the others and feed them until the guardsmen return. Then we will decide."

At Northwall there was a great deal to do. The Tantal were put to digging graves in the Pelbar cemetery on the hill. At first it was thought to separate the tribes, but then they were all put together, according to rank. A special place was reserved for Manti, who had been thrown from the wall by the Tantal blast.

Sima Pall seemed as much distressed by that as by anything. Her own wound was not severe. Tia had held a shield in front of her, and thrown a spear at the man who shot the Protector. Three arrows were left in the shield, one piercing it and just scratching Tia's knuckle.

She joked about "my wound, and the special treatment I deserve." She would sit with Jestak and say, "See, husband? I am wounded. Why do you lie there, with your scratches? Are you not going to take care of me? Make up a bed, for I must lie down." He would try to laugh, but then wince. Tia was very concerned about him, spending all the time she could with him. But she was needed elsewhere much of the time. She would come in at odd moments and sit with him. He generally lay very still, but on the fourth day he began to rouse himself a little.

As they sat in the dusk, he said, "Think, Tia. If there were no time of fire, all this horror would not have been. The place of learning was another Northwall, but at that time it was like that all over, from here to Emerta and beyond."

"It is the way men are, Jes."

"I have been lying here thinking about that. Are we going to do the whole thing over again? Would it be worth it?"

"You and I together are worth it."

"That is not what I mean. And I am not sure it is the way men are. It is the way their cultures are. They are not all like that. Look how different the Tantal are from the Pelbar."

"But look how much more deadly the Pelbar proved to be than the Tantal."

"Not by choice."

"Nevertheless, they are."

"Let us not talk about it anymore now."

"All right. Do you want some soup? I can get you some before I go and work on the wall."

The Shumai were anxious to leave. The herd animals had long ago begun their southward migration, and they were eager to catch up with their people. In the end, it was decided that the Sentani winter hunt would go, as usual, but with twenty Shumai on it, all young men eager for something new. Waldura and another twenty-five would stay at Northwall. The others would go south, under Thro, traveling with the Pelbar guard as far as Pelbarigan. Ten of the guardsmen stayed behind for the winter. Reming stayed to care for the horses. Stantu stayed for Jestak, and was often seen on the walls in the company of Tag.

Before Thro left, Jestak had a talk with him, trying to convince him to help form a council of the Heart River peoples. "We have not heard the last of the Tantal, I fear. We must get this new weapon of theirs so we may defend against it. Now that we have a start at friendship, we must tie it fast so that all are safe. We could turn the Pelbar cities into centers for all the peoples, and open farms that all could benefit from. Don't you get tired of meat?"

Thro laughed. "Yes," he said. "Sometimes. But not of open sky out on the great prairies. Did you not love it, Jes? Is it not a paradise?"

Jestak thought. "Yes," he replied. "It is. Except when it is snowing, or in a cold rain. Or in the great heat. Or when I am very hungry, or would like something to read, or some music, or some iron to work, or . . ."

Thro held up his hand. "Enough," he said. "We are different."

"We are, but we are still the same people," said Jestak. "We are not divided anymore, and we ought to begin the process of melding ourselves into a single unit, for trade, for exchange of knowledge, for marriage, and eventually, perhaps, even in government."

"That is too much for me," said Thro. "At least right now. I will have to think."

In the hall, he met Tag, the acting chief of defenses. Her arm was in a sling. Stantu was with her. "Thro," she said, wearily. "It takes so short a time to break something—in a fight—and so long to put it back together."

Thro nodded. He shot a look at Stantu. "Some things will never be the same," he said.

The Pelbar had raised the ship in Arkan Creek, repaired it, and all the returning Pelbarigan guard, with the Shumai, were to crowd on it for the trip downriver. On their way, they found that two of the other ships left to burn were comparatively undamaged, though they had not much on them.

Though they were not sailors, they managed to bring all three ships to Pelbarigan, even racing, gleefully, part of the way. Finally, they heard the warning horn from the Pelbarigan towers, and the guard leader picked up his own horn and returned three long blasts.

The guardsmen were met at the river bank by laughing families. Even the Shumai managed to kiss a few of the young women, who were surprised, but managed to join in the spirit of the celebration. As they made their way up the hill to the city, which was much closer to the river than Northwall, they presented a strong contrast to the forlorn Tantal by the south wall in their tents. The children looked on in some fear. Only the older woman, whose arm was bandaged, approached the guardsmen.

"Tell us," she said, "what of our men? Our men. Did you not bring them? What have you done with them?"

"They have remained for the winter to work, while we decide what to do with them," said one man.

"Who are they? What are their names?"

"We will see that you are given a list when we have one."

"A list? That is what you will give us? A list?"

"What did you expect, a medal for your grace and courtesy?"

She said nothing, but turned and walked away.

The Tantal were a problem. The Pelbar were not inclined to call anyone irredeemable. But here was a culture it was difficult to trust. Even though hostile, the Heart River peoples all had a strong sense of honor. When a messenger came from Threerivers, he said that only three Tantal ships had passed there. He saw the wrecks of the others on his way, and there were some dead on them.

At Northwall they knew the importance of learning the secret of the charging dust. Finally, they made that the chief condition of the release of the Tantal. They were given evasive answers for a time, but finally a formula. It could not be tested without a trip to the caves across the Heart and south, but the Shumai gladly went for the white powder from the caves.

When they tested it, it did not seem to work, but they worked on it for a time in the blacksmith shop. Finally, with further questioning of the Tantal, they thought they had it. Aku applied a sliver lit afire. When the noise ceased, and dust and objects stopped falling, Allo said, "By Aven, that must be it."

Aku was still trying to clear her eyes, and said, "What?" as several guardsmen ran in the door. Then they all began to laugh.

The Tantal were escorted to Pelbarigan by the returning

Sentani in the spring, and given two of the ships. The third would follow as far as the mouth of the Koorb, giving the Sentani a ride home. Then the enemies would be on their own.

The reunion with the women and children was not as happy as it might have been, but four couples were reunited, and the men and women held each other, as children clung to their legs. The Pelbar gave each of the Tantal a sturdy cloth bag, with necessities, but no weapons except a small knife and sheath. It was a subdued group that left with their escort. One child was left behind. His mother, who had been hurt while trying to get to the Tantal ships in late fall, had died. None of the others would accept him. He watched them leave cradled on the arm of a guardsman, his arm around the man's neck.

Jestak and Tia had come downriver with the party. He was standing on the wall with his mother when the Tantal departed. "I wonder," he mused, "if we have seen the last of them—as aggressors. I have asked Mers to let us know if the lake Sentani have further troubles. We are hoping at Northwall for a party from the central Sentani to make a permanent truce with us. But I still wonder."

 XIX

As the leaves began to turn again the following year, Northwall looked considerably changed. The walls had been repaired, but doors were now obvious. On the front of the wall was a large stone structure, still being roofed. This was Jestak's idea. It was to be called the hall of the hunters, and was to be open for any passing Shumai or Sentani to occupy as long as they needed it.

Much of the forefield and north shorefield was cultivated, and the small herd of Pelbar horses grazed south of Arkan Creek in a large enclosure. There was one colt. Further east, south of the orchard, were the beginnings of a herd of wild cattle, also in an enclosure. The Pelbar were attempting to domesticate them as the Emeri had.

By the shore was a ship under construction, along the lines of the Tantal craft, though of a flatter bottom and shallower draft. Waldura had returned from his summer on the plains to watch its completion. His leg had never really healed after the fight for Northwall, and he was growing more sedentary. Shumai shelters were scattered along the river bank. It was still quite warm, and none wanted to move inside the hall of the hunters. Besides, there was still some work to do there.

Guards were still maintained on the wall, but the gate was open. High on a central position, specially constructed, overlooking the whole area, was the Tantal tube weapon, which had been repaired and tested.

For the time, Jestak had been made chief of defenses, but this position had changed, and he was more diplomat and less a military man. Northwall was increasingly visited by curious Shumai and Sentani, including the delegation from the central bands. To all, the whole battle had to be described. The new walling was shown them, and the function of both Shumai and Sentani in the victory was explained. They were taken through the city, and such things as the fight for the judgment hall and the defense by the ten brave old ones were described. The Shumai loved the descriptions of the fire rafts, the catapults, and the final arrival of the people from the west bank. They took boats over to see the catapults, which were decaying among the willows and butternuts. Some swam out to the remains of the Tantal ships in the shallows, but the four that had settled in the mud after they were drilled had been raised and were in use on the river.

On the first day of Colormonth—new style, for Tia's astronomy had modified the Pelbar calendar, which she had thought hilariously cumbersome—Jestak was on the wall. As usual, Tag was with him. But she was not only being conscientious. "When did he say he would be here?"

Jestak looked at her. "You know. Sometime in the fall. You know how casual the Shumai are about time, accurate as they may be about where they are in it."

"Is that all? Did he not say in the first week? Did he not say we should be sure to have all the hay in?"

"Hmmm. Perhaps he did. Why?"

"Well, then he meant right now. Are there any hostiles at all between here and Ottan?"

"No, Tag. Only Shumai, and all are his friends. Of course there are wild cattle, and he may have fallen off a horse and broken his neck, but—"

"Jestak, do not say things like that. He is your friend, your oldest Shumai friend."

"And of course Reming may have done him in. I saw Reming looking at you last spring. He may want his chance."

"You are awful," she spat, and started to go.

"Wait, Tag." She stopped. He walked over to her and turned her around. "You will have to think very carefully about this. He is a good man. But he will not be like a Pelbar man. You will not have all the say. Do you really know what that means?"

She thought and nodded. "My mother never had everything her way," she said.

"All right. But remember, there may be times when he says, 'Come here,' and he will mean it. Right then. He will never think much about not being obeyed, and he may not like it when you take your time."

"Stantu? He will not do that."

"I think he will. He is less likely to misunderstand than Waldura, or even Thro perhaps. But when you take him, you are taking the whole tribe. Are you ready for that?"

"I thought you said we were all one people."

"So we are, but there are differences, even in families. You well know that if you marry a Jestan, you marry the attitudes of the whole family, even if your husband is resisting them. He will have them in him."

"What about you? What about Tia?"

"I know. But you see, I have all the advantages. I am being freed by that. A Pelbar woman would expect to be able to make all the decisions. Tia does not. I do not expect mastery. She has been raised to expect more or less to obey. We are both being helped."

"Stantu will understand. Look, is that him?"

"No, Tag. It is only a few wild cows."

It was nearly a week before Stantu came, wearily, with Reming and Reor, and twenty-five horses. Kod had come, with his family, and all were surprised to see the old Emer, Esis, from Ilet.

"Well, Esis, you are a long way from home," said Jestak, holding out his hands.

The old man got down stiffly from his horse and sighed. "It is not the same with the old Krugistoran around. He is an ache in the head, and Acco is always scolding him, and even me. I heard that you had some cattle that needed caring for, and I thought I could do that. Now where is this famous city?"

"There," said Jestak.

"Oh. That? I thought it must be three times the size of Emerta. It is only a small place."

"You will see it grow, Esis." Jestak turned and saw Ary grinning at him, waiting for a hug.

"I can even play the pellute a little bit now," she announced.

"Hello, Kod. Hello, Iben," said Jestak, holding Ary on an arm, big as she was growing. "Have you come to winter with us?"

"No," Kod replied. "We thought we would come to see Northwall after the fight. I am sorry I missed it. Are those the ships?" He whistled. "How many did we sink? You mean we took those with only a few men?"

Soon Jestak had to leave his friends to say good-bye to the central Sentani. They were taking with them an old man, Icton, who had been one of the Tantal prisoners, but who had stayed nearly a year, at first to recover, then to work, then because of his fascination with Pelbar choir singing.

"He has a terrible voice," Jestak whispered to Stantu. "But he understands the harmonies, and he will teach it well."

Icton had requested the choir to sing once more for him, and also for the central Sentani, and they had been brought from fields and shops, brushing their hands on leather aprons and smoothing their hair. Icton was so radiant that they sang for him the long chorus of the love of Aven, as he stood wistful and enraptured. The chapel had filled with a conglomeration of the Heart River people, and the afternoon light, streaming through the high narrow windows, making wide stripes of the dusty air, gave the place a hush and reverence that one would not have expected of an impromptu gathering.

As the crowd left, Stantu said, his arm around Tag, "I would like to be married here."

Jestak turned. "Here it would have to be a Pelbar wedding."

"That is all right. That is fine with me," he said.

"Do you know what that means?"

"Yes. I have thought it over. I have had a whole summer to think it over." Jestak went away wondering if he really knew Stantu at all. During this last trip across the plains, they had looked rather desolate to the Shumai, and he decided that he really wanted to settle at Northwall, where so much of the core of his life seemed centered. Jestak hoped all would go well, but at least Stantu and Tag were both people of much goodwill.

Stantu caught up with him. "We have heard that you and Tia are building a house outside the wall, on the north bluffside."

"Yes. We have started. But it will be a long process with all the other work. It will be the first family house outside the walls."

"We would like to build near you."

"Good. We will help. If you have not picked a place, I know a good one. Ary, did you like that singing?"

She, who had seen no architecture more substantial than the loghouses at Black Bull Island, said, "Yes," very softly.

That evening they were testing the new chimneys on the hall of the hunters. Even the Protector was there to see. "Hangings will make those walls warmer," she said. The hunters present, who slept in skin or bough shelters even in deep winter, grinned at each other. "Well," said the Protector, "it is very nice indeed. Now, Tia, if you will help me back, please."

She had taken the events of the past year in stride, but it was clear to all, including herself, that she was near retirement. "Tia," she said, as they walked slowly up the stairs, "I never knew how much I would miss Manti. It is as if half the world were gone, as if the river flowed out of nowhere and into nowhere. How long I treated him in such an official manner on so many occasions."

"But look what you have accomplished, Sima. Could that have been possible had you been married? I mean among the Pelbar?"

They climbed in silence. Finally the Protector said, "No, I suppose not. He was the right chief of defenses, and he could not have been that were I not the Protector. But how fragile it all was. Look how easily Jestak snapped that thread. Why could I not have done that?"

"Look at the help you all gave him. Was it not the council who sent him east in the first place?"

"Yes. The three councils. But what would that have done to a lesser man? It was a matter of his response. It was like the great harp that sets all the pellutes humming."

"Yes, Sima. But how far back will you take the great harp? What set the harp in the chapel thrumming, and what set that one going? The Shumai have a story about Olleg, the stargroup in the south that forms an arc. Our deity, who is really the same as Aven, lit the central star in order to see a beautiful fawn he had created. The other stars were close enough to blaze up from that one fire. But they were all alike, and it was the creator who lit them. All burned from the creator's fire."

Sima Pall stopped and turned. "I hope that you will love Jestak enough. He is a rare man, Tia."

She only laughed. "Well, I will tell you a secret."

"No need. I have been always able to tell."

"You are a sly old woman. No wonder they call you the 'Perceptor of Northwall.'"

"Who says that?"

"Oh, some people. Perhaps I heard it wrong. Here is your door."

At the hall of the hunters, Reor was telling of their trip west. "Prestiginagi has held the peace. Some of the Shumai have gone to work on the farms, but only for harvest help. But one did not leave. Eriam has stayed and married a farmer's daughter. He will settle and raise cattle for milk."

"I never thought I would see all these changes," said Waldura. "Only two years ago I chased you into Northwall, Jestak. What has happened? The whole world is falling apart."

"It is being remade. I hope it will be more peaceful, more cooperative. But we have a lot to do."

"What now?"

"I can't say. If there is a communication between all the people from the lakes to the mountains, then the Tantal will be nullified. We must get to the learning of the eastern cities, and perhaps help them with their spiritual dullness. Somehow we must bring the Tantal themselves into our sphere, and then open the whole Heart River to travel and trade."

"You are going to do all this?"

"No. Not me. Whatever I do will be the first stroke of the axe."

"What is that?" said Thro. Ary was hanging on his arm, swinging her legs.

"When I was at Saltstream, and they were telling me that I had some function in the harmonizing of the peoples, I did not believe them. I asked them if they realized the magnitude of the thing they were expecting. One of them, a woman named Arthil, said, 'Imagine a tree that has grown a thousand years. It is so big that twenty people can ring it only with arms outstretched. You are going to build a house from it. Imagine the complex of feelings you have when you take the first stroke of the axe.'"

"But Jessi," said Ary, "that would take until I am an old woman." She held out her arms to indicate great fatness. They all laughed and turned to leave the hall, with its fresh smells of new wood, new stonework, and the newly built fire.

DEL REY GOLD SEAL SELECTIONS... SCIENCE FICTION CLASSICS IN QUALITY PAPERBACK EDITIONS.

Major works of imaginative fiction that have become modern literary classics.